PRAISE FOR
SARAH MacLEAN

"Sarah MacLean's books are *fierce*."

—Julia Quinn, #1 *New York Times* bestselling
author of the Bridgerton series

"For a smart, witty, and passionate historical romance, I recommend anything by Sarah MacLean."

—Lisa Kleypas, *New York Times* bestselling author

"Propulsive escapism at its absolute finest. We are lucky to be living and breathing in the Sarah MacLean era."

—Christina Lauren, *New York Times* and #1 internationally
bestselling authors of *The Unhoneymooners*

"When a new Sarah MacLean novel comes out, I drop everything to read."

—Emily Henry, *New York Times* bestselling author

"The elegantly fuming, utterly intoxicating queen of historical romance."

—*Entertainment Weekly*

"MacLean works magic, crafting . . . magnificent romance that's as satisfying as it is subversive."

—*New York Times Book Review*

"Romance novelist Sarah MacLean has reignited the genre with a bolder edge."

—*New Yorker*

"When it comes to historical romance, she's one of the best."

—*Vulture*

Nine
Rules to Break
When Romancing
a Rake

By Sarah MacLean

HELL'S BELLES
Bombshell

THE BAREKNUCKLE BASTARDS
Wicked and the Wallflower
Brazen and the Beast
Daring and the Duke

SCANDAL & SCOUNDREL
The Rogue Not Taken
A Scot in the Dark
The Day of the Duchess

THE RULES OF SCOUNDRELS
A Rogue by Any Other Name
One Good Earl Deserves a Lover
No Good Duke Goes Unpunished
Never Judge a Lady by Her Cover

LOVE BY NUMBERS
Nine Rules to Break When Romancing a Rake
Ten Ways to Be Adored When Landing a Lord
Eleven Scandals to Start to Win a Duke's Heart

The Season

Nine
Rules to Break
When Romancing
a Rake

SARAH MacLEAN

AVON
An Imprint of HarperCollins*Publishers*

P.S.™ is a trademark of HarperCollins Publishers.

NINE RULES TO BREAK WHEN ROMANCING A RAKE. Copyright © 2010 by Sarah Trabucchi. All rights reserved. Printed in the United States of America. No part of this book may be used or reproduced in any manner whatsoever without written permission except in the case of brief quotations embodied in critical articles and reviews. For information, address HarperCollins Publishers, 195 Broadway, New York, NY 10007.

HarperCollins books may be purchased for educational, business, or sales promotional use. For information, please email the Special Markets Department at SPsales@harpercollins.com.

A mass market edition of this book was published in 2010 by Avon, an imprint of HarperCollins Publishers.

FIRST AVON PAPERBACK EDITION PUBLISHED 2022.

Designed by Diahann Sturge

Library of Congress Cataloging-in-Publication Data has been applied for.

ISBN 978-0-06-323035-4

22 23 24 25 26 LSC 10 9 8 7 6 5 4 3 2 1

For the spy and the Italian,
who, it should come as no surprise,
gave me all my stories.

For Eric, my rock.

In Loving Memory of
Barbara Delhi Joan MacLean,
Thomas Pearson, Ada Fiori,
and Giuseppe Trabucchi.

Prologue

London, England
April 1813

ady Calpurnia Hartwell blinked back tears as she fled the ballroom of Worthington House, the scene of her most recent and most devastating embarrassment. The welcome night air was crisp with the edge of spring as she rushed down the great marble steps, desperation shortening her footsteps and propelling her forward into the shadows of the vast, darkened gardens. Once hidden from view, she let out a deep sigh and slowed her pace, finally safe. Her mother would be livid if she discovered her eldest daughter outside without a chaperone, but nothing could have kept Callie inside that horrible room.

Her first season was an utter failure.

It hadn't even been a month since she'd made her debut. The eldest daughter of the Earl and Countess of Allendale, Callie should by all rights have been the belle of the ball; she'd been raised for this life—all graceful dancing and perfect manners and stunning beauty. That was the problem, of course. Callie might be a fine dancer with impeccable manners, but a beauty? She was nothing if not pragmatic, and she knew better than to believe she was one of those.

I should have known this would be a disaster, she thought as she plopped herself down onto a marble bench just inside the Worthington hedge maze.

She'd been at the ball for three hours and had not yet been asked to dance by a suitor who wasn't entirely *un*suitable. After two invitations from renowned fortune hunters, one from a crashing bore, and another from a baron who couldn't have been a day under seventy, Callie hadn't been able to continue feigning enjoyment. It was obvious that she was worth little more to the *ton* than the sum total of her dowry and her ancestry—and even that total was not enough to garner a dance with a partner she might actually like. No, the truth was, Callie had spent the better part of the season overlooked by eligible, coveted, young bachelors.

She sighed.

Tonight had been the worst. As if it weren't enough that she was visible only to the boring and the elderly, tonight she'd felt the stares of the rest of the *ton*.

"I never should have allowed my mother to pour me into this monstrosity," she muttered to herself, looking down at the gown in question, at its too-tight waistline and its too-small bodice, unable to contain her breasts, which were a good deal larger than fashion dictated. She was positive that no belle of the ball had ever been crowned in such a vibrant shade of mandarin sunset. Or in such a hideous frock, for that matter.

The dress, her mother had assured her, was the very height of fashion. When Callie had suggested that the gown was not the most flattering to her figure, she had been informed by the countess that she was incorrect. Callie would look stunning, her mother had promised as the *modiste* had flitted around her, poking and prodding and squeezing her into the gown. And, as she watched her transformation in the dressmaker's mirror, she'd begun to agree with them. She did look stunning in this dress. Stunningly awful.

Wrapping her arms tightly around her to ward off the evening chill, she closed her eyes in mortification. "I cannot return. I shall just have to live here forever."

A deep chuckle sounded from the shadows, and Callie shot up, gasping in surprise. She could barely make out the figure of a man as she pulled herself up to her full height and attempted to slow her pounding heart. Before she could think to escape, she spoke, allowing her distaste for the entire evening to lace her tone. "You really shouldn't sneak up on people in the dark, sir. It isn't gentlemanly."

He responded quickly, the deep tenor of his voice sweeping over her. "My apologies. Of course, one might argue that lurking in the darkness isn't exactly *ladylike*."

"Ah. There you have it wrong. I am not lurking in the darkness. I am *hiding* in it. Quite a different thing, altogether." She pressed back into the shadows.

"I shan't give you away," he spoke quietly, reading her mind as he advanced. "You might as well show yourself. You're well and truly trapped."

Callie felt the prickly hedge behind her even as he loomed above and knew that he was right. She sighed in irritation. *How much worse could this night get?* Just then, he stepped into a sliver of moonlight, revealing his identity, and she had her answer. *Much worse.*

Her companion was the Marquess of Ralston—charming, devastatingly handsome, and one of London's most notorious rakes. His wicked reputation was matched only by his wicked smile, which was aimed directly at Callie. "Oh no," she whispered, unable to keep the desperation from her voice. She could *not* let him see her.

Not like this, trussed up like a Christmas goose. A *mandarin sunset* Christmas goose.

"What could be so bad, moppet?" The lazy endearment warmed her even as she looked about for an escape route. He was close enough to touch now, towering over her, a good six inches taller than she. For the first time in a long time, she felt small. Dainty, even. *She had to escape.*

"I . . . I must go. If I were found here . . . with you. . . ." She left the sentence unfinished. He knew what would happen.

"Who are you?" His eyes narrowed in the darkness, taking in the soft angles of her face. "Wait . . ." She imagined his eyes flashing with recognition, "You're Allendale's daughter. I noticed you earlier."

She could not contain her sarcastic response, "I'm sure you did, my lord. It would be rather difficult to overlook me." She covered her mouth immediately, shocked that she had spoken so baldly.

He chuckled. "Yes. Well, it isn't the most flattering of gowns."

She couldn't help her own laughter from slipping out. "How very diplomatic of you. You may admit it. I look rather too much like an apricot."

This time, he laughed aloud. "An apt comparison. But I wonder, is there ever a point where one looks *enough* like an apricot?" He indicated that she should resume her place on the bench and, after a moment's hesitation, she did so.

"Likely not." She smiled broadly, amazed that she wasn't nearly as humiliated by his agreement as she would have expected. No, indeed she found it rather freeing. "My mother . . . she's desperate for a daughter she can dress like a porcelain doll. Sadly, I shall never be such a child. How I long for my sister to come out and distract the countess from my person."

He joined her on the bench, asking, "How old is your sister?"

"Eight," she said, mournfully.

"Ah. Not ideal."

"An understatement." She looked up at the star-filled sky. "No, I shall be long on the shelf by the time she makes her debut."

"What makes you so certain you're shelf-bound?"

She cast him a sidelong glance. "While I appreciate your chivalry, my lord, your feigned ignorance insults us both." When he failed to reply, she stared down at her hands, and replied, "My choices are rather limited."

"How so?"

"I seem able to have my pick of the impoverished, the aged, and the deadly dull," she said, ticking off the categories on her fingers as she spoke.

He chuckled. "I find that difficult to believe."

"Oh, it's true. I'm not the type of young lady who brings gentlemen to heel. Anyone with eyes can see that."

"I have eyes. And I see no such thing." His voice lowered, soft and rich as velvet as he reached out to stroke her cheek. Her breath caught, and she wondered at the intense wave of awareness coursing through her.

She leaned into his caress, unable to resist, as he moved his hand to grasp her chin. "What is your name?" he asked softly.

She winced, knowing what was to come, "Calpurnia." She closed her eyes again, embarrassed by the extravagant name—a name with which no one but a hopelessly romantic mother with an unhealthy obsession with Shakespeare would have considered saddling a child.

"Calpurnia." He tested the name on his tongue. "As in, Caesar's wife?"

The blush flared higher as she nodded.

He smiled. "I must make it a point to better acquaint myself with your parents. That is a bold name, to be sure."

"It's a horrible name."

"Nonsense. Calpurnia was Empress of Rome—strong and beautiful and smarter than the men who surrounded her. She saw the future, stood strong in the face of her husband's assassination. She is a marvelous namesake." He shook her chin firmly as he spoke.

She was speechless in the wake of his frank lecture. Before she had a chance to reply, he continued. "Now, I must take my leave. And you, Lady Calpurnia, must return to the ballroom, head held high. Do you think you can do that?" He gave her chin a final tap and stood, leaving her cold in the wake of his departure.

She stood with him and nodded, starry-eyed. "Yes, my lord."

"Good girl." He leaned closer and whispered, his breath fanning the hair at her nape, warming her in the cool April night. "Remember, you are an empress. Behave as one, and they will have no choice but to see you as such. I already do . . ." He paused, and she held her breath, waiting for his words. "Your Highness."

And with that, he was off, disappearing deeper into the maze and leaving Callie with a silly grin on her face. She did not think twice before following him, so keen was she to be near him. At that moment, she would have followed him anywhere, this prince among men who had noticed *her,* not her dowry, or her horrible dress, but *her!*

If I am an empress, he is the only man worthy of being my emperor.

She did not have to go far to catch him. Several yards in, the maze opened on a clearing that featured a large, gleaming fountain adorned with cherubs. There, bathed in a silvery glow was her prince, all broad shoulders and long legs. Callie caught her breath at the sight of him—exquisite, as though he himself had been carved from marble.

And then she noticed the woman in his arms. Her mouth opened in a silent gasp—her hand flying to her lips as her eyes widened.

In all her seventeen years, she'd never witnessed something so . . . wonderfully scandalous.

The moonlight cast his paramour in an aethereal light, her blond hair turned white, her pale gown gossamer in the darkness. Callie stepped back into the shadows, peering around the corner of the hedge, half-wishing she hadn't followed, entirely unable to turn away from their embrace. My, how they kissed.

And, deep in the pit of her stomach, youthful surprise was replaced with a slow burn of jealousy, for she had never in all her life wanted to be someone else so very much. For a moment, she allowed herself to imagine it was she in his arms: her long, delicate fingers threading through his dark, gleaming hair; her lithe body that his strong hands stroked and molded; her lips he nibbled; her moans coursing through the night air at his caresses.

As she watched his lips trail down the long column of the woman's throat, Callie ran her fingers down the same path on her own neck, unable to resist pretending that the feather-light touch was his. She stared as his hand stroked up his lover's smooth, contoured bodice and grasped the edge of the delicate gown, pulling it down, baring one high, small breast to the night. His teeth flashed wickedly as he looked down at the perfect mound and spoke a single word, "Gorgeous," before lowering his lips to its dark tip, pebbled by the cool air and his warm embrace. His paramour threw her head back in ecstasy, unable to control her pleasure in his arms, and Callie could not tear her eyes from the spectacle of them, brushing her hand across her own breast, feeling its tip harden beneath the silk of her gown, imagining it was his hand, his mouth, upon her.

"Ralston . . ."

The name, carried on a feminine moan, sliced through the clearing, shaking Callie from her reverie. In shock, she dropped her hand and whirled away from the scene upon which she had intruded. She rushed through the maze, desperate for escape, and stopped once more at the marble bench where her garden excursion had begun. Breathing heavily, she collected herself, shocked by her behavior. Ladies did not eavesdrop. And they *certainly* did not eavesdrop in such a manner.

Besides, fantasies would do her no good.

She pushed aside a devastating pang of sorrow as the truth coursed through her. She would never have the magnificent Marquess of Ralston, nor anyone like him. She felt an acute certainty that the things he had said to her earlier were not truth, but instead the lies of an inveterate seducer, carefully chosen to appease her and send her blithely off, easing his dark tryst with his ravishing beauty. He hadn't believed a word of it.

No, she was not Calpurnia, Empress of Rome. She was plain, old Callie. And she always would be.

One

London, England
April 1823

The incessant pounding woke him.

He ignored it at first, sleep clouding the source of the irritating noise.

There was a long pause and a thick silence fell over the bed-chamber.

Gabriel St. John, Marquess of Ralston, took in the early-morning light washing over the decadently appointed room. For a moment, he remained still, registering the rich hues of the chamber, adorned with silk wall coverings and gilded edges, a garish haven of sensual pleasure.

Reaching for the lush female beside him, a half smile played over his lips as she curved her willing, naked body into his—the combination of the early hour and her heated flesh returning him to the edge of slumber.

He lay still, eyes closed, trailing his fingertips idly across his bedmate's bare shoulder as one lithe, feminine hand stroked down the rigid planes of his torso, the direction of the caress a dark erotic promise.

Her touch became stronger, firmer, and he rewarded her skill with a low growl of pleasure.

And the pounding began again—loud and constant on the heavy oak door.

"Cease!" Ralston surged from his mistress's bed, entirely prepared to terrify his intruder into leaving him in peace for the rest of the morning. He had barely pulled on his silk dressing gown before he tore the door open with a wicked curse.

On the threshold stood his twin brother, impeccably dressed and perfectly manicured, as though it were entirely normal to call upon one's brother, at the home of his mistress, at the crack of dawn. Behind Nicholas St. John stood a sputtering servant, "My lord, I did my best to keep him from—"

An icy look from Ralston stopped the words in the man's throat. "Leave us."

Nick watched as the footman scurried away, one brow arched in amusement. "I had forgotten how charming you are in the morning, Gabriel."

"What in God's name brings you here at this hour?"

"I went to Ralston House first," Nick said. "When you weren't there, this seemed the most likely place to find you." He let his gaze slide past his twin to land on the woman seated in the center of the enormous bed. With a lazy grin, Nick gave a nod of acknowledgment in the direction of his brother's mistress. "Nastasia. My apologies for the intrusion."

The Greek beauty stretched like a cat, sensual and sybaritic, allowing the sheet she held in feigned modesty to slip, revealing one luscious breast. A teasing smile played across her lips as she said, "Lord Nicholas. I assure you, I am not the least bit put out.

Perhaps you would like to join us . . ." She paused suggestively. "For breakfast?"

Nick smiled appreciatively. "A tempting offer."

Ignoring the interaction, Ralston prodded. "Nick, if you are in such need of female companionship, I am certain we could have found you a destination that did not so summarily disturb my rest."

Nick leaned against the doorframe, allowing his gaze to linger on Nastasia before returning his attention to Ralston. "Resting, were you, brother?"

Ralston stalked away from the door, toward a basin in the corner of the room, hissing as he splashed bracing water on his face. "You are enjoying yourself, aren't you?"

"Immensely."

"You have mere seconds to tell me why you are here, Nick, before I grow weary of having a younger sibling and toss you out."

"Intriguing that you would select such a relevant turn of phrase," Nick said casually. "As it happens, your position as eldest sibling is why I am here."

Ralston lifted his head to meet his brother's gaze as droplets of water coursed down his face.

"You see, Gabriel, it appears that we have a sister."

"A HALF SISTER."

Ralston spoke flatly, staring down his solicitor, waiting for the bespectacled man to overcome his nerves and explain the circumstances of this surprise announcement. Ralston had perfected the intimidation tactic in gambling hells across London and expected that it would work quickly to get the little man talking.

He was correct.

"I—that is, my lord—"

Ralston cut him off, stalking across the study to pour himself a drink. "Spit it out, man. I haven't got all day."

"Your mother—"

"My mother, if one may use such a word for the unloving creature who bore us, departed England for the Continent more than twenty-five years ago." He swirled the amber liquid in his glass, affecting a look of boredom, "How are we to believe this girl is our sister and not some charlatan eager to capitalize on our goodwill?"

"Her father is a Venetian merchant with plenty of money, all of which he left to her." The solicitor paused, adjusting his spectacles, warily eyeing Ralston. "My lord, he had no reason to lie about her birth. Indeed, by all accounts, it appears that he would prefer not to have alerted you to her existence."

"Then why do so?"

"She has no other family to speak of although I am told that friends were willing to take her in. According to the documents that were sent to my offices, however, this is your mother's doing. She requested that her"—he paused, uncertain—"husband . . . send your . . . sister . . . here in the event of his death. Your mother felt certain that you would . . ." He cleared his throat. "Do right by your family."

Ralston's smile held no humor. "Ironic, is it not, that our mother has called upon our sense of familial obligation?"

The solicitor did not pretend to misunderstand the comment. "Indeed, my lord. But, if I may, the girl is here and very sweet. I'm not certain what to do with her." He spoke no more, but his meaning was understood. *I'm not certain I should leave her in your hands.*

"Of course, she must stay here," Nick finally spoke, drawing the grateful attention of the solicitor and an irritated look from his brother. "We shall take her in. She must be rather in shock, I'd imagine."

"Indeed, my lord." The solicitor readily agreed, latching onto the kindness in Nick's eyes.

"I had not realized that you were able to make such decisions in this house, brother," Ralston drawled, his gaze not wavering from the solicitor.

"I'm simply shortening Wingate's agony," Nick replied, with a nod to the lawyer. "You won't turn away blood."

Nick was, of course, correct. Gabriel St. John, seventh Marquess of Ralston would not deny his sister, regardless of his deep-seated desire to do so. Raking a hand through his black hair, Ralston wondered at the anger that still flared at the thought of his mother, whom he hadn't seen in decades.

She had been married at a young age—barely sixteen—and had borne twin sons within a year. She was gone a decade later, escaped to the Continent, leaving her sons and their father in despair. For any other woman, Gabriel would have felt sympathy, would have understood her fear and forgiven her desertion. But he had witnessed his father's sorrow, felt the pain that the loss of a mother had caused. And he had replaced sadness with anger. It had been years before he was able to speak of her without a knot of fury rising in his throat.

And now, to discover that she had destroyed another family, the wound was refreshed. That she would bear another child—a girl no less—and leave her to a life without a mother infuriated him. Of course, his mother had been correct; he would do right by his family. He would do what he could to atone for her sins. And perhaps that was the most maddening part of this whole situation—that his mother still understood him. That they might still be connected.

He set his glass down, resuming his place behind the wide mahogany desk. "Where is the girl, Wingate?"

"I believe she's been placed in the green room, my lord."

"Well, we might as well fetch her." Nick moved to the door, opening it and sending an unseen servant to retrieve the girl.

In the ensuing, pregnant silence, Wingate stood, smoothing down his waistcoat nervously. "Indeed. If I may, sir?"

Gabriel fixed him with an irritated look.

"She is a good girl. Very sweet."

"Yes. You've mentioned as much. Contrary to your clear opinion of me, Wingate, I am not an ogre with a taste for young girls." He paused, one side of his mouth kicking up. "At least not young girls to whom I am related."

The arrival of their sister prevented Gabriel from taking pleasure in the solicitor's disapproval. Instead, he stood as the door opened, his eyes narrowing as he met the eerily familiar blue gaze leveled at him from across the room.

"Good Lord." Nick's words mirrored Gabriel's thoughts.

There was no question that the girl was their sister. Aside from her eyes, the same rich blue as her brothers', she shared the twins' strong jaw and dark, curling hair. She was the image of their mother—tall and lithe and lovely, with an undeniable fire in her gaze. Gabriel cursed beneath his breath.

Nick regained his composure first, bowing deeply, "*Enchantée,* Miss Juliana. I am your brother Nicholas St. John. And this"—he gestured to Ralston—"is *our* brother Gabriel, Marquess of Ralston."

She curtsied gracefully, rising and indicating herself with a delicate hand, "I am Juliana Fiori. I confess, I was not expecting—" She paused, searching for the word, "*I gemelli.* My apologies. I do not know the word in English."

Nick smiled. "Twins. No, I imagine that our mother did not expect *i gemelli* either."

The dimple in Juliana's cheek was a perfect match for Nick's. "As you say. It is quite striking."

"Well." Wingate cleared his throat, drawing the attention of the rest, "I shall take my leave, then, if my lords have no further need of me." The little man looked from Nick to Ralston, eager to be set free.

"You are free to go, Wingate," Ralston said, his tone icy. "Indeed, I look forward to it."

The lawyer exited, bowing quickly, as if afraid that he might never escape if he tarried too long. Once he had left the room, Nick consoled Juliana, "Don't let yourself be fooled by Gabriel. He's not as wicked as he seems. Some days, he simply likes to play the lord of the manor."

"I believe that I *am* the lord of the manor, Nicholas," Ralston pointed out dryly.

Nick winked at their sister. "Four minutes older, and he cannot help but hold it over me."

Juliana offered Nick a small smile before turning her clear blue gaze on her eldest brother, "My lord, I should like to leave."

Gabriel nodded. "Understandably. I will have your things brought to one of the chambers above stairs. You must be weary from your travels."

"No. You do not understand. I would like to leave England. To return to Venice." When neither Gabriel nor Nick spoke, she continued, her hands moving in time with her words, her accent thickening as emotion crept into her speech. "I assure you, I cannot comprehend why my father insisted I come here. I have friends at home who would happily welcome me—"

Gabriel cut her off, firmly. "You will stay here."

"Mi scusi, my lord. I would prefer not to."

"I'm afraid you do not have a choice."

"You cannot keep me here. I do not belong here. Not with you . . . not in . . . England." She spat the word as though it were foul-tasting.

"You forget that you are half-English, Juliana," Nick said, amused.

"Never! I am Italian!" Her blue eyes flashed.

"And your personality shows it, kitten," Gabriel drawled. "But you are the very portrait of our mother."

Juliana looked to the walls. "Portraits? Of our mother? Where?"

Nick chuckled, charmed by her misunderstanding. "No. You will not find pictures of her here. Gabriel was saying that you *look* like our mother. Exactly like her, actually."

Juliana slashed one hand through the air. "Never say such a thing to me again. Our mother was a—" She stopped herself, the silence in the room heavy with the unspoken epithet.

Ralston's lips twisted in a wry smile. "I see we have found something upon which we can agree."

"You cannot force me to stay."

"I am afraid I can. I've already signed the papers. You are under my protection until you marry."

Her eyes widened. "That is impossible. My father would never have required such a thing. He knew I have no intention of marrying."

"Whyever not?" Nick asked.

Juliana spun on him, "I should think you would understand better than most. I will not repeat my mother's sins."

Gabriel's eyes narrowed. "There is absolutely no reason that you would be anything like—"

"You will forgive me if I am not willing to take such a chance, my lord. Surely we can reach an accord?"

In that moment, Gabriel's decision was made.

"You did not know our mother?"

Juliana held herself perfectly straight and proud, meeting Ralston's gaze without flinching. "She left us nearly ten years ago. I believe it was the same for you?"

Ralston nodded. "We were not even ten."

"Then I imagine neither of us has much love lost for her."

"Indeed."

They stood like that for a long moment, each testing the truth of the other's words. Gabriel spoke first. "I will offer you a bargain." Juliana shook her head in an instant denial before Ralston lifted one hand and halted her words. "This is not a negotiation. You will stay for two months. If, after that time, you decide that you would prefer to return to Italy, I will arrange it."

She tilted her head as though considering the offer and the possibilities for escape. Finally, she nodded once in agreement. "Two months. Not a day more."

"You may have your pick of the bedchambers above stairs, little sister."

She dropped into a deep curtsy. "*Grazie,* my lord." She turned toward the door of the study and was stopped by Nick's curiosity.

"How old are you?"

"Twenty."

Nick cast a fleeting look at his brother before continuing. "You will need to be introduced to London society."

"I hardly think it necessary as I am only here for eight weeks." Her emphasis on the last words was impossible to mistake.

"We shall discuss it when you are settled in." Ralston ended the conversation and escorted her across the room, opening the door to the study and calling for the butler. "Jenkins, please escort Miss Juliana upstairs and have someone assist her maid in unpacking her things." He turned back to Juliana. "You do have a maid, do you not?"

"Yes," she said, amusement crossing her lips. "Must I remind you that it was the Romans who brought civilization to *your* country?"

Ralston's eyebrows rose. "You plan to be a challenge, do you?"

Juliana smiled angelically. "I agreed to remain, my lord. Not to remain silent."

He turned back to Jenkins. "She will be with us from now on."

Juliana shook her head, meeting her brother's eyes. "For two months."

With a nod, he revised his statement. "She will be with us *for now.*"

The butler did not blink at the surprising announcement, instead offering a calm, "Very good, my lord," and sending several footmen scurrying to remove Juliana's trunks above stairs before leading the young woman away.

Satisfied that his bidding would be done, Ralston closed the door to the study and turned back to Nick, who was leaning against the sideboard, a lazy smile on his face.

"Well done, brother," Nick said. "If only the *ton* knew that you have such an inflated sense of familial obligation . . . your reputation as a fallen angel would be shattered."

"You would do well to stop talking."

"Truly, it's heartwarming. The Marquess of Ralston, in all his wickedness. Laid low by a child."

Ralston turned away from his brother, stalking across the room to his desk. "Don't you have a statue somewhere that must be cleaned? An elderly woman from Bath with a marble in desperate need of identification?"

Nick extended his legs and crossed one shining Hessian over the other, refusing to rise to his brother's bait. "As a matter of fact, I do. However, she—along with my legions of fans—shall have to wait. I should much rather spend the afternoon with you."

"Do not stay on my account."

Nick became serious. "What happens in two months? When she still wants to leave and you cannot allow it?" When Ralston did not reply, Nick pressed on. "It has not been easy for her. Deserted by her mother at such a young age . . . then losing her father as well."

"No different than our own circumstances." Ralston feigned disinterest as he sorted through a pile of correspondence. "In fact, I would remind you that we lost our father along with our mother."

Nick's gaze did not waver. "We had each other, Gabriel. She has no one. We know better than anyone what it is like to be in her position; to be deserted by everyone you have ever had—everyone you have ever loved."

Ralston met Nick's eyes, somber with the memories of their shared childhood. The twins had survived their mother's desertion, their father's descent into despair. Their childhood had not been pleasant, but Nick was right—they had had each other. And that had made the difference. "The one thing I learned from watching our parents is that love is overrated. What matters is responsibility. Honor. Juliana will be better for understanding that at such a young age. She has us, now. And likely she thinks it not much. But it will have to be enough."

The brothers fell into silence, each lost to his own thoughts. Eventually, Nick said, "It will be difficult to get the *ton* to accept her."

Ralston swore roundly, recognizing the truth in his brother's words.

As the daughter of a woman who had not received a proper divorce, Juliana would not be immediately accepted into society. At best, Juliana was the child of a lady exiled from polite society, and she would struggle to cast off the heavy mantle of her mother's soiled reputation. At worst, she was the illegitimate daughter of a fallen marchioness and her common-born Italian lover.

Nick spoke again. "Her legitimacy will be questioned."

Gabriel thought for several moments. "If our mother married her father, it means that the marchioness must have converted to

Catholicism upon arriving in Italy. The Catholic Church would never have acknowledged her marriage in the Church of England."

"Ah, so it is we who are illegitimate." Nick's words were punctuated with a wry smile.

"To Italians, at least," Gabriel said. "Luckily, we are English."

"Excellent. That works out well for us," Nick replied, "but what of Juliana? There will be many who will refuse to socialize with her. They shan't like that she is the daughter of a fallen woman. And a Catholic no less."

"They wouldn't have accepted Juliana to begin with. We cannot change the fact that her father is of common birth."

"Perhaps we should attempt to pass her off as a distant cousin rather than a sibling."

Ralston's response brooked no refusal. "Absolutely not. She is our sister. We shall present her as such and face the consequences."

"It is she who will face the consequences." Nick met his brother's eye as the words hung in the air, heavy with importance. "The season will soon be in full swing. If we are to succeed, our activities must be entirely aboveboard. Our reputation is hers."

Ralston understood. He would have to end his arrangement with Nastasia—the opera singer was renowned for indiscretion. "I shall speak with Nastasia today."

Nick nodded in acknowledgment before adding, "And Juliana will need an introduction into society. From someone with an impeccable character."

"Yes, I thought of that myself."

"We could always call on Aunt Phyllidia." Nick shuddered even as he referred to their father's sister who, despite being certain to arrive full of loud opinions and brash instructions, was a dowager duchess and a pillar of the *ton*.

"No." Ralston's response was short and immediate. Phyllidia

would not be able to manage such a delicate situation as this—a mysterious, unknown sister arriving on the doorstep of Ralston House at the start of the season. "None of our female relatives will do."

"Then who?"

Twin gazes locked. Held. Their determination matched, their commitment equal.

But only one was the marquess. And his words left no room for questions. "I shall find someone."

Two

Then with a burst of tears she ran straight toward him,
and flung her arms about the neck of Odysseus,
and kissed his head, and spoke:
"Lo, thou dost convince my heart, unbending as it is."
And in his heart aroused yet more the desire for lamentation;
and he wept, holding in his arms his dear and true-hearted wife.

Callie Hartwell paused in her reading, and released a deep, satisfied sigh. The sound rent the silence of the Allendale House library, where she had escaped hours earlier in search of a good book. In Callie's opinion, a good book required an enduring love story . . . and Homer delivered.

Oh, Odysseus, she thought soulfully, turning a yellowed page in the leather-bound book and wiping away a stray tear. *Twenty years later, back in the arms of your love. A well-deserved reunion if ever I've read one.*

She paused in her reading, leaning her head back on the high padded chair and breathing deeply, inhaling the rich scent of long-loved and well-oiled books and imagining herself the heroine of this particular story—the loving wife, the object of an heroic quest to return home, the woman who, through love, inspired her wonderfully flawed husband to fight the Cyclops, to resist the Sirens, to conquer all for a single goal—to resume his place by her side.

What would it be like to be such a woman? One whose unparalleled beauty was rewarded with the love of the greatest hero of his time? What would it be like to welcome such a man into one's heart? Into one's life? Into one's *bed*? A smile played across Callie's lips as the wicked thought flashed through her mind. *Oh, Odysseus indeed.*

She chuckled. If only others knew that Lady Calpurnia Hartwell, proper, well-behaved spinster, entertained deep-seated and certainly unladylike thoughts about fictional heroes. She sighed again with self-deprecation. She was well aware of how silly she was, dreaming of the heroes in her books. It was a terrible habit, and one she had harbored for far too long.

It had begun when she had first read *Romeo and Juliet* at age twelve and followed her through heroes great and small—from Beowulf and Hamlet and Tristan to the dark, brooding heroes of gothic novels. It didn't matter the quality of the writing—Callie's fantasies about her fictional heroes were entirely democratic.

She closed her eyes and imagined herself far from this high-ceilinged room, filled to the brim with books and papers collected by a long line of Allendale earls. She imagined herself not the spinster sister of the Earl of Allendale, but instead, as Penelope, so deeply in love with her Odysseus that she had spurned all suitors.

She conjured her hero into the vision, she, seated at a loom, he, standing strong and intense in the doorway to the room. His physical appearance came easily—it was one that had been used again and again in her fantasies for the last decade.

Tall, towering, and broad, with thick dark hair that made women itch to touch it and blue eyes the color of the same sea that

Odysseus had sailed for twenty years. A strong jaw, marred only by a dimple that flashed when he smiled—that smile—a smile that held the equal promise of wickedness and pleasure.

Yes . . . they were all modeled on the only man about whom she'd ever dreamed—Gabriel St. John, the Marquess of Ralston. One would think that after a full decade of pining, she would have given up her fantasy . . . but it appeared that she had fallen for the rake quite squarely and most regretfully, and she was doomed to spend the rest of her life imagining him the Antony to her Cleopatra.

She laughed outright at the comparison. The fact that she was named for an empress aside, one would have to be severely touched to think Lady Calpurnia Hartwell anything close to Cleopatra. For one thing, Callie had never laid a man low with her beauty— something Cleopatra was reported to have been extraordinarily skilled at doing. Cleopatra did not share Callie's ordinary brown hair and ordinary brown eyes. Nor could the Queen of Egypt have been described as plump. Nor did Callie imagine that Cleopatra had ever been left on the edge of a ballroom for the entirety of a ball. And, Callie was certain there was absolutely no evidence that the Queen of Egypt had ever worn a lace cap.

Unfortunately, the same things could not be said of Callie.

But, for now, in this moment, Callie was the beautiful Penelope and Ralston the devastatingly handsome Odysseus, who had rooted their marital bed to the ground with a living oak tree. Her skin grew flushed as the fantasy played out, and he approached her and that legendary bed, slowly lifting his tunic, baring a chest bronzed from years in the Aegean sun—a chest that could have been molded from Grecian marble. When he reached her and gathered her into his arms, she imagined the heat of him wrapping around her, dwarfing her with his size. He had spent years waiting for this moment . . . and so had she.

His hands stroked her skin, leaving trails of fire wherever they touched, and Callie imagined him leaning down to kiss her. She could feel his body pressed against her, his hands on her face, his strong, sensual lips parting just a hairsbreadth from her own. Just before he claimed her mouth in a searing kiss, he spoke in a low whisper, the words private, the sound barely reaching her ears.

"CALLIE!"

She jerked up in her chair, dropping her book, startled by the piercing sound outside the door to the library. She cleared her throat, heart pounding, silently wishing that whoever it was would go away and let her finish her daydream. The thought was fleeting—quashed with a sigh—Callie Hartwell was nothing if not impeccably mannered, and she would *never* reject a caller out of hand. No matter how much she might like to.

The door to the library flew open, and her sister bounded in, all energy and excitement. "Callie! There you are! I've been looking everywhere!"

Callie took one look at her sister's bright, eager face and couldn't help but smile. Mariana had always been a charming, ebullient force—immediately adored by all who met her. At eighteen, Mariana was the belle of the season . . . the debutante who had earned the attentions of the entire *ton*—and the nickname The Allendale Angel.

Today, she was bathed in the diffused sunlight of the library, swathed in gossamer chiffon the color of buttercups, her sweet, loving smile perfectly framed by chestnut ringlets. Callie could easily understand why London society adored her sister. It was hard not to love Mariana.

Even if her perfection could be rather trying at times to a much older, much less perfect sister.

With a teasing smile, Callie spoke. "Whatever could you possibly need me for? I think you've done quite well on your own today, Mari!"

A pretty pink blush spread across Mariana's porcelain skin—one Callie would have envied for its demureness and evenness if she hadn't lived with such perfect flushes for her entire life. "Callie! I can't believe it! I've been pinching myself all day!" Mariana flew across the room and threw herself into the leather chair opposite her sister. In a dreamy, dazed voice, she continued, "He proposed! Can you believe it? Isn't it wonderful?"

"He" in this case was James Talbott, the sixth Duke of Rivington and the single most coveted catch in all of Britain. Young, handsome, wealthy, and titled, the duke had taken one look at Mariana at a preseason ball and become quite thoroughly infatuated. A whirlwind courtship had followed, and the duke had arrived at Allendale House that morning to ask for her hand in marriage. Callie had been barely able to contain her amusement at Rivington's nervousness; for all his title and wealth, he had been obviously eager for Mariana's answer—a fact that had only served to endear him further to Callie.

"I can, indeed, believe it, sweet." She laughed. "He arrived with stars in his eyes . . . very similar to the ones in your own right now!" Mariana dipped her head shyly as Callie continued, "But you must tell me! How does it feel to have caught a man who loves you so very much? And a duke no less!"

"Oh, Callie," Mariana gushed, "I don't give a farthing about James's title! I care only for James! Is he not the most wonderful, pillar of a man?"

"And a duke no less!" Both women turned in surprise at the statement, spoken in a shrill pitch of barely contained excitement from the doorway of the room. Callie sighed as she recalled what had sent her into hiding earlier in the day.

Her mother.

"Callie! Is it not the most wonderful news?" Wryly wondering just how many times she would have to answer that particular question that day, Callie opened her mouth to reply. Not quickly enough, however. "Why, Rivington is deeply in love with Mariana! Can you imagine? A duke! In love with our Mariana!" Again, Callie began to answer, only to be cut off. "There is so very much to do! A wedding to plan! A betrothal ball to host! Menus to design! Invitations to send! Not to mention Mariana's gown! And trousseau! Oh! Mariana!"

The utter bliss on the dowager countess's face was rivaled only by the utter terror on Mariana's. Callie bit back a smile and entered the fray to rescue her sister. "Mother, Rivington only proposed this morning. Don't you think we should allow Mariana some time to enjoy this momentous occasion?" Laughter entered her tone as she continued, offering a knowing look to her sister, "Perhaps, a day or two?"

It was as though she had not spoken. The dowager countess pressed on, her volume becoming more and more earsplitting. "And you, Callie! We shall have to think carefully about what kind of gown *you* shall wear!"

Oh, no. The Dowager Countess of Allendale was many things, but a reliable *modiste* for her elder daughter was not one of them. If Callie did not provide a distraction for her mother soon, she would be destined to attend her sister's wedding in a feathered monstrosity complete with matching turban.

"I think we should tackle first things first, don't you, Mother? Why not hold a small celebratory dinner party this evening?" She paused, waiting to see if her mother would take the bait.

"A wonderful idea!" Callie let her breath out slowly, pleased with her quick thinking. "We should! It will be family only, of course—because we must hold the official announcement for the betrothal ball—but I think a dinner tonight is just the thing! Oh! So much *more* to do! I must send invitations out and speak with Cook!" The dowager countess swiveled around and rushed to leave, propelled by her excitement. At the entrance to the room, she turned back abruptly. Unable to contain her exuberance, her face red and her breathing heavy, she exclaimed, "Oh! Mariana!" And, with that, she left.

In the silence that followed their mother's departure, Mariana sat stunned by the scene that had just taken place. Callie couldn't help but smile. "You didn't think it would be easy, did you, Mari? After all, our mother has been waiting thirty-two years for a wedding, since Benedick was born. And now, thanks to you, she's got one."

"I don't think I can survive this," Mariana said, shaking her head in bemusement. "Who was that woman?"

"A mother with a wedding in her future."

"My God," Mariana spoke, dazed. "How long do you think she's going to be like that?"

"I can't be certain, but I'd guess at least the season."

"A whole season! Is there a way out of it?"

"There is one," Callie paused for dramatic effect, thoroughly enjoying herself.

Mariana pounced. "What is it?!"

"Do you think Rivington would consider Gretna Green?"

Mariana groaned in anguish as Callie dissolved into laughter.

This was going to be an extraordinarily entertaining season.

THIS WAS GOING to be the most painful season of her life.

Callie stood at the corner of the sitting room, where, after dinner and postmeal rituals of cigars for men and gossip for women, the entire family had resumed showering Mariana and her duke with well-wishes. Dozens of candles cast a lovely soft glow over the room's inhabitants, transforming the space into an intimate scene. Ordinarily, Callie adored events that could fit into the sitting room, for they were typically cozy, happy occasions that made for warm memories.

Not so, tonight, however. Tonight, Callie was ruing the moment that afternoon when she had suggested a small, intimate dinner. Tonight, even the ancestors watching from the portraits lining the sitting-room walls seemed to be mocking her.

She swallowed a sigh and forced a smile as her aunt Beatrice approached her, beaming. Callie knew exactly what was coming . . . knew, too, that it was unavoidable.

"Isn't it wonderful? Such a happy couple! Such a fine match."

"Indeed it is, Aunt," Callie intoned, turning her head to gaze upon the happy couple in question. She had discovered over the course of the interminable evening that looking at an elated Mariana and Rivington made stomaching this particular conversation slightly easier. *Very* slightly easier. "It is a treat to see Mariana so very happy."

Her elderly aunt rested a wrinkled hand on Callie's arm. *Here it comes,* Callie thought to herself, gritting her teeth. "I'm sure your mother is happy finally to have a wedding to plan!" the old woman cackled with amusement as she spoke. "After all, between you and Benedick, there was little guarantee that she'd ever see the day!"

Callie forced a laugh that came out a little too loud as she cast a desperate eye around the room in search of someone, *anyone,* to save her from a seemingly endless string of rude and impertinent family members. In the three hours since the guests had arrived for dinner, Callie had had some variation of this conversation with twelve different people. Dinner had been particularly difficult, considering she'd been sandwiched between Rivington's opinionated grandmother and a particularly callous cousin, both of whom seemed to believe that Callie's unmarried state was well within the bounds of proper conversation. She was beginning to believe that there was not a single person in either the Rivington or Allendale families with even a modicum of tact. Did they really believe that she would take no offense to being consistently reminded that she was a dusty old spinster set firmly upon the shelf? It was really too much.

Seeing no salvation in her future, she settled for waving down a footman with a tray of sherry. Selecting a glass for herself, she turned to her aunt, asking, "May I offer you a refreshment, Aunt Beatrice?"

"Dear me, no! I cannot stomach the stuff," the elderly woman spoke, a note of indignation in her tone. "You know, Calpurnia, drinking wine in company is liable to damage your reputation."

"Yes, well, I should think there's no need for me to worry about that this evening, don't you agree?"

"No, I suppose your reputation is not at risk, Calpurnia." Aunt Beatrice patted her arm with unconscious condescension. "It is a tragedy, that, isn't it? You couldn't have predicted it. With your dowry, no one would have expected you never to marry."

The implication that only her dowry served to recommend Callie as a wife clouded her consciousness with shock and anger. Before she could respond, Aunt Beatrice had pressed on.

"And now, at your age, we should simply give up hope. It's virtually impossible to imagine someone offering for you. Unless, of course, it was an older gentleman seeking companionship as he shuffles off this mortal coil. *Perhaps* that could happen."

A vision flashed through Callie's mind, a pleasing fantasy that ended with Aunt Beatrice doused in sweet red wine. Shaking herself from her reverie, she carefully set down her glass and returned her focus to her aunt, who was still speculating on Callie's spinsterhood.

"Of course, it does not help that your figure is—well—rather less than desirable? After all, we are long past the days of Rubens, Calpurnia."

Callie was struck mute. She could not have possibly heard the odious woman correctly.

"Have you considered a diet of boiled eggs and cabbage? I hear it works wonders. Then you would be less . . . well, more!" Aunt Beatrice cackled, entirely amused by and thoroughly oblivious to her own rudeness. "And *then*, perhaps we could find you a husband!"

Callie had to escape before she did serious damage either to a member of the family or to her own sanity. Without meeting Beatrice's eyes—she could not guarantee that she wouldn't say something thoroughly nasty to the horrible woman—Callie made her excuses, "Pardon me, Aunt, I think I should see to the . . . kitchens." She didn't care that the explanation made little sense, what with dinner long over; she simply had to flee.

Holding back tears, Callie escaped to her brother's study—the nearest room where she knew wayward guests would not disturb her. Guided by the moonlight spilling in through the enormous windows that lined one wall of the study, she made her way to the sideboard and retrieved a glass and a bottle of sherry before moving to a large chair in the far corner of the room that had long been a sanctuary for Allendale men.

It will have to serve the purpose for an Allendale female tonight, she thought, letting out a long, slow breath as she poured herself a glass of sherry, set the heavy crystal decanter down on the floor, and threw her legs over one arm of the chair, making herself comfortable.

"What has you sighing, sister mine?"

Callie gave a little start, turning in the direction of the imposing mahogany desk at the other side of the room. She saw the shadowed figure behind it and smiled broadly into the darkness. "You startled me."

"Yes, well, forgive me if I don't apologize. You entered *my* lair." Benedick Hartwell, Earl of Allendale, rose and moved across the room to seat himself in the chair opposite Callie. "I hope you have a good reason, or I shall have to send you back."

"Oh? I should be interested in seeing how you accomplish that, as you cannot reveal my escape without calling attention to your own," she teased.

"Too true." Benedick's white teeth flashed. "Well, then, you can stay."

"Thank you." She toasted him with her glass of sherry. "You are too kind."

Benedick swirled a glass of scotch lazily as Callie drank deeply and relaxed in the chair with her eyes closed, enjoying their companionable silence. After several minutes, he spoke. "And so, what sent you fleeing the familial rite?"

Callie did not open her eyes. "Aunt Beatrice."

"What did the old bird do now?"

"Benedick!"

"Are you about to tell me that you don't think of her in a remarkably similar way?"

"Thinking of her in such a manner is one thing. Saying it aloud is quite another."

Benedick laughed. "You are too well behaved for your own good. So what did our dear, revered, valued aunt do to send you fleeing to a darkened room?"

She sighed, refilling her glass. "She did nothing that no other member of the two families represented in that room failed to do. She simply did it more rudely."

"Ah. Marriage."

"She actually said—" She paused, taking a deep breath. "No. I will not give her the pleasure of repeating it."

"I can imagine."

"No, Benny. You cannot." She sipped her sherry. "I vow, had I known that this was how spinsterhood would be, I would have married the first man who proposed to me."

"The first man who proposed to you was an idiot vicar."

"You shouldn't speak ill of the clergy."

Benedick snorted and took a long pull of scotch.

"Fine. I would have married the *second* man who proposed. Geoffrey was quite attractive."

"If you hadn't turned him down, Callie, Father would have. He was an inveterate gambler and a notorious drunk. He died in a gambling hell, for goodness sake."

"Ah, but then I would be a *widow*. No one insults widows."

"Yes, well, I'm not sure that's true, but if you insist . . ." Benedick paused. "Do you really wish you were married to one of them?"

Callie drank again, letting the sweet wine linger on her tongue as she considered the question. "No, not to anyone who has ever asked me," she said. "I wouldn't like to be chattel to some horrible man who married me only for money or land or to be aligned with the Allendale earldom . . . but I wouldn't refuse a love match."

Benedick chuckled. "Yes, well, a love match is an entirely different thing altogether. They don't come along every day."

"No," she agreed, and the two lapsed into silence. After several long moments of contemplation, Callie said, "No . . . what I would really like is to be a man."

"I beg your pardon?"

"I would! For example, if I told you that you had to spend the next three months suffering unfeeling remarks related to Mari's wedding, what would you say?"

"I should say, 'Hang that,' and avoid the whole thing."

Callie used her sherry glass to point in his direction. "Exactly! Because you are a man!"

"A man who has succeeded in avoiding a great number of events that would have led to criticism of my unmarried state."

"Benedick," Callie said frankly, raising her head, "the only reason you were able to avoid those events is *because* you're a man. I, unfortunately, cannot play by the same rules."

"Whyever not?"

"Because I am a woman. I cannot simply avoid the balls and dinners and teas and dress fittings. Oh, God. Dress fittings. I'm going to have to suffer through all these horrid piteous stares again . . . while Mariana is in her wedding gown . . . in a *modiste*'s shop. Oh, God." She covered her eyes against the image.

"I still fail to see the reason why you cannot just avoid the horrid events. Fine, you have to be at the ball announcing their engagement. You must attend the wedding. But beg off everything else."

"I cannot do that!"

"Again, I ask, whyever not?"

"Decent women no more beg off events like that than they take lovers. I have a reputation to worry about!"

Now it was his turn to snort. "What utter nonsense. Calpurnia. You are twenty-eight years old."

"It's not very gentlemanly of you to speak of my age. And you know I hate it when you call me Calpurnia."

"You'll suffer through. You are twenty-eight years old, unmarried, and have, quite possibly, the most pristine reputation of any member of the *ton,* no matter their gender or their age. For God's sake, when was the last time you went anywhere without your lace cap?"

She glared at him. "My reputation is all I have. That's what I'm trying to tell you, Benedick." She reached down to pour another glass of sherry.

"Indeed, you're right. It's all you have *now.* But you could have more. Why not reach out and take it?"

"Are you encouraging me to tarnish our good name?" Callie asked incredulously, freezing, decanter in one hand, glass in the other. Benedick raised one eyebrow at the tableau. Callie set the bottle down. "You do realize that if I do so, you, as the earl, will likely suffer the repercussions?"

"I'm not suggesting you take a lover, Callie. Nor am I hoping that you'll cause a scene. I'm simply arguing that you hold yourself to a rather high standard for . . . well . . . someone who need not worry so much about a slight mark on her reputation. I assure you, skipping odious wedding-related events will not impact the state of the earldom."

"While I'm at it, why not drink scotch and smoke a cheroot?"

"Why not?"

"You don't mean that."

"Callie, I feel certain that the house will not crumble around us if you have a drink. Though I'm not certain you would enjoy it." He let silence stretch out for several minutes before continuing. "What else would you want to do?"

She thought carefully about the answer to that question. What if there were no repercussions? What would she do? "I don't know. I've never allowed myself to think of such things."

"Well, allow yourself now. What would you do?"

"As much as I could." The answer came fast, surprising them both, but once the words were spoken, Callie realized the truth in them. "I don't want to be impeccably mannered. You're right. Twenty-eight years of perfect behavior is too long." She laughed as she heard herself say the words.

He joined her. "And, so? What would you do?"

"I would throw away my lace cap."

"A given, I would hope." He scoffed at her. "Come now, Calpurnia. You can be more creative than that. No repercussions, and you choose three things you can do in your own home?"

She smiled, cuddling deeper into her chair, warming to the game. "Learn to fence."

"Now you've got it," he said, encouragingly. "What else?"

"Attend a duel!"

"Why stop there? Use your newfound fencing skills to fight one," he pointed out matter-of-factly.

She wrinkled her nose. "I don't think I actually want to hurt anyone."

"Ah," he said, all seriousness, "so we have found the line you do not wish to cross."

"One of them, it seems. But I should enjoy firing a pistol, I think. Just not at another person."

"Many do enjoy that particular activity," he allowed. "What else?"

She looked up at the ceiling, thinking. "Learn to ride astride."

"Really?"

She nodded. "Really. Sidesaddle seems so . . . missish."

He laughed at her disdain.

"I would—" She stopped as another item flashed through her mind. *Kiss someone.* Well. She certainly couldn't say *that* aloud to her brother. "I would do all the things men take for granted. And more," she said. Then, "I would gamble! In a men's club!"

"Oh ho! And how would you manage that?"

She thought for a moment. "I suppose I should have to masquerade as a man."

He shook his head in amusement, "Ah . . . mother's Shakespeare fascination finally becomes relevant to our lives." She giggled as he continued, "I think that's where I would draw the line. The Earls of Allendale could lose privileges at White's if you tried that."

"Well, lucky for you, I am not about to attempt to sneak into White's. Or do any of those other things, either." Was that disappointment in her tone?

Silence descended again, both siblings lost in their own thoughts, until Benedick raised his glass to his lips to finish his drink. Before it reached his mouth, he paused and, instead, held the glass out, arm extended toward his sister in a silent offer. For a fleeting moment, Callie considered the crystal tumbler, knowing full well that Benedick's offer was for more than the finger of scotch left in the glass.

She shook her head finally, and the moment passed. Benedick threw back the liquid and spoke again. "I am sorry about that," he said, rising from his chair. "I should be happy to hear of you taking a risk or two, sister."

The comment, spoken carelessly as he moved to leave, landed heavily on Callie's ears. She barely listened to the dry question that followed, "Do you think I'm safe in leaving this room? Or will we have to hunker down until the wedding?"

She shook her head distractedly, and replied, "I should think you're safe. Tread carefully."

"Will you join me?"

"No, thank you. I think I shall remain here and ponder a life of adventure."

He grinned at her. "Excellent. Let me know if you decide to set sail for the Orient on the morrow."

She matched his smile with her own. "You shall be the first to hear of it."

With that, he made his exit, leaving Callie to her thoughts.

She sat for a long while, listening as the sounds of the house quieted, guests leaving, the family retiring to bed, the servants clearing the rooms that were used for the dinner, all the while playing the last moments with Benedick over and over in her mind and wondering, *What if?*

What if she could live a life other than the staid, boring mockery of one that she currently lived? What if she could do all the things that she would never dream of doing? What was to keep her from taking such a leap?

At twenty-eight, no one much thought about her. Her reputation had been impeccable for years—for all the years that it had mattered that she retain such an untarnished name. It wasn't as if she were about to traipse off and completely destroy that reputation, anyway. She wasn't going to do anything that a well-respected *male* member of the *ton* wouldn't do on any given day without a second thought. And if they could, why shouldn't she?

She reached up and removed the pins securing her lace cap. Once it came free from its moorings, she plucked it from her head, several long curls of hair tumbling free as she did so, and held it in her hands, turning it over and over as she considered her next move. When had she become the type of woman who wore lace caps? When had she given up hope of being *en vogue*? When had she become the type of person to allow Aunt Beatrice's malice to send her into hiding?

She stood, slightly unsteady, and moved slowly to the fireplace, wringing the cap in her hands, the heady combination of her conversation with Benedick and the sherry offering a heightened sense of power. She stared down at the dying embers, the hiss of the orange coals taunting her.

What *would* she do if she could change it all?

Without pause, she tossed the lace cap into the fireplace. For a few long moments, nothing happened; the round disk of cloth simply lay there, its pristine whiteness in stark contrast to the hot, charred wood. Just as Callie began to wonder if she should reach in and retrieve the now-ruined garment, it burst into flames.

She gasped, taking a small step back in the face of the angry orange fire that engulfed the small piece of lace, but was unable to stop herself from crouching low and watching as the finely wrought fabric took on a life of its own, curling and coloring until every inch of it was aflame.

Watching her lace cap burn, Callie started to laugh, feeling at once scandalous and wonderful—as though she could do anything she had ever dreamed.

Spinning on one heel, she marched across the room to the earl's desk. After lighting a stubbed candle, she opened the top drawer and removed a clean sheet of paper from its place. Smoothing her hand across it, she pondered the vast, ecru expanse before nodding emphatically, opening the silver inkpot that sat nearby, and reaching for a pen.

She dipped the nib of the pen in the black ink and considered the list of things that she would do . . . if she had the courage.

The first answer was obvious and, while she hadn't wanted to share it with Benedick earlier, she felt strongly that she should be honest with herself and commit it to paper. After all, it was the only item she could think of that she truly dreaded never being able to complete.

Setting the nib to the parchment, she wrote, her script strong and certain.

Kiss someone

She looked up as soon as the words were written, half-afraid that she would be discovered writing such a scandalous thing. Returning her attention to the words on the paper, she cocked her head to one side. It didn't seem enough, did it? "Kiss someone" didn't seem to capture exactly what she meant.

Biting her lower lip, she added one word.

Kiss someone—Passionately

Callie let out a long breath—one that she hadn't known she was holding in. *No turning back now,* she thought to herself, *I've already written the most scandalous thing.*

The next few items came easily, born of her conversation with Benedick.

Smoke cheroot and drink scotch
Ride astride
Fence
Attend a duel
Fire a pistol
Gamble (at a gentleman's club)

After a flurry of activity, Callie brought her head up and sat back, looking at the words she had written. A hint of a smile played across her lips as she considered each item, imagining herself seated in a smoky room at White's, scotch in one hand, playing cards in the other, sabre lying at her feet, discussing the duel she was to attend the next morning. The image brought a deep chuckle from far within. Imagine!

She almost stopped there, with the seven items that had come quickly. But for all that the list was a flight of fancy, Callie knew that it was much more. It was a chance for her finally to be honest with herself. To write down the things that she would most desperately like to experience. The things that she had never admitted to anyone—not even herself. With a heartfelt sigh, she eyed the list, knowing that the next few items would be the most difficult to write.

"Right, then." She spoke the words in a strong tone, as if preparing herself for battle. Then, she set pen to paper.

Dance every dance at a ball

Her lips twisted in a self-deprecating smile. *Well, Callie, that item proves that this is an imaginary list.* She adored dancing.

She always had. When she was a child, she used to sneak from her bedchamber to watch the balls her parents had hosted. There, high above the ballroom, she would twirl and twirl in time to the music, imagining that her night rail was a beautiful silk gown to rival the ones swirling below. Dancing was the one thing that Callie had looked forward to when she had her first season; but as she had aged into spinsterhood, invitations had tapered off. She hadn't danced a country dance in—well, it had been a long, long time. Too long.

There in the darkness, she allowed herself to admit that all those years of standing on the edges of ballrooms across London had taken their toll. She loathed being a wallflower, but she had never been able to lift herself out of that position. And, in the ten years since her debut, she had become so comfortable as a witness to the elegance of society that she couldn't imagine actually being at the center of it. Of course, she would *never* be at its center. The women at the nexus of the *ton* were beautiful. And Callie was too plain, too plump, too boring to be considered beautiful. Blinking back tears, she scrawled the next item on the list.

Be considered beautiful. Just once.

It was the most unlikely item on the list . . . she could only remember one time, one fleeting moment in her life when she had even come close to achieving the goal. But, thinking back on that night long ago, when the Marquess of Ralston had made her feel beautiful, Callie was certain that he hadn't perceived her that way. No, he was just a man who did what he could to make a young girl feel better so that he could escape to a midnight tryst. But in that moment he had made her feel beautiful. Like an empress. How she wanted to be that girl again; how she wanted to feel like Calpurnia again.

Of course, she couldn't do it. It was just a silly exercise.

With a sigh, Callie stood from the desk, folding the paper carefully and tucking it just inside the bodice of her gown before she replaced the ink and pen. Snuffing the candle, she moved quietly toward the door. Just as she was about to exit the study and make her way upstairs, she heard a noise from outside—quiet and unfamiliar.

Opening the door carefully—just a crack—Callie peered into the darkened hallway, squinting to make out anyone who might be there. The blackness beyond made it impossible to see, but there was no question that she was not alone; the open door allowed a soft giggle to reach her.

"You are beautiful tonight. Perfect. The Allendale Angel indeed."

"You're required to say so . . . to flatter your fiancée."

"My fiancée." The reverence in the words was palpable. "My future duchess . . . my love . . ."

The words trailed off on a feminine sigh, and Callie's hand flew to hold in her shocked laughter as she realized that Mariana and Rivington were in the darkened foyer. She froze for a moment, eyes wild, uncertain of her next move. Should she close the door quietly and wait for them to leave? Or should she contrive to stumble upon them and end what was most definitely a lovers' tryst?

Her thoughts were interrupted by a little gasp, "No! We shall be caught!"

"And what then?" the words came on a masculine chuckle.

"I suppose then you shall have to marry me, Your Grace." Callie's eyes widened at the blatant sensuality in her little sister's tone. *When had Mariana become a doxy?*

Rivington groaned in the darkness. "Anything that gets you into my bed more quickly."

It was Mariana's turn to laugh, entirely inappropriately. And then there was silence, punctuated only by the soft sounds of lips on flesh and silk on skin.

Callie's mouth dropped open. Yes, she should definitely close the door.

Then why didn't she?

Because it wasn't fair.

It simply wasn't fair that her baby sister—who had looked up to her for so long, who, for so many years, had turned to her for advice and guidance and friendship—was now experiencing this remarkable new world of love.

Mariana had come out with a vengeance, the star of the season, and Callie had been so very proud of her. And when Mari had caught the eye of Rivington, the catch of the *ton,* Callie had celebrated alongside her little sister.

And Callie *was* happy for Mariana.

But how much longer could she happily stand by as Mariana lived the life that Callie herself had longed for? Everything would change. Mariana would do all that Callie had never done. She would marry, and bear children, and run a household, and grow old in the arms of a man who loved her. And Callie would remain here in Allendale House, a spinster.

Until Benedick found a wife. And she was relegated to the country. Alone.

Callie swallowed back the sting of tears, refusing to allow herself to feel self-pity in the face of Mariana's happiness. She moved to close the door to the study softly, to leave the lovers in peace.

Before she could, however, Mariana spoke, breathlessly. "No, Riv. We cannot. My mother would horsewhip us both if we ruined her chance for a wedding."

Rivington groaned softly. "She has two other children."

"Yes, but . . ." There was a pause, and Callie did not have to see her sister to read her thoughts. *What are the odds that either of them will marry anytime soon?*

"Benedick will marry," Rivington said, humor in his tone. "He's simply waiting until the last possible moment to do so."

"It is not Benedick about whom I worry."

"Mari, we've discussed this. She is welcome at Fox Haven."

Callie's mouth dropped open in outrage at the mention of Rivington's country seat. *She?* Could they mean *her*? They had discussed her fate? As though she were an orphaned child in need of care?

As though she were an unmarried female with no prospects.

Which, of course, she was.

Her mouth closed.

"She will make a wonderful aunt," Rivington added.

Excellent. He's already sloughing off the heirs to the dukedom on the spinster aunt.

"She would have made a wonderful *mother*," Mariana said, and her emphatic words brought a watery smile to Callie's face. She tried to ignore her sister's use of the past tense as Mari added, "I only wish she could have had what we have. She so deserves it."

Rivington sighed. "She does. But I am afraid that only Callie can seize such a life for herself. If she remains so . . ." He paused, searching for the word, and Callie strained to hear—the angle of her body so unnatural that she risked toppling over entirely. "Passive . . . she shall never have those things."

Passive?

Callie imagined Mariana nodding her agreement. "Callie needs an adventure. Of course, she shall never seek one out."

There was a long pause as their words—so lacking in malice and still so painful—echoed around Callie, suffocating her with the heavy weight of their meaning. And all at once, she could not seem to catch her breath or stop the tears from welling.

"Perhaps you would like an adventure for yourself, my beauty." Rivington's sensual tone was restored, and Mariana's responding giggle proved too much to bear. Callie closed the door quietly, blocking out the sound.

If only she could block out the memory of their words.

Passive. What a horrible word. What a terrible sentiment. Passive and plain and unadventurous and destined for a boring, staid, utterly uninteresting life. She choked back tears, leaning her forehead against the cool mahogany door and considering the very real possibility that she was about to cast up her accounts.

Taking great, heaving breaths, she attempted to calm herself, the powerful combination of sherry and emotion threatening to bring her low.

She did not want to be that woman—the one of whom they spoke. She had never planned to be that woman. Somehow, it had happened, however . . . somehow, she had lost her way and, without realizing it, she had she chosen this staid, boring life instead of a different, more adventurous one.

And now her younger sister was mere feet away, on the brink of self-induced ruin, and Callie had never even been kissed.

It was enough to drive a spinster to drink.

Of course, she'd done enough of that tonight.

It was enough to drive a spinster to *action*.

Reaching into her bodice, she produced the folded piece of paper she had placed there only minutes earlier. Fingering the rounded edges of the square, she considered her next move.

She could go to bed, drown herself in tears and sherry, and spend the rest of her life not only regretting her inaction but— worse—knowing those around her believed her *passive*.

Or, she could change.

She could complete the list.

Now. Tonight.

She smoothed back an errant lock of hair; noted her missing lace cap.

Tonight. She would begin with an item that was a challenge. An item that would set her squarely on this new, bold, un-Callie-like course.

Taking another deep breath, she pulled open the door to the study and stepped into the darkened foyer of Allendale House, no longer caring if she stumbled upon Mariana and Rivington. In fact, she barely registered that they were gone.

She hadn't time for them, anyway, she thought as she hurried up the wide marble staircase to her bedchamber. She had to change her gown.

Lady Calpurnia was going out.

Three

Callie watched the hackney cab drive off down the darkened street, leaving her utterly stranded.

She gave a little sigh of dismay as the clatter of horses' hooves faded into the distance, replaced by the pounding of her heart and the rushing of blood in her ears. She should have begun with the scotch. And she certainly should *not* have had so much sherry.

Had she remained abstemious, she would most definitely not be standing here, alone, in front of the home of one of London's most notorious rakes, in the middle of the night. *What had she been thinking?*

Clearly, she hadn't been thinking—at all.

For a fleeting moment, she considered turning back to the street and hailing the next hackney that passed, but fast on the heels of that thought came the realization that her reputation would be thoroughly destroyed should she be discovered.

"I shall have Benedick's head for this," she muttered to herself, pulling the hood of her dark cloak lower over her face. "Mariana's as well." Of course, it was neither Benedick nor Mariana who had forced her into a hack, risking her safety and good name. She'd done that all on her own.

With a deep breath, she accepted the truth . . . that she had landed herself squarely in the midst of this mess, that her reputation was mere minutes from being in tatters, and that her best chance of surviving this situation intact lay inside Ralston House. She winced at the thought.

Ralston House. Dear Lord. What had she done?

She had to go inside. She had no choice. Standing on the street for the rest of the night was not an option. Once indoors, she would beg the butler to ferry her from the house to a hack, and, if all went well, she could be in her bed within the hour. He would certainly feel obligated to protect her. She was a lady, after all. Even if her actions that evening were not precisely bearing that out.

And what if Ralston were to open the door?

Callie shook her head at the thought. First, marquesses did not go around opening their own doors. And secondly, the odds of this particular marquess being home at this particular hour were slim to none. He was likely off with a paramour somewhere. An image flashed through her mind, pulled from a decade-old memory of him locked in a heated embrace with a breathtakingly beautiful woman.

Yes. She had made a horrid mistake. She would just have to escape as quickly as possible.

She squared her shoulders and approached the imposing entrance of Ralston House. She had barely let the knocker fall when the large oak door swung open, revealing an aged servant who seemed not at all surprised to find a young woman standing outside his master's home. Stepping aside, he allowed her to enter, closing the door behind her as she took in the warm, inviting entryway to the long-established London home of the Marquesses of Ralston.

Instinctively, she began to push the hood of her cloak back from her face only to realize that the events to follow would be easier if she were shielded from recognition. Resisting the impulse, she turned to the servant, and said, "Thank you, good sir."

"Indeed, milady." The butler offered a short, respectful bow and began to shuffle toward the wide staircase leading to the upper floors of the house. "If you will follow me?"

Follow you where? Callie recovered quickly from her surprise, "Oh, I do not mean to—" she paused, not sure of the end of the sentence.

He stopped at the foot of the staircase. "Certainly not, milady. It is no trouble. I shall simply provide you escort to your destination."

"My—My destination?" Callie stopped abruptly, her question laced with confusion.

The butler cleared his throat. "Above stairs, milady."

"Above stairs." She was beginning to sound like a ninny even to herself.

"That is where his lordship is at the moment." The butler gave her a curious look, as though questioning her mental faculties, before turning back to the staircase and beginning the climb to the second floor.

"His lordship." Callie watched the servant mount the stairs as understanding dawned and her eyes went wide as saucers. Good lord. He thought her a lightskirt! The shocking realization was quickly followed by another—the butler thought her *Ralston's* lightskirt. Which meant that Ralston was *here.* In the house.

"I'm not . . ." her words trailed off.

"Of course not, milady." He spoke the words with perfect decorum, but she had the distinct sense that he had heard the same, meek protest from countless other women, countless times before. Women who had feigned innocence for propriety's sake.

She had to escape.

Unless . . .

No. She quashed the little voice. No unless. Her reputation was hanging by a thread. She'd be safer hailing a hackney by herself on the dark London streets than following this ancient butler to Lord knew where.

To Ralston's rooms.

Callie nearly choked at the thought. She would never drink sherry again.

"Milady?" The word, delivered with all decorum, held an unspoken query. Was Callie going to follow?

This was her chance. Misguided or not, this was what she had hoped for when she'd sneaked from the house and hailed a hack. She'd wanted to see Ralston—to prove that she had the courage for adventure. And here she was, her objective squarely within reach.

This is your chance to prove yourself more than passive.

She swallowed, staring mutely up at the old man. Fine. She would follow him. And she would ask Ralston to help get her home. It would be embarrassing, but he would come to her aid. He had to. She was the sister of a peer of the realm, and he was a gentleman.

She hoped.

Maybe not, though. A thrill coursed through her at the thought.

She pushed it aside, giving a silent prayer of thanks that she had thought to change into her most flattering gown before making the trip. Not that Ralston would see the lavender silk beneath her plain black traveling cloak—she had absolutely no intention of revealing her identity to the marquess except as a last resort—but knowing that she wore her prettiest dress gave her an extra ounce of confidence as she lifted her skirts and began to climb.

As she moved up the staircase, Callie detected the sound of faraway, muffled music that became louder as the butler led her sedately down a long, dimly lit corridor. He stopped in front of a large mahogany door that did nothing to contain the music that spilled from the room. Callie couldn't help the flash of curiosity that, for a brief moment, overpowered her nervousness.

The butler rapped twice, and a strong, clear "Enter" sounded above the music. He opened the door, but did not cross the threshold. Instead, he moved aside to let Callie enter alone, which she did, tentatively.

The door closed behind her. She was in the lion's den, wrapped in a cloak of shadow and sound.

The large room was barely lit, a hint of light from a few spare candles illuminating the space in a quiet, intimate glow. Even without its enveloping darkness, it was the most masculine room she had ever seen—decorated in rich, dark wood and deep, earthen colors. The walls were covered in a wine-colored silk; the floor boasted an enormous woven carpet that could only have come from the Orient. The furniture was large and imposing—bookshelves lined two walls, each one full to bursting. On the third wall was a large mahogany bed draped in midnight blue fabrics. As her gaze fell to it, her mind flashed to her earlier fantasy of Odysseus and Penelope and a very different but equally alluring bed.

Callie swallowed nervously, averting her gaze from the scandalous furnishing, her eyes alighting on the master of the house, seated on the far end of the room, his back to the door, at a pianoforte. She had never imagined a piano outside of a conservatory or a ballroom—certainly never as an addition to a bedchamber. He had not turned away from the instrument at her intrusion, instead raising a hand to stay any words that might have interrupted his playing.

The piece he played was dark and melodic, and Callie was immediately captivated by its blend of talent and emotion. She watched, riveted by his tanned and corded arms, bare to the elbows, where his white-linen shirtsleeves had been haphazardly rolled; by his strong hands dancing deliberately, instinctively across the keys; by the curve of his neck as his head dipped low in concentration.

When he finished the piece, the last of the notes lingered in the heavy air as he lifted his head and turned toward the door, revealing long, muscled legs in tight breeches and knee-high riding boots; his shirt, open at the collar, without cravat or waistcoat to hide the sliver of skin there; the rippling muscles of his shoulders as he straightened on the stool.

When he noticed her, the only sign of his surprise was a slight narrowing of his gaze, barely perceptible as he searched for her identity in the dim light of the room. She was never more thankful for her hooded cloak than at that moment. He stood calmly and folded his arms.

An untrained eye would have thought that his position was one of carelessness, but Callie's years of watching rather than participating in London society had given her a keen sense of awareness. He appeared all at once angular . . . more tense, the muscles in his arms taut with coiled strength. He was not happy to have a visitor. At least, not a female one.

She opened her mouth to speak, to apologize for her intrusion, to escape, but before she could say anything, his words cut across the room. "I should have guessed that you wouldn't accept my ending our acquaintance. Though, I confess I am surprised that you would be so bold as to visit me here."

Callie's mouth closed in surprise as he continued, his tone firm, his words cold. "I had not wanted to make this more difficult than it had to be, Nastasia, but I see you will not accept my decision. It is over."

Dear Lord. He thought her a tossed-over paramour! Granted, she wasn't exactly presenting herself as a gentlewoman, arriving as she had—unbidden—on the doorstep, in the dead of night, but this was really too much! She should correct him.

"Nothing to say? That's rather out of character, is it not?"

Then again, remaining silent required far less courage than revealing herself to this imposing man.

He gave an irritated sigh, clearly through with the one-sided
conversation. "I think I was more than generous with the end of
our agreement, Nastasia. You retain the house, the jewels, the
clothes—I've given you more than enough rein with which to bri-
dle your next patron, have I not?"

Callie gasped, outraged at the way he was so callously and cav-
alierly ending a romance.

Her response garnered a humorless laugh from the marquess.
"There is no need to play the shocked miss. We both know that na-
ïveté escaped you long ago." His tone was cool and emotionless as
he dismissed her, "You may find your own way out." He resumed
his seat, turning his back to her and beginning to play once more.

Callie had never thought she would feel for one of the courtesans who lurked on the edges of the *ton* as mistresses of the aristocracy, but she couldn't help but take offense on this particular
woman's behalf. And to think, she had thought Ralston a pillar
among men!

She stood, fists clenched in womanly outrage, wondering just
what she should do. No . . . she knew what she *should* do. She
should leave this room immediately and flee this house. She
should return to her quiet, calm life and forget her silly list. But
that was not what she *wanted* to do.

What she *wanted* to do was teach this man a lesson. And her
anger made her brave enough to stay.

He did not look back as he said, "I beg you not to make this
situation any more awkward than you have."

"I'm afraid this situation can only become more awkward, my
lord."

His head whipped toward her as he shot from his seat. If she were not so irritated, she would have been vastly entertained. "You see, I am not who you quite obviously believe me to be."

She had to give him credit. His surprise was almost immediately replaced by shuttered calm. "Indeed you are not, Miss . . ." He paused, waiting for her to identify herself. He continued after a long silence, "It appears that you have the advantage of me."

"Indeed, it does seem that way." Callie was shocked by her own boldness.

"May I assist you in some way?"

"I had thought so. However, after witnessing the manner in which you address the women in your life, I find I would rather not join their ranks."

One of his dark eyebrows kicked up at her words. Callie took that as her cue to escape. Without another word, she turned abruptly and grasped the door handle. She had opened the door not a quarter of an inch when a large, strong hand shot over her shoulder and closed it again. *Dear Lord . . . he was fast.* She tugged at the handle with both hands, but her strength was no match for his; that single, strong arm kept the door firmly shut.

"Please," she spoke, her words barely above a whisper, "let me go."

"You speak as though I brought you here, my lady. On the contrary. 'Tis you who entered my domain. Don't you think you owe me the courtesy of an introduction?" His reply was quiet, spoken just at the edge of her hood, sending a shiver of panic through her. His body was scant inches away from hers—any closer, and they would be touching. They might as well have been for the way the heat of him was overwhelming her senses. Callie stared at the doorjamb, wondering just how she was going to escape her fate.

She had started this evening as Calpurnia. She couldn't give up now. "We've—" She cleared her throat and started again. "We've met before, my lord."

"I cannot be expected to know that with you shrouded in cloth." He tweaked the edge of her sleeve, his fingertips carelessly brushing the back of her hand. She sucked in a breath at the touch. His tone turned cajoling. "Come now, do you really think that I will allow you to leave without learning your identity? You have come too far now."

He was right, of course, and Callie was nothing if not pragmatic. Taking a deep breath, she let go of the handle and began to turn toward him. He took a step back, letting go of the door as she lowered her hood, revealing herself. He tilted his head just slightly at the sight of her, as though trying to place her. After a brief moment, recognition dawned, and he stepped back again, unable to keep the surprised confusion from his face and his voice. "Lady Calpurnia?"

"The very same." She closed her eyes, cheeks burning, feeling sick with regret. She would never leave the house again.

His breath expelled on a humorless half laugh. "I confess, had I been given a thousand guesses, I would never have imagined that you would be my midnight visitor. Are you quite well?"

"I assure you that, contrary to how it might appear, I am not at all mad, my lord. At least, I don't believe I am."

"Forgive me for asking, then, but, what on earth are you doing here?" He seemed all at once to realize where they were. "This is not at all the appropriate place for a lady. I recommend we remove this conversation to a more . . . acceptable . . . location." He waved an arm to indicate the room at large before making a move to reach around her to open the door.

Not interested in dragging out this disastrous meeting any longer, Callie stepped to the side, avoiding his arm and putting more distance between them as she spoke. "Nonsense, my lord. I do not think it necessary to continue this conversation at all. I found myself here at Ralston House under rather . . . peculiar . . .

circumstances, and I think it would be best for us to forget this ever happened. It shouldn't be so difficult, I should think." She pasted a bright smile on her face and fiddled with a tassel on her cloak.

Ralston took in her words, allowing a silence to fall around them. In the long moments of quiet, Callie looked anywhere but at him, and he took note of her nervousness. It wasn't long before his surprise and confusion turned to intrigue, and he assumed a less threatening pose, casually leaning against the wall by the door. "I am not so certain of that, my lady. Contrary to what you may believe, I do not so easily forget women who visit me in my bedchamber." Heat flared high on her cheeks again as he continued, "What brings Lady Calpurnia Hartwell to my doorstep in the middle of the night? Frankly, you do not seem the type."

Callie scrambled for a response. "I was . . . nearby."

"In the middle of the night."

"Yes. I found myself . . . outside . . . and . . . in need of transport home."

"Outside of my home." The words were dry with his obvious disbelief.

"Indeed." Perhaps if she held her own, he would not press her for further explanation.

"How did you come to be outside my home in need of transport?" The sound of his casual curiosity set her on edge.

"I would prefer not to discuss it," she said, averting her eyes and willing him to leave that particular subject alone. Silence descended and, for a brief moment, she thought he was satisfied by her evasive response.

She was wrong.

He crossed his arms arrogantly as he let amused disbelief seep into his words. "And so, you naturally decided that knocking on my door was a safer course of action than hailing the nearest hackney."

In for a shilling, in for a pound. "Indeed, my lord. You are a peer of the realm, after all."

He snorted. She snapped an indignant gaze to meet his mocking one, and blurted out, "You do not believe me?"

"Not a word of it." He leveled her with a piercing, blue look. "Why not tell me the truth this time?"

She dropped her eyes to the floor once more, desperate for another fib to tell, something, *anything* that would get her out of this situation.

He seemed to read her mind. "Lady Calpurnia."

"I'd rather you call me Callie," she said hurriedly.

"You don't like Calpurnia?" The words were lazily curious.

She shook her head, refusing to meet his eyes.

"Callie . . ." He coaxed, the words spoken in a deep, liquid tone that she was certain he used whenever he wanted something from a woman. She would not be surprised to discover that it always worked. "Why are you here?"

And then, whether from courage or cowardice or too much sherry she would never know, she decided to answer him. After all, the evening couldn't possibly become any worse.

In a whisper, she announced, "I came to ask you to kiss me."

IT WASN'T THE answer he'd been expecting. He was surprised by the timid words, barely audible in the silent room. For a moment, he thought he had misheard her, but the crimson flush that raged across her face was enough to convince him that, yes, he had just received an entirely indecent proposition from Lady Calpurnia Hartwell.

The evening had begun innocuously. Having refused all invitations, Ralston had dined with his siblings, still fresh from the discovery of Juliana, then retired to his chamber, hoping that the privacy of his sanctuary and his piano would offer welcome distraction. Eventually, it had worked, and he had lost himself in his music.

Until the knock at the door, announcing Lady Calpurnia's arrival. He gave her a frank perusal. She was not unattractive—slightly plump and a touch plain, but he imagined that was more a result of her simple black cloak than anything else. She had full lips and flawless skin and wide, lovely eyes that flashed with emotion. He wondered at their color briefly before he forced himself to return to the matter at hand.

This was obviously the first time she'd ever done something so forward—so adventurous; if he hadn't already been aware of her pristine reputation, he would have sensed it from her obvious discomfort. Little Calpurnia Hartwell, whom he knew only tangentially from her years of blending into the edges of balls and drawing rooms, was a wallflower of the first water.

Of course, she wasn't much of a wallflower this evening.

He watched her calmly, years of practice hiding his thoughts. She refused to meet his eyes, instead focusing her gaze on her tightly clasped hands while darting quick glances at the door as if to measure the potential success of an attempt to flee the room. He couldn't help the burst of sympathy he felt for her, this little mouse who had obviously found herself in a situation far beyond her experience.

He could be a gentleman about the whole thing—take pity on her, provide her an exit, and offer to forget that this evening had ever happened. But he sensed that, despite her obvious nervousness, there was a part of her that wanted to play this out. He wondered how far she would go.

"Why?"

Her eyes went wide at the question, meeting his for the briefest of moments before she looked away again. "My— my lord?" she stammered.

"Why such a request? Not that I am not flattered, of course, but you'll admit it's rather odd."

"I— I don't know."

He shook his head slowly, a predator on the hunt. "That, my darling, is the wrong answer."

"You shouldn't call me that. It is too familiar."

One side of his mouth lifted in a hint of a smile. "You are in my bedchamber asking me to kiss you. I should think we are rather past the bounds of propriety. Now, I ask again, why?"

She closed her eyes against a wave of embarrassment. For a moment, he thought she wouldn't reply. And then her shoulders rose and fell on a deep breath, and she said, "I've never been kissed. I thought it was time."

The words shocked him—they were not filled with self-pity, nor did they plead. Instead, they were so honest, so matter-of-fact, that he couldn't help but admire her courage. Such a statement could not be an easy one to make.

He did not reveal his surprise. "Why me?"

Her confession seemed to bolster her confidence, and she replied without pause, as though stating the obvious. "You're a notorious rake. I have heard the gossip."

"Oh? What gossip?"

Heat flooded Callie's cheeks.

He pressed on, "Lady Calpurnia. To which gossip do you refer?"

She cleared her throat. "I—may have heard—that you left a certain viscountess half-naked in her husband's conservatory as you climbed out the window to escape his wrath."

"That's an exaggeration."

"They say you left your shirt. And he burned it in effigy."

"A *gross* exaggeration."

She met his eyes. "What about the vicar's daughter who followed you across Devonshire in the hopes of ruining herself?"

"Where did you hear that?"

"It is amazing what one hears on the edges of ballrooms, my lord. Is it true?"

"Let's just say that I am quite lucky that she did not catch up to me. However, I hear she is happily married in Budleigh Salterton these days." She chuckled at his words, the laugh catching in her throat when he added, "Well, considering the gossip, who is to say I would stop at kissing you?"

"No one. But you would stop."

"How do you know?"

"I know."

He recognized the self-deprecation in her tone, but ignored it. "Why now? Why not wait for a man to come along and . . . sweep you off your feet?"

She gave a short laugh. "If the man you speak of had ever planned on coming, my lord, I'm afraid he has obviously lost his way. And, at twenty-eight, I find I have grown tired of waiting."

"Perhaps you should exhibit some of the character you are showing this evening in a more public forum," he said. "I'll admit you seem far more intriguing than I have ever given you credit for, my lady, and intrigue is the spark of desire."

His words hit their mark, and she flushed again. Ralston was unable to deny the enjoyment he felt at this unexpected turn of events. Indeed, this was just the diversion he needed in the face of Juliana's introduction into society.

Quickly on the heels of that thought came another.

Lady Calpurnia Hartwell was the answer to his problems. And she had been delivered to his doorstep—well . . . rather farther than his doorstep—on the same day as his long-lost sister. He felt a wave of satisfaction.

He would kiss her. For a price.

"I wonder if you would be willing to consider a trade?"

Callie turned skeptical. "A trade?" She stepped backward, putting more distance between them. "What kind of trade?"

"Nothing so awful as what you are clearly thinking. You see, it appears I have a sister."

Her eyes widened. "A sister, my lord?"

"Yes, I was rather surprised by the fact myself." He gave her a brief description of the day's events—Juliana's arrival, his decision to claim her as a sibling instead of a distant relative, his commitment to finding her a proper sponsor with an impeccable reputation to ease her entry into society.

"So, as you can see, it's rather lucky that you are here tonight. You are the perfect solution. Assuming, that is, that you do not make it a habit to visit unmarried gentlemen in the dead of night."

She gave a slight, self-conscious laugh. "No, my lord. You are the first."

He'd known that was the case and made a mental note to discover at a later date what exactly had prompted her nocturnal visit. "And the last, I would hope, at least until Juliana is successfully introduced."

"I haven't agreed to your request, yet."

"But you will." His tone was arrogant. "And, as payment, you'll get your kiss."

"Forgive me," she said with humor in her voice, "but you must place a rather high value on your kisses."

He tipped his head, conceding the point. "Very well. Name your price."

Callie looked up at the ceiling thoughtfully before replying. "The kiss will do for now, but I reserve the right to a favor in the future."

"I'm to be indebted to you, then?"

She smiled. "Think of it as a business transaction."

An eyebrow rose. "A business transaction that begins with a kiss."

"A *unique* business transaction." She blushed again.

"You seem shocked by your boldness," he said.

She nodded. "I'm not quite sure what has come over me."

Once more, her honesty surprised him. "Very well, my lady, you are a formidable negotiator. I accept your terms." He approached her, his voice taking on a seductive tenor. "Shall we seal it with a kiss, then?"

Callie caught her breath and stiffened at the question. Ralston smiled at her obvious nerves. He ran a finger along the edge of her hairline, tucking a rogue lock of hair behind her ear gently. She looked up at him with her wide brown eyes, and he felt a burst of tenderness in his chest. He leaned close, moving slowly, as though she might scare at any moment, and his firm mouth brushed across hers, settling briefly, barely touching before she jumped back, one hand flying to her lips.

He leveled her with a frank gaze and waited for her to speak. When she didn't, he asked, "Is there a problem?"

"N—No!" she said, a touch too loudly. "Not at all, my lord. That is—Thank you."

His breath exhaled on a half laugh. "I'm afraid that you have mistaken the experience." He paused, watching the confusion cross her face. "You see, when I agree to something, I do it wholeheartedly. That was not the kiss for which you came, little mouse."

Callie wrinkled her nose at his words, and at the nickname he had used for her. "It wasn't?"

"No."

Her nervousness flared, and she resumed toying with her cloak tassel. "Oh, well. It was quite nice. I find I am quite satisfied that you have held up your end of our bargain."

"Quite nice isn't what you should be aiming for," he said, taking her restless hands into his own and allowing his voice to deepen. "Neither should the kiss leave you satisfied."

She tugged briefly, giving up when he would not free her and instead pulled her closer, setting her hands upon his shoulders. He trailed his fingers down her neck, leaving her breathless, her voice a mere squeak when she replied, "How should it leave me?"

He kissed her then. Really kissed her.

He pulled her against him and pressed his mouth to hers, possessing, owning in a way she could never have imagined. His lips, firm and warm, played across her own, tempting her until she was gasping for breath. He captured the sound in his mouth, taking advantage of her open lips to run his tongue along them, tasting her lightly until she couldn't bear the teasing. He seemed to read her thoughts, and just when she couldn't stand another moment, he gathered her closer and deepened the kiss, changing the pressure. He delved deeper, stroked more firmly.

And she was lost.

Callie was consumed, finding herself desperate to match his movements. Her hands seemed to move of their own volition, running along his broad shoulders and wrapping around his neck. Tentatively, she met Ralston's tongue with her own and was rewarded with a satisfied sound from deep in his throat as he tightened his grip, sending another wave of heat through her. He retreated, and she followed, matching his movements until his lips closed scandalously around her tongue and he sucked gently—the sensation rocked her to her core. All at once she was aflame.

He was right. This was the kiss for which she had come.

He broke off the kiss then, running his lips across her cheek and setting them to her ear, taking the soft lobe between his teeth and biting gently, sending waves of pleasure coursing through her body as he laved the sensitive skin there. From far away, Callie heard a whimper . . . and belatedly realized that it was her own.

His lips curved at her ear as he spoke, his harsh breathing making the words more a caress than a sound, "Kisses should not leave you satisfied."

He returned his lips to hers, claiming her mouth again, robbing her of all thought with a rich, heady caress. All she wanted was to be closer to him, to be held more firmly. And, as though he could read her thoughts, he gathered her closer, deepening the kiss. His heat consumed her; his soft, teasing lips seemed to know all of her secrets.

When he lifted his mouth from hers, she had lost all strength. His next words pierced through her sensual haze.

"They should leave you wanting."

Four

allie woke late, an instant feeling of nervous apprehension roiling deep within her. For a few, brief moments, her scrambled thoughts failed to pinpoint the reason for the odd sensation—until the events of the previous evening came flooding back, hurling her into vivid consciousness. She shot straight up in bed and froze, eyes wide, hoping that the whole night had been a wild, ridiculous dream.

No luck there.

What had she been thinking traipsing off in the middle of the night to Ralston House? Had she honestly approached the Marquess of Ralston in his bedchamber? Had she really made an overture toward London's most notorious rake? Surely she hadn't asked him to kiss her. Remembering her actions, Callie flushed, feeling a wave of heat wash across her face, causing her to drop her head into her hands, groaning in abject mortification.

She would never touch another drop of sherry. Ever again.

Her thoughts raced for a few brief moments, until she raised her head and spoke aloud to the room in horror. "I asked him to *kiss* me." Callie flopped back to the bed with a sigh and willed the universe to strike her dead or, at the very least, infirm. She simply could not risk ever facing Gabriel St. John again. Not after that kiss.

But what a kiss it had been. She squeezed her eyes tightly closed at the thought but was unable to avoid the flood of memories that came with it. The kiss had been everything she had ever imagined. It had been more. Ralston had been larger than life, looming above her, his dark hair tousled, his eyes glittering in the soft candlelight of the room, then he had kissed her, all warm lips and strong hands and exquisite man.

Moving of their own volition, Callie's hands ran down her torso as she remembered the soft stroke of his tongue, the firm grip of his arms. She felt a flood of warmth as she remembered the delicate way his lips had played across hers, the shiver of excitement she'd felt at his breath on her neck. He had been everything she'd ever dreamed.

And when he was through, she had been reduced to rubble. He had said that kisses should leave one wanting . . . but she had not been prepared for the emptiness that spread through her when he'd stepped back from their embrace, looking as calm and collected as though they'd just been to Sunday services.

She had wanted. She still did.

The whole experience, as embarrassing as it had been, was so fierce and freeing and like nothing she'd ever experienced before, and like everything she'd ever dreamed. And it had been Ralston! It had been a kiss to make up for ten long years spent on the edges of ballrooms, watching him with an endless run of beauties on his arm, a decade of her ears pricking up anytime she heard whispers in ladies' salons about his latest affairs, an age of tracking his long line of mistresses with what she'd always told herself was idle interest. Of course, there had never been anything idle about her interest.

She shook her head. But men like Ralston were not for women like Callie. If anything, she'd learned that last night. Ralston was all darkness and excitement and adventure . . . and despite what sherry-laden Callie might have seemed to be the night before. . .

Well, by the light of day, Callie was none of those things.

But, for one evening, for a fleeting moment, she had been. And what a lovely moment it had been. She'd been bold and forward and decidedly *un*passive—reaching for what she knew she might never otherwise have. And, while the previous evening might have taught her that Ralston was not for her, there was certainly no reason why the rest of the things she longed to do couldn't be entirely attainable.

I could have the list.

The thought emboldened her. She turned instinctively to look at the dainty bedside table upon which she had set the scandalous sheet of paper before climbing into bed. Reaching for the list, she scanned it, a ghost of a smile crossing her lips as she reviewed the words scrawled across it. If the events of last night were any indication, she would enjoy every minute of completing the other items. These nine items were all that stood between Callie and living. All she had to do was take the risk.

And why not do so?

Energized, Callie pushed back the coverlet and emerged from the bed. Squaring her shoulders, she moved across the room to the little writing desk in the corner. Setting down the list, she smoothed out the wrinkled paper and considered the words one more time before reaching for a pen and dipping it in a nearby inkpot. She had kissed someone. And passionately.

In a single fluid motion, she drew a thick, black line through the first item, unable to keep the wide grin from her face. *What next?*

A quick knock sounded, and Callie watched in her looking glass as the door swung open to reveal her maid. Registering the stern look on the older woman's face, Callie felt her grin fade as the door clicked shut.

"Good morning, Anne." She quickly slid the list under a book of Byron's poetry.

"Calpurnia Hartwell," Anne said, slowly, "what have you done?"

Callie's eyes slid away from the older woman, settling on a large mahogany wardrobe. "I should like to get dressed," she said, brightly, "I have an appointment this morning."

"With the Marquess of Ralston?"

Callie's eyes widened. "How did you—What?—No!"

"Really? I find that difficult to believe, considering there is a man from Ralston House downstairs waiting for a response to the missive that just arrived for you."

Callie's breath caught as she noticed the piece of paper in the older woman's hands. She stood, moving across the room. "Let me see."

Anne crossed her arms across her ample bosom, hiding the missive under one arm. "Why is the Marquess of Ralston sending you messages, Callie?"

Callie flushed. "I—I don't know."

"You are a terrible liar. Have been since you were in swaddling clothes." Anne was like a dog with a bone. "You've been pining for Ralston for years, Callie-girl. Why has he suddenly taken an interest?"

"I—he hasn't!" She attempted a firm tone, extending her hand. "I should like my correspondence, Anne."

Anne smiled before asking casually, "Were you with Ralston last night?"

Callie froze, heat flooding her cheeks, before blurting out, "Of course not!"

Anne gave her a knowing look. "Well, you were somewhere. I heard you sneak through the servants' entrance just before sunrise."

Callie headed for the wardrobe, throwing open the doors to distract herself from the conversation at hand. "You know, Anne, just because you've cared for me since birth does not give you leave to speak to me so freely."

Anne gave a little laugh. "Of course it does." The maid took advantage of Callie's movement away from her dressing table, removing the list from its hiding place and reading it.

Callie turned back at Anne's scandalized gasp. Noting the paper in her maid's hand, she cried out, "No! Give it back!"

"Callie! What have you done?"

"Nothing!" She snatched the paper back, then paused, taking in Anne's look of disbelief. "Well, nothing *really.*"

"That paper doesn't appear to be nothing."

"I would prefer not to discuss it."

"I'm sure you would."

"It's nothing. It's just a list."

"A scandalous list. Of things that young unmarried females *do not do.*"

Callie turned back to the wardrobe, shoving her head deep into the piece of furniture in the hopes of ending the conversation. When she pulled a peach day dress out and turned back, Anne was still waiting for a response. With a sigh, she muttered, "Well, perhaps young unmarried females should take advantage of their youthful and unshackled state and try some of those things."

Anne blinked at the frank words. And then she laughed. "You completed one of these items already."

"I did." Callie blushed.

Anne squinted at the paper, making out the obscured words. When she looked up in shock, Callie turned away. "Well, Calpurnia Hartwell. You didn't waste any time taking what you've wanted for years."

Callie couldn't help the little smile that played across her lips.

"You *were* with Ralston last night!"

Callie's flaming cheeks spoke volumes.

"I shall tell you one thing," Anne said, a hint of pride in her voice. "You're the only girl I've ever known to make a list like that and actually follow through on it." Her tone shifted, "Of course, if you're not ruined in a week, I shall be even more surprised than I am now."

"I have plans to be very careful," Callie protested.

Anne shook her head. "Unless you work for the War Office, Callie-mine, you can't do half of the things on that list without your reputation collapsing into the gutter." She paused. "You do know that, don't you?"

Callie gave a little nod. "Is it wrong that I don't much care this morning?"

"Yes. You cannot do it all, Callie. Gamble? At a men's club? Are you mad?"

Callie grew serious. "No." The two fell silent for a long moment. Finally, Callie seemed to find the words she was looking for. "But, Anne, it was so *wonderful*. It was the most incredible, freeing *adventure*. Can you blame me for wanting more?"

"It appears that you are already getting more than you've bargained for. Give me that." Anne took the peach muslin from Callie and exchanged it for a grass green jaconet day dress.

"What was wrong with the one I chose?"

"Oh, stop pouting. If we are going to Ralston House, this is the gown you'll wear. You look lovely in green."

Callie accepted the dress, watching as Anne rummaged for underclothes. "We are not going to Ralston House."

Anne said nothing, still engrossed by the contents of the wardrobe. Instead, she thrust the missive toward Callie. Ignoring her shaking hands, Callie broke the wax seal, at once desperately curious and filled with dread.

Lady Calpurnia,

My sister will expect you at half eleven.

R.

There was no turning back now.

"Anne," Callie said, unable to pull her gaze from the text, "we are going to Ralston House."

THE DAY AFTER her first visit, Callie found herself on the steps of Ralston House again—this time, quite respectably, by light of day, lady's maid in tow—to meet Miss Juliana Fiori, the mysterious younger sister of the marquess.

Callie took a deep breath, sending a silent prayer to the fates that Ralston be away from the house in the hopes that she could avoid the inevitable abject mortification. Of course, she knew that she could not avoid future interactions . . . she had, after all, agreed to shepherd his sister into society. She could at least hope that she would be able to avoid him *today*, however.

A footman opened the door, revealing a stone-faced Jenkins in the foyer beyond. *Please, don't recognize me*, she pleaded silently as she looked up into the butler's weathered, wrinkled face, attempting to appear cool and collected.

"Lady Calpurnia Hartwell, to see Miss Juliana." Drawing herself up to her full height, Callie spoke, willing the words to come in the most even-mannered of tones. She offered an ecru calling card to the butler, who received it with a low bow.

"Certainly, my lady. Miss Juliana is expecting you. Please, follow me."

Once Jenkins had turned his back, Callie let out a long, silent sigh of relief. She followed him to an open doorway off the main marble corridor and offered him the most regal of nods as he stepped aside to let her pass into a lovely green receiving room.

Callie took in the grassy green silk that lined the walls, the detailed chaise and chairs, all beautifully crafted from mahogany and upholstered in the finest of fabrics. The lightness of the room was complemented by a stunning marble statue that stood to one side—a tall, limber female figure, carved as though holding a wide swath of fabric above her head, billowing out behind her. Callie caught her breath at the beauty of the statue; she was unable to resist moving toward it, drawn in by the quiet, secret smile that graced the goddess's lovely face, by the liquid movement of the marble. She was admiring the fall of the figure's gown, reaching out to touch the drape of it, half-expecting to feel warm fabric rather than cool stone, when a voice sounded from the doorway.

"She is beautiful, is she not?"

Callie whirled toward the sound with a little gasp. In the doorway was Ralston, flashing a rakish grin, as though he was amused by her discomfort.

No—not Ralston.

The man in the doorway was Lord Nicholas St. John, tall and broad, with a chiseled jaw and glittering blue eyes, identical to Ralston in every way but one. St. John's right cheek was marked with a wicked scar, a long, thin white line that tore across his bronzed skin in stark contrast with the rest of the man, an impeccable gentleman. Where the scar should have given St. John a dangerous countenance, instead it made him more alluring. Callie had seen respectable women of good *ton* turn into utter imbeciles when near St. John—something he seemed not to notice.

"Lord Nicholas," she said with a smile, offering a short dip of the head as he crossed the room to take her hand and bow deeply.

"Lady Calpurnia"—he smiled warmly—"I see you have discovered my lady love." Nicholas indicated the statue.

"Indeed, I have." Callie turned her attention back to the marble. "She is stunning. Who is the artist?"

St. John shook his head, a gleam in his eye revealing his pride. "Unknown. I found her off the southern coast of Greece several years ago. I spent seven months collecting marbles there, came home with far too many and donated this beauty to the betterment of Ralston House, on the condition that my brother give her a proper home." He paused, transfixed by the statue. "I believe she is Selene, goddess of the moon."

"She looks so content."

"You sound surprised."

"Well," Callie said tentatively, "Selene's is not the happiest of stories. After all, she is doomed to love a mortal in eternal sleep."

St. John turned at her words, obviously impressed. "Her own fault. She should have known better than to ask favors of Zeus. That particular course of action never ends well."

"A truth of which Selene was likely acutely aware upon receiving her favor. I assume that this statue depicts a happy Selene *before* Zeus meddled."

"You forget," St. John said, a teasing gleam in his eye, "she and Endymion did have twenty children despite his somnolence, so she couldn't have been so very unhappy with her situation."

"With due respect, my lord," Callie said, "bearing and raising twenty children alone does not sound like the happiest of circumstances. I hardly think she would appear so very rested were this a statue depicting her maternal bliss."

St. John laughed loudly. "Exceptionally well put, Lady Calpurnia. If this conversation is any indication, Juliana's debut should be tremendously entertaining . . . for me, at the very least."

"And it is, of course, your entertainment that is of the utmost importance, Nicholas."

Callie stiffened as the irritated words sailed across the room, dark and ominous, setting her heart to racing. She attempted to maintain the illusion of calm but knew before turning that Ralston had joined them.

Seeming to sense her nervousness, St. John winked at her before turning a wide, open smile toward the marquess, and saying, "Indeed, it is, brother."

Ralston's scowl deepened. He turned to Callie, spearing her with a piercing blue stare. A bright blush colored Callie's cheeks, and she tore her gaze from his, looking anywhere else. Nick noticed her discomfort and came to her aid. "There is no need for you to be rude, Gabriel. I was simply keeping Lady Calpurnia occupied while we waited for Juliana to arrive. Where is the girl?"

"I stopped Jenkins from fetching her. I would like to speak to Lady Calpurnia before they meet." He paused. "Alone, if you please, Nick."

Callie's heart began a rapid hammering. What could he possibly have to say to her that his brother could not hear?

Nick bowed low over her hand, and said, "I look forward to next time, my lady." He straightened, offering Callie a bright smile and another reassuring wink.

She couldn't help but smile back. "As do I, my lord."

Ralston waited for the door to the room to close before waving Callie into one of the nearby chairs, seating himself across from her. Callie tried to ignore the way he dwarfed the furniture—and the room itself—as though the entirety of Ralston House was designed for a lesser creature. She dipped her head, pretending to be enthralled by the upholstery on the chair in which she sat—eager to appear as though he were outside her notice. It was a fool's errand. He was not a man who went easily unnoticed.

"I want to discuss Juliana before you meet her."

Callie quashed a pang of disappointment. Must he be so perfunctory? She did not look up, instead turning her attention to her gloved hands, clenched together in her lap, and desperately trying to forget that mere hours ago those hands had touched Ralston intimately. But, how could she forget? His warm skin, his soft hair, his strong, muscled arms—she had touched all those places. And he seemed entirely unmoved.

She cleared her throat delicately, and said, "Certainly, my lord."

"I think it best you come to Ralston House to work with Juliana. She is in need of significant guidance, and I would not like for her to make a misstep in front of the Countess of Allendale."

Her eyes widened as she lifted her head to meet his gaze. "My mother would never betray the confidence of your sister's lessons."

"Nevertheless, the walls have ears."

"Not Allendale House walls."

He leaned forward in his chair, close enough to touch her, his muscles bunched with tightly leashed power. "Let me make myself plain. I will not cede this point. Juliana is resistant to joining society and eager to return to Italy. She is likely to wreak a bit of havoc before she accepts that her new home is here. Your mother and her friends are pillars of the *ton*—women for whom ancestry and reputation are paramount and, while Juliana does not have a family line that can be traced back to William the Conqueror, and she is quite likely to be tarnished with the soiled reputation of our mother, she will meet London's aristocracy. And she will make a smart match. I will not jeopardize that opportunity."

He spoke with complete certainty, as though the one true path to Juliana's success was the one he had planned. And, yet, there was no mistaking the urgency that laced his tone. He was right— Juliana Fiori would need far more than Callie's support if she was to succeed in society. She was the daughter of a ruined marchioness and an Italian merchant—not aristocratic, barely legitimate in the eyes of the *ton*.

But Gabriel St. John, the Marquess of Ralston, would not allow the dark history of his family tree to tarnish his sister's future. The fact that the brothers St. John had committed to bring Juliana into society's fold showed their mettle and, as a proud and committed sister herself, Callie respected their decision. These were not men who failed.

"I am eager to meet your sister, my lord." A simple enough sentence, but one that carried an unmistakable meaning. *I am with you.*

He paused, watching her with the piercing, knowing gaze and, for the first time in a decade, she did not look away. When he spoke moments later, it was with a softer tone. "I did not think that you would come today."

A hint of a smile played across her lips. "I confess, my lord, I did consider avoiding the visit."

"And yet, here you are."

Her cheeks pinkened as she dipped her head, shyly. "We have a bargain."

When he replied, his voice was quieter, more thoughtful. "Indeed. We do."

The deepened tenor of his voice sent a flood of heat through Callie, and she cleared her throat nervously, making a show at looking to a clock on a nearby table. "It is getting late, my lord. I think it is time I meet Miss Juliana. Don't you agree?"

He held her gaze for a long moment, as if reading her innermost thoughts. Eventually, he seemed satisfied by what he saw. Without speaking, he stood and went to send for his sister.

THE FIRST THING one noticed about Juliana Fiori was not her beauty, although she was most certainly beautiful—with arresting blue eyes, porcelain skin, and a mass of rich chestnut curls that most women would commit serious bodily harm to have for themselves. It was not her delicate features, or her lilting voice, accented with her native Italian. It was not her height, although she towered above Callie and would do so over many.

No, the first thing one noticed about Juliana Fiori was her frankness.

"What silliness that we must consider the proper order of milk and tea when pouring a cup."

Callie swallowed back a laugh. "I suppose you do not place much stock in such ceremony in Venice?"

"No. It is liquid. It is warm. It is not coffee. Why worry?" Juliana's smile flashed, showing a dimple in her cheek.

"Why indeed?" Callie said, wondering, fleetingly, if Juliana's brothers had such an endearing trait.

"Do not be concerned." Juliana held a hand up dramatically. "I shall endeavor to remember tea first, milk second. I should hate to cause another war between Britain and the Continent."

Callie laughed, accepting a cup of perfectly poured tea from the younger woman. "I am certain that Parliament will thank you for your diplomacy."

The two shared a smile before Juliana continued, "So, were I to meet a duke or a duchess—" Juliana said as she carefully placed a piece of cake on a small plate for Callie.

"Which you most certainly shall do," Callie pointed out.

"Allora, when I meet a duke or a duchess, I shall refer to either as 'Your Grace.' With all others, it is safe for me to call them 'my lord' or 'my lady.'"

"Correct. At least, all others who are either titled or who have courtesy titles because of their parentage."

Juliana cocked her head, considering Callie's words. "This is more complicated than tea." She laughed. "I think it is a very good thing for my brothers that I am only here for a short time. Certainly, they can quickly repair any damage their scandalous Italian sister might do in a mere two months."

Callie offered a reassuring smile. "Nonsense. You shall set the *ton* on its ear."

Juliana looked confused. "Why would I impact society's hearing?"

Callie's smile broadened, shaking her head. "It is a figure of speech. It means you will be a great success in society." She lowered her voice to a conspiratorial whisper. "I predict that gentlemen will clamor to meet you."

"Just as they did with my mother, no?" Juliana's blue eyes flashed, and she slashed her hand through the air. "No. Please put the idea of a marriage for me out of your head. I shall never marry."

"Whyever not?"

"What if I turn out to be just like her?" The quiet words gave Callie pause; before she could find the right response, Juliana continued. "I am sorry."

"There is no need for you to apologize." Callie reached out, setting one hand on Juliana's arm. "I can imagine how difficult this must be."

The younger woman paused, eyes on her lap. "For ten years, I have pretended that my mother did not exist. And now I discover that the only family I have left is because of *her*. And these men . . . my *brothers* . . ." Her voice trailed off.

Callie watched the younger woman carefully before saying, "They do not seem much like family now, do they?"

A flash of guilt crossed Juliana's face. "It is that obvious?"

Callie shook her head. "Not at all."

"I do not think they like me."

Callie shook her head firmly. "Impossible. You are an exceedingly likeable young woman. I, for one, enjoy your company immensely."

Juliana smiled a half smile before saying, "I believe that Nicholas has warmed to me. But Ralston . . ." She met Callie's eyes, and her voice quieted. "He does not smile."

Leaning forward, she placed a hand on the younger woman's arm. "I should not read much into that. I believe I could count on a single hand the number of times I have seen Ralston smile." *And not for lack of watching.*

Juliana shifted her gaze to where Callie was touching her, staring for a brief moment before placing her own hand on top of Callie's. When she met Callie's eyes, the younger woman's expression was filled with doubt. "I am rather a lot of trouble for him, do you not think? The orphan daughter of a woman who deserted them appears one day, looking for a new family."

Callie knew she should end this inappropriate conversation. After all, the intricacies of the Ralston family matters were just that—Ralston family matters—but Callie couldn't help herself. "Not a new family. An old one," she corrected. "One you were always a part of . . . you simply had to claim your place in it."

Juliana shook her head. "No. They know nothing of me. I do little more than remind them of our mother. She is our only connection. I am certain that Ralston sees only her when he looks at me. I think he will be happy to see me go in two months."

Despite her immense curiosity about their mother, Callie refrained from probing more deeply about the woman who had so callously abandoned three such remarkable children, instead saying, "Your brothers may not know you, Juliana, but they will. And they will love you. I would guess they have already begun. I predict that they will not let you leave in two months. And even if they would allow it, I hope that you will change your mind and stay."

Juliana's brilliant blue eyes filled with tears. "Seven weeks and six days."

Callie's heart clenched with sympathy for the young woman.

She smiled softly, "Honestly, after spending an afternoon with you, I find that I am rather committed to your future as well. I think we shall be very good friends."

Juliana offered Callie a watery smile. Taking a deep breath, the young woman straightened and brushed her tears away, choosing to put her insecurities aside. "Have you been a friend to my brother for a very long time?"

Callie froze at the question. "A friend?"

"*Si*. It is clear that Ralston holds you in high regard and considers you a friend. He was quite eager to inform me this morning that he had secured your agreement to sponsor me in society. If you were not friends, why would you be here, risking your own status to guide me through my every misstep?"

Callie knew she couldn't tell the truth. *You see, Juliana, there comes a point in a woman's life when she's willing to do anything to be kissed.* She paused, searching for the appropriate words; Juliana misread the meaning of the silence.

"Ah," she said, a knowing tone seeping into the single syllable, "I understand. You are more than a friend, *si*?"

Callie's eyes widened at the words, "Whatever do you mean?"

"You are his . . ." Juliana thought for a moment, seeking the correct phrase. "His *inamorata*?"

"I beg your pardon?" The question ended in a strangled squeak.

"His lover, yes?"

"Juliana!" Outrage took over, and Callie pulled herself up into her most regal of poses, adopting her very best governess tone. "One does not refer to lovers or paramours or . . . any other personal matters with guests!"

"But you are not simply a guest!" Juliana looked confused. "You are my friend, are you not?"

"Of course I am. However, one does not refer to such personal matters with friends either!"

"I apologize. I did not know. I thought that if you and Ralston were—"

"We are not!" The words came pouring out as Callie's voice trembled. "Not lovers. Not even friends! I am here to help you because I like you. I enjoy your company. The Marquess of Ralston has nothing to do with it."

Juliana looked Callie directly in the eye, waiting several moments before responding. "I enjoy your company, as well, Lady Calpurnia, and I am happy to have you with me on this journey." She then leaned forward, one side of her mouth up in an impish smile. "However, I believe there is more to your being here than goodwill. Else, why should you so passionately deny it?"

Callie's eyes widened, her mouth opening in surprise, then closing without sound.

"Do not worry. Your *segreto* is safe with me."

Shaking her head, Callie said, "But, there is no secret! Nothing to be kept safe!"

Juliana smiled more broadly. "As you say." She tilted her head thoughtfully. "I shall keep it safe nonetheless."

Callie leaned back in her chair, eyes narrowing on her pupil, who was grinning as though she were a cat with a bowlful of cream.

And to think, just yesterday she had considered the marquess the most cunning resident of Ralston House.

Five

To a casual observer, the Marquess of Ralston, lounging in an oversized armchair in an elegantly styled room at Brooks's men's club, appeared every inch the spoiled aristocrat—legs extended carelessly, boots gleaming, in the direction of the room's great marble fireplace; cravat loosened, but not undone; hair artfully disheveled; eyes half-lidded, watching the flames flicker and dance. From one hand, a crystal tumbler of scotch dangled, but the two fingers of amber liquid in the glass had been neglected, hovering on the brink of spilling upon the thick blue carpet.

Here, the untrained eye would note, was the portrait of a lazy dandy.

Such an observation, however, would be a gross untruth, as Ralston's casual sprawl belied his true state—mind racing, pent-up frustration making his stillness a battle of will.

"I had a feeling I would find you here."

Gabriel turned from the fire to meet his brother's gaze. "If you are here to announce the existence of another St. John sibling, now is not the best of times."

"Alas, we remain a meager trio. As hard as it is to believe." Nick took the chair next to Gabriel with a sigh. "Have you spoken with Nastasia?"

Ralston took a deep drink. "Yes."

"Ah. That would explain your mood. Attempting to rectify years of profligacy in mere hours is no easy task."

"I did not agree to changing my ways—only to an increase in discretion."

"Fair enough." Nick tilted his head in amusement. "That is something of a beginning, I should think, with your legacy."

Ralston's scowl deepened. For years after his father's death, he had cut a wide, indecorous, and rather legendary swath across London, building a reputation as a rake and a libertine, which currently stood as significantly more scandalous than was actually deserved.

"She looks so much like our mother."

Gabriel turned his head at the words. "For all of our sakes, I hope that is the only similarity between the two of them. Else we would do well to send her back to Italy now. As it is, I expect our mother's reputation will be difficult enough to overcome."

"It's lucky that you are rich and titled. Juliana will not lack for invitations to the most-anticipated events of the season. Of course, you'll be required to attend those events with her."

Gabriel took a drink of scotch, refusing to rise to his brother's bait. "And how do you intend to escape a similar fate, brother?"

Nick flashed a quick smile. "No one will notice the absence of the second, lesser son of St. John."

"They shan't have an opportunity to, Nicholas, as you will be at every one of those events."

"Actually, I have been asked to journey north, into Yorkshire. Leighton believes my skills are vital in finding and retrieving a statue he has misplaced. I am toying with honoring the request."

"No. You will not rush off to play with your marbles and leave me to keep the wolves at bay."

Nick raised an eyebrow. "I shall attempt not to take offense at your assessment of my work . . . how long before you will allow me my freedom?"

Gabriel took a pull of scotch. "How quickly do you think we can get her married?"

"That will depend on how quickly we can disabuse her of the notion that she should not marry. She's terrified of our mother's influence, Gabriel. And can you blame her? The woman has left her mark on each of us. And this is Juliana's cross to bear."

"She is nothing like our mother. Her fear proves it."

"Nevertheless. It is not we who must be convinced. It's she. And the rest of London." The brothers fell silent for several long moments before Nick added, "Do you think Juliana is the type to hold out for a love match?"

Ralston gave a little grunt of irritation. "I certainly hope the girl has more sense than that."

"Women do tend to believe that love is their due. Particularly younger women."

"I cannot imagine Juliana would ascribe to such fairy tales. You forget, we were raised by the same woman . . . it simply isn't possible that Juliana yearns for love. Not after seeing the damage it can do."

The twins were quiet for a long moment, before Nick said, "For all our sakes, I hope you are correct." When Ralston remained quiet, Nick added, "Lady Calpurnia was an excellent choice of shepherd."

Ralston offered a noncommittal grunt.

"How did you secure her participation?"

"Is it relevant?"

One of Nick's brows shot up. "Now, I sense that it is extremely relevant." When Ralston did not respond, Nick stood from his chair, straightening his cravat. "Marbury is hosting a card game in the next room. Care to join me?"

Ralston shook his head, instead taking a long sip of scotch.

Nick nodded and took his leave. Ralston watched under hooded lids, cursing his twin's uncanny ability to strike at the heart of any delicate situation.

Lady Calpurnia.

He had thought her a boon—a woman with an unparalleled reputation who had simply *appeared*. She was the perfect solution to the problem of preparing Juliana for her first season—or so he had thought. But then he had kissed her.

And the kiss had been rather extraordinary.

He scoffed at the thought. He had been frustrated and taken aback by the arrival of his sister. Any kiss would have been a welcome distraction.

Especially one so freely given by such an enthusiastic, enjoyable partner.

Ralston hardened almost instantly, remembering the way Callie felt in his arms, her soft sighs, the way she had so willingly given herself up to the kiss. He wondered if her excitement for kissing would translate into eagerness for other, more passionate, acts. For a moment, he allowed himself to imagine her in his bed, all enormous brown eyes and full, welcoming lips, wearing nothing but a willing smile.

A burst of laughter came from across the room, yanking him from his reverie. He shifted in his chair to ease the uncomfortable tightness of his breeches, shaking his head to clear it of the vision he'd conjured and making a mental note to find himself a willing female. Quickly.

He took another drink of scotch, watching the warm liquid swirl in the glass as he considered the strange events of the night before. He could not deny the fact that Lady Calpurnia Hartwell, a plain little wallfower with a strange name—to whom he could honestly say he'd never given much thought—was rather intriguing. She certainly was not the type of female who would ordinarily interest him. In fact, she was quite the opposite of his standard preference—ideally exquisite, confident, and experienced.

Then why did she so intrigue him?

Ralston was saved from having to consider the question further by another eruption of raucous noise from across the room. Eager for some distraction from his disconcerting thoughts, he turned his attention to a group of men eagerly calling out wagers. Finney, the bookmaker, was scribbling the bets in the Brooks's betting book as quickly as he could.

Leaning forward in his chair for a better view, Ralston quickly deduced the focus of the men's interest, Baron Oxford. With Oxford at the center of the betting, there was little question as to what the topic must be—the baron's seemingly endless search for a wife. For several months, Oxford, deep in debt largely because of his penchant for gambling, had publicly announced to the membership of Brooks's that he was looking to marry—the richer the bride, the better.

Typically, Ralston found the boisterous Oxford—more often than not deep in his cups—to be insufferable, but considering the marquess's need for diversion, he made an exception. He stood and approached the group.

"Ten guineas on Prudence Marworthy."

"She's got the face of a horse!" This, from Oxford himself.

"Her dowry is worth keeping the lights out!" came a voice from the back of the crowd. Ralston was the only man in the room who did not laugh at the joke.

"I've got twenty guineas that says none but Berwick's daughter will have you!" The Earl of Chilton threw his bet into the pool, garnering a round of groans at the insensitive wager, interspersed with surprise for the size of Chilton's wager.

"She may be simple," Oxford said with a laugh, "but her father *is* the richest man in England!"

Uninterested in the base conversation, Ralston turned to leave the room. He had almost reached the door when a voice called out, above the rest.

"I've got it! The Allendale chit!"

He stilled, then turned back to hear the response. The woman was haunting him.

"No good. She's just been betrothed to Rivington," someone said. "And you're touched if you think The Allendale Angel would settle for Oxford."

"Not the pretty one . . . the other."

"The fleshy one?"

"With the ridiculous name?"

Oxford held court with a swagger that was likely the result of too much drink, enjoying every minute of the immature attention. "That said, Rivington did make a smart move marrying into the Allendale fortune . . . Lady Cassiopeia wouldn't be the worst ending to my story."

"Calpurnia." Ralston said the name softly, too softly to be heard, at the same time one of the other men corrected Oxford.

The baron continued, waving his glass in the air dismissively. "Well, whatever her name, I'd be wealthy again—wealthy enough to keep a stellar mistress and never bother with the wife. Except to get her with the heir and the spare. And I imagine that, at her age"—he paused for bawdy emphasis—"she'll be grateful for whatever I give her."

Oxford's statement brought a round of cacophonous laughter.

A visceral distaste coursed through Ralston. *There was no way Calpurnia Hartwell would marry Oxford.* No woman with that kind of passion would settle for such an ass. Ralston had never been so certain of anything in his life.

"Who is willing to match a wager that she's mine by June?"

Several of Oxford's friends entered the pool, with others wagering that the Earl of Allendale would step in and refuse the match, and at least one man betting that Oxford would have to elope with Lady Calpurnia in order to achieve his gains.

"I'll take all the wagers." Ralston's words, despite their being spoken quietly from across the room, silenced the other men who, to a man, turned to look at him.

Oxford offered him a broad smile. "Ah, Ralston. I hadn't noticed you. You'd like to place a bet on my future bride?"

Ralston couldn't imagine a single situation in which the woman who had marched herself into his home last evening would consider Oxford anything more than an irritation. He'd never seen a wager so easily won as this one. *Like taking sweets from a babe.* "Indeed, Oxford. I'll take every one of the bets on Lady Calpurnia. There is not a chance in hell that she'll marry you." He turned to the bookmaker. "Finney, mark my words. If Oxford even has an opportunity to offer for Lady Calpurnia, she'll most certainly refuse."

A rustle of surprise went through the crowd as Finney asked, "How much, my lord?"

Ralston met Oxford's eyes as he spoke. "One thousand pounds will keep it interesting, I would imagine," he said, turning and exiting the room, leaving the group of men utterly dumbfounded.

The gauntlet had been thrown.

Six

Callie had thought that tonight would be different.

She had expected Mariana and Rivington's betrothal ball to be perfect. And it was—every inch of the room had been polished until it shone, from the floors and windows, to the enormous crystal chandeliers and wall sconces that held thousands of twinkling candles, to the marble columns that lined one length of the room, supporting the most impressive feature of the Allendale House ballroom—an upper viewing corridor that allowed guests in need of a respite to find one without ever leaving the ballroom.

She'd expected that Mariana would sparkle, and she did—a glittering gem on Rivington's arm, swirling through the dozens of other couples in a rousing country dance. And the other guests seemed to agree with Callie; they were thrilled to be there, at the first major event of the season, to fête Mariana and her duke. The *ton* was at its best, dressed in the height of fashion, eager to see and be seen by those whom they had missed while away from London for the winter months.

Callie had imagined that this ball would be special for *both* Allendale sisters, however.

And yet, here she sat, in Spinster Seating. As usual.

She should be used to it, of course—used to being ignored and sloughed off with the rest of the women who were on the shelf. Truthfully, in the early years, she'd preferred it here. The women had accepted her into their fold, graciously making room for her on whatever furniture happened to be arranged for their kind. Callie had found it much more enjoyable to watch the season unfold while trading gossip with the older women than to stand awkwardly on the other side of the room waiting patiently to be asked to dance by an eligible young gentleman.

After two seasons of fortune hunters and aging widowers, Callie had welcomed the companionship of the spinsters.

And then, she'd turned into one of them.

She wasn't even really sure when or how it had happened, but it had. And now, she had very little choice in the matter.

But tonight was Mariana's betrothal ball. Tonight was Calpurnia's first ball since she had begun crossing items off her list. And tonight she had honestly thought that things might be different. After all, as the bride's obvious choice for maid of honor, did she not earn special recognition at an event wholly designed to celebrate the pending nuptials?

Watching the dancers, she let out a little sigh. *Evidently not.*

"Oh, Calpurnia." Miss Genevieve Hetherington, a middle-aged spinster with kind eyes and a complete lack of sensitivity, patted Callie's knee gently with one lace-gloved hand. "You must move beyond that, my dear. Some of us are not made for dancing."

"Indeed not." The words were wrung from Callie, who took the opportunity to stand and excuse herself. Certainly that would be a more preferable course of action than strangling one of the *ton*'s most beloved spinsters.

Keeping her head down to limit the number of people she might be required to acknowledge, Callie made her way to the refreshment room.

She was waylaid by Baron Oxford mere feet from her destination. "My lady!"

Callie pasted a too-bright smile on her face and turned toward the baron, who flashed her the toothiest grin she had ever seen. Unable to keep herself from doing so, she took a small step back from the beaming man. "Baron Oxford. What a surprise."

"Yes, I rather suppose it is." His smile did not waver.

She paused, waiting for him to continue. When he didn't, she said, "I am happy to see that you could join us tonight."

"Not so happy as I am to have been able to join you, *my lady.*"

The emphasis on the honorific sent a wave of confusion through Callie. Did the baron mean for his words to sound so suggestive? Surely not, considering that Callie couldn't recall the last time she'd spoken with the incurable dandy. She cleared her throat delicately. "Well. Thank you."

"You look quite lovely tonight." Oxford leaned in, and his smile broadened. *Was it possible that the man had more than the usual number of teeth?*

"Oh." Belatedly, Callie remembered to dip her head and appear flattered instead of thoroughly bewildered. "Thank you, my lord."

Oxford looked entirely proud of himself. "Perhaps you would do me the honor of a dance?" When she did not immediately respond, he lifted her hand to his lips and lowered his voice, adding, "I've been meaning to ask you all evening."

The unexpected interaction set Callie back on her heels. *Is he soused?*

As she considered the eager invitation, Callie heard the orchestra tuning to the first tentative notes of a waltz and was immediately resistant to the idea of dancing with Oxford. The waltz had not come to England until after Callie had been labeled a spinster, and she had never had a chance to dance it—at least, not with anyone other than Benedick in the privacy of their home. She certainly did not want her first waltz in public to be with Oxford, grinning like a fool. With a quick look into the refreshment room, she considered her best avenue for escape.

"Oh. Well. I—" she hedged.

"Calpurnia! There you are!" Miss Heloise Parkthwaite, in her fifties and quite nearsighted, came from nowhere to clutch Callie's arm. "I've been searching *everywhere* for you! Do be a dear and escort me to have my hem repaired, would you?"

A wave of relief coursed through Callie; she was saved. "Of course, Heloise, dear," she said. Tugging her hand from Oxford's grasp, she offered a regretful smile in his direction. "Perhaps another time, my lord?"

"Indeed! I shan't allow you to escape me next time!" Oxford punctuated his sentence with a booming laugh, and she responded with a tiny, stilted chuckle before turning away to lead Heloise in the direction of the ladies' salon.

Callie took Heloise's arm, and the older woman began chattering about the daring bodices that were clearly in fashion that year. Between nodding and murmuring in a manner she hoped appeared both intrigued and entertained, Callie allowed her mind to wander—turning from the odd interaction with Oxford to thoughts of her list.

She promptly decided that if she was to suffer through an entire evening of bizarre conversation and Spinster Seating, she well deserved another attempt at adventure. In fact, she was sorely tempted to drop Heloise safely in the ladies' salon and take the opportunity to escape immediately to her list.

If, of course, they ever arrived at the ladies' salon. The older woman had stopped midstride and was squinting into the crowd. "Is that Ralston I see there? How odd!"

Callie's heart skipped a beat at the words, and she turned to follow the direction of Heloise's attention but, because of her lack of height, could see nothing through the mass of people surrounding them. Reminding herself of Heloise's terrible eyesight, Callie shook her head, returning herself to the task of navigating through the crowds. *It couldn't be Ralston.*

Heloise evidently agreed. "No, it cannot be Ralston. He rarely attends balls. It must be St. John."

Callie let out a breath that she hadn't known she'd been holding. Of course. It could be Lord Nicholas. *Please, let it be Lord Nicholas.*

"How curious that he be approaching us, though."

Unable to keep herself from doing so, Callie snapped her head back to the crowd just in time to see the tall, magnificent gentleman moving gracefully toward them, determination in his blue eyes.

It wasn't Lord Nicholas.

Even if the lack of scar had not revealed his identity, Callie would have known. Nicholas's shoulders weren't quite as broad, his jaw wasn't quite as strong, his eyes weren't quite as all-consuming as his brother's. St. John had never made her breath catch, had never set her pulse racing, had never made her think absolutely unthinkable thoughts.

No, the man approaching them was most definitely *not* Lord Nicholas St. John.

But how she wished he were.

Callie glanced quickly from side to side, attempting to judge the quickest and least crowded escape route, by which she could avoid a meeting with Ralston. Bodies seemed to close in upon them from all sides—with the exception of the direction from which he approached. She met his knowing gaze as he raised one dark, perfectly arched brow.

She was trapped. Trapped alongside the sputtering Heloise, who, one might believe, hadn't been approached by a handsome gentleman in years.

Not that it was a common occurrence for Callie.

"Lord Nicholas!" Heloise cried, a touch too loudly. "How lovely to see you!"

"Heloise, dear," Callie spoke quietly to her companion. "'Tis Ralston."

Heloise squinted, her gaze falling obviously to Ralston's cheek, searching for the telltale difference between the brothers. "Oh! Of course! My apologies, Lord Ralston." She dropped a quick curtsy.

"No apologies necessary, Miss Parkthwaite." He bowed low over Heloise's gloved hand, before adding, "I assure you, I consider it a great compliment. My brother is the better-looking of the pair."

"Oh, no, my lord," Heloise tittered, blushing and waving her fan like a drunken hummingbird. "Certainly not!"

Ralston offered the older woman a wink before saying, "Well, far be it from me to disagree with a lady."

The words sent Heloise into a fit of giggles as Ralston turned to Callie, who offered her hand to Ralston. Ralston bowed low, sending a shiver of heat up her arm. "Lady Calpurnia, I had hoped to secure your next available dance."

Heloise gasped in surprise as Callie blurted out, "I beg your pardon?"

"The next dance." Ralston repeated, looking from one woman to the other as if they were both slightly touched. "I will admit I do not attend as many balls as I likely should these days, but people do still dance at them, do they not?"

"Oh! Yes, indeed, my lord," Heloise interjected helpfully.

"In that case," Ralston's eyes sparkled with checked humor, "may I have your dance card, Lady Calpurnia?"

"I do not have a dance card." She so rarely danced, she did not need one.

There was a beat as he took in her words.

"Excellent. That makes it much easier to claim a dance, then, doesn't it?" Ralston turned back to Heloise. "Do you mind if I thieve your companion, Miss Heloise?"

Dumbfounded, Heloise could do little more than shake her head, and sputter, "Not at all!"

Callie stood still, feet rooted to the floor, refusing to be led onto the dance floor. She couldn't waltz with Ralston. He couldn't be her first waltz. It would most definitely ruin her for all others.

Men like Ralston are not for women like you, Callie.

No. Indeed they were not. Especially not when they were threatening to waltz with her. In the interest of self-preservation, Callie shook her head firmly. "Oh, I couldn't possibly, my lord. You see, I've promised Heloise I would accompany her to—"

"Nonsense!" Heloise said, her tone high-pitched and breathless. "I shall be quite fine! You *must* waltz, Lady Calpurnia." At the last, the older woman beamed up at Ralston, nodding excitedly.

And the decision was made.

Ralston swept her into the center of the room for her first waltz.

As he guided her across the floor, Callie saw her mother at the opposite end of the room, standing with a beaming Mariana, watching them. The dowager countess looked utterly shocked. Callie gave her a little nod of acknowledgment, trying her best to appear as though handsome marquesses approached her at every ball she attended.

Desperate to lighten the situation—for her own good sense— Callie said dryly, "You've certainly given everyone something to talk about tonight, my lord."

"I suppose you mean my attendance. Well, I rather thought that with Juliana on her way out, I had better start ingratiating myself to the *ton*." After a long pause, he added, "Why do you not dance?"

Callie considered his question for a moment before replying. "I did, for several years. And then . . . I stopped."

Unsatisfied with her answer, he pressed on. "Why?"

She gave a small, self-deprecating smile. "The partners were not altogether ideal. Those who weren't fortune hunters were elderly or boring or . . . simply unpleasant. It became easier to avoid the invitations altogether than to suffer their company."

"I hope you do not consider me so distasteful."

She allowed herself to meet his amused gaze. No. Ralston was not distasteful. Not by any stretch of the imagination.

"No, my lord," she said, the softness in her tone betraying her thoughts before she added, "And neither does Miss Heloise, it appears. She was quite charmed by you."

"One must use one's talents to one's advantage, Lady Calpurnia."

"Something I am certain you do quite well."

His voice deepened. "I assure you, I do it very well."

Refusing to allow herself to be flustered, she said, "Your reputation precedes you, my lord." Callie failed to notice the double meaning in her words until they were out of her mouth.

He raised one brow. "Indeed?"

Callie's cheeks flamed as she redirected her gaze to his elaborate cravat, wishing that she were as erudite and alluring as the women with whom he was accustomed to dancing. They, of course, would know exactly how to play his flirtatious game.

"Come now, Lady Calpurnia," he teased quietly, "to which of the nefarious deeds of my past do you refer?"

She met his eyes again, noting the challenge there. "Oh, any number of them, my lord," she said lightly, enjoying herself. "Is it true you once leapt from a countess's balcony quite unfortunately into a holly bush below?"

Ralston's eyes widened slightly at her quiet question before amusement flashed. "A gentleman would neither confirm nor deny such an occurrence."

Callie laughed. "On the contrary, my lord. A gentleman would most certainly *deny* such an occurrence."

He smiled, a rakish grin, and Callie was thankful for the companionable silence that fell between them, for she was not certain she could find words in the face of his rare smile. She lost herself in the dance, in the sound of the music, in the sway of their bodies. If this was to be her first and only waltz, she wanted to remember every moment. She closed her eyes, allowing Ralston to guide her around the room, and Callie became keenly aware of his gloved hand barely touching her waist, the brush of his long, muscled leg against her own as they swirled across the floor. After several moments, she became disoriented and opened her eyes, uncertain whether the source of her light-headedness was the movement or the man. Meeting Ralston's blue eyes, she accepted the truth.

It was, of course, the man.

"I was hoping we could talk of Juliana."

Callie swallowed her disappointment. Despite her visiting with Juliana three times that week, she had not seen Ralston during her visits—a fact that was likely for the best, considering she turned into something of a cabbagehead when he was nearby.

Unaware of her thoughts, he pressed on. "I wonder when you think my sister will be ready to take to the ballrooms of London?"

"I would think no longer than another week. Juliana is a wonderful pupil, my lord. Very eager to please both you and your brother."

He nodded, satisfied with her answer. "I should like for you to take her shopping. She will need new gowns."

Callie's surprise was obvious. "I'm not certain I'm the appropriate companion for dress shopping, my lord."

"You seem quite appropriate to me."

She tried another tack. "You should have someone who is at the height of fashion accompany her."

"I want you." The words were frank and imperious.

Callie knew she would not win. After a pause, she nodded her agreement. "I shall have to have a look at her current wardrobe, to assess her needs."

"No. She needs everything. I want her outfitted in entirety. The best and most current of fashions." His tone did not encourage discussion. "I will not have her out of place."

"With her only here for two months—"

"You cannot honestly believe that I would allow her to return to Italy."

"I—" Callie noted the firm resolve in his tone. "No, I suppose not. But, my lord," she said delicately, uncertain of how to point out the expense of such an extravagant request.

"Money is of no import. She is to have the *best*."

"Very well." She acquiesced quietly, deciding that she'd much rather dance than argue the point.

He allowed her a few moments of silent movement before saying, "I would also like to discuss the necessary requirements to secure entrance to Almack's for her."

Callie's eyes widened at his words. She replied, choosing her response carefully. "Almack's may not be the best place to enter Juliana into society, my lord."

"Whyever not? Acceptance there makes for a much easier entrée into the rest of the *ton,* does it not?"

"Certainly," Callie agreed. "However, the Lady Patronesses do not give vouchers freely. There are considerable hoops through which one must jump."

Ralston's eyes narrowed. "Are you saying you do not believe that Juliana will receive a voucher?"

Callie paused, thinking before she said, "I believe the ladies of Almack's will find your sister impeccably mannered—"

"Ah, but impeccable manners are not enough, are they, Lady Calpurnia?"

She met his eyes directly. "No, my lord."

"Is it me? Or my mother?"

"This is really not the place to discuss—"

"Nonsense. This is society. Aren't all matters of import discussed in ballrooms?" His tone was laced with heavy sarcasm. If she were not so keenly aware of his frustration with the situation, she would have been offended by his flippancy.

He looked away from her, over her head, his eyes unseeing. She paused, judging his response before speaking carefully. "If she were titled . . . or if she weren't living at Ralston House . . ." She changed tack. "It might be easier to garner acceptance for Juliana if we avoid Almack's altogether."

He fell silent, but she could sense the change in him. The arms that held her were stiff with corded tension. After several moments, he met her gaze. "I don't want to hurt her."

"Neither do I." And she didn't.

He paused, as if he could read her thoughts. "Will this work?"

"I shall do my best." The truth.

The corner of his mouth raised quickly—if she hadn't been so focused on him, she might have missed it. "So certain of yourself."

"One does not spend one's life on the edge of ballrooms and not learn exactly what it takes to be belle of the ball, my lord."

"If anyone can help Juliana navigate these shark-infested waters, I think it quite possibly could be you, Lady Calpurnia." The words, laced with respect, caused a warmth to spread through Callie, which she tried, unsuccessfully, to ignore.

As the waltz came to an end and her skirts swirled back into place, she risked asking, "May I suggest you escort me to my mother?"

He immediately recognized the logic behind her words. "You think a single conversation with your mother will convince them that I am reformed?"

"It cannot hurt." She smiled up at him as they promenaded around the edge of the ballroom. "You forget one of the most important tenets of London society."

"Which is?"

"Wealthy, unmarried marquesses are always welcome back into the light."

He paused, letting one finger stroke slowly across her knuckles as he spoke softly in her ear. "And if I am not sure I want to exit the darkness?"

A shiver pulsed down her spine at the words, more breath than sound. She cleared her throat delicately. "I am afraid it is too late."

"Lord Ralston!" Her mother's voice came, high-pitched and excited, as they approached her and Mariana, who appeared to have been watching the entire waltz, waiting for this particular moment. "How fortunate we are to have you join us this evening."

Ralston offered a low bow. "It is I who was fortunate to have received an invitation, my lady. Lady Mariana, you are radiant. May I offer my best wishes on your coming marriage?"

Mariana smiled warmly at Ralston's flattery, offering him a hand. "Thank you, my lord. And, may I say that I am quite eager to meet your sister? Callie has said wonderful things about her."

"Lady Calpurnia has been a good friend to Juliana in the week since her arrival." He looked to Callie, and added, "I am of the opinion that there is no one better to ensure my sister's success."

"You are absolutely correct, of course, my lord," said Lady Allendale. "Callie's reputation is impeccable. And, considering her age and situation, hers is the ideal tutelage for Miss Juliana."

Callie winced inwardly at her mother's words, which—whether intentionally or not—drew attention to her status as untouchable spinster. The real meaning of Lady Allendale's statement couldn't have been more obvious if she had announced that Callie had taken vows as a nun.

Lady Allendale plunged onward. "May I ask, my lord, how you and Callie came to such an agreement regarding your sister's introduction into society?"

Callie's gaze flew to Ralston, her heart in her throat. How was he going to avoid the truth? He replied calmly, "I confess, Lady Allendale, the agreement was entirely my idea. I was extraordinarily lucky that Lady Calpurnia happened to be in the right place at the right time, as they say. I do not know how I will repay her for such a generous offer." Callie's eyes widened at his reply; did she detect a teasing tone in his words? She turned her attention back to her mother, who appeared entirely pacified with the marquess's answer, as though it were perfectly ordinary for rakes to request the company of her unmarried daughter for purposes not altogether clear.

She had to end this embarrassment. Immediately. Before her mother did something truly mortifying. As if it weren't enough that she was dressed in a shimmering aubergine silk adorned with peacock feathers. Many peacock feathers.

"Mother, Lord Ralston has agreed to escort me to the refreshment room," she said, avoiding Ralston's gaze as she attempted to lie as prettily as he seemed to do. "May we fetch something for you?"

"Oh, no, thank you." The dowager countess waved her fan in the air dismissively before placing a hand on Ralston's arm and meeting his gaze directly. "Lord Ralston, I look forward to meeting this sister of yours very soon. Perhaps she will come to luncheon?" It was not a question.

Ralston tipped his head graciously, accepting the countess's offer of support, saying, "I am certain Juliana would enjoy that, Lady Allendale."

Callie's mother nodded firmly. "Excellent."

With that, Lady Allendale was off, poor Mariana in tow, to greet more guests. Ralston offered Callie an arm.

"I should very much like to escort you to the refreshment room, Lady Calpurnia," he said wryly.

She took the arm. "I apologize for the untruth."

"No need." They walked in silence for several moments before he added, "Thank you." He recognized how important the interaction with her family and the invitation from her mother would be in securing Juliana's acceptance into society.

She did not immediately respond, her thoughts instead focused on the evening's surprising turn of events. Keenly aware of the heat of Ralston's arm under her hand, of the eyes of London's best and brightest following their path around the ballroom, Callie couldn't stop herself from wondering just how different this particular evening could become.

"Do not thank me too quickly, my lord," Callie began tentatively. "After all, as you so tactfully stated, I have not yet made my request for payment."

Ralston glanced down at her. "So I've noticed. I don't suppose you'll out with it now, so we can get it over with?"

"I'm afraid not. I do have a rather strange question, however, if you wouldn't mind humoring me."

"Not at all. I would be happy to oblige."

She swallowed, shoring up her courage, and attempting to sound as casual as possible, asked, "Are you able to recommend a good tavern in town?"

As questions went, it was neither the most tactful nor the most delicate, but Callie was too eager for his response to attempt anything other than a direct approach.

Ralston was to be credited for not betraying the surprise he must have felt at the query. In fact, with the exception of a quick

glance in her direction, he continued navigating the couples blocking their path deftly, without pause.

"I beg your pardon? A tavern?"

"Yes. A public house." She nodded, offering him a smile, hoping he wouldn't press her.

"What for?"

She really should have expected his curiosity. Callie grasped for
an explanation. "You see . . . my lord," she paused, thinking. "My
brother . . . Benedick?" She waited for Ralston's nod of recognition
before continuing. "Well . . . *Benedick* is seeking a new haunt . . .
and I thought you might have an answer to his conundrum."

"I'm sure I could recommend somewhere. I shall discuss it with
him."

"No!"

One eyebrow rose at her vehement response. "No?"

She cleared her throat quickly. "No, my lord." She paused,
seeking inspiration. "You see . . . my brother . . . he would not appreciate my discussing taverns with you."

"As well he shouldn't."

"Quite." She attempted to appear properly chagrined. "So, you
see, it might be better for you to name an appropriate location . . .
for a gentleman, of course . . . and I will make the recommendation quietly. When the appropriate time presents itself."

She had been so engrossed in weaving her tale that Callie hadn't
noticed that they had stopped their passage. Ralston had guided
her into one of the alcoves on the far edge of the ballroom, out of
the way of the throngs of guests.

Turning to face her, he said, "You are a terrible liar."

Callie's eyes widened. She did not have to feign shock. "My
lord?"

"Your fibs. Even if the words had rung true—which they
didn't—you hide your thoughts poorly."

She opened her mouth to respond, could think of nothing to say, and closed it again.

"As I thought. I don't know why or for whom you would be seeking a public house, it seems a rather odd request, especially coming from a lady—" She opened her mouth again; he held up a hand to stop her from speaking. "However, I am feeling rather magnanimous this evening . . . and I am inclined to indulge you."

She couldn't help the smile that flashed. "Thank you, my lord."

"Don't thank me too quickly."

Callie's eyes narrowed as she recognized the words that she had spoken to him just moments ago. "What do you want?"

She expected a number of things from him at that moment—another request relating to Juliana's lessons, an entrée to Almack's, a dinner invitation from her mother, from Rivington's mother, even. She was prepared for those things. At this moment, they seemed an even trade for the name of a tavern where she could continue her adventures.

She was not expecting him to smile. And so, when he did—a wicked, wolfish grin that shook her to her toes—she was completely unprepared. A burst of heat spread through her, and her heart began to pound. She couldn't stop staring at his white teeth, his wide, soft lips, the single dimple that appeared in one cheek.

He was more handsome than he had ever been.

Ralston took advantage of her unguarded state, closing in on her until her back was pressed against the wall. She noticed belatedly that the small alcove was remarkably quiet, considering the mass of humanity that was just out of sight. He had selected a space that was almost entirely blocked by a massive column and a cluster of large ferns, affording them a measure of privacy.

He did not seem to care that the entire *ton* was mere inches away.

She grew nervous.

He reached out and ran a finger down the length of her arm, leaving a trail of fire where he touched her. Taking her gloved hand in his, he turned it over, baring her wrist to his gaze. He brushed his thumb over the delicate skin there, sending her pulse racing. Callie's entire world had been reduced to this single moment, this single caress. She could not tear her eyes from the point where they touched. The warmth of his hand, the even stroke of his thumb, consumed her as it threatened her sanity.

She did not know how long he stood caressing her before he lifted her hand to his lips and pressed his mouth to the bare skin of her wrist. Her eyes closed against the flood of sensation that came with the touch—the softness of his lips, parted just enough to breathe a hot, moist kiss upon her before he scraped his teeth against the sensitive spot. She heard her own gasp and opened her eyes just in time to feel his tongue soothing the skin. He boldly met her gaze as he wreaked havoc on her senses, and she couldn't help but watch him, knowing that he knew exactly what he was doing to her.

With one final kiss, Ralston let go of her hand, holding her gaze as he leaned toward her. When he spoke, his words were more air than sound as they brushed softly over the skin of her temple. "The Dog and Dove."

At first, she was confused. While she hadn't been certain of precisely what he would say, she had not been expecting that. And then, from deep within the haze of sensuality that he had created around them, understanding dawned. Her eyes widened. Before she could say anything, he was gone, leaving her to regain her sanity in private.

When she exited the alcove, flushed with anticipation, she was not surprised to discover that the marquess had taken his leave entirely.

He had, however, given her the name of a tavern.

Seven

"Anne, you must help me." Callie's tone was pleading as she watched her outraged maid unravel the long strands of hair that she had carefully arranged prior to the betrothal ball.

"I must do no such thing," the older woman scoffed. "You do realize that, if it were discovered, I could lose my position!"

"You know that I would never allow that to happen," Callie said. "But I cannot do this without you!"

Anne met Callie's eyes in the looking glass. "Well then, you shall have a very difficult time of it, Callie-mine. If you were caught . . . think of your reputation!"

"I shan't be caught!" Callie spun to face Anne, her half-unraveled hair flying out behind her. "First, everyone is so distracted by the ball that no one would even notice that I have gone. With *your* help in securing a disguise, the odds of my being caught would be virtually nil! Just one night, Anne. I will be back in no time, with none the wiser." Callie paused, her hands coming together, as she added, "*Please.* Don't *I* deserve an evening of excitement, as well?"

The older woman paused to consider Callie's quiet words, then heaved a resigned sigh. "This list shall be the death of both of us."

Callie grinned broadly. She had won. "Excellent! Oh, Anne, thank you!"

"You shall have to do more than thank me when the earl comes for my head."

"Done." Callie couldn't stop smiling as she turned to provide the maid with better access to the row of buttons down the back of her gown.

As Anne began to unhook the fastenings, she shook her head again, muttering to herself. "A tavern. In the dead of night. I must be mad to help you."

"Nonsense," Callie said vehemently. "You are merely a very good friend. A very good friend who should have Sunday, Monday, and Tuesday free."

The maid offered a noncommittal grunt at the obvious bribe. "Have you ever even *seen* the inside of a tavern?"

"Of course not," Callie said. "I've never had the opportunity to do so."

"One might think there was a reason for that," Anne said dryly.

"Have *you* ever been inside a tavern?"

The maid nodded brusquely. "I've had reason to visit a public house a time or two. I simply hope that the Marquess of Ralston has recommended one with a respectable clientele. I do not like that he was so willing to help you tarnish your reputation, Callie."

"Do not blame Ralston, Anne. I'm sure that he would not have made the recommendation had he thought I might be the one to patronize the Dog and Dove."

Anne snorted in disbelief. "The man must be something of a dunderhead then, Callie, because anyone with a brain can see through your fibs."

Callie resolutely ignored her. "Either way, I'm in for an adventure, don't you think? Do you imagine there will be a ruddy-cheeked barkeep with a missing tooth or two? Or a tired, winsome barmaid, working to keep her children fed and clothed? Or a group of young workmen eager for a pint of ale to chase away their tiring day?"

Anne spoke dryly. "The only thing I imagine there will be in that tavern is an overly romantic lady doomed to be disappointed by reality."

"Oh, Anne. Where is your sense of adventure?"

"I think you have more than enough of that for both of us." When Callie ignored her, she pressed on. "Promise me one thing?"

"Yes?"

"If you become uncomfortable in any way, you will leave immediately. Perhaps I should send Michael with you," she said, referring to her son, one of the Allendale coachmen. "He would make certain that you were safe."

The idea set Callie on edge. She whirled around to face the maid, clutching the loosened gown to her breast, urgency on her face. "Anne, no one aside from you must ever know that I've done this. Not even Michael. I cannot risk discovery. Surely, you understand that."

Anne paused, considering her next move. With a firm nod, the maid spoke matter-of-factly, "A plain brown wool should do. And you'll need a cloak to hide your face."

Callie smiled broadly. "I defer to your superior understanding of disguise."

"Well, I don't know about disguise, but I should think I'd be rather an expert on dressing you as a commoner." Anne pointed to the dressing screen nearby before continuing. "I shall go to fetch you a frock and cloak. You remove that gown while I am gone."

"And I'll need a cap."

Anne sighed. "I thought we were rid of lace caps."

"We are. But tonight, I need as much disguise as possible."

With a huff, Anne left, muttering to herself, likely about the challenges that long-suffering maids must endure.

Once Anne was gone, Callie removed the dress she had worn for the ball earlier that evening. As she slipped out of the blue satin gown, she swayed gently to the faint music that drifted up from the floor below, where revelers continued to dance and celebrate Mariana and Rivington.

There was little question that this was the greatest ball of her life. It wasn't just the waltz with Ralston—although that certainly was a factor—or the decadent, rather scandalous interaction with the marquess in the midst of the festivities, where anyone could have found them. It was that, for the first time in her life, she had been filled with an undeniable strength—as though she could do anything.

As though the adventure she craved was hers for the taking.

The powerful feeling had been almost too much to bear, and Callie had escaped above stairs soon after Ralston had left the ball. Her secret encounter, paired with the thrill that came with the tavern recommendation Ralston had provided, had rendered her unable to continue her sedate interactions with the *ton*. How could she discuss the season when there was scotch to be tried? A tavern to visit? A new Callie to encourage?

She couldn't, of course.

It was not the first ball she had left early; she doubted that anyone would notice or care that she had disappeared—a truth that made for an easy escape to adventure. *At long last, some good comes of being a wallflower.*

She smiled at the thought as a sharp rap announced Anne's return. The maid bustled back into the room, arms laden with brown wool.

Consumed with excitement, Callie couldn't stop herself from clapping her hands, eliciting a scowl from her companion.

"I should think you're one of the first people to ever applaud brown wool."

"Perhaps I am the first person to recognize brown wool for what it really is."

"Which is?"

"Freedom."

THE DOG AND Dove was, evidently, a popular haunt.

Callie peered out the window of the hansom cab she had hired to take her to the tavern, curiosity bringing her to the edge of her seat, nose nearly pressed against the glass window. She had ridden down Jermyn Street countless times by day, never realizing that it was an entirely different place at night. The transformation was really quite fascinating.

There were dozens of people on the street in front of the tavern, bathed in the yellow light that poured from its windows. She was surprised to see aristocrats in their starched cravats mingling with gentlemen and members of the merchant class, the "cits" who were so publicly criticized in ballrooms across London for working.

Interspersed among the men was a handful of women, some clearly the companions of the men upon whom they hung, others who seemed to be without an escort. The last filled Callie with apprehension; there had been a small part of her that had hoped to arrive at the tavern and, finding no unchaperoned women, to be required to ask the hack to return her home immediately.

Frankly, she wasn't sure if she was miserable or thrilled that she had been provided with no viable excuse to turn back.

Callie sighed, the exhaled breath clouding the window, turning the light beyond into a hazy yellow fog. She could just go home and drink scotch in Benedick's study. With Benedick. After all, he'd offered before. At Allendale House, where she would not risk her reputation.

At Allendale House, there would be no adventure. Callie winced at the thought, clutching the square sheet in her gloved hand, feeling the rich, thick paper crinkle in her palm as doubt assailed her.

She should have let Anne come with her. Solitary adventure was fast becoming overrated.

She couldn't go home now, however. Not after she'd gone through the trouble of asking Ralston for the name of a tavern *and* securing an appropriate disguise. She fidgeted under the rough wool of the gown, which irritated her skin despite the linen chemise she wore. With the hood of her cloak up, no one would even look twice at the plain young woman who entered, ordered a tumbler of whiskey and sat quietly at a table at the back of the taproom. She'd begged Anne for information about the inside of taverns as well. She was fully prepared. All she had to do was exit the hack.

Unfortunately, her legs did not seem to be willing to cooperate. *To list? Or not to list?*

The door opened. And she no longer had a choice. The driver spoke, exasperation filling his tone. "Miss? Ye did say The Dog and Dove, did ye not?"

Callie crushed the list in her hand. "I did."

"Well, here y'are."

She nodded. "Quite." And, stepping down onto the block he had set on the ground for her to exit, she thanked him.

She could do this. Shoring up her courage, Callie took the last step down to the street and planted her kidskin boot right into a puddle of murky water. With a little, involuntary cry of distress, she hopped to dry land and looked back at the now-amused driver. He offered her a cocky grin. "Ye should be watchin' where ye step, miss."

Callie scowled. "Thank you for the advice, sir."

He tilted his head at her as he added, "Are ye certain ye want to be here?"

She squared her shoulders. "Quite certain, sir."

"Right, then." He tipped his cap, leapt up to the driver's seat, and, with a click to his horses, was off to find his next fare.

Adjusting her hood, she faced the tavern. *To list, it seems.* Carefully checking the cobblestones in front of her for additional pitfalls, she made her way through the crowd of uninterested people outside, toward the door.

HE SAW HER the moment she entered the tavern.

There had been no question that she'd been lying earlier in the evening about her brother's looking for a tavern in town. There was little chance that the Earl of Allendale needed his sister's interference to find his way to a pub.

Which begged the question, why on earth was Lady Calpurnia Hartwell looking for a tavern?

And what on earth was she doing *inside* a tavern in the middle of the night? Had she no concern for her reputation? For that of her family? For that of his *sister,* for God's sake? He'd placed Juliana's reputation in her care, and here she was prancing into a public house, bold as brass. She was certain to get herself into trouble.

Ralston leaned back in his chair, whiskey in hand, his attention focused entirely on Callie, who was frozen just inside the doorway of the tavern, looking equal parts fascinated and terrified. The room was packed with people, most in various stages of drunkenness. He'd selected one of the more reputable establishments in St. James. While he could have sent her to Haymarket or Cheapside to teach her a lesson, he had predicted—correctly—that this place would be enough to set her back on her heels.

She pulled her cloak tight around her, eyes darting around the room, not sure where to direct her gaze to retain the calm demeanor that her upbringing required. A burst of masculine laughter startled her into turning toward a large group of men seated at a long table to her left. The men were eyeing a barmaid as she set tankards of ale on the scarred oak tabletop, revealing her ample bosom to the appreciative patrons. Callie's eyes widened as one particularly forward man grabbed the buxom server and pulled her, squealing, onto his lap for a rude grope. Callie snapped her eyes away from the scene before she could see the next, certainly more scandalous, scene in the tableau.

Unfortunately, she turned toward another, more mutually accommodating couple. To her immediate right, a young woman showing an indecent amount of skin was running a long, feminine finger along the jaw of a gentleman clearly in search of companionship. The two were whispering to each other, lips scant inches apart, eyes locked in a passionate gaze that could only result in one thing . . . something even the innocent Lady Calpurnia Hartwell could understand. The couple did not notice Callie's quick intake of breath before she catapulted herself farther inside, heading for the back of the tavern, straight to an empty table in a dimly lit corner   and to him.

If he weren't so angry with the ridiculous woman, he would be amused.

As she made her way through the crowded room, she tried desperately to avoid touching or even brushing accidentally against the other patrons—an impossible task in the crush of humanity that stood between her and the sanctuary of the empty table within her sights. She seated herself without looking at the people nearby, in an obviously desperate attempt to regain some semblance of calm. She sat with her back to him, but the hood of her plain woolen cloak had fallen back, and he watched as she collected herself and waited for a barmaid to approach. Her hair was up, tucked into a horrid lace cap, but a few auburn curls had escaped and were brushing against the nape of her neck, drawing his attention to the lovely, straight column, flushed with excitement.

For a fleeting moment, he considered what it would be like to kiss the skin there. The scene at the Allendale ball earlier in the evening had confirmed his suspicions that Lady Calpurnia Hartwell was an eager and passionate woman. Her responses were irresistibly uninhibited—so different from those of the women he usually partnered—he couldn't help but wonder how she would react to his touch in other, more scandalous places.

What was she doing here?

She could be discovered at any moment, by any number of people with connections to London society—she was in St. James, for God's sake! If that weren't enough, she had also entered the tavern alone, without protection; were she discovered by the wrong sort of man, she could find herself in a very serious and unpleasant situation. He noticed she held a square of paper firmly in both hands, as if it were a talisman. *Could it be a love letter? Was it possible she was meeting a man here?*

Of all the irresponsible things she could have done, this might well be the most rash. She tucked the parchment into the pocket of her cloak as a barmaid approached.

"I shall have a whiskey please. A scotch whiskey."

Had he heard her correctly? Had she just calmly, from her position alone at a darkened table in a London tavern at an ungodly hour, ordered a scotch as though it were the most normal thing in the world?

Had the woman taken leave of her senses?

One thing was certain. He had entirely misjudged little Callie Hartwell. She was most definitely *not* the appropriate sponsor for Juliana. He'd been looking for a woman of impeccable character and, instead, he had found Callie, who calmly ordered whiskey in London taverns.

Except—

Except there was nothing calm about her. His eyes narrowed as he watched her carefully. She was as stiff as a board. Her breathing, which he measured by the rise and fall of her shoulders, was uneven and shallow. She was nervous. Uncomfortable. And, yet, here she was, in a place he could have told her would make her both of those things. *Why?* He was going to have to ask her. To confront her. And he knew she wasn't going to enjoy it.

The barmaid returned with the drink, and Callie paid for it; Ralston noticed she included a handsome addition for the woman's service. When the server left, he leaned forward to watch as Callie lifted the glass and took a long whiff of the alcohol within. He couldn't see her face, but he saw her physically recoil with a single harsh cough, shaking her head as if to clear it before repeating the action. This time, she restrained herself from an obvious response, but from the way she bent her head to address the glass, he could tell she was skeptical of the beverage. It was clear she'd never had a drop of scotch in her life. After several moments of her investigation, during which she appeared to be debating whether or not she should drink, Ralston could no longer contain his curiosity.

"That is what you get for ordering whiskey."

Callie nearly dropped the glass. Ralston couldn't help feeling a touch vindicated by that. It served the chit right.

She had turned instantly toward him, scotch jostling violently in her glass, and he rose to move to join her at her table.

He gave her credit for quickly recovering from her surprise enough to respond, "I suppose I should have guessed you would be here."

"You will admit, a lady of good breeding requesting a recommendation for a tavern is not exactly the most common of occurrences."

"I suppose not." She looked back at her glass. "I do not suppose I could convince you to return to your table and pretend that you never saw me?"

"I am afraid that would be quite impossible. I could not leave you alone here. You could easily find yourself in a compromising situation."

She gave a half laugh. "I find that difficult to believe, my lord."

He leaned forward, lowering his voice. "Are you honestly unable to see the damage that your being found alone here would do to your reputation?"

"I would imagine that the damage would be significantly less than that of being discovered here with *you*." She gave a little wave, indicating the rest of the tavern. "There are plenty of unaccompanied ladies here."

Ralston's eyes darkened. "I highly doubt that those particular 'ladies' expect to remain unaccompanied."

She did not immediately take his meaning, furrowing her brow in confusion. When, after a few seconds, understanding dawned, she looked to the unattached women around the pub and then back to him, wide-eyed. He nodded, as if to confirm her suspicions.

She gasped, "But— I am not . . ."

"I know."

"I would never—"

He tipped his head in acknowledgment of her words. "It begs the question . . . Why *are* you here?"

She was silent long enough for him to think she might not answer the question. Then she said, "If you must know, I am here to drink scotch."

One dark eyebrow rose. "Forgive me if I do not believe you."

"It's true!"

"It does not take a master investigator to see that you are not a scotch drinker, Lady Calpurnia."

"It's true," she repeated.

He gave an irritated sigh, leaning back in his chair. "Really," he said, as though it was nothing of the sort.

"Yes!" She grew indignant. "Why is that so difficult to believe?"

"Well, first, I can assure you that the scotch at Allendale House is likely legions better than whatever swill they've given you here. So why not simply have a drink there?"

"I want to drink here. I find the atmosphere . . . engaging."

"You didn't even know *here* existed until two hours ago," he pointed out.

She was silent. Realizing she was not going to respond, he continued. "Secondly, you seem to be thoroughly averse to actually *drinking* the scotch in front of you."

The gleam in her eyes became defiant. "Do I?" And with that, she lifted the glass, saluting him with it before taking an enormous swallow of the amber liquid.

She immediately began coughing and sputtering, clutching a hand to her chest and blindly setting the glass on the table. It took her several moments to regain control of her faculties; when she did, it was to find that he had not moved except to assume a look of smug superiority.

His voice was dry as sand when he said, "It is an acquired taste."

"Evidently," she replied, peevishly. Then adding, "I believe my throat is on fire."

"That particular sensation will abate." He paused, then added, "It would probably be best if your next taste is more of a sip than a gulp."

"Thank you, my lord, I hadn't considered that," she said dryly.

"What are you doing here?" The words were quiet and cajoling, matched with a warm curiosity in his blue eyes.

"I already told you." She took a little sip of the liquid in her glass, grimacing.

He sighed again, gaze locked on her. "If that is true, you are more careless than I thought. You are taking a serious risk with your reputation tonight."

"I wore a disguise."

"Not a very good one."

She lifted a hand to her lace cap, nervously. "No one recognized me."

"I recognized you."

"You're different."

He paused, watching her. "You are right. I am different. Unlike most of the men an unchaperoned female would meet in an establishment such as this, I have a marked interest in preserving your honor."

"Thank you, Lord Ralston," she scoffed, "but I do not need your protection."

"It appears that you need precisely that. Or, shall I remind you that you and your family are about to be linked to my sister? She has enough against her. She doesn't need you ruining your reputation and her chances at success in one fell swoop."

The whiskey made her bold. "If you have such concern for the quality of my reputation, my lord, may I suggest you find another to guide your sister into society?"

His eyes narrowed on hers. "No, Lady Calpurnia. We have an agreement. I want you."

"Why?"

"Because she trusts you and enjoys your company. And because I do not have enough time to return to the beginning and find someone else." His tone turned to steel.

The barmaid returned then, leaning close enough to provide Ralston with an excellent view of her more-than-ample charms. "Is there anything else yer needin' this evenin', milord?"

"Not tonight," Ralston said with a careless smile, registering Callie's shock at the woman's overt invitation.

"I've got other ways of makin' ye comfortable, luv."

Callie's eyes were wide as saucers.

"I'm certain you do," Ralston said wickedly, producing a crown and slowly sliding the coin into the barmaid's palm. "Thank you."

Callie inhaled sharply. Her tone iced. "I grow weary of being told how to behave, as though I am unable to think for myself, especially by someone like *you*."

"Whatever do you mean?" he asked innocently.

"You cannot mean to suggest that you did not notice her . . . her . . ."

A smile played across his lips. "Her . . . ?"

Callie made a little sound of frustration. "You, sir, are incorrigible."

"Indeed. As we can agree that my reputation is beyond repair, may I suggest we return our attention to yours?" He did not wait for her response. "You will cease risking your reputation, Calpurnia, at least until Juliana is out. That means no unchaperoned visits to London public houses. Strike that. No visits to London public houses whatsoever. And, if you could see to it that you avoid leaving the house in the dead of night, that would be excellent."

"Certainly, my lord." Callie turned willful, her courage bolstered by drink. "And how would you suggest I prevent men from inappropriately accosting me in my ancestral home?"

The brashness of her statement surprised him, and he was immediately chagrined. "You have an excellent point. Please accept my—"

"Don't you dare apologize." Callie's voice shook as she interrupted him. "I am not a child, nor will I be made to feel as though

I have no control over my actions. Not by you, or by anyone else. And I could not—"

She stopped short. *And I could not bear hearing that you regretted our kiss.*

Of course, she knew in her heart that it was true, that he had trapped her in that alcove to prove his superiority, to pass the time, or for some other decidedly unromantic reason. But, for the first time in her life, she had felt sought after. And she would not have him ruin it with an apology.

In the silence that fell between them, mind reeling, Callie finished the last of her scotch. Ralston had been right, of course. The liquid seemed to go down much more easily with practice. She set the glass down, watching a droplet of whiskey make its slow, meandering way down the inside of the glass to settle at the bottom. She traced its path on the outside of the glass and waited for him to speak.

When he didn't, she was flooded with a desire to escape the now-too-small space. "I am sorry to have spoiled your evening, my lord. As I have completed the task for which I came, I believe I shall leave you in peace."

She stood, replacing her hood and pulling her cloak around her. He stood with her, immediately swinging his cloak around his shoulders and taking his hat and walking stick in hand. She offered him a direct look, and said, "I do not need a chaperone."

"I would not be much of a gentleman if I did not escort you home, my lady." She noted a slight emphasis on the last two words, as if he was reminding her of her position.

She refused to argue with him, refused to let him further ruin an evening that should have been bright with possibility—after all, she had succeeded in crossing yet another item off her list. Instead, she turned and began the long journey through the crowded taproom to the door, eager to exit the tavern ahead of him, certain that, if she could only reach the street first, she could hail a hackney and leave him—and this horrid interlude—behind. This time, however, she seemed less able to avoid being jostled by the crowd; her balance seemed somehow off, her thoughts slightly fuzzy. Was it possible that that small amount of scotch had gone to her head?

She exited the room into the cool spring evening beyond and marched to the street, head high, to search for a cab. Behind her, she was aware of Ralston calling up to the driver of his coach, who was waiting for him. *Excellent,* she thought to herself, *perhaps he has decided to leave me alone after all.* Ignoring the pang of disappointment that came with the thought, Callie stepped off the edge of the sidewalk to peer around another parked carriage. At the last minute, she recalled the puddle that she had met with earlier in the evening, and she increased the length of her stride, avoiding the muck. She landed off-balance and felt herself pitching forward onto the cobblestones. Flinging her hands out to catch herself, she prepared for impact.

An impact that never came.

Before she could grasp what had happened, she felt the earth shift and was caught against a rigid wall of warmth. She heard Ralston's mutter of "Infuriating female" as his arms came around her like stone, and she gave a little shriek when he lifted her into the air, flush against his chest. His very broad, very firm chest. The hood of her cloak fell back, and she found herself staring straight into his angry blue gaze. His lips were scant inches from her own. *Such marvelous lips.* She shook her head to clear it of such silly thoughts.

"You could have killed yourself," he said, his voice thick with an emotion she could not quite place. *Likely fury,* she thought to herself.

"I would think 'killed' is rather unlikely," she said, knowing as she spoke them that the words would not engender his goodwill.

"You could have fallen and been run over by a passing coach. I think killed is a fair statement."

She opened her mouth to speak, but he shifted her, distracting her from continuing their argument. Setting her down on the sidewalk in front of the open door to his carriage, he pointed a single finger toward the dimly lit interior of the vehicle. The single word he offered brooked no refusal. "In."

Taking his offered hand, she stepped up into the carriage, settling herself on the seat. Noticing that several curls had come down and were brushing against her cheek, she lifted a hand to check the positioning of her cap, only to discover it was missing. "Wait!" She called to Ralston just as he was about to lift himself into the coach. He paused, offering her a questioning look. "My cap. It is gone."

At the words, he ascended into the vehicle, taking the seat next to her and nodding to the footman to close the door behind him. She watched in shock as he removed his gloves and hat and set them on the seat across from them before banging on the roof of the carriage, signaling to the coachman to drive on.

"Did you not hear me?" she asked.

"I heard you," he said.

"My cap—" she started.

"I heard you," he repeated.

"But, you didn't—"

"No. I didn't."

"Why?"

"The loss of that cap is no loss at all. You should be thankful that it is gone. You're too young to be wearing such a loathsome thing."

"I like it!" she said, indignantly.

"No, you don't."

She turned her face away from him, looking out the window to the street passing beyond. He was right of course. She hated the lace cap and everything it represented. After all, hadn't she incinerated one of the awful things already? She couldn't help the little smile that crossed her face. Fine. She was happy to be rid of it.

Not that she would allow Ralston to know that.

"Thank you," she said quietly, the words echoing in the silence of the carriage. When he did not reply, she added, "For saving me."

Ralston gave a noncommittal grunt in response. Clearly, he was put out by her actions. Fair enough.

After several minutes of silence, Callie tried again, offering what she hoped would be a conversational olive branch. "I look forward to Juliana's coming out, my lord. I have every hope that she will find a love match."

"I hope she finds no such thing."

Her eyes flew to him in surprise. "I beg your pardon?"

"Love does not bode well for the Ralston family. I do not wish it upon any of us."

"Surely you cannot believe that."

He responded matter-of-factly, "Why would I not? My mother left a trail of broken hearts through Europe, cuckolding two husbands and deserting three children—all of whom she claimed to love—along the way. And you suggest that a love match should be the standard by which I measure my sister's success in society? No. I shall measure Juliana's success by her marriage to a man of character and kindness—two qualities with far higher value than love."

Were they in any other place at any other time, Callie would have likely allowed the conversation to end at that. Whether because of the whiskey or the adventure as a whole, she turned on the carriage seat to face him. "My lord . . . are you saying that you do not believe in love?"

"Love is merely an excuse to act without considering the consequences," he said with disinterest. "I've never seen evidence of its being anything more than a precursor to pain and anguish. And, as a concept, it does more harm than good."

"I must disagree."

"I would expect no less," he said frankly. "Let me hazard a guess. You think that love exists in all the poetic glory of Shakespeare and Marlowe and the wretched Lord Byron and whomever else."

"You needn't say it with such disdain."

"Forgive me." He waved a hand in the air, meeting her gaze directly in the dim light. "Please, go on. Educate me in the truth of love."

She was immediately nervous. No matter how academically he seemed to be able to discuss it, one's views on love were rather . . . well . . . personal. She attempted a scholarly tone. "I would not go so far as to believe that love is as perfect as those poets would like us to believe, but I believe in love matches. I would have to. I am the product of one. And, if that weren't enough proof, I should think tonight would have been at least moderately convincing. My sister and Rivington have eyes only for each other."

"Attraction is not love."

"I do not believe that what is between them is simple attraction."

The words faded into silence, and he watched her intently for a long moment before leaning in, stopping mere inches from her. "There is nothing simple about attraction."

"Nevertheless—" She stopped, unable to remember what it was she was trying to say. He was so close.

"Shall I show you how complicated attraction can be?" The words were deep and velvety, the sound of temptation. His lips were nearly on hers, she could feel their movement as he spoke, barely brushing against her.

He waited, hovering just above her, for her to respond. She was consumed with an unbearable need to touch him. She tried to speak, but no words came. She couldn't form thoughts. He had invaded her senses, leaving her with no other choice but to close the scant distance between them.

The moment their lips touched, Ralston took over, his arms coming around her and dragging her into his lap to afford him better access to her. This kiss was vastly different than their first one—it was heavier, more intense, less careful. This kiss was a force of nature. Callie moaned as his hand ran up the side of her neck cupping her jaw, tilting her head to better align their mouths. His lips played across hers, his tongue running along them before he pulled away just barely and searched her half-lidded eyes. A ghost of a smile crossed his lips.

"So passionate," he whispered against her lips as he drove his fingers into her hair, scattering hairpins and sending her curls tumbling around them. "So eager. Open for me."

And then he claimed her mouth in a searing kiss, and she did open for him, matching him stroke for stroke, caress for caress. She became caught in a web of long, slow, drugging kisses, and all she could think was that she had to be closer to him. She wrapped her arms around his neck as he opened her cloak and set his hands on a path to her breasts, cupping and lifting the heavy flesh there. She tore her mouth from his in a gasp as he ran his thumbs over the tips, hardened beneath the strained wool of the borrowed dress, freeing him to set his lips to the taut muscles in her neck, his tongue tracing a line along the column to her shoulder. He ran his teeth over the sensitive skin there, sending a jolt of pleasure through her, then laved the spot with his tongue. She sighed at the sensation and felt the curve of his lips against her shoulder, just as the taut wool of her bodice came loose, and her breasts spilled into his hands.

She opened her eyes at the sudden freedom, at the cool air rushing across her chafed skin, and she met his searing gaze for an instant before he pulled back to look at her bare breasts. Her skin shimmered in the flickering light from the streets beyond, and when he set one hand to her, she found herself unable to tear her gaze from the image of his fingers, stark against her paleness. The picture was more erotic than she could have imagined. She watched as he soothed the abraded skin and rubbed a thumb across her bare nipple, circling it gently, causing it to harden.

She shifted in his lap at the sensation, and he let out a low hiss as her hip pressed against the firm length of him. She was consumed by a feeling of feminine power, and she repeated the motion, this time rocking deliberately against him. He breathed deeply and stilled her with an iron grip, meeting her eyes. When he spoke, his voice was rough. "It's a dangerous game you play, Minx. And I am a formidable opponent."

Her eyes widened in surprise at the words. When he set his mouth to her breast, it was her turn to gasp. His tongue circled one peaked nipple before his lips closed around it and he sucked gently, working the hardened tip with mouth and teeth until she cried out, putting her hands to his head, clutching his hair.

He lifted his mouth from her, blowing a stream of cool air across her pebbled nipple, teasing her with the lightness of the caress. "Ralston." His name on her lips was harsh, pleading.

"Yes?"

"Don't stop," she whispered into the darkness. "Please."

His teeth flashed in a wicked grin. He shook his head, watching her, fascinated by her request. "So bold. You know exactly what you want, despite never having had it before."

"Ralston," she said again, writhing on his lap, frustration in her tone. "Please."

He kissed her, unable to deny the keen satisfaction he felt at her honest response to his caresses. How long had it been since he'd been with a woman who was so open? He could become addicted to her eagerness, to her enthusiasm. He pulled away from the rough kiss to reward her. "With pleasure, my lady," he said, and set his lips to her other breast. Callie cried his name, the sound echoing in the darkness, sending a jolt of pleasure through him, straight to his core.

He wanted her. In the carriage. He wanted to bury himself deep within her and show her what passion could be.

The thought shocked him from the moment, and he lifted his mouth from her breast, turning his attention to the street beyond. He swore roundly. This was not a woman one took in a carriage. This was Lady Calpurnia Hartwell, sister of the Earl of Allendale. She was half-undressed, and they were mere minutes from her home. How had he so lost control?

He began to set Callie to rights, straightening the bodice of her dress as she sat, confused, on his lap, watching him with wide, searching eyes. "We are almost at Allendale House," he said.

The words spurred Callie into motion. She leapt from his lap onto the seat across from him, yanking at her bodice. Her gloves made dexterity impossible and she clawed at them, freeing her hands to tighten her laces. She scrambled to collect her hairpins, which were scattered across the coach, to restore her hair to its former state. He watched as she did it, trying not to notice the swell of her breasts straining against the rough wool of her dress. He resisted the urge to stop her from taming her mane of hair, instead reaching down to collect several more pins from the floor and offer them to her.

She took them, brushing her fingers across his, releasing more of the searing heat that had built between them. "Thank you," she said quietly, flustered. She secured the last of her errant curls and placed her hands in her lap.

Gone was the passionate woman he had uncovered; returned was the prim and proper Lady Calpurnia. Ralston leaned back on the seat, watching her as the carriage pulled to a stop just outside of the Allendale driveway.

"I was not certain if the driver should take you to the door," he said. "Are you planning a clandestine reentry?"

She gave him a small smile. "Indeed, I am, my lord."

"Ah, so we are back to 'my lord.'"

She did not reply, instead dipping her head shyly. He couldn't see in the darkness of the coach, but he knew she blushed.

"I should like to escort you to the door."

"There is no need."

"Nevertheless—"

She interrupted. "I think it best I go alone. If we were found together . . ." The sentence did not have to be finished. With a nod, Ralston swung open the door and alighted to hand her down to the street.

He stood unmoving, watching until she had safely entered the house through the darkened front door before he climbed back up into the carriage and, with a sharp rap to the ceiling, signaled the coachman to drive on.

Eight

allie closed the wide oak door to Allendale House with a soft click before releasing a long sigh and leaning back against the cool wood. She slipped her key back into the hidden pocket of Anne's cloak and placed one bare hand to the pulse at her throat, attempting to stem the pounding there.

The great marble entryway was dark and quiet; the ball had ended hours earlier, and the servants, having finished tidying the space, had taken to their beds, leaving Callie in a silence that offered her a chance to address her racing thoughts. She had set out for an adventure that evening . . . and an adventure she had had!

A giggle escaped her at the thought, and her hand flew to her mouth to stem the noise as she surprised herself. Ladies of her age most certainly did not giggle . . . but for some reason it seemed an appropriate response tonight . . . as she sneaked back into her home after an evening filled with excitement. She felt another laugh bubbling up and quashed it. She had to get herself above stairs and into bed before she was discovered. She had worked too hard to keep her activities that night a secret—she would not allow herself to be caught!

Creeping across the marble foyer toward the wide staircase

that promised protection from discovery, Callie felt her way in the darkness, hands outstretched, searching for the thick mahogany banister. She had just set foot on the first stair when a hinge creaked behind her and a sliver of golden candlelight fell across her face. Turning with a gasp toward the now-open library door, Callie met her brother's eyes . . . and instantly recognized the irritation in them.

"I can explain—"

"Where the devil have you been?" His tone was equal parts frustration and incredulity.

She paused, frozen in midmovement, and considered her options for escape. Not many, and, if one eliminated the idea of leaving the house and never returning, none whatsoever.

Pasting a smile on her face, Callie whispered, "I don't suppose you'd believe I was in the conservatory?"

"Not a chance," Benedick said dryly.

"The morning room? Catching up on my correspondence?"

"Again. Likely not."

"The orangery?"

"Sister"—Benedick's tone was laced with warning as he extended his arm and widened the library door—"may I suggest you join me?"

Recognizing defeat when faced with it, Callie sighed and trudged toward her brother, who did not move from his place leaning against the doorjamb. Dipping under his arm to enter the warm library, lit by two fireplaces and a dozen or so candles, Callie muttered to herself, "One would think I would have noticed all these lights on the way in."

"One would think, indeed," Benedick said dryly, closing the door. Callie swirled to face her brother as she heard the latch click.

Seeing his sister in the well-lit room did not soften Benedick's mood. "Good God! What the hell are you wearing?"

"Mother would not approve of your using such language in the company of a lady, Benedick."

He was not going to be distracted. "First, I'm not entirely uncertain that Mother wouldn't use that language herself, considering the circumstances. And second, the current situation does raise a question or two about your status as a lady, Callie. Would you care to offer an explanation as to your whereabouts this evening?"

"I was at the betrothal ball this evening," Callie hedged, failing to endear herself to her elder sibling.

"My patience is wearing thin." His deep brown eyes flashed. "After the betrothal ball. More specifically, where did you go wearing this"—he waved an arm to indicate her attire—"*disguise . . .* I can only imagine you would call it? Where did you get such a hideous thing, anyway?"

"I borrowed it."

"From whom?"

"I shan't tell you."

He slashed one hand through the air. "From Anne, I imagine. I should toss her out for encouraging your behavior."

"Probably. But you shan't."

Warning flashed in his eyes. "I would not test me, Calpurnia. Now, answers. Where did you go?"

"Out."

Benedick blinked. "Out."

"Indeed," Callie said with a firm nod. "Out."

"Out where, Calpurnia?"

"Really, Benedick," she said in her haughtiest of tones, "I don't harangue you about your comings and goings."

"Callie—" The word was laced with warning.

She sighed again, realizing that there was no path to escape. "Oh, fine. I sneaked out. I went to—" She stopped. There really was no easy way to say it.

"You went to—?"

"I can't say," she whispered.

Benedick's eyes narrowed, his patience having run out. "Try."

She took a deep breath. "I went to a public house."

"You did what?" The words came out at a near roar.

"Shh! Benedick! You'll wake the whole house!"

"I'm not so sure I shouldn't!" He lowered his voice to a crazed whisper. "Tell me I've misunderstood you. Did you just say you went to a public house?"

"Shh! Yes!"

"With whom?"

"By myself!"

"By yourse—" He paused, thrusting one hand through his hair before cursing. "Whatever for?"

"To have a drink, of course," she said as if it were perfectly normal.

"Of course." Benedick repeated slowly, shocked. "Have you gone mad?"

"I don't think so."

"Were you recognized?" She was quiet, setting him further on edge. "Callie. Were you recognized?"

"Not by anyone important."

Benedick froze, spearing her with a rich brown gaze. "By whom, then?"

She hedged. "It's not entirely important. Suffice to say, it won't be a problem."

"Calpurnia."

"Fine. Ralston saw me. He was there."

Benedick sat heavily in a brocade chair. "Good God."

Callie followed his lead, flopping into the chair across from him. "Well, I shouldn't have really been surprised, considering he recommended the tavern in the first place," she said quickly, attempting to assuage her brother before realizing that his eyes were round as saucers and her words had done more harm than good.

"Ralston recommended a *tavern* to you?"

"Well, to be fair, I did ask him for a recommendation."

"Ah, well. That changes everything."

"There's no need for sarcasm, Benedick," she said curtly. "It isn't very becoming."

"Unlike an unmarried lady—the daughter of an earl—asking one of London's most notorious rakes for a recommendation to a tavern. That, of course, is the very epitome of becoming."

"When you put it that way—I can see how it might appear— problematic."

"*Might* appear?" Benedick ran a hand through his hair again. "What would possess you? What on earth were you thinking? What on earth was *he* thinking?" He stopped, struck by a thought. "Good God, Callie. Was he improper? I shall have his head!"

"No!" She exclaimed, "No! I approached him!"

"To ask for a tavern recommendation."

"Yes."

"He shouldn't have given it to you."

"He thought it was for you."

"For me?" Surprise and confusion laced his tone.

"Indeed. I couldn't very well ask him for myself, could I?"

"Of course not." Benedick looked at her as though she were mad. "Why the hell not drink here? What did you need a tavern for?"

"Well, for one thing," Callie said matter-of-factly, "drinking here wouldn't be nearly as much of an adventure."

"An adventure."

"Indeed." She pressed on. "And, if you take a moment to con- sider it, it was really all your idea."

"*My* idea?" Benedick began to turn red.

"Yes. Wasn't it you who was encouraging me to experience life mere days ago?"

The words hung in the air as Benedick leveled his sister with his most incredulous look. "You are jesting."

"Not at all. You started it. Categorically." She smiled, rather pleased with herself.

Benedick looked to the ceiling as though begging for divine patience. Or for the Lord to strike his sister down. Callie couldn't quite discern which. When he spoke, his tone brooked no discussion.

"Then allow me to finish it. Categorically. I am happy for you to pursue all the adventure you like. Here. In this house. Under this roof. Drink until you can no longer stand. Curse like a dockside sailor. Set your embroidery aflame, for God's sake. But, as your elder brother, the head of the family, and *the earl*," he stressed the last words, "I forbid you from frequenting taverns, public houses, or other establishments of vice."

She snorted in amusement. "Establishments of vice? That's a rather puritanical view of things, isn't it? I assure you, I was quite safe."

"You were with Ralston!" he said, as though she were simple-minded.

"He was perfectly respectable," she said, the words coming out before she remembered that the carriage ride home was anything *but* respectable.

"Imagine—my sister and the Marquess of Ralston together. And *he* turns out to be the respectable one," Benedick said wryly, sending heat flaring on Callie's cheeks, but not for the reason he thought. "No more taverns."

Callie considered her brother. She wouldn't need a tavern again, of course. "No more taverns," she agreed.

"If you want adventure, take it here."

"Really?" She turned a hopeful smile on him.

"Oh, no. Now what?"

"I don't suppose you would give me a cheroot."

Benedick burst into incredulous laughter. "Not on your life, sister mine."

"Benedick! You just said—"

"I've changed my mind."

"Have I not done enough to convince you that, if you do not assist me in experiencing life, I shall find someone else to do so?"

Benedick's eyes narrowed. "That is blackmail."

"And that is your opinion." She smiled broadly. "I think it would be a nice moment, a brother helping his old, spinster sister to have an adventure."

"I think you hold rather too-high expectations of the experience of smoking."

"Well, no time like the present to dash those expectations, don't you think?" She paused, offering him a pleading look. "Please? I've never even *seen* someone smoke."

"As well you shouldn't have!" Benedick argued imperiously, "A gentleman does not smoke in the presence of ladies."

"But I'm your sister!"

"Nonetheless."

"Benny . . ." she said, using his nickname from their childhood, "No one will ever know. You said I could have adventure inside the house!"

He watched her, not speaking, for several minutes, until she was entirely certain that she was not going to smoke a cheroot that evening. Just as she was about to stand and make her exit from the room, he heaved an enormous sigh. Hearing it, Callie's face broke into a grin.

She had won.

She clapped her hands in excitement. "Excellent!"

"I shouldn't push my luck if I were you," Benedick said with warning as he reached into his breast pocket and removed a thin silver rectangle. Setting the box on the table next to his chair, he threw a catch on its underside, revealing a hidden drawer.

Callie sat forward with a gasp as the drawer came into view, craning to see. "I never knew!"

Benedick withdrew a small crystal ashtray, a tinderbox, and bundle of wooden matches. "Again, as well you shouldn't have. I'm rather certain I shall regret showing you in the morning."

Callie watched, fascinated, as Benedick opened the silver box and removed two long, slender brown cheroots. Putting one to his lips, he inserted the match into the tinderbox, lit the small stick of wood, and lifted the flame, producing a cloud of smoke.

"Fascinating!" Callie cocked her head to one side, watching the orange tip of the cheroot glow.

Closing his eyes briefly to both her innocence and his own bad behavior, Benedick took a long pull on the cigar, as though shoring up his confidence, then removed it from his mouth and offered it to his sister.

Giddy with excitement, she reached for it. Of course, once the burning tube was held gingerly between her fingers, she hadn't any idea how to proceed. Meeting her brother's amused gaze through the long column of smoke that was rising from the end of the cheroot, she said, "Now what?"

"Not much to it, really," Benedick said nonchalantly. "Now you smoke it."

"Like this?" she asked, carefully bringing the cheroot to her lips and inhaling deeply.

She noted Benedick's eyes widening as she did so, and that was the last thing she registered before she began to cough. Horrible racking coughs that consumed her strength. She was vaguely aware of Benedick taking the burning stick from her hand, allowing her to pound upon her chest. Desperate for fresh air, she took huge gulps of breath, which only caused her to cough more, leading Benedick to bang on her back until she stopped him with a wave of her hand, fearing that the blows would simply knock any usable air from her lungs.

When she was once again able to focus on something other than her need for air, she registered her brother towering above her, trembling. Certain that he was quaking with concern for her well being, she looked up to allay his fears only to discover that he was instead shaking with barely controlled laughter. Her reassuring look immediately became a scowl as she noted his broad grin. His teeth gleamed white in his face, which was now red with exertion.

"You, sir, are no gentleman."

The words sent Benedick over the edge. He could not contain his great rolling laughs at her prim displeasure. In the face of his infectious amusement, Callie began to see the humor in the situation, and she began to laugh as well, which brought on another fit of coughing, more pounding, and an additional round of laughter.

After several moments, Benedick resumed his seat and stamped out Callie's cheroot in the ashtray as she watched. "And so we discover why women do not smoke," he said, humor still lacing his voice.

"What a vile habit!" Callie said. "How can you do it?"

"Suffice it to say that it is an acquired taste."

"That's precisely what Ralston said about scotch."

"And he was right," Benedick said. After a few moments, he asked, "You did not enjoy that part of the evening, either, then?"

"On the contrary," Callie said. "I enjoyed every bit of the evening. I may not drink scotch or smoke a cheroot again, but I shall always cherish the fact that I *did* those things. The adventure is well worth the disappointing experience."

"I do not like this taste for adventure you have developed, sister."

"I am afraid I cannot guarantee I shall be rid of it anytime soon. It's a shame that women are not able to even try the experiences that men so take for granted. You lot really are quite lucky." Benedick turned a skeptical look on her, but she pushed on. "Come now, Benedick, you're not really going to tell me you don't think I deserve an adventure or two, do you? After all, you provided me with the most recent instrument of my demise."

"A point I should like to forget."

"Coward."

They smiled at each other.

"Mother will have my head if she finds out."

"She won't find out," Callie said, "and, even if she did, it's not as though she has anything to worry about. I'm well and truly on the shelf. I should think I'm allowed an eccentricity or two."

Benedick snorted with laughter. "Smoking and drinking are rather remarkable eccentricities, Callie. I'm not sure the *ton* would accept them—despite your having one foot in the grave." He paused, thinking. "I'm rather shocked that Ralston would encourage you, what with you being so kind as to sponsor his sister. What was he thinking? He should have packed you into a carriage and brought you home immediately."

Callie had the good sense to avoid telling her brother that Ralston had in fact packed her into a carriage and brought her home. Instead, she said, "I imagine he felt, as you did, that he would better serve my reputation by staying with me while I pushed the boundaries. At least, then, I had a chaperone."

"I would not exactly refer to him as a 'chaperone,'" Benedick growled. "I should call him out."

"I would prefer you didn't. I rather like him."

He met her eyes. "You don't—You can't—" He leaned forward.

"What does that mean?" She did not respond, leaving Benedick to try again. "Ralston . . . he isn't . . . Callie, women don't 'rather like' the Marquess of Ralston."

Her voice was barely audible when she said, "No, I don't suppose they do."

As he registered the sadness in his sister's voice, Benedick swore softly. "I saw that he danced with you tonight. I know how that must have felt. I understand that he played the part of protector at the ridiculous tavern you went to—Lord knows I'm glad he found you there or who knows what might have happened to you—but you must understand . . . Ralston . . . men like Ralston . . ." He stopped again, uncertain of how to say delicately what he was thinking.

Callie took pity on him and offered him an exit from the awkward conversation. "I know, Benedick. I'm not silly. Men like Ralston are not for women like me."

Perhaps if I say it enough, I'll begin to believe it.

She forced a chuckle, attempting to lighten the mood. "I should think Ralston would be far more adventure than I could endure."

He smiled. "Not only you. Think of your poor old brother."

Returning his smile, she stood, placing a kiss on his cheek. "Thank you for the cheroot, Benny." And, with that, she left the room, climbing the great marble stairs to her bedchamber.

Callie prepared herself for sleep slowly and methodically, refusing to allow Benedick's words to upset her. Certainly, he was right. She was no match for Ralston; she never had been. But that night, she had come close. And, if one night were all she could have, it would have to be enough.

She replayed the events of the evening in her mind as she took down her hair, moved through her toilette and changed into her billowing white nightgown. She then smoothed out her wrinkled list and considered it frankly. For several long minutes, she sat at her desk, unmoving, reading over the items. With a sigh, she lifted her pen and drew a dark line through *Smoke cheroot and drink scotch.*

She snuffed the last candle and slid into bed and dreamed of the woman in Ralston's carriage—in Ralston's arms.

Nine

$\mathcal{S}$everal days later, Callie arrived at Ralston House promptly at noon, prepared for a day of dress shopping.

If there was one thing that Callie loathed, it was dress shopping.

Thus, she brought reinforcements in the form of Mariana who, aside from her unnatural love of Bond Street, was also consumed with curiosity over Ralston's mysterious younger sister.

"I've never been to Ralston House!" Mariana whispered excitedly, as they approached the door.

"As well you should not have done," Callie pointed out, primly. "Until the arrival of Ralston's sister, this was most certainly *not* the place for young unmarried women."

Nor an old, unmarried woman, but that did not prevent you from visiting the marquess.

Callie ignored the little voice in her head and started up the steps to the front door of the house. Before she reached the top stair, the door burst open, revealing an eager Juliana. "Hello!" she said, breathless with excitement.

Behind her stood a wild-eyed Jenkins, looking thoroughly appalled by the fact that the young woman had not waited for a footman to open the door and announce the arrival of her guests. His mouth opened a fraction, then closed, as though he were entirely unsure of how to deal with such an egregious breach of conduct. Callie swallowed back a smile, certain that the stoic butler would not at all appreciate the humor of the situation.

Mariana, however, took in the scene before her and burst into laughter. Clapping her hands together in glee, she crossed the threshold, took Juliana's hands warmly in her own, and said, "You *must* be Miss Juliana. I am Callie's sister, Mariana."

Juliana dropped a small curtsy—as much as she could curtsy without the use of her hands—and said, "Lady Mariana, it is an honor to meet you."

Mariana shook her head with a wide smile. "We can dispense with the 'Lady' altogether; you must call me Mariana. Can you not see that we are going to be excellent friends?"

Juliana matched Mariana's smile with a brilliant one of her own. "Then you must call me Juliana, no?"

Callie grinned at the picture they made, heads already bent as if in confidence. Behind them, Jenkins looked to the ceiling. Callie had no doubt that the butler was longing for the days when there were no female residents of Ralston House.

Taking pity on him, she turned to the girls to say, "Shall we be off?"

Within moments, they had piled into the Allendale coach and were on their way to Bond Street, where they were to spend much of their afternoon. Of course, getting there was much easier said than done in the crush of carriages and shoppers. As the coach crept along, Juliana quieted, pressing her nose to the window to watch the bustling activity in the street beyond: scores of aristocrats moving in and out of shops; footmen loading carriages with boxes and packages; gentlemen tipping their hats as they passed clusters of chattering ladies. There was nothing quite like Bond

Street at the start of the season. Callie could imagine that Juliana would find the entire experience of shopping alongside the *ton* rather daunting. Frankly, she couldn't blame her for it.

Mariana seemed to sense the other girl's nerves and chattered brightly. "We shall begin, of course, with Madame Hebert." She placed her hand on Juliana's, leaning across the carriage to whisper excitedly, "She's French, of course, and the finest dressmaker in London. *Everyone* wants her . . . but she's *very* particular about her clientele. In her creations, you'll be the talk of the season!"

Juliana turned wide eyes on Mariana, and said, "If she is, as you say, particular, why would she accept me as a patron? I have no title."

"Oh, she shall accept you without question! First, she's designing my entire trousseau—so she will not be able to turn away a friend of mine. And, if that weren't enough," she added, matter-of-factly, "Ralston is a marquess and rich as Croesus. She won't turn him down."

"Mariana!" Callie exclaimed in outrage.

Mariana gave Callie a frank look. "Well, it's true!"

"Nevertheless! It is vulgar to discuss the marquess's finances."

"Oh, posh, Callie. Everyone does it among friends." Mariana waved a hand in dismissal and flashed a grin at Juliana. "It's true. I'd imagine he's outfitted several mistresses there."

"Mariana!" Callie's voice turned shrill. Juliana laughed, drawing a warning look from Callie. "Don't encourage her!"

The carriage pulled to a stop, and Mariana adjusted the bow of her bonnet, tying it at a jaunty angle under her chin. She winked impishly at Juliana before hopping down from the carriage to the street below, calling back, "It's true!"

And, with another laugh, Juliana joined her and the pair rushed ahead, into the *modiste*'s shop.

Callie followed them, amused. Mari had been the perfect addition to the outing—her natural exuberance was a match for Juliana's—and Callie was rather proud of herself for making such a wonderful match. Ralston would be happy to hear that his sister had become fast friends with the future Duchess of Rivington; there was no question that such an alliance would smooth Juliana's entry into society. Assuming, of course, that he never discovered that Mariana was more than willing to discuss his private affairs—all of them, evidently—without a care for discretion. Callie could only hope that the marquess's own sister was slightly more careful with her words.

Mari was, of course, correct. Most men of London society kept their mistresses well housed and well dressed. Ralston would be no different. At the thought, a memory flashed in Callie's mind— Ralston in his darkened chamber on that first night, when everything had begun, listing off the things that he had given his mistress at the end of their relationship. *You retain the house, the jewels, the clothes.* The vision chilled her. She shouldn't be surprised, of course, but . . . the pang of jealousy she felt at the thought of his buying *clothing* for another woman was sharp.

How many had there been?

"Lady Calpurnia!"

The words startled her from her morbid reverie, and she turned to find Baron Oxford approaching from the opposite side of the street. His snug buckskin breeches and dark blue topcoat were offset by his crimson waistcoat, which was perfectly matched to the knob on his cane and the heels of his boots—the brilliance of which was rivaled only by his wide, white smile. Oxford was the height of fashion.

Aside, of course, from the fact that he just bellowed at me from halfway across London.

"Lady Calpurnia!" he repeated as he bounded out of the street to join her on the steps to Madame Hebert. "What tremendous good luck! Why, I was just considering paying a visit to Allendale House . . . and here you are!"

"Indeed," Callie said, resisting the urge to ask the baron why he would be at all interested in visiting Allendale House, "here I am!" When Oxford continued to smile at her without speaking, she added, "It is a lovely day for shopping."

"Only made lovelier by your being here."

Callie's eyebrows snapped together. "Oh. Well. Thank you, my lord."

"Perhaps I could tempt you to forgo your shopping for a fruit ice?"

Was he pursuing her?

"Oh, I couldn't . . . You see, my sister is inside." She waved a hand to indicate the *modiste*'s shop. "She will be waiting for me."

"I'm sure she would understand." He offered one arm to her and, with a wide smile, winked at her.

Callie froze at the gesture. He was most definitely pursuing her. *Why?*

"Callie!" Startled, Callie spun toward Mariana, who had popped her head out of the door to the shop to look for her sister. Taking in the scene before her with a look of utter confusion, Mari added, "Oh, hello, Baron Oxford."

Oxford dipped into an extravagantly low bow, pointing one red-heeled boot in Mariana's direction. "Lady Mariana, a pleasure, as ever."

Callie lifted one gloved hand to her lips to cover the smile that escaped at the bizarre interaction. Lips twitching, Mari added, "Yes, well. You will not mind if I steal my sister away, will you?"

Oxford straightened and smiled broadly, "Not at all! Indeed this turn of events will only serve to make it more imperative that I call upon Lady Calpurnia at Allendale House."

"That would be lovely, my lord." Callie added in a tone that any but the baron would have noted as too bright. Seizing the opportunity for escape, she hurried up the stairs to Mariana, turning back to wave briefly at Oxford before following her sister into the shop.

"I cannot believe that he kept you waiting in the *street*! Do you think there is anything in that man's head at all?" Mari asked under her breath.

Callie grinned. "Aside from teeth?"

The sisters laughed loudly as they approached Juliana, who had already waylaid Madame Hebert. The *modiste* had clearly decided, as Mariana had predicted, that designing an entire wardrobe for Juliana would be good for business.

Soon, they were surrounded by a gaggle of seamstresses, several of whom had already started measuring the girl, while others scrambled to collect bolts of fabric in every imaginable color and material. One small, bespectacled young woman perched on a nearby stool, taking notes as Mariana joined the conversation.

"She'll need at least six dinner dresses to start . . . six day dresses, three riding habits, a dozen morning gowns, five walking dresses . . ." She paused, allowing the dressmaker's assistant to catch up with her scribbling. "Oh! And three ball gowns . . . no, four. They must be stunning, of course," Mariana said, giving a meaningful look at Madame Hebert. "She must take London by storm."

Callie smiled as she took in the scene. Mariana had indeed been the perfect choice of companion. Juliana appeared thoroughly dumbstruck. Poor thing.

Mariana looked to Callie. "What have I forgotten?"

Turning to the *modiste*, Callie spoke up, "Spencers, pelisses, cloaks, and shawls to go with everything, as necessary . . . and she'll need undergarments for all, of course. And night rails."

Juliana spoke for the first time. "I do not see why I need new night rails. Mine are perfectly acceptable."

"You need them because your brother is willing to buy them for you," Mariana pointed out, matter-of-factly. "Why not have them?"

Juliana looked to Callie. "It is too much. I am only here for seven weeks."

Callie shook her head sympathetically, immediately understanding the younger woman's discomfort. She had barely met Ralston, and now she was ordering a fortune in clothing on his account. Callie moved closer to Juliana, placing a reassuring hand on her arm. Softly, so no one but Juliana could hear, Callie said, "He *wants* to do this for you. It was *his* idea. I know it seems too extravagant . . ." She met the young woman's clear, worried gaze. "Let him play the elder brother today."

After a moment, Juliana gave a little nod. "*Bene.* However, I should like the dresses to be in a more . . . Italian style."

Madame Hebert overheard from her place nearby and scoffed, "You think I would take a wild lily and trim it to appear an English rose? You shall meet the *ton* as a bright Italian star."

Callie couldn't help but chuckle. "Capital. Shall we choose some fabrics?"

The words sent the cluster of women around them into a flurry, rolling out yards of muslins and satins, jaconet and crepe, velvet and *gros de Naples* in every imaginable color and pattern.

"Which do you like?" Callie asked.

Juliana turned her attention to the pile of fabrics, a bemused smile on her face. Mariana approached and locked their arms together. Leaning close, she said, "*I* adore that mulberry crepe. It would go beautifully with your hair." Turning to Callie she said, "And you, sister?"

Callie cocked her head in the direction of a willow green satin, and said, "If you don't leave here with an evening dress in that satin, I shall be very disappointed."

Juliana laughed. "Well, then I shall have to have it! And I *do* like that rose muslin."

Madame Hebert lifted the bolt and passed it to a seamstress. "Excellent choice, *signorina*. May I suggest the gold satin as well? For evening, of course."

Mariana squeezed Juliana's arm, and said brightly, "This is fun, isn't it?" sending Juliana, nodding, into a fit of laughter. Ralston's sister warmed quickly to the process, and within an hour she had selected colors and fabrics for all of her gowns. She and Mariana were taking tea and discussing hems and waists as Callie found herself fingering an aethereal blue satin that had caught her eye several times since she entered the shop. For the first time in a very long time, Callie was drawn to the idea of having a gown made. For herself.

"The fabric, it has been calling to you, *non*?" The deeply accented words of the *modiste* drew Callie from her thoughts. "It would make a beautiful gown. For your next ball. This satin, it is made for waltzing."

"It is gorgeous!" Mariana had materialized beside her as the dressmaker had spoken.

"Indeed! You must have it!" Juliana added.

She smiled, shaking her head. "Thank you, but I have no need of a gown like that."

Madame Hebert's eyebrows rose in surprise. "You do not attend the balls?"

"Oh, I do . . ." Callie struggled for the words. "But I do not dance."

"Perhaps you do not have the right gown, my lady. May I say . . . if *I* were to design you a gown of that fabric, you would most certainly dance." Throwing an excess of the fabric out onto her table, the Frenchwoman worked several moments, pleating and folding. Stepping back, she allowed Callie a look at her work, which barely hinted at being a gown. It was gorgeous.

"We shall lower the line of the neck to show you off, the waist as well. You hide yourself among these flounces and frill—like so many other Englishwomen," Madame Hebert spat the last words out as if they had a foul taste. "You need the French design. The French, they celebrate the woman's shape!"

Callie blushed at the dressmaker's bold speech, but she was tempted by it, nonetheless. Meeting the little Frenchwoman's gaze, she said, "All right. Yes."

Mariana and Juliana let out little exclamations of delight.

Madame Hebert nodded, all business. "Valerie," she said sharply, calling to her assistant, "take Lady Calpurnia's measurements. She will have the aethereal blue satin. She will also need a cloak."

"Oh, I don't think—"

The *modiste* did not look at Callie, instead pushing forward as though she hadn't spoken. "The midnight satin. We shall line it with chinchilla. And then the aethereal comes off the shelf. The fabric belongs only to this lady."

At the words, the girls around the shop tittered. Callie looked to Mariana in confusion. Her sister whispered, "Madame Hebert only removes fabric from sale when she constructs a gown without the help of her staff! Callie! How exciting!"

Callie swallowed audibly. What had she gotten herself into?

Madame Hebert turned back to Callie. "Three weeks."

She nodded in understanding. "And Juliana's?"

"The same. We shall send them to her as they are finished."

"She will need the gold evening gown on Wednesday," Mariana said, "for the opera."

Juliana, who had been idly stroking a lavender muslin that was to become one of her new walking dresses, looked up in surprise.

"She must be at the opera on Wednesday, Callie," Mariana repeated, then said to Juliana, "You will come with us, of course."

Of course, Mariana was right. Wednesday was opening night at the Theatre Royal and the perfect event at which to launch Juliana into society. She would be introduced as delicately as possible, only having to interact with the *ton* before and after the opera, and during its intermission.

Callie nodded her agreement. "Wednesday is, of course, the perfect day."

The *modiste,* who had remained quiet through the conversation, finally spoke. "It is Monday, my ladies. I can finish the gown for Wednesday, but not without having my girls work through the night." The meaning was clear.

Callie smiled. Ralston *had* put her in charge. And he *had* said money was no object. "Her brother is the Marquess of Ralston. I am certain he will approve the charge."

Madame Hebert did not press the issue and sharply ordered two of her girls to begin the dress immediately.

Once outside, the trio began a whirlwind tour of the shops of Bond Street and beyond. After visiting the milliner, they made their way down a small, narrow street, and Juliana stopped to gaze through a bookshop window. Turning back to her companions, she said, "Would you mind terribly if we went in? I should like to purchase something for my brothers. To thank them for their kindness."

"What an excellent idea!" Never one to avoid a bookseller, Callie opened the door with a wide smile, motioning for Juliana to enter ahead of her.

The tinkling of a small bell welcomed the young women into the shop and alerted its proprietor to their presence. With a polite nod, he quickly returned to his work, and Callie and Mariana moved to browse the latest novels, leaving Juliana to consider an appropriate gift for her brothers.

The younger girl had never considered how difficult it might be to choose the perfect gift for Ralston and St. John—something that spoke to their unique interests and would hold additional meaning as the first gift they received from their new, unexpected sister.

After a quarter of an hour of browsing, Juliana had finally selected a large book of illustrations of Pompeii for Nick, hoping that his love of the ancient world would make it the perfect gift.

Ralston, however, presented a challenge. She knew so little of him, aside from the long hours he spent at his piano late at night. Moving through the shop, Juliana ran her fingers along the spines of large, leather-bound tomes, wondering what might be the right choice for her eldest brother.

Finally, she paused, lingering over a German volume on Mozart, nibbling on her lower lip as she considered the book.

"If one is looking for a biography of Mozart, there is none better than that. Niemetschek knew the maestro personally."

Juliana started, spinning toward the voice.

Scant inches away, stood the most beautiful man she had ever seen.

He was tall and broad, with eyes the color of honey warmed in the sun. The late-afternoon light that streamed into the bookshop played on his golden curls and underscored the perfect lines of his straight nose and strong jaw.

"I—" She stopped, her mind racing as she attempted to remember the rules of conduct for such a situation. Callie and she had never discussed proper conduct when approached by an angel in regard to musical biographies. Certainly it would not be inappropriate to thank him. Would it? "Thank you."

"My pleasure. I hope you will enjoy it."

"Oh, it is not for me. It is a gift. For my brother."

"Ah, well then I hope *he* will enjoy it." He paused, and they stared at each other for a long moment.

Juliana grew nervous in the silence, eventually saying, "I am sorry, sir. I am fairly certain that we are not allowed to converse."

He gave her a small, crooked smile, sending a wave of warmth through her. "Only fairly certain?"

"Almost positive. I am new to London and your rules, but I seem to remember something about our needing to be introduced." Her blue eyes flashed.

"That is a pity. What do you think will happen if we were discovered? Discussing books in a public place by light of day?"

The scandal in his tone drew a little laugh from her. "One never knows. The earth might well swallow us whole for such a dangerous activity."

"Well, I would hate to place a lady in such imminent danger. And so, I will take my leave, and hope that someday we will have cause for proper introductions."

For a fleeting moment, she considered calling Callie or Mariana over to make the introductions, but she felt certain that kind of thing was not done. Instead, she blinked up at the golden man. "I shall hope the same."

He bowed low then, and was gone, the only sign that he had been there at all the faint tinkling of the bell above the bookshop's door announcing his exit.

Unable to stop herself, Juliana moved to the window, watching him as he strode down the street.

"Juliana?" Callie spoke from nearby. "Have you selected your books?"

Turning with a smile, Juliana nodded. "I have. Do you think that Gabriel will enjoy a biography on Mozart?"

Callie considered the title. "I think that is a fine choice."

Juliana took a deep breath, pleased. "Tell me, do you know that man?"

Mari followed the direction of Juliana's gaze, taking in the tall, golden man moving quickly away from the shop. Wrinkling her nose, she looked back at Juliana and said, "Why?"

"No reason," Juliana hedged. "He is . . . familiar."

Mari shook her head. "I doubt you know him. I can't imagine his even deigning to visit Italy, let alone actually *speak* to someone Italian."

"Mari . . ." Callie said, caution in her tone.

"But, who is he?" Juliana pressed.

Callie waved one hand dismissively, heading for the sales counter. "The Duke of Leighton."

"He is a duke?" Juliana asked in surprise.

"Yes," Mari nodded, guiding her friend to the front of the book-shop. "And a thoroughly awful one. Considers anyone with a lesser title to be entirely beneath him. Which doesn't leave him many equals."

"Mariana! Must you insist on gossiping in public?"

"Oh, come, Callie. Admit that you cannot suffer Leighton."

"Well, of course not," Callie said in a low voice. "No one can. I do try not to announce my distaste to entire bookshops, however."

Juliana considered their conversation. He hadn't seemed at all distasteful. But, then, he hadn't known who she was. Certainly if he had discovered she was a merchant's daughter . . .

"Are there many like him? Many who will discount me imme-diately, simply because of my birth?"

Mariana and Callie exchanged a brief glance at the question be-fore Callie waved a hand in the air, and said, "If there are, they are not worth the effort. There are plenty who will adore you. Never fear."

"Indeed," Mari added with a smile. "And do not forget that I am soon to be a duchess myself. And then . . . hang them all!"

"I should not like them to be killed," Juliana said, worriedly.

The other women looked confused for a brief moment before Callie laughed, understanding that Mariana's words had been lost in translation. "It is an expression, Juliana. No one shall be hanged. It simply means that Mariana will not care about them."

Understanding dawned. "Ah! *Capisco*. I understand! *Si*. Hang them!"

The three women all laughed together and Juliana paid for her brothers' gifts. After a footman had been charged to deliver their wrapped packages to the carriage, she turned a bright smile on the other women. "Where shall we go next?"

Mariana smiled broadly and announced, "The glover, of course. A woman cannot very well make her debut without opera gloves, can she?"

$\mathcal{C}$allie stood at the edge of the Rivington box at the Theatre Royal, unable to contain her satisfied smile as she scanned the rest of the audience, noting the scores of opera glasses pointed in the direction of Miss Juliana Fiori.

If the attention were any indication, title or no, daughter of a fallen marchioness or no, Juliana would make a remarkable debut.

The opera had not even begun and, already, the box was mobbed with visitors, from pillars of the *ton* who came, ostensibly, to visit with the dowager duchess, and, as such, happened to meet the lovely young Juliana, to young men of society who were less discreet about the reason for their visit to the box—arriving and promptly falling over themselves for an introduction.

The evening could not have been more perfectly orchestrated, and Callie was taking full responsibility for its success.

Juliana had arrived at opening night in the Allendale carriage and, to Callie's delight, the young woman had alighted with grace and aplomb, as though being set on display for the judgment of London's aristocracy were the most natural thing in the world. Once inside the theatre, Juliana had removed her cloak to reveal her stunning satin evening dress, which had been delivered to

Ralston House in perfect condition that morning; Madame Hebert had outdone herself on the gown, which was shot through with gold threads and sure to be the envy of every other woman in the house.

And then she had been escorted—on this, the most important night of the London theatrical season—to the Duke of Rivington's personal box, where she was to be the personal guest of the dowager duchess, the future duchess, and the duke himself. For this evening, the Allendale box would stand empty; the Earl and Dowager Countess of Allendale and Callie would view the opera from the Rivington box—showing the world that Juliana was accepted by two of the most powerful families in Britain.

And, as if all that weren't enough, Ralston and St. John had arrived—giving the matchmaking mamas of the *ton* even more gossip to feed upon. The elusive twin brothers were rarely seen at such blatantly social events as this one, and even more rarely seen together. Callie turned her attention to them, standing sentry, side by side, several feet behind their sister, thoroughly intimidating in their identical height and handsomeness.

Callie's pulse quickened as she studied Ralston. He was impeccably dressed, forgoing the brilliant waistcoats preferred by the dandies of the *ton* in favor of perfectly tailored black breeches and dress coat over a classic white waistcoat without a single crease. His cravat was perfectly starched, and his boots gleamed, as though he had arrived via some magical route other than London's muddy streets. He was flawless. That is, until one noted the tightly coiled tension in his square shoulders, the fisted hands at his sides, the tiny muscle that flexed in his jaw as he watched his sister navigate her way through the intricate dance of London's social scene. It was clear that he was prepared to do battle to ensure his sister's acceptance this evening.

As though sensing her attention, Ralston turned his head to

look at her. She inhaled sharply as their gazes collided, trapped by his glittering blue eyes, intent and unreadable. He tipped his head, almost imperceptibly. She understood the meaning implicitly. *Thank you.*

She mirrored the action.

Not trusting herself to disguise her emotions, she turned back to stare unseeingly at the crowd building in the theatre, impatient for the opera to begin and distract her from his presence in the box.

The performance should have begun a half an hour earlier, but, sadly, society rarely attended the Theatre Royal for the opera . . . most certainly not on the opening night of the season. No, one attended the opera to see and be seen, and the owners of the theatre knew well how to keep their patrons happy.

Callie returned her gaze to Juliana, watching with pride as she spoke gracefully to the dowager duchess and, in full view of the entirety of London society, made the older woman laugh. *Perfect.*

"You appear rather proud of yourself."

A flutter of excitement coursed through her at the rich, amused voice so close to her ear. Willing herself to be calm, she met Ralston's blue eyes, and said, "Indeed, I am, my lord. Your sister is doing exceedingly well, don't you think?"

"I do. The evening could not have been more perfectly arranged."

"It was Mariana's idea to use Rivington's box," Callie pointed out. "Our sisters seem to have become fast friends."

"Due, in large part, to your intervention, I imagine."

Callie dipped her head in silent acknowledgment.

"Very well done."

She quashed an odd desire to preen at the praise as the theatre's chimes rang, signaling the beginning of the performance. On cue, the visitors took their leave, and Ralston offered Callie his arm. "May I accompany you to your chair, Lady Calpurnia?"

Callie slid her hand along his arm, accepting his escort, attempting to ignore the sizzle of awareness that shot through her as they touched. It was the first time they had seen each other since the evening in the tavern. In the carriage. The first time they had touched since she had been in his embrace.

Once she was seated beside Benedick, Ralston claimed the seat next to her, his nearness overwhelming her senses. She was enveloped by his scent, a combination of sandalwood and lemon and something thoroughly male. She resisted the temptation to lean toward him and breathe deeply. That certainly wouldn't do.

She searched for a conversation that would distract her from his nearness. "Do you enjoy the opera, my lord?"

"Not particularly." His words were laced with indifference.

"I am surprised to hear that," she said, "I was under the impression that you enjoyed music. After all, you have a pianoforte—" She stopped short, darting a quick glance around the box to determine if anyone were listening to their conversation. She couldn't well discuss his pianoforte in mixed company.

He raised an eyebrow at her statement, saying dryly, "Indeed I do, Lady Calpurnia."

The man was taunting her. She would not rise to it. "Well, of course everyone has a pianoforte these days." She pressed on, refusing to look at him, instead babbling, "I have heard that the performance tonight is unparalleled. *The Barber of Seville* is a lovely opera. I am particularly fond of Rossini. And I have heard that the singer portraying Rosina is brilliantly talented. I cannot remember her name . . . Miss . . ." she trailed off, comforted that they were on safer conversational ground.

"Kritikos. Nastasia Kritikos," he provided.

The words washed over her. *Nastasia*. Understanding dawned.

I had not wanted to make this more difficult than it had to be, Nastasia.

Dear Lord. The opera singer was his *mistress*. She looked up at him, meeting his calm, unreadable gaze.

"Oh," she said almost inaudibly, unable to contain the syllable.

He remained silent.

What did you expect him to do? Announce to all within hearing that the mezzo-soprano was his mistress? The same mistress for whom he mistook you on the evening you arrived indelicately in his bedchamber?

No, it was for the best that he not pursue the conversation, she decided. Cheeks aflame, she leaned forward in her chair and looked over the edge of the box, wondering if she would survive an escape attempt over the side. *Likely not,* she thought with a sigh. She turned back, meeting his now-amused gaze. He was enjoying her embarrassment!

"Too far to jump, I should think," he said conspiratorially.

He was infuriating.

Luckily, she was saved from having to respond by the rising curtain. She turned her attention resolutely to the stage, willing herself to stop thinking of Ralston.

Of course, that was impossible, particularly when the opera began in earnest, and Nastasia Kritikos appeared. The Greek singer played Rosina, the beautiful woman upon whom the entire plot of mistaken identity and love at first sight hinged, and she was the perfect choice for the role, all unparalleled buxom beauty. Callie could not stop imagining the glamorous woman in Ralston's arms, could not shake the vision of his dark hands on her flawless skin, could not stanch the vicious envy that burned deep within as she cataloged the actress's remarkable attributes against her own.

As if the singer's incredible beauty were not enough, it appeared that she also had the most magnificent voice to grace the stage—likely ever.

There was no way a man could resist this paragon of womanhood.

The positioning of the Rivington box was such that audience members seated there could see into the wings of the theatre and, at several points, Callie was certain that Nastasia Kritikos was looking at Ralston, as though waiting for him to return her attention. *Was it possible they had resumed their acquaintance?* Callie closed her eyes against the thought, only to open them and steal a glance at Ralston. She had to give him credit for discretion; his concentration did not appear to waver from the stage.

When Nastasia's aria in the first act began, however, he—along with the rest of the audience—was rapt with attention. Callie could not help but see the irony in the words of the song: *Yes, Lindoro shall be mine! I've sworn it! I'll succeed! If I am thwarted I can be a viper! I can play a hundred tricks to get my way.*

"I can just imagine what a viper she can be," Callie muttered under her breath, as the aria stopped the show, sending the entire theatre to its feet, calling, *"Brava! Bravissima!"*

It was decided. Callie would never again enjoy the opera.

As the first act ended and the curtain fell, signaling the performance's intermission, Callie sighed, wishing she were anywhere else and wondering how difficult it would be to escape before the second act tortured her further.

Juliana's laughter sounded behind her, and Callie realized she could not leave. She had promised to bring Ralston's sister out successfully, and she would do just that.

Steeling herself, she stood, eager to interject herself into a conversation that did not involve Ralston, and nearly collided with Baron Oxford, who had appeared inside the box almost immediately upon the close of the first act.

Perfectly manicured, the handsome dandy offered one of his trademark smiles to the box at large before settling his gaze on

Callie. As he moved toward her, she took in his rich green topcoat, a lovely contrast to his shimmering satin waistcoat of aubergine. She immediately noticed that his heels and the tip of his walking stick once more matched his waistcoat, and she wondered if he had boots and canes in every color. The idea was so ridiculous; she couldn't help the curving of her lips.

"My lord," she said, hiding her face with a demure curtsy as he bowed low over her hand, "it is a pleasure to see you."

"The pleasure is entirely mine." The words, spoken slightly too close, sent a wave of color to Callie's cheeks as she took a deliberate half step backward. He continued. "I took the liberty of ordering champagne." He paused, indicating a footman nearby who held a tray of champagne coupes. "For you . . . and for the rest of your party."

Callie cocked her head slightly at his words. Surely she had misunderstood his emphasis. "Thank you, my lord." She watched as the footman passed the champagne through the box, uncertain of how to proceed. "Are you enjoying the performance?"

"Indeed. I am particularly impressed with Miss Kritikos's performance, she is—quite—something." Oxford said with a broad grin in the direction of the stage that Callie found not altogether pleasant. He reached for a glass of champagne and held it out to her. When she took it, he ran a finger over the back of her hand and leaned close, deepening his voice to a flirtatious whisper. "Of course, I am enjoying the intermission immensely as well."

This time, she was certain that he was inebriated. He had to be. Callie removed her hand from the inappropriate touch and considered giving the Baron a thorough set down. Certainly that would be the proper course of action, but she could not deny a certain amount of pleasure that, even as she suffered through an evening of Ralston's mistress endearing herself to the entire *ton,* she was receiving some attention of her own. She cast a sidelong glance toward Ralston, who was in conversation with his brother. He met her eyes and lifted his champagne in a silent salute. She snapped her head back around to Oxford and offered him a bright smile. "I, too, am enjoying intermission, my lord."

"Excellent." He took a deep drink from his glass, then said, his words slightly slurred, "Do you care for art?"

Slightly taken aback by his question, Callie said, "I— Well, yes, my lord."

Oxford traded his empty glass for a full one, and said, "I should like to escort you to the Royal Art Exhibition next week."

Resisting the urge to question the Baron's motives, Callie realized there was no easy way to escape this invitation. Instead, she said, "That would be lovely, my lord."

"What would be lovely?" The lazy drawl indicated the arrival of Ralston. Callie refused to rise to his bait.

Oxford, however, seemed more than eager to share their conversation with the marquess. "I shall be escorting Lady Calpurnia to the Royal Art Exhibition next week," he said, and Callie couldn't help noticing the boastfulness in his tone.

"Is that so?" Ralston said.

He didn't have to sound so disbelieving. "Indeed, it is, my lord. I am eager to see this year's exhibition." She placed a hand lightly on Oxford's sleeve. "I shall be lucky to have such an escort."

"Not as *lucky* as I shall be," Oxford said, his gaze not straying from Ralston.

Before Callie could wonder at the strange emphasis, the theatre chimes rang, signaling the end of intermission. Oxford took his leave, first bowing low over Callie's hand, and saying, "Good evening, my lady. I shall look forward to next week."

"And I, Baron Oxford," she replied with a little curtsy.

He then turned a broad grin on a stone-faced Ralston. "Good night, old chap."

Ralston did not reply, instead staring down the young dandy, who laughed off the cut direct and tipped his cane at the marquess before leaving the box. Callie watched him go before saying. "You didn't have to be so very rude to him."

"He's got nothing in his head but teeth," he said, matter-of-factly.

Ignoring the fact that she had said the exact words only days ago, Callie ignored his and resumed her seat. When Ralston took his place next to her, she ignored him, instead looking resolutely at the stage, willing the curtain to rise.

Out of the corner of her eye, she noticed the arrival of a footman with a silver tray, upon which was a folded message. Ralston took the proffered note with a nod of thanks for the messenger and turned the sealed parchment over in his hand, sliding a finger under the wax to open it.

Callie couldn't stop herself from peeking at the page as he looked at it. It was a short missive, only visible for a flash before he folded it closed. But Callie could not have missed the message—or its meaning.

Come to me.

N.

Ralston and Nastasia were still lovers.

Callie choked back a gasp, turning sharply away and pretending to be completely absorbed by the performance, which had just begun.

Her mind reeled. She shouldn't be surprised, of course. She should not be thinking of the other evening—of the betrothal ball, of their embrace in his carriage. She should not be wondering why, if he was involved with Nastasia, he had thought to kiss *her*.

But, of course, she did wonder.

And what of his sister? Surely he wouldn't accept the invitation. Not tonight, of all nights. It was Juliana's first night in society!

Sadness and outrage warred within her for the first two scenes of the second act. When, at the start of the third scene, he stood and abruptly left the box, outrage won.

No. She would not allow him to ruin his sister's first night out. Not after all that Juliana had done to ensure its success. Not after all that *Callie* had done to ensure its success. Not to mention the others, who had also cast their support for his sister.

How dare he risk it all? And for what?

Her anger rose. She squared her shoulders. Someone had to think of Juliana.

Turning to Benedick, she whispered, "The champagne appears to have gone to my head. I am going to rest in the ladies' salon."

Her brother leaned forward, taking note of Ralston's disappearance. Meeting her eyes, he said quietly, "No adventures, Callie."

She forced a smile. "No adventures."

And she left the box.

Hurrying along the dimly lit hallways of the theatre, her mind raced, wondering if she would find Ralston before he destroyed Juliana's chances at success. Callie would wager Allendale House itself that he'd escaped to meet his paramour in this very theatre more than once in the past—he likely knew the shortest path to Miss Kritikos's dressing room. She could not help the little exclamation of disgust that came with the thought.

She tore around a corner into the upper colonnade to find Ralston heading for the wide, grand staircase. A glance around revealed the space empty of people, and Callie could not resist calling out to him, "Ralston! Stop!"

He froze on the top stair, casting a disbelieving look at the arcade, where she was hurrying to catch him. Once he registered her purpose, his obvious disbelief turned to fury, and he retraced his steps until he was face-to-face with her.

Before she had a chance to speak, he grabbed her arm and pulled her into a darkened corridor. Voice filled with anger, he whispered, "Are you mad?"

Breathing heavily with both exertion and irritation, she yanked her arm from his grasp, and whispered back, "I could ask you the very same thing!"

He ignored her words, "What are you doing out here? If you were discovered—"

"Oh, please," she cut him off. "It is a public theatre. What do you think would happen if I were discovered? Someone would point me in the direction of the ladies' salon, and I would be on my way. But what if *you* were discovered?"

He looked at her as though she were crazed. "What are you talking about?"

"You aren't the most discreet, Lord Ralston," she spat his name. "For someone who is so very concerned about his sister's reputation, one would think you would have more care with it." She poked his shoulder with a single, gloved finger. "I *saw* the note! I *know* you are off to meet your . . . your . . ."

"My?" he prompted.

"Your—your mistress!" With each word, she poked him harder.

He grabbed her finger on the last word and flung it away from him. His blue eyes flashed dangerously. "You *dare* to chide me? You *dare* to question my behavior? Who do you think you are?"

"I'm the woman you chose to guide your sister into society. I will not have you ruin her chances for one night of . . ."

"*You* will not have *me*? Was it not you who was flirting shamelessly with a drunken dandy in full view of the entire *ton*?"

Her mouth fell open. "I most certainly did not!"

"Well that is how it appeared, *my lady.*"

"How dare you!" she said, furious, "How dare you speak to me about shameless flirting! *I* was not the one making eyes at an *actress* while she was in the midst of a performance!"

"That's enough," he said, his tone barely even.

"No. I don't think it is!" Callie pressed on, unable to control herself. The floodgates had opened. "*I* am not the one rushing off to tryst with my . . . painted paramour . . . while my sister faces the most difficult challenge of her life! Have you any idea what the *ton* will do to her if you are discovered, you insensitive . . . beast!" The last word was shrill.

His eyes shuttered as his face turned to stone. Fists clenched at his sides, he spoke, and his tone betrayed his barely leashed temper. "If you are quite through, Lady Calpurnia, I believe this conversation is over. I find I no longer require your assistance with my sister."

"I beg your pardon?" she was outraged.

"It's quite simple, really. I don't want her near you. You are too much of a risk."

Her eyes widened in shock. "*I*, a risk?" she replied, her voice was shaking with fury. "Oh, I shall see your sister, my lord. I won't see her chances ruined. And, furthermore"—she held a single finger up to his nose—"I will not be told what to do by a notorious— and now proven—rake and libertine."

He lost his temper then, capturing her hand, wagging finger and all, in his own and using it to pull her flush against him. "If I am to be labeled as such, I may as well stop resisting the part." And, with that, he kissed her.

She should have fought him, all strong arms and firm muscle and hard, unyielding mouth. Should have pounded on his shoulders as he grasped her waist with both hands and lifted her from the ground. But she didn't. Instead, she wrapped herself around him, clinging to him as he pressed her against the wall. She gasped in

surprise at the sudden movement. Surprise, and something else as
he plundered her mouth, both hands cupping her face, stealing her
breath. Setting her aflame.

She matched his movements with lips and tongue and teeth,
refusing to allow him the upper hand, even in this. Stroke for
stroke, where he went, she followed. He captured her sighs with
his mouth; she reveled in his low hum of pleasure. After several
intense moments of the sensual battle, his lips gentled, caressing hers as his tongue stroked along the soft, sensitive skin of her
lower lip, ending the kiss infinitely more gently than it had begun.

The caress wrung a little cry from Callie, and Ralston smiled
at the sound, pressing a final, soft kiss at the corner of her mouth.
He pulled back a fraction of an inch, and their gazes collided.
There was no sound in the hallway save their labored breathing—
reminding them both of the intensity of the argument that had
preceded the kiss.

He raised a single dark eyebrow in a silent, victorious gesture.

The arrogant expression renewed her fury.

Pulling herself up to her full height, she said, "I am not one of
your women, to be mauled in public. You would do well to remember that."

"Forgive me," he said, mockingly, "but you did not seem so
very opposed to playing the role."

She could not help herself. Her hand flew of its own volition,
in a direct line for his cheek. Even as she moved to slap him, she
dreaded the blow, unable to stop the motion. When he caught her
hand in a viselike grip, mere inches from his face, she gasped in
surprise, meeting his eyes and immediately recognizing the anger
in them.

She had overstepped her bounds. Dear Lord. She'd tried to
strike him. What had possessed her? She struggled to free her
hand, only to discover his hold was thoroughly unyielding.

"I—I'm sorry."

He narrowed his gaze but remained silent.

"I shouldn't have . . ."

"But you did."

She paused. "But, I didn't mean to."

He shook his head, dropping her hand and taking a moment to straighten his coat. "One cannot have one's cake and eat it, too, Lady Calpurnia. If you plan to make a habit of acting without care of the consequences, I would recommend taking ownership of those actions. You meant to strike me. At least have the courage to admit it." He paused, waiting for her to respond. When she didn't, he shook his head. "Amazing. I hadn't thought you a coward."

His words sent an angry wash of color across her cheeks. "Stay away from me," she said, voice shaking with emotion, before she spun away from him, fleeing in the direction of the lit foyer and Rivington's box.

Ralston watched her go, his expression betraying none of his thoughts.

Eleven

knew you would come."

The words, spoken with soft sensuality, reeked of a feminine arrogance that immediately set Ralston on edge. He remained casually draped over a chintz-upholstered armchair in Nastasia Kritikos's dressing room, refusing to allow her to see his irritation. He had spent enough time around the woman to know that she would take particular satisfaction in her ability to provoke him.

Ralston cast a heavy-lidded gaze over her as she moved to her dressing table and began to take down her hair in a ritual he had watched dozens of times before. He took her in: her breasts, heaving from the exertion of singing for nearly three hours straight; the heightened color on her cheeks marking her exhilaration at her performance; her bright eyes signaling her anticipation for the next part of the evening, which she clearly believed would be spent in his arms. He had seen this exact combination of heightened emotion in the beautiful singer before—it had never failed to raise his own excitement to a fever pitch.

Tonight, however, he was unmoved.

He had debated leaving her note unanswered, considered remaining in the box until the end of the performance and exiting with his family, as planned. Ultimately, however, the note had served to underscore the fact that the opera singer was unable to be discreet. He was going to have to articulate their new relationship more explicitly.

He supposed he should have known that she would not be cast aside so easily, should have seen that her pride would not allow it. That much was clear now.

"I came to tell you that tonight's note will be the last."

"I do not think so," she purred, as the last of her ebony tresses fell around her shoulders in a cloud of silk. "You see, it worked."

"It won't work next time." His cold blue gaze emphasized the truth of his words.

Nastasia considered his reflection in the mirror as a silent maid moved to remove the elaborate costume the singer had been wearing. "If you did not come for me tonight, Ralston, why are you here? You loathe the opera, my darling. And yet, your eyes did not leave the stage tonight."

For all she declared herself an artist, Nastasia was always acutely aware of her audience. He'd often admired her ability to recall the precise location of certain members of the *ton* in the theatre—she had a gossiper's eye for who was watching whom through their opera glasses, for who exited the theatre midperformance with whom, and for what excitement and drama was occurring in which box, and when. He was not surprised she had noticed him and sent the note.

The Greek beauty pulled on a scarlet dressing gown and dismissed the servant curtly. Once they were alone, she turned to Ralston, her dark eyes flashing beneath kohl-thickened lashes, her lips curved in a crimson pout.

Your painted paramour. . .

Callie's words came unbidden to Ralston as he watched Nastasia stalk toward him, so sure of the power of her feminine wiles, so calculated in her approach. His eyes narrowed as she shifted her shoulders and arched her neck to show off the ridge of her collarbone, a spot that was so often his weakness. He felt nothing.

When she stopped in front of him, bending over to reveal her ample bosom in a move calculated to send him over the edge, he met her cool, confident gaze and spoke, his words dry as sand.

"While I appreciate the effort, Nastasia, I am no longer interested."

A patronizing smile crossed the opera singer's face. She reached out to stroke his jaw with expert fingers; he resisted the urge to flinch. "I am happy to play this game of cat and mouse, my darling, but you must admit you haven't given me much of a challenge. After all, *you* are in *my* dressing room."

"Find someone else, Nastasia."

"I do not want someone else," Her voice became a sultry whisper. "I want you."

He met her brazen gaze, unimpressed. "Then it seems we find ourselves at an impasse. I am afraid I don't want you."

The heat in her gaze cooled, so quickly that he realized she had been prepared for his rebuff. She slid past him, all grace, to her dressing table. When she spoke, it was with casual interest. "It is because of her, isn't it? The girl in the Rivington box."

Suspicion flared. "That girl is my sister, Nastasia, and I won't have you ruin her coming out."

"You think I would not know your sister, Ralston? I recognized her immediately, all dark hair and gorgeous eyes; a beauty—just as you are. No, I am talking about the wallflower. The woman seated next to you. The one with the plain hair and the plain eyes and the plain face. She must be very rich, Ralston, because you cannot possibly want her for anything else," she ended with a smug smile.

He refused to rise to her bait, instead drawling, "Jealous, Nastasia?"

"Of course not," she said, simply. "She is no match for me."

A vision of Callie came unbidden, all heated words and angry looks and heightened emotion. Callie, who couldn't coolly calculate if she were given a decade of lessons. Callie, who had chased him down in a public theatre, for God's sake, without a care in the world for how it might be perceived, simply to serve him a scathing set down. Callie, who was so very alive and changing and unpredictable—and so very much the opposite of the cold and untouchable Nastasia.

One side of his mouth lifted in a wry smile. "There you are right. There is no comparison between you."

Her eyes widened. "Fascinating," she said on a half laugh. "I would not have guessed you would turn to a mouse."

"That mouse is a lady, Nastasia," he hedged, "sister to an earl. You will refer to her with respect."

Her lips twisted in a knowing smile that faded into a perfect pout. "You would leave me with a broken heart?"

He raised an eyebrow. "I feel confident that your heart shall not remain broken for long."

She held his unreadable gaze for a long moment—her long history as mistress to aristocratic men telling her that Ralston was lost to her. She could war with him, but she knew that society's opinion would always err on the side of a wealthy marquess when a foreign actress was involved.

She smiled. "My heart is ever resilient, Ralston."

He tipped his head, acknowledging her surrender.

"You know, of course, that a girl like that knows nothing of the world in which you and I live."

He could not resist. "What does that mean?"

"Only that she will want love, Ralston. Girls like her always do."

"I have little interest in whatever fairy tales the girl believes in, Nastasia. She is nothing to me but a chaperone to my sister."

"Perhaps," Nastasia said thoughtfully. "But what are you to her?" When he did not respond, one side of her mouth curved in a wry smile. "You forget that the best seat in the theatre is mine."

Ralston stood from his chair, making a production of straightening his cravat and smoothing his sleeves before gathering his hat, gloves, and greatcoat from the chaise where he had tossed them upon entering the room. He withdrew Nastasia's note and set it on the dressing table before turning back to the singer. Bowing low, he took his leave.

And he did it all without saying a word.

Twelve

"*H*ow dare he call me a coward!"

Callie paced the floor of her bedchamber, livid at the events of the evening. She had arrived home an hour before but hadn't stopped moving long enough to allow Anne to help her undress.

Instead, the maid had taken up residence on the end of Callie's bed, watching her mistress walk up and down the room as though she were watching a tennis match. "I'm not sure," Anne said dryly, "particularly considering the fact that you attempted to strike him in a public theatre."

Callie missed Anne's amusement, instead grasping the maid's words, throwing her hands into the air in frustration, and saying, "Exactly! There's nothing cowardly about that!"

"Nothing ladylike about it either."

"Yes, well, that's beside the point," Callie said. "What *is* the point is that Gabriel St. John, Marquess of Ralston, accosted me in a public theatre on the way to meet his mistress, and somehow contrived to place *me* in the wrong!" She stamped her foot. "How *dare* he call me a coward!"

Anne couldn't keep the smile from her face. "To be fair, it does sound like you provoked him."

Callie stopped pacing, turning to the maid incredulously. "For someone who, mere days ago, was concerned about my reputation being ruined for sneaking out to a tavern, you seem awfully quick to take Ralston's side in this! You are supposed to defend me!"

"And I shall do so until the end of time, Callie. But you've set out to find yourself some adventure, and you have to admit that Ralston seems to have given you exactly the kind you were looking for."

"I most certainly was not looking for him to haul off and kiss me in public!"

One of Anne's eyebrows raised in a disbelieving gesture. "I suppose you didn't enjoy it?"

"No!"

"Not at all?"

"Not a bit."

"Mmm-hmm." The maid's response was rife with disbelief.

"I didn't!"

"So you've said." Anne stood, turning Callie toward the dressing table and setting to work unhooking the long row of buttons on the back of Callie's dress.

They stood in silence for several long minutes before Callie spoke again. "All right, I may have liked it a little."

"Ah, just a little."

Callie sighed, turning in spite of Anne's still working on the fastenings of her dress. The maid resumed her place on the bed as Callie began pacing again.

"Fine. More than a little. I enjoyed it immensely, just as I have all the other times he's kissed me." She caught the maid's surprised look before saying, "Yes, there have been other times. And why wouldn't I enjoy it? The man is clearly an expert kisser."

Anne cleared her throat. "Clearly."

Callie snapped her head around to look at her maid. "He is! Anne, you've never been kissed like that."

"I shall have to take your word for it."

Callie nodded seriously. "You shall. Ralston's everything you'd imagine he would be . . . one moment he's all tempting words and wicked glances, then his arms are around you, and you can't quite understand how it all happened . . ."

She trailed off dreamily, looking up at the ceiling and clasping her gown to herself. Anne stood, thinking to take the opportunity to finish helping Callie undress, but before she could step away from the bed, Callie's look had gone from dreamy to irritated, and she was at it again. "And then the rounder pulls away and looks at you with all the smug satisfaction of a complete and utter cad! And when you try to defend yourself—"

"By striking him?"

"And when you try to defend yourself," Callie repeated, "do you know what he does?"

"He calls you a coward?" Anne asked wryly.

"He calls you a coward! He's utterly infuriating!"

"It seems so," Anne said, making her way to work on Callie's buttons once more.

This time, Callie allowed her access, standing still as the gown came loose in her hands and she stepped out of it. Anne then set to work on the laces of her corset, and Callie sighed as the tight garment came undone. A modicum of Callie's anger was released with the stiff confines of the stays.

Standing in her chemise, she wrapped her arms around her middle and took a deep breath. Anne guided her to sit at the dressing table and began to comb Callie's long brown hair. The feeling was rather glorious, and Callie sighed, eyes closed.

"Of course, I enjoyed the kiss," she muttered after a while.

"So it seems," Anne said, matter-of-factly.

"I wish I wasn't such a fool around Ralston."

"You've always been a fool about Ralston."

"Yes, but now I am near him far more. It's different."

"Why?"

"Before I merely daydreamed about Ralston. Now I find myself actually with him. Actually talking to him. Actually discovering the *real* Ralston. He is no longer a creature I invented. He is flesh and blood and . . . now I can't help wondering . . ." She trailed off, unwilling to say what she was thinking. *What if he were mine?*

She did not have to say the words aloud; Anne heard them anyway. When Callie opened her eyes and met Anne's gaze in the looking glass, she saw Anne's response there. *Ralston is not for you, Callie.*

"I know, Anne," Callie said quietly, as much to remind herself as to reassure her friend.

Of course, she didn't know. Not anymore. Mere weeks ago, Callie would have laughed at the idea that Gabriel St. John even knew her name . . . let alone was willing to engage in conversation with her. And now . . . Now he was kissing her in darkened carriages and darkened hallways . . . and reminding her why she had been such a fool for him since the beginning.

He had been on his way to see his opera singer that evening— Callie was sure of it—and there was no question that she was no match for the Greek beauty. He could not be attracted to her.

She faced herself in the looking glass, cataloging her flaws: her brown hair, so very common and uninteresting; her too-large brown eyes; her round face, so unlike the heart-shaped faces of the beauties of the *ton*; her too-wide mouth, not at all the perfect bow that it should have been. With each feature, she considered the women to whom Ralston had been linked before, all Helens of Troy, with faces that stopped men in their tracks.

He had left her and gone to his mistress, who had most definitely welcomed him with open arms. What woman in her right mind wouldn't?

And Callie had returned home to her cold, empty bed . . . and dreamed of the impossible.

Tears sprang to her eyes, and Callie tried to dash them away before Anne could see, but soon they were coming fast, on top of each other, and she couldn't hide her sadness. She sniffled, drawing attention from the maid, who, with one look, stopped combing and crouched low next to her lady.

Callie allowed the older woman to put her arms around her, and she placed her head upon Anne's shoulder and allowed the tears to come. She sobbed into the rough wool of the maid's gown, exposing the sadness that had consumed her for years. Through a decade of seasons, the weddings of all of her friends, Mariana's betrothal—a decade of being moved higher and higher upon the shelf—she had hidden her sorrow, refusing to allow her regret to shadow the happiness of others.

But now, with Ralston wreaking havoc on her senses and reminding her of everything she had always wanted and would never have, it was too much. She could no longer hold it in.

She cried for long minutes, Anne murmuring soothing sounds as she stroked Callie's back. When she was done, unable to find the energy to continue with tears, Callie sat up straight, pulling back from Anne and offering a watery smile of self-conscious thanks. "I don't know what's come over me."

"Oh, Callie-mine," Anne said, her voice taking on the tone she'd used when Callie was a little girl and crying over some injustice, "your white knight, he will come."

One side of Callie's mouth kicked up in a wry smile. Anne had said the words countless times over the last two decades. "Forgive me, Anne, but I'm not so certain that he will."

"Oh, he will," Anne said firmly. "And when you least expect."

"I find I'm rather tired of waiting." Callie laughed halfheartedly. "Which is probably why I've turned my attentions to such a dark knight."

Anne cupped Callie's cheek in her hand with a smile. "I think I'd rather see you ticking off items on your ridiculous list than keeping company with Ralston. I should steer clear of him if I were you."

"Easier said than done," Callie said. There was something so very compelling about the man—it didn't seem to matter that he infuriated her. To the contrary, his arrogance only served to make him more attractive. She sighed. "Perhaps you're right. Perhaps I should steer clear of Ralston and focus on my list again." She lifted the list from the dressing table, where she'd set it earlier that evening. "Of course, it appears I'm rather out of simple tasks."

Anne gave a little grunt of disbelief before saying dryly, "Of course, because drinking at a tavern makes for a perfectly simple outing. What's left?"

"Fencing, attending a duel, firing a pistol, gambling at a gentlemen's club, and riding astride," she said, leaving off the rest of the items—the items that she was embarrassed to share with even her closest confidant.

"Hmm. That *is* a challenge."

"Indeed," Callie said distractedly, biting her bottom lip and considering the paper.

"One thing is for sure, however," Anne said.

"What's that?"

"No matter which of those things you tackle next, no one will call you a coward for doing them."

Callie met Anne's eyes at the words, and, after a beat of surprised silence, the two women laughed.

* * *

"OOF!" CALLIE GRASPED the bedpost firmly as Anne tugged on the length of linen that she was wrapping around Callie's torso. "I think you could be slightly more gentle, Anne."

"Likely so," the maid said, passing the fabric under Callie's arms and arranging it flat against her breasts, "but I am not feeling very gentle at the moment."

Callie looked down at her fast-reducing bosom and smiled through the discomfort. "Yes, well, I appreciate your putting those feelings aside to assist me."

Anne responded with a grunt of displeasure and a harsh yank on the linen. She shook her head as she worked. "Binding your breasts and dressing like a man . . . I think you've gone mad."

"Nonsense. I'm simply trying something new."

"Something that would give your mother the vapors if she knew."

Callie turned her head sharply toward the maid. "Which she won't."

"You cannot be thinking *I* would tell her," Anne said, outraged, "I'd lose my position before the words were out!"

"Not if she had a fit of the vapors beforehand," Callie teased.

It was late in the afternoon, and Callie and Anne had sequestered themselves in Callie's bedchamber to prepare her to tackle the next item on her list—fencing.

Callie had worked out an elaborate plan to gain entrance to Benedick's fencing club, disguised as a young dandy, just out of university, and looking for a new sporting ground. She had practiced deepening her voice and developed a background story for her character—Sir Marcus Breton, a baronet from the Lake District. She'd had Anne pilfer some old clothes from Benedick's wardrobe, including a fencing suit that would not be missed, and the two women had spent a week altering the clothes to fit Callie.

She was already wearing a newly tailored pair of men's breeches, which, she had to admit, were surprisingly comfortable despite her feeling thoroughly indecent wearing them. Underneath, she wore thick stockings and a pair of boots that they had bribed from a stable boy.

As her stomach tumbled with nerves and Anne swaddled her in linen, Callie refused to consider the absolute humiliation that would come of her being discovered dressed as a man in one of London's most male of establishments. She had come too far to quit now.

Taking a deep breath as Anne tucked the tail of the fabric under her arm, Callie lifted her list from the bed and inserted it between the linen bindings and her skin, unwilling to leave the house on this particular mission without the talisman. She then took up a billowing linen shirt and slipped it over her head, tucking it into the waistband of her breeches. Turning to Anne, she asked, "Well? Can you tell I'm a lady?"

Anne raised a solitary brow at the question, at which point Callie added, "Fine. Can you tell I am *female*?"

"Yes."

"Anne!" Callie rushed to the mirror. "Really?"

"Let's finish the transformation, then see where we are," the maid said, matter-of-factly.

"Fair enough." Callie allowed Anne access to her neck as the maid worked to tie a cravat in some approximation of one of the elaborate knots that were the current style. Then, she put on a beige waistcoat and slipped into a dark green topcoat before sitting at the dressing table and allowing Anne to hide her hair. "It's a pity that I shan't have you on the way home, Anne. How will I remember it all?"

"Oh, you'll remember. You'll have to."

Callie swallowed, watching as the maid placed a hat upon her head, working diligently to tuck any stray tendrils inside the cap. "You cannot take this off until you put your fencing mask on."

"Believe me, I shan't." Callie shook her head tentatively, testing the stability of the hat. "Will it stay?"

Anne opened her mouth to respond as a knock sounded and the door to the room opened.

"Callie? Mother said you were feeling ill? Is there something—" Mariana's question ended on a scream as she registered the man sitting in her sister's bedchamber.

The sound spurred Callie and Anne into motion, both spinning away from the dressing table and toward Mariana. Anne closed the door to the room firmly, pressing her back against the wood and spreading her arms out to block Mari's exit. Callie headed for her sister, who was frantically shaking her head at the image that Callie made, dressed head to toe in men's clothing.

"Shh! Mariana! You'll bring the house running!"

Mari cocked her head at her sister's words, and Callie waited as understanding dawned. "What are you doing dressed like that?" the younger girl whispered.

"It's rather complicated," Callie hedged.

"My Lord!" Mari went on, eyes wide. "It's incredible! I actually thought you a man when I entered!"

"I noticed! I suppose I have that to be thankful for, at least!" Callie turned her attention to Anne. "Is anyone out there?"

Anne shook her head. "I think it is too late in the day for there to be many people above stairs."

Mari could not contain her curiosity, "Callie, why are you dressed as a man?"

"I— I—" Callie looked to Anne for help. The maid crossed her arms defiantly and raised both eyebrows, leaving Callie with no aid. "Mari—I'll tell you—but you *must* keep my secret."

"Of course!" Mari's eyes lit up with excitement. "I love secrets!" She hopped up on the bed and waved a hand at Callie. "Turn around so I can see the whole disguise!" Callie did as she was told.

"Amazing! What did you do to your . . ." Mari waved her hand in the general direction of Callie's chest.

Callie sighed. "We bound them."

Mari turned to Anne. "Excellent work!" The maid nodded in acknowledgment of the praise. Mari turned a bright smile on Callie. "Now, go on."

Taking a deep breath, Callie began, "Several weeks ago, I made a list of the things I would do if I had the courage to risk my reputation." Mariana's jaw dropped, and Callie discovered that was the hardest part of the tale—once it was out, the rest seemed rather easy to tell. Skipping the visit to Ralston's home, she told her sister about her visit to the Dog and Dove.

"What was it like?"

"The tavern?" At Mari's eager nod, Callie said, "Fascinating."

"And the scotch?"

"Horrid. But not as horrid as the cheroot."

"The *cheroot*?" Mari's mouth gaped again.

Callie blushed. "After the tavern, I came home and Benedick and I smoked a cheroot."

"*Benedick* let you smoke a cheroot?" Mari's response was incredulous.

"Shh! Yes, but you cannot tell him you know."

"Oh, I won't." Mari paused, an impish grin crossing her face. "At least, not yet, not until I need something from him."

"So," Callie pushed on, "I decided that this afternoon is the time for the next item on the list."

"Which is?"

"Fencing."

Mariana blinked, absorbing Callie's words. "Fencing!" She looked Callie up and down. "You can't wear that fencing."

"I have a fencing suit tailored to fit me. I shall change into it at the club. Once I'm safely inside."

"You've thought of everything!" Mari said with pride.

"I hope so," Callie said nervously. "Do you really think I can pass as a man?"

Mari clapped her hands twice in excitement, "Oh, yes! I'm your sister, and *I* was fooled!" She leaned forward. "Callie, let me come with you!"

Anne and Callie shared a nervous look. "What? No!" Callie looked at her sister in horror.

"I could steal some clothes from one of the footmen. We could go together!"

"Absolutely not! Think of your reputation!"

"That doesn't seem to be stopping you!"

"Mari," Callie said slowly, as though speaking to a child, "I'm on the shelf. You're to marry a *duke* in a month. I don't think the *ton* would take well to a ruined duchess."

Mari tilted her head, considering Callie's words for a moment before heaving a giant sigh. "Fine. But at least let me help you get to a carriage."

Callie smiled. "That, sister, you can do."

"Excellent." Mari met Anne's eyes. "You realize that if you aren't back before dinner, we shall have to send Benedick to find you."

Callie went pale at the thought. "You wouldn't!"

"Indeed, we would," Mari said, turning to the maid for confirmation. "Wouldn't we, Anne?"

Anne nodded vehemently. "Of course! We couldn't very well ignore your not returning. What if something were to happen to you?"

"What could happen to me at a fencing club?"

"You could be run through," Mariana speculated.

Callie gave her sister an exasperated look. "I shall be fencing in a practice room. With a bag of sand." Was it her? Or did Mariana look disappointed? "I shall be home by dinner."

"If you aren't back . . ." Mari started.

"I shall be." Callie straightened her coat. "Now, if you'll help me get out of this house, I have fencing to do."

Mari clapped her hands again, eager for Callie's adventure to begin. She leapt from her spot on the bed and clasped Callie to her. "I'm so proud of you, sister. I cannot wait for you to return with tales of the foil!" She stepped back and assumed the *en garde* position, then giggled. "Oh, Callie! To be you!" she said dreamily.

Callie shook her head at her sister's response before accepting gloves and a cane from Anne. *Yes, to be me. An aging spinster with a newfound penchant for the ruin of her reputation*

It did appear that Mariana no longer considered her passive, however.

That was something.

Thirteen

Callie took a deep breath, bolstering her courage as the carriage slowed to a stop in front of Benedick's sporting club.

After waiting several long moments for the driver to open the door to the vehicle and help her out, then realizing that he would do no such thing for a man, she scrambled out of the hack, landing unceremoniously on the gravel roadway. Keeping her head down for fear of being discovered, Callie peeked at the gentlemen around her on the street. She recognized the Earl of Sunderland heading straight for her, and she snapped her head away, eyes closed, certain he would discover her. When he passed by, paying her no mind, she let out the long breath she hadn't realized she'd been holding.

She approached the door to the club, remembering to brandish the cane as though it were an extension of her arm rather than a cumbersome thing to carry. The door opened, revealing a footman standing to the side of the entryway, the portrait of disinterest. *The disguise was working!*

Entering the foyer, she gave a quick prayer of thanks that it was empty, save the club steward, who approached her immediately. "Sir? May I assist you in some way?"

Now came the hardest part.

She cleared her throat, willing the deep voice she had practiced to come. "You may." *No going back now.* "I am Sir Marcus Breton, of Borrowdale. Lately of Cambridge. I'm new to town and in search of a sporting club."

"Indeed, sir." The steward seemed to expect her to continue.

"I so enjoy the foil." She blurted out, uncertain of what else she should say.

"We boast the finest fencing facility in town, sir."

"I've heard as such from friends." The steward's gaze turned politely curious, and Callie realized she had to press on, "Like Allendale."

Invoking Benedick's name opened the gates. The steward dipped his head graciously, then said, "We, of course, welcome any friend of the earl. Would you care to visit a practice room and test out the facilities?"

Thank God. Callie pounced on the offer. "I should like that very much."

The steward gave a little bow and, with the wave of a hand, guided her through a mahogany door to one side of the foyer. On the other side of the door was a long, narrow hallway with chambers on either side, each numbered. "These are the practice rooms," the steward intoned, before turning a corner and pointing to a large door, "That is the club's social room. Once you have donned your fencing attire, you may wait there for another member with whom to practice."

Callie's eyes widened at the thought of entering a room filled with men, any number of whom might recognize her. Quashing her alarm she attempted a calm reply, "And if I do not wish a partner? Have you any rooms that include a sandbag for practice?"

The steward cast a questioning look in her direction before saying, "Indeed, sir. You may use room number sixteen. Once you have completed your solo practice, should you decide you would like to parry with a partner, simply use the bellpull by the door, and we will be happy to find another athlete to join you."

He paused outside another row of doors, opening one to reveal a small, private room. "I shall leave you here to outfit yourself in your fencing suit." He indicated the small bag she held in her hand. "I see you did not bring your own foil; there are practice foils in each of the rooms."

She knew she'd forgotten something. "Thank you."

He dipped his head. "Enjoy your practice."

She stood aside, waiting for him to pass before entering the dressing room and closing the door firmly. She released a long sigh. The walk to the dressing room had felt like a fencing match in itself.

Shoring up her confidence, Callie began to dress, opening the canvas bag that Anne had packed and removing the pieces of the fencing uniform. Once the suit was laid out, she went through the challenging process of changing from one set of clothes completely foreign to her into another outfit, equally bizarre.

Once stockings and special fencing breeches were on, she wiggled her way into her plastron, designed to provide added protection on her sword-arm side. Callie struggled to tie the bows of the one-armed shirt herself, but found that between the discomfort of the bindings on her breasts and her own lack of experience, she could not fasten the garment.

She stopped, leaning against the wall of the dressing room breathing heavily for a moment before realization dawned. She was only fencing in a practice room; she wouldn't be facing an opponent. Why wear the unwieldy garment?

She cast the plastron aside, instead reaching for the tight canvas jacket that would cover all of her upper body. Callie looked askance at the jacket and the peculiar croissard that connected its front and back pieces—snugly between the legs. Taking a deep breath and ignoring the wave of embarrassment she felt at the idea of wearing such a revealing piece of clothing, she stepped through the strap and pulled the jacket on, buttoning it carefully up to the high collar.

She pulled on her mask next. Pulling the mesh hood over her head, she took care to ensure that every bit of her hair was tucked inside the bib of the helmet. She smiled within her dark, wired cocoon. She hadn't put fencing on the list because it was a sport that lent itself to disguise, but she was thrilled that she could walk among the male members of the club completely covered, unafraid of discovery.

Gloves were the final touch, covering the last, small areas of skin—one long, complete with gauntlet to prevent blades from entering her sleeve, the other smaller, but still ensuring that her pale, delicate hands were invisible.

"Excellent," she whispered, the words echoing around her in the chamber of the fencing hood. With a deep breath and pounding heart, she exited the room and made her way back down the empty hallway to practice room number sixteen.

She pushed open the door to the room and had hurriedly entered before she realized that the sandbag at the side of the room was in use. Swaying back and forth, the bag blocked the fencer who had obviously just delivered a blow of considerable force to the hanging sack.

Catching her breath, Callie spun around to exit the room as quickly as possible, so as not to be discovered by the room's occupant.

"I was wondering when they would find me a partner," he said dryly.

She stilled at the words.

The fencer continued, "I see you are already masked and ready. Perfect."

Callie turned slowly toward the sound, eyes squeezed tightly shut, willing her instincts to be wrong. Willing him not to be who she thought he would be. Forcing them to open, she cursed her luck.

Standing before her, wearing an identical uniform to hers, handsome as ever, was Ralston. Callie tried to revive the anger she had felt at their last meeting but found herself distracted by the white suit he wore—snug and revealing, showing off his remarkable body. He looked like an ancient Olympian, all lean, corded muscle and perfect physique. She felt heat consume her as she traced the straight lines of his legs and back to the curve of his rear.

She swallowed, pressing a gloved hand to her chest. What was she thinking? She'd never in her life marveled at a man's rump!

She had to get out of this room.

She watched, paralyzed, as he moved to the edge of the room to don his own mask and adjust the gauntlet of his sword-arm glove. Facing her, he waved in the direction of the mat that marked the boundaries of a standard fencing match. "Shall we?"

She stared blankly at the mat, her mind crying, *Flee!*

Unfortunately, her feet refused to comply.

"Sir," Ralston said, as though speaking to a child, "is there some problem?"

At his words, she shifted her gaze to him, unable to see his face or eyes through his wire mask. That truth reminded her that the same was true of him—he would not be able to identify her. *Here's your chance! To really fence!*

She shook her head to clear the insane thought from her head. Ralston took the movement to have a different meaning. "Capital. Let's get started, then."

He marched to the far corner of the mat to wait for her as she moved to the rack of foils in the corner of the room and tested the weight of several of them, making a show of selecting one. She took the time to bolster her own nerves. *He can't see me. I'm just another man to him right now.*

Of course, he was most definitely *not* another man to her . . . but she took courage in her invisibility, her mind racing to recall every bit of meager experience she'd had with fencing—watching Benedick show off as a youth, mostly.

This had been a terrible mistake.

She approached the practice area, facing Ralston as he assumed the classic fencing position, left arm up, right arm extended, the foil held perfectly steady, unmoving in his firm grip. His legs were bent, the muscles tense with coiled strength, left leg beautifully extended behind him, right leg bent in a perfect right angle. He nodded to her, and said, *"En garde."*

Taking a deep breath, Callie mirrored his position, blood rushing in her ears. Drunken men dueled with swords. How hard could this really be?

One of those men is killed much of the time.

She pushed the thought aside, waiting for him to make the first move.

He did, lunging toward her, thrusting his foil toward her torso. Swallowing back a cry of alarm, Callie allowed her terror to take over, hacking at the air with her foil to block his blow. The sound of steel on steel rang loudly between them.

Ralston immediately retreated in the face of her obvious lack of skill. When he spoke, his words were dry with humor behind the dark, mesh mask.

"I see you are no swordsman."

Callie cleared her throat, deepening her voice and speaking softly. "I am a beginner, my lord."

"An understatement, I daresay."

At the words, Callie assumed the initial position of swordplay once more. Ralston followed suit, saying, "When your opponent thrusts, try not to attack with all your force. Do not show how far you are able to go. Instead, lead up to a full-on battle."

Callie nodded as Ralston came at her, more gently this time. He allowed her to parry several times before crowding her off the mat. Once both of her feet were on the wooden floor of the practice room, he released her from his charge, turning back to take his place once more on the mat and wait for her to join him. They repeated the exercise several times, Ralston coaching her on the basics of combat, each time bolstering her confidence enough for her to ward off his thrusts more firmly and with more conviction.

"Much better," he said encouragingly, after the fourth go, and Callie felt a wave of warmth at his praise. "This time, you come at me."

Attack Ralston? Callie shook her head at the idea. "Oh—I—" she hedged.

He laughed. "I assure you, young sir, I can take it."

This entire exercise was more than she had bargained for. But she could not very well back out now, could she? She let out a long breath before taking up the now-familiar stance and lunging at him with a strong, "Ha!"

He deftly deflected her blade with a light force that threw her off, sending her to her knees. He gave an amused snort at her lack of grace, sending a wave of irritation through her. Once she was on the ground, he reached down to offer to help her back up. With one look at his gloved hand, she shook her head, refusing his aid, eager to attack him once more.

She tried again, this time getting several strong thrusts in before he went on the attack, and she found herself backed off the mat once more. Frustrated with his deft maneuvering—did the man have to do *everything* so well?—she lunged at him, whacking his blade to the side with her foil, sending it sliding off course. The movement ended in the sharp edge of his weapon sliding along the arm of her fencing jacket, slicing open the stiff cotton and grazing her upper arm.

She dropped her foil, grasping her arm, the sting of the wound sending her reeling backward, a bit off balance, only to land firmly, and painfully, on her backside. "Ow!" she exclaimed loudly, forgetting her disguise and turning her attention to the tear in her uniform, focused on her injury.

"What the devil?"

Callie registered the confusion in Ralston's voice and looked up, alarmed, to find him heading for her, one hand pulling off his mask and throwing it to the edge of the room, the hard clash of metal on wood ringing ominously. She scooted backward on the mat, the use of only one hand making her rather clumsy, as he removed his gloves and tracked her from above, eyes narrowed.

In a desperate attempt to deflect him, she deepened her voice, and said, "It's just a scratch, my lord. I—I shall be fine."

Ralston's brows snapped together at the words and he swore roundly. She could hear the recognition in his voice, could see it in the thunderous look he gave her. He was upon her now, towering over her. Leaning down, one strong hand reached for the cowl of her mask. Terrified of discovery, she attempted to stay his action. The movement was futile. With one fluid motion, he lifted the mask from her face, sending her hair tumbling around her shoulders.

His eyes widened in recognition and he dropped the mask to the floor. His blue eyes flashed darkly, almost navy with anger.

"I—" she began, uncertain.

"Do not speak." The words were clipped, demanding obedience as he knelt next to her and took her arm in his hands. He inspected her wound gently, breathing harshly. She could feel his hands, carefully testing the skin of her arm, trembling with barely contained fury. He tore at the arm of her jacket, the sound of rending fabric causing her to flinch. He then reached into his pocket and withdrew a perfectly folded linen handkerchief, which he used to clean, then bind, the wound. She watched as he worked, transfixed by his deft movements. She sucked in a breath of air when he tied the bandage off tightly, and he met her eyes, raising one eyebrow at her, daring her to complain at his ministrations.

The air between them thickened. She couldn't suffer it. "I—"

"Why aren't you wearing a plastron?" The question was deadly quiet.

Of all the things she had imagined he would say, this was not one of them. She looked to his face, so close to her own, and said, "My—my lord?"

"A plastron. The piece of the fencing uniform designed to protect one's sword arm. From precisely this type of wound." He spoke as though he were reading from a fencing rulebook.

"I know what a plastron is," she grumbled.

"Oh? Then why aren't you wearing one?" The question was edged with an emotion she could not place, but did not like.

"I . . . I did not think I needed one."

"Of all the damn fool things!" He exploded. "You could have been killed!"

"It's just a flesh wound!" she cried.

"What the hell would you know about flesh wounds? What if I had thrust at full force?"

"*You* were not supposed to be here!" The words escaped before she could stay them. Their gazes locked, blue against brown, and Ralston shook his head at her, as though he could not quite believe what he was seeing.

"*I? I* was not supposed to be here?" His voice shook. "The last I checked, this is my sporting club! A men's sporting club! Where men fence! The last I checked, you were a woman! And women did not fence!"

"Those are all fair points," she hedged.

"What the hell are you doing here? Where the hell are your wits?"

Callie sniffed primly, as though she weren't flat on her bottom dressed in men's clothing in the midst of a situation that, if she guessed correctly, would be her ruin. "I would prefer you not use such language with me."

"*You* would prefer? Well, *I* would prefer you stayed the hell out of my fencing club! And, while we're at it, out of my taverns and my bedchamber! But it seems that neither of us is going to get what we want!" He paused, amazed. "For God's sake, woman, are you *trying* to get yourself ruined?"

Tears sprang to Callie's eyes at the words, turning them into mahogany pools. "No," she whispered, her voice cracking. She looked away, suddenly desperate to be anywhere other than here, next to him, about to cry.

At her tears, he cursed roundly beneath his breath. He hadn't meant to upset her. Well, he had meant to *scare* her into stopping her damn foolishness, but he hadn't meant to make her cry. He softened his tone. "What, then?" When she didn't answer, he pressed on, cajoling, "Callie."

She looked at him again, shaking her head. Taking a deep breath, she said, "You don't understand."

His blue gaze locked with hers as he relaxed next to her, seating himself at her side so that they were facing each other, his knee supporting her wounded arm. "Explain it to me." The words were firm.

"It's really quite fine, you know," Callie said, her tone belittling the importance of her words. "It's just that . . . even in this moment, while I'm faced with certain ruin, and your anger, and my own fear, and not a small amount of pain from my wound—not that you didn't do a lovely job binding it, my lord." He nodded his acknowledgment of her praise. "Even with all that," she plunged on, "I am having one of the best days of my life."

She could see the confusion in his eyes as she tried to explain. "You see, today I am *living*."

"Living?"

"Yes. I've spent twenty-eight years doing what everyone around me expected me to do . . . being what everyone around me has expected me to be. And it's horrid to be someone else's vision of yourself." She paused, then, "You were right. I am a coward."

His eyes softened at her impassioned statement. "I was an ass. I shouldn't have said it."

"You're not an . . ." She stopped, unable to say the word aloud.

"I'm not certain I agree. Go on."

"I'm not a wife, or a mother, or a pillar of the *ton*." She waved her unharmed arm as though the life she was describing was just beyond the room. "I'm invisible. So, why not *stop* being such a craven wallflower and *start* trying all the things that I've always dreamed of doing? Why not go to taverns and drink scotch and fence? I confess, those things have been much more interesting than all the loathsome teas and balls and needlepoint with which I have traditionally occupied my time." She met his gaze again. "Does this make sense?"

He nodded seriously. "It does. You're trying to find Callie."

Her eyes widened. "Yes! Somewhere along the way, I lost Callie. Perhaps I never had her. But today, here, I found her."

He smiled wryly. "Callie is a fencer?"

She matched his smile with one of her own. "Callie is many things, my lord. I also found her in the tavern."

"Ah," he said, knowingly. "So Callie is a rake."

She blushed. "I don't think so."

Silence fell between them as he watched the wash of pink across her cheeks. He lifted her wounded arm in his hand, placing a soft kiss on the back of her hand. She breathed deeply at the feel of his lips on her skin, so warm and soft, and her eyes flew to his, intently focused on her. He held her gaze, and she felt a shock of liquid heat as his tongue circled one of her knuckles.

He registered her surprise, smiling against her and turning her hand palm up, then setting his tongue and lips to work on the soft, sensitive spot at its center. Her breath quickened, and she closed her eyes to the sensation, unable to watch the erotic movement of his mouth across her skin.

He lifted his lips from her hand and, when she opened her eyes again, it was to find him watching her, a wicked smile on his lips. Reaching out, he traced one finger along the line of her jaw, sending a shiver through her. When he spoke, his voice was thick and liquid, and it sent a shock of heat down her spine. "I shouldn't give up on that part of her just yet, Empress."

She caught her breath at the endearment, which brought with it a hazy memory from long ago. He chased the vision away with the vivid present as he clasped her chin, bringing her face closer to his. "You forget, I've met the woman several times . . . In carriages . . ."

His lips hovered just above hers, sending a tremor of anticipation through her, "And in theatres . . ."

She tried to close the distance between them and he pulled back just enough to drive her slightly mad. "And in bedchambers.

"In fact," he added, his words a caress along the sensitive skin of her lips, "I rather like the rakish side of her."

And then he settled his lips upon hers, and she was lost. She was consumed by the softness of his mouth, the gentleness of the caress—so very different than the kisses they had shared before. This kiss consumed her, made her forget herself, their surroundings, everything but the magnificent pressure of his lips on hers. His thumb stroked her jaw as his mouth ate at hers, sending waves of pulsing pleasure through her.

She gasped at the feeling, and he took advantage of her open lips to plunder her mouth with deep, drugging kisses that made her dizzy. She reached for him, her anchor in a sea of sensuality, wrapping her arms around his neck and plunging her fingers into his heavy, soft hair. He made a deep, satisfied sound at the feeling of her wrapped around him, and traced a path across her cheek and down the column of her throat with soft, moist kisses that sent explosions of pleasure through her.

The high neck of the fencing jacket she wore hindered his progress, and he deftly unbuttoned it as he made love to the sensitive skin of her neck, following the path of her skin as the widening collar revealed it. When he finished unfastening the jacket, he pulled back from the embrace to open the coat. His heavy-lidded gaze fell to her bound breasts, rising and falling against the tightly wound linen that had bound them for the afternoon.

He shook his head at the bindings before meeting her gaze once more. "This," he said, running his hands over the edge of the linen, "is a travesty."

Registering the need in her eyes, her lips parted in passion, her flushed cheeks, Ralston took her lips in another ravenous kiss before setting his hands to the bindings, seeking the end of the linen. Finding it, he pulled it from its place and began to unwrap the length of fabric.

Callie watched as his eyes followed the movement of his hands, nervous. She registered the roughness of his breathing, the darkened blue of his eyes, and she realized that she was here, in Ralston's arms. In the arms of the only man she had ever wanted. The only man of whom she had ever dreamed. And now, as he laid her body bare, she knew with an unquestionable certainty that her soul, too, was his. She would never stop wanting him.

As the words floated through her mind, she gasped from the glorious feeling of the last of the bindings falling away, releasing her breasts from their tight confines. His eyes darkened further, and she looked down at herself, noting the harsh red lines that ran across her normally pale skin. She moved to cover herself, embarrassed by her nakedness. He caught her hands in his.

"No," he said, his voice thick and seductive. "You have treated these beauties most unkindly. As their rescuer, they now belong to me."

Callie felt heat flare at his words, pooling deep within her as he released her hands and moved to caress her. His warm, strong hands cupped and molded her abraded flesh, coaxing sighs of pleasure from her as he soothed and gentled her chafed skin. He set his lips to the red marks left by the linen, running his tongue along the oversensitive skin, placing soft, gentle kisses across her breasts.

He laved the skin for long minutes, deliberately avoiding the straining tips of her breasts, allowing them to grow tighter and more sensitive with every stroke of his fingers and tongue. Callie began to squirm under his ministrations, straining for his touch on the areas where she was most desperate for it.

He noticed her movement, lifting his head to meet her gaze. "What is it, Empress?" he asked, the words a caress in themselves, his breath breaking across her aching skin. "Do you want me here?" He ran one finger across a straining nipple, and she gave a little cry at the explosion of sensation that came at the featherlight touch. He moved to the other tip, repeating the caress. "Or here?"

"Yes . . ." The word came on a pant.

He smiled wickedly at the sound. "You have only to ask."

And then he set his lips to one turgid peak, and she thought she might drown in the pleasure of it. He soothed the sensitive skin with his roughened tongue, his head clutched in both of her hands as he suckled gently, sending a burst of liquid heat to the very core of her. The sensation, so foreign and wonderful, consumed her as he turned his attention to the other breast, repeating his actions, this time more firmly. He scraped his teeth across the peak, then soothed it with tongue and lips, and she cried out, anxious for something that she could not name.

He seemed to sense her need, one hand grazing along the inside of her thigh, gently tracing a path to the core of her. He cupped her in one hand, sending a dart of pleasure through her, making her keenly aware of the fabric that blocked his access to that spot where she so desperately wanted his touch. She squirmed, trying to get closer to him, and he lifted his head again, meeting her gaze.

He kissed her soundly, stealing her breath, before saying, "Tell me what you want, my lovely."

"I—" She stopped, too many words coming at once. *I want you to touch me. I want you to love me. I want you to show me the life that I have been missing.* She shook her head, uncertain.

He smiled, pressing firmly with his hand against her, watching the wave of pleasure course through her. "Incredible," he whispered against the side of her neck. "So responsive. Go on . . ."

"I want—" She sighed as he set his lips to the hardened peak of one breast again. "I want . . . I want you," she said, and, in that moment, the words, so utterly simple in the face of the roiling emotions that coursed through her, seemed enough.

He moved his fingers firmly, deftly against her, and she gasped. "Do you want me here, Empress?"

She closed her eyes in embarrassment, biting her lower lip.

"Are you aching for me here?"

She nodded. "Yes."

"Poor, sweet love." His words were liquid fire against her ear as he slipped one arm of her jacket off and pushed aside her croissard, gaining access to the buttons of her breeches. Sliding a warm hand inside the fabric, he coaxed another sigh from her as he met the soft down of her sex. Parting the slick folds there, one finger pushed inside the heat. "Here?"

She gasped, grasping his forearm with her hand.

He growled low in his throat as he watched her attempt to understand the feelings coursing through her. When he spoke, his voice was rough with his own response. "I think you want more than that."

His fingers began to move against her as he set his mouth to the straining tip of one breast, and Callie lost the ability to think. He stroked against her pulsing flesh, nudging her legs wider, gaining access to her slick heat. One finger circled the very center of her, and she writhed against him, uncertain of the emotions roiling through her. The movement of his firm, knowing hands—in perfect tandem with the lush pull of his mouth—pushed her further and further toward a precipice she couldn't identify. Pleasure spiked as he found the soft, wet place where the world seemed to end, and she cried out as he stroked there, pushing her higher and higher.

She tensed as waves of pleasure washed over her in concert with his movements, and he felt the change in her. He released her breast, plundering her mouth, stroking with tongue and teeth, drugging her with his kiss before pulling away and meeting her gaze, and noting the confusion and passion mingling there. He inserted a finger deep within her, and she gasped, the coiled tension deep within her, threatening to release.

He set his lips to her ear, whispering, "Let go, my lovely . . ."

She turned to him at the words, seeing ripe understanding in his eyes as the finger inside her was joined by a second, thrusting rhythmically, as he circled the core of her faster, more firmly, as though he knew just where she ached, just where she needed his touch. She cried out at the wave of feeling—like nothing she'd ever felt before.

"I will catch you when you fall." The words, liquid with passion, were her undoing.

He held her gaze as she plunged over the edge, clinging to him.

She throbbed beneath his touch, writhing against him, begging for more even as he gave it to her. His fingers moved inside her, knowing just how to touch, where to stroke, when to flex. And when he had wrung the last, pulsing movement from her, had captured the last of her cries with his firm lips, he *did* catch her, his knowing hands guiding her safely back to his arms, back to earth.

He held her as she regained her senses, his lips brushing against her temple, his hands stroking her back and arms and legs gently. When her breathing returned to normal, Callie dropped her hands from around his neck, allowing her wounded arm to rest on him again. Ralston hissed as her hand settled on his lap, and he quickly grabbed her hand and lifted it away from him.

Recognizing only that he had moved her hand from where it had touched him, Callie became immediately insecure. Ralston instantly understood her uncertainty. Placing a warm kiss on her now-clenched hand, he met her wounded gaze, and said, "It's rather difficult to watch such a thoroughly enthralling display of passion and not be moved, lovely."

Her concern turned to confusion and he pressed her hand to the outside of his breeches, allowing her access to the hard ridge of him. Understanding dawned and, though she blushed, she did not pull her hand away from the heat of him. Instead, she tentatively pressed against him, reveling in his soft groan of response, and in the way he held her hand to his body. "Can—" She swallowed, then tried again, "Can I . . . do something?"

One side of his mouth kicked up in a pained smile before he pulled her to him and kissed her again, not stopping until she was clinging to him once more, breathless with excitement. "While I would like nothing more than for you to do something, Empress, I think we have done rather too much as it is, considering someone could enter at any time."

The words shook her from her reverie like a splash of ice water. Her attention flew to the door—unlocked—just waiting for another fencer to make the same mistake she had and to stumble upon them.

"Oh!" She leapt up, wincing at the pain that shot through her arm at the movement. Stuffing her free arm into the sleeve of the ruined jacket, she turned away from him and hurried to the far corner of the room, working on the long row of buttons fastening the garment. *What had she been thinking?*

She hadn't, of course, been thinking of anything but him.

"You seem to have forgotten a critical piece of your disguise."

She whirled toward the lazy words to find him walking calmly toward her, running the length of linen that had flattened her breasts between his fingers. As he closed in on her, he whispered, "No one will believe you're a man with those gorgeous breasts left to their own devices. Frankly, no one should believe it with your magnificent—"

"Thank you," she said firmly, staying his words, ignoring the wash of heat on her cheeks and taking the linen from his hands.

"You'll need my help, lovely."

No. She couldn't allow him such an intimate task. She would simply have to risk discovery—Benedick's coat allowed a modicum of coverage. Unwittingly, she looked down at herself, as though measuring the obviousness of her cleavage.

It was quite obvious.

Ralston seemed to read her thoughts, taking the linen back from her. "You should be discovered in seconds, Empress. Best let me help." His gaze took on a wicked gleam. "I promise to be the perfect gentleman."

She couldn't help the laugh that bubbled at his words, so ridiculous were they. His face broke into a wide grin and, after a moment's thought, she gave in. Slipping out of the jacket once more, she shyly turned her back to him, holding one end of the fabric tight against her breasts. She waited for him to begin wrapping her in the linen, but he did not move. After a long minute, she looked over her shoulder to find him mere inches away, watching her. She offered him a questioning look.

"Turn."

It took her a moment to realize what he meant. He wanted her to spin into the bandages, instead of standing still and allowing him to wrap her. She did so, slowly, understanding almost immediately the seductive nature of the situation. Something about the movement, about his dark blue eyes on her as she spun, made her feel like a temptress—his Salome. He did not touch her as she turned, dancing only for him; instead, he allowed her to choose the speed and the strength with which she was bound. And when she reached the end of the fabric, she spun right into his arms.

Holding her gaze, Ralston tucked the end of the linen into the bindings before he took her face in one hand and tilted it up for another kiss. This one was soft and sweet, his lips brushing gently across hers in an excruciatingly slow caress, leaving her heart pounding and her mind reeling. With his other hand, he stroked one flattened breast gently, teasing the protected skin until she wanted to tear off the bindings again.

He broke off the kiss and leaned down, setting his lips to the edge of the linen, softly laving the sensitive skin straining above the bindings. "Poor, lovely darlings," he murmured, worshipping her with hands and mouth, raising her temperature and sending another wave of passion pooling deep within her.

Just as she thought she might not be able to stand if he continued, he stopped, bending to retrieve her fencing jacket, carefully pulling it over her bandaged arm and tucking her into it, deftly fastening the buttons as she watched, her emotions wreaking havoc on her ability to accomplish anything useful.

When he was done, he stepped away, toward the pile of fencing accoutrements they had abandoned earlier. She watched as he stopped just off the mat to pick up the piece of paper that had fallen unseen when he had removed her bindings. She immediately recognized it and was spurred into motion, calling out, "Wait. Don't."

He paused in the act of opening the folded sheet and, curiosity in his blue eyes, watched her approach. She placed one hand over his, taking hold of the paper and attempting to pull it from his fingers, but his grip tightened.

"Why not?" he asked, his words smooth and teasing.

"It's mine."

"It seems you misplaced it."

"I wouldn't have if you hadn't taken it upon yourself to unbind my—" She stopped, unwilling to finish the sentence.

He raised a brow. "Yes, well, I'm certainly not going to apologize for that."

She squared her shoulders, attempting her most regal of poses. "Nevertheless, it's my property."

With a quick move of his wrist, Ralston ensured that she had lost her grip on the paper and he, once more, was in full possession of her list. Her heart jumped into her throat as he moved to open it once more. "Please, Gabriel. Don't."

Whether because of the use of his given name, or because of her pleading tone, he would never know, but Ralston stayed his movement, instead meeting her gaze, and saying, "What is it, Callie?"

She shook her head, looking away from him, and stammered, "It's nothing . . . It's silly . . . It's personal."

"Tell me what it is, and I shan't look at it."

Her eyes flew to his. "That rather defeats the purpose of your not looking at it, doesn't it?" she said, peevishly.

He was silent, turning the crinkled paper over and over in his hand. She sighed, irritated. "Fine. It's a list." She put out one hand, as though he would place the paper in her palm, and that would be that.

His look turned quizzical. "What kind of list?"

"A *personal* list," she said, attempting to infuse her voice with ladylike disdain, hoping the tone would make him feel ungentlemanly and relinquish this particular battle.

"A personal shopping list? A list of inappropriate books you'd like to read? A list of men?" She blushed at the thought, and he paused, his eyes widening. "Dear God, Callie, is it a list of men?"

She stomped her foot in irritation. "Good heavens, no! It isn't really relevant what the list contains, Ralston. What is relevant is that it belongs to me."

"Not a good answer, Empress," he said, and began to unfold the paper.

"Wait!" She placed a hand over his once more. She couldn't bear the idea of him seeing her secret desires. Refusing to meet his gaze, she said, "If you must know, it is a list of . . . activities . . . that I would like to try."

"I beg your pardon?"

"Activities. Most of which men can partake in but women are barred from for fear of our delicate reputations. I've decided that, considering few care a whit for my reputation, I have no reason to sit quietly whiling away the rest of my days doing needlepoint with my sisters in spinsterhood. I am tired of being thought of as passive."

He raised a brow. "You may be many things, Empress. But I would never label you as passive."

What a lovely thing for him to say.

She swallowed, closing her fingers over the edge of the paper.

He watched her fingers, so closely entwined with his own, as he considered her words. He could not help but be intrigued. "So, this is a list of actions that Lady Calpurnia believes constitute living."

She recognized the words from their earlier conversation. Perhaps if he had spoken them prior to their interlude on the floor of the practice room, she would have agreed with them. Those few, precious moments in Ralston's arms, however, had changed everything. In that embrace, Callie had *really* lived. She had finally experienced the life she'd dreamed of since that first chance meeting with Ralston, a decade—a century—ago. And now, drinking scotch rather paled in comparison—tavern or no. Of course she couldn't tell him *that*.

"The list is mine. I would appreciate your returning it, unopened. This conversation is embarrassing enough, I should think."

He neither responded nor released the paper, forcing her to meet his eyes. He must have seen the truth in hers, because he relinquished his prize. She refolded the paper and inserted it into the pocket of her jacket with all speed. He watched her movements carefully before saying, "I gather fencing is on this list?"

She nodded.

"And scotch?"

Another nod.

"What else?"

Kissing. "Gambling."

"Dear Lord. And?"

"Cheroot."

He snorted. "Well that shall be a difficult one. Not even I would let you smoke a cheroot. And my morals are questionable at best."

His words, so supercilious, set her on edge. "Actually, my lord, I have already crossed that particular item off my list."

"How? Who gave you a cheroot?"

"Benedick."

"Of all the irresponsible things—" Ralston paused, amazed. "I shall have his head."

"That's what he said about you and scotch."

He let out a bark of laughter. "Yes, I imagine he did. So he knows about this ridiculous list?"

"Actually, no. Only my maid knows." She paused. "And, well . . . now you."

"I wonder what your brother will say when he finds out I wounded you at his fencing club?"

The question, so calm, sent her eyes flying to his. "You wouldn't!" she said incredulously.

"Oh, I don't know," he said, retrieving her gloves and passing them to her.

Taking the gloves, she let them hang from distracted fingers. "You can't!"

"Whyever not?"

"Think of—" She paused, considering her words. "Think of what it would say about you!"

He smiled, making a production of pulling on his own gloves. "It would say I am a rake and a libertine. And I think we've already established the truth in that." The words were spoken in a tone that only underscored their truth, and Callie's ears burned as she recognized them as those she had flung at him in anger at the theatre several evenings earlier.

He pressed on. "Not to mention the fact that you have to exit the club without being discovered by any number of *other* men who would be more than happy to regale your brother—and legions of others—with tales of your indiscretion. You may have arrived at a quiet time of day, Empress, but it's nigh on five o'clock now. The hallways will be teeming with men, eager to have their afternoon exercise before returning home for dinner and the evening's festivities."

She hadn't considered that. She'd been so focused on getting *into* the fencing club that she hadn't really imagined that leaving would be just as much of a challenge—perhaps more. Now that he had drawn her attention to their presence, she could hear shouts of male laughter and raucous conversation coming from other members of the club as they passed, unknowing, just outside the room. She quashed a flood of embarrassment at the notion that any one of those men could have entered minutes ago and caught them in the midst of a highly inappropriate act.

"Of course, I would be happy to keep quiet"—his words broke into her thoughts—"and to help you escape from the difficulty in which you seem to have found yourself. For a price."

Her brows snapped together, and she looked at him warily. "What price?"

He lifted her mask and handed it to her. "I shall protect your reputation today if you allow me to do so for the duration of your list."

Her jaw dropped.

"Ah," he said genially, "I see you take my meaning. Yes. If I discover that you've completed another item on that list without my escort, I shall tell your brother everything."

She was silent for a long moment, emotions flaring. "That's blackmail."

"A loathsome word. But if you must label it such, so be it. I assure you it's for the best. You obviously need a chaperone and, for the good of both of our families, I am offering my services."

"You can't . . ."

"It would seem that I can," he said, matter-of-factly. "Now, you can either put on your mask and let me help you exit this club, or you can put it on and take your chances on your own. Which will it be?"

She met his eyes for a long moment. As much as she wanted to leave him there, smug expression on his face, and find her own way out of the mess, she knew that his would likely be the quickest and easiest exit strategy.

Callie donned her mask, taking her time as she tucked her hair up under the cowl, away from view. When she was done, she spoke, her words muffled by the wire mesh.

"It would seem I haven't much of a choice."

He smiled wickedly, sending a shock of excitement through her. "Capital."

Fourteen

"No! No! *Non!* Miss Juliana, ladies should be *all daintiness* while dancing! You are meeting my gaze altogether too often!"

As the dance master spoke, his affront clear as day, Callie turned toward the massive floor-to-ceiling windows overlooking the impressive Ralston House gardens and hid her smile. The small, effete Frenchman was Juliana's least favorite teacher despite being one of the finest dancing masters in England; the two had very different opinions on the importance of dancing in the life of a young woman, and Callie had a sneaking suspicion that young Miss Fiori enjoyed irritating him.

"Apologies, Monsieur Latuffe," Juliana said, her tone indicating absolutely no remorse. "I was merely trying to ensure that I knew your whereabouts—and did not tread upon your toes."

The dance master's eyes widened. "Miss Juliana! Neither do young ladies presume to discuss *toe treading*. If such a horrible thing should occur, I assure you that your partner will not notice. For, ladies, when dancing, should be *light as air*."

Juliana's laugh was rife with disbelief, sending Latuffe into a fit of sputtering hysterics. Callie covered her mouth to keep her own laughter from spilling out—thereby ruining her image as an impartial bystander.

Callie had been overseeing the lesson from a settee on the far end of the ballroom for the better part of an hour, but as Juliana and Monsieur Latuffe had progressed through the steps of several country dances, a quadrille, and now a minuet, the patience of both parties had worn thin, and Callie was finding herself unable to hide her amusement at their bickering. Affixing what she hoped was a neutral expression upon her face, she turned back to Juliana and Latuffe.

The Frenchman was stalking across the bare floor, arms flailing, toward the pianoforte, where the pianist who had been hired for the afternoon's lessons was looking more than a little uncertain. Placing one hand to his heart and the other on the edge of the piano, Latuffe made a show of taking several deep, calming breaths between harried French muttering. One side of Callie's mouth twitched as she almost certainly heard him take the names of the Island of Great Britain, Italian females, and the quadrille in vain. She had to admit to a modicum of surprise at the last— Juliana must be quite a trial if he was ready to give up his faith in dance.

Approaching Juliana, Callie met the younger woman's blue eyes, which were immediately rolled in exasperation. Flashing a grin, Callie whispered, "You've only another twenty minutes. Do attempt to suffer through."

Juliana spoke through gritted teeth. "I'm doing this for you, you realize."

Callie squeezed the younger woman's arm, and said, "A fact for which I shall be forever grateful."

Juliana snickered as the dance master turned abruptly. "It is no matter," he said, firmly. "We shall move on to the waltz. Surely, even a young lady such as you must respect the waltz."

Juliana's eyes widened. She looked at Callie, and whispered, "A young lady such as I?"

It was Callie's turn to snicker as the Frenchman swept a surprised Juliana into his arms and, in an act that belied his diminutive size, whirled her across the ballroom floor to a rousing tune. Callie smiled genially at the obviously relieved pianist and watched as the pair swayed and turned with the music. As they danced, Latuffe kept up his litany of do's and don'ts—Juliana was chastised in quick succession for having too firm a grip, too rigid a form, and, finally, too wild a look in her eye. Callie had a rather firm suspicion that the wild look would be less of an issue once the younger woman was out of her dance master's grasp.

Callie couldn't help the wide grin that had settled on her face, especially when Juliana looked her instructor square in the eye and stomped quite deliberately upon his foot. *I rather expect that belied the theory that young ladies are light as air while dancing.*

"Is it I, or is my sister requiring her exorbitantly expensive dancing instructor to earn every shilling?" The words, spoken at a close proximity, surprised Callie, and she whirled toward the sound to discover Nicholas St. John standing nearby, his amused attention focused on Juliana.

Callie ignored the burst of emotion in her chest, unwilling to define it as either disappointment or relief that *this* was the St. John who had made an appearance that afternoon. Instead, she offered Nick a bright smile, and said, "I think that given the opportunity, your sister would enjoy roundly trouncing Monsieur Latuffe."

Nick watched silently for a long moment, during which Juliana and her dance master had rousing words about the appropriateness of young ladies smiling at other gentlemen—even her brothers—while waltzing. Turning back to Callie, Nick said, "Yes, well, I'm not entirely certain I would reprimand her for doing so."

Callie laughed. "Between us, I'm rather tempted to allow her free rein."

"Retribution for past dance masters?"

"That . . . and the supreme enjoyment of the circus that would almost certainly ensue."

Nick raised one brow. "Why, Lady Calpurnia. I confess, I hadn't pegged you for such a wicked sense of humor."

"No. No! *Non!*" The explosion of negativity from the far end of the room interrupted Nick and Callie's banter, causing them to share an amused look as the dance master blustered. "It is the *gentleman* who leads the young lady. *I* am the gentleman. *You* follow! You are merely a leaf in the wind!"

The analogy spurred a burst of irate Italian. While Callie did not wholly understand the words, Juliana's meaning was unmistakable.

Nick flashed a grin at Callie. "I do not imagine women take well to being compared to foliage."

"Certainly not Italian women, it seems."

Her words drew a bark of laughter from him which, in turn, drew a pair of angry looks from the other couple. Clearing his throat, Nick turned to Callie and, holding out a hand, said, "Shall we show them how it is done?"

Callie looked down at the proffered hand, dumbfounded. "My lord?"

"Come now, Lady Calpurnia," he whispered teasingly, "never tell me you are afraid that Latuffe will critique your form."

Callie squared her shoulders in mock affront. "Certainly not."

"Well then?"

She placed her hand in his.

"Excellent."

And, with a wave of the hand at the pianist, who began another waltz, Nick swept her into his arms and they started across the room. As they dipped and turned their way through the sun-drenched ballroom, Callie craned her neck to keep watch over the bickering Juliana and Latuffe.

"Lady Calpurnia," Nick said finally, "I would be offended by your lack of interest were I not so very sure of myself."

Callie snapped her attention back to Nick at the words, only to laugh at the twinkle in his eye. "Apologies, my lord. I am merely preparing to enter the fray should the two of them come to blows."

"Never fear. I shall be the first to leap to Latuffe's aid should my sister act on the emotions with which she so clearly struggles." He tilted his head toward Juliana, and Callie looked in that direction, to find his sister looking thoroughly annoyed.

"'Twould be a pity if Italy and France were to war so soon after Napoleon was bested," Callie said, wryly.

Nick grinned. "I shall do my best to foster a universal peace."

"Excellent," Callie said, with mock seriousness. "But you do understand that may require playing dance master yourself?"

Nick pretended to consider the proposition. "Do you think the pianist would come back?"

Enjoying their game, Callie tilted her head and made a show of considering the wiry young man at the pianoforte. "Likely not, my lord. Aren't you lucky that your brother is a virtuoso?"

The words were out before she could consider their implication. To Nick's credit, he did not miss a step of their waltz, instead fixing her with an intrigued look, and quietly asking, "And, how do you know that my brother plays, my lady?"

Callie hedged, desperate for an escape from the conversation. "It is . . . quite . . . well-known, is it not?" She attempted a curious, innocent look.

One side of Nick's mouth kicked up in amusement. "No. It isn't. Yours would have been a convincing effort, however, were I not his twin brother." He paused, watching as defeat fell across her face. "When have you heard him play?"

Callie's mouth opened, then closed.

"Or should I ask, *where* have you heard him play?"

Was he teasing her? She was caught, but would not go down without a fight. Meeting Nick's eyes again, she said, "Nowhere."

He leaned close and whispered. "Liar."

"My lord," she protested, "I assure you that Lord Ralston has not . . ."

"There's no need for you to defend him," Nick said casually. "You forget I know my brother well."

"But we haven't—" Callie stopped, feeling a telltale spread of heat across her cheeks.

Nick raised one eyebrow. "Indeed."

Callie turned her gaze to Nick's cravat, attempting to distract herself with the cambric knot. He allowed her to remain quiet for several moments before he let out a rich laugh. "Never fear, my lady, your secret is safe with me, although I confess a twinge of jealousy. After all, it is well-known that I am by far the handsomer St. John."

She could not contain her own laughter as he turned her quickly, pulling her almost off her feet and lightening the moment. Smiling up into eyes twinkling with boyish amusement, Callie's eyes lingered on Nick's scar briefly before she caught herself and looked away.

"It's a horrid-looking thing, isn't it?"

Callie looked back at him, giving his cheek a frank perusal. "Not at all. Indeed, it is a surprise, but I have heard many women say they think you all the more handsome because of it."

He made a show of grimacing at the words. "They romanticize it. I am no pirate to be reformed."

"No? That is a pity. I heard that you spent half a decade sailing the Mediterranean, plundering ships and abducting innocents."

"The truth is much less exciting."

She feigned a look of horror. "Don't tell me. I prefer my version."

They laughed together, and Callie wondered at the fact that she could be so at ease with Nicholas St. John when his mirror image held such power over her emotions.

It had been just over a week since she had seen Ralston last — since he had smuggled her out of his fencing club and into his carriage to return her to Allendale House. She had been to Ralston House several times in the eight days, both to oversee Juliana's lessons and with Mariana to take tea with the young woman, and, each time, she had hoped to have an excuse to see Ralston; hoped that he might seek her out. For, certainly, with a houseful of servants and such an openly social sister, he must have known when Callie was in the building.

Twice, she had considered excusing herself to hunt him down and talk with him; she'd divined dozens of ways to force an interaction between them, from accidental entry to his study to fabricated reasons why she might need to discuss his sister. Unfortunately, Juliana's entry into society looked to be going quite smoothly— she would be ready for her first ball in a week's time—and Callie hadn't been able to get up the nerve to enter Ralston's study.

Ironic, that, considering that the first time she'd entered Ralston House, she'd brazenly entered Ralston's bedchamber. But that had been different. That had been about the list. This was about something altogether different.

She'd considered using the list to gain access to Ralston—after all, she had promised not to attempt another item without his chaperone, and she was rather chomping at the bit to try something else. But, frankly, she felt rather pathetic whenever she thought of using it to see him. It made her feel like something of a lapdog— eagerly chasing after its master. No. The truth was that she didn't want to *have* to seek him out. She wanted their interlude in the fencing club—which had changed everything for her—well, she wanted it to change something for him.

She wanted him to come to her. Was that too much to ask?

"Well . . . isn't this a cozy portrait."

The music halted as the dry words shot across the ballroom, and Callie caught her breath as the object of her reverie cast a bored look at her.

My God. I conjured him up.

She shook her head at the silly thought and moved instantly to separate herself from Nick, only to discover that he would not let her leave his embrace. When she looked to him in confusion, he winked at her and leaned entirely too close to whisper, "Don't show your hand. We were only dancing."

Her eyes widened as Nick released her slowly, bending into a deep, somewhat overdone bow and making a show of kissing her hand. Callie's eyes darted to Ralston, leaning casually in the entry to the ballroom, watching them with an entirely unreadable look. She felt immediately uncomfortable—and indignation flared. Nick was right, of course. They had only been dancing. *So why did she feel as though she were an errant child caught doing something naughty?*

"My lord Ralston!" Latuffe exclaimed, hurrying across the room toward the marquess. "It is an honor to have you grace us with your presence at Miss Juliana's lessons!"

"Indeed." The word rolled off Ralston's tongue lazily, his gaze not straying from Nick and Callie.

"Indeed! Indeed! *Oui!*" The dance master repeated eagerly, following the marquess's gaze. "Lord Nicholas and Lady Calpurnia have been a great help in adding levity to these challenging lessons."

"Is that what they were doing? Adding . . . levity?" Ralston's dry tone struck true. Callie sucked in a breath, feeling Nick stiffen next to her.

"Oh yes!" the dance master said. "You see, your sister is not the most malleable student, and they . . ."

"Is that a *criticism*?" Juliana interrupted pertly from her place across the room, causing Callie to turn in surprise at the younger woman's brashness, at which point Juliana added, "Well, would *you* like to be called malleable?"

"This is what I am trying to say! *Précisément!*" Latuffe's hands flapped desperately. "What kind of a young lady speaks to her teachers with such disrespect?"

Juliana's eyebrows snapped together. She turned toward the Frenchman, and said, hands flying through the air, "Perhaps if you were more of a *teacher* and less of *un idiota*, you would *deserve* my additional respect!"

The entire room froze at Juliana's outburst. Before anyone could speak, Monsieur Latuffe spun on one heel to face Ralston. He spoke, his voice growing louder with each word. "This is why I make it a practice never to take on *common* pupils! Her lack of breeding is alarmingly clear!" He pulled a handkerchief from his pocket and mopped his brow dramatically.

The silence in the room was palpable. A muscle twitched in Ralston's cheek before he spoke, anger turning his voice to steel. "Get out of my house."

The Frenchman turned surprised eyes on Ralston. "Surely you cannot be angry with *me,* my lord."

"It is refreshing to hear that you remain aware of your place with me, Latuffe," Ralston said coolly. "I will not have you speak of my sister in such a disrespectful manner. You are relieved of your duties."

Latuffe succumbed to a fit of inarticulate sputtering before flouncing from the room, the pianist following meekly behind.

The foursome that remained watched mutely as Latuffe exited before Juliana clapped her hands with glee. "Did you see his face? I wager no one has ever said anything like that to him! Marvelously done, Gabriel!"

"Juliana . . ." Callie began, stopping when Ralston raised a hand to stay her words.

"Juliana. Leave this room."

The girl's eyes widened. "You cannot mean to . . . I did not mean—"

"You did not mean to chase away the best dance master in all of London?"

Juliana scoffed, "He could not possibly be such a thing."

"I assure you he is."

"That is a sad truth for London."

Nick's lips twitched as Ralston's flattened into a thin line. "You are going to have to learn to keep your thoughts to yourself, sister, else you shall never be ready for society."

Juliana's eyes darkened, signaling that her will was equal to that of her brother. "May I suggest you allow me to return to Italy then, brother? I assure you I shall be far less trouble there."

"While I have no doubt of that, we agreed on eight weeks. You owe me another five."

"Four weeks and five days," she corrected tartly.

"Would that it were less. Leave this room. Do not return until you have decided to behave more like the lady that I was assured you were."

Juliana looked at her eldest brother for a long moment, her eyes flashing fire before she spun on one heel and stormed from the room.

Callie watched her go before turning an accusing look on Ralston. He met her gaze with a cool one of his own, daring her to protest his actions. With a barely perceptible shake of her head to indicate her disappointment, Callie followed her charge into the depths of Ralston House.

He watched her go before looking to Nick. "I should like a drink."

CALLIE FOUND JULIANA in her bedchamber, yanking dresses from her wardrobe. Eyeing the growing pile of silks and satins at the younger woman's feet and the wide-eyed maid who stood, uncertain, in the corner of the room, Callie smoothed the skirts of her gown and perched on the edge of the bed, waiting for Juliana to notice her arrival.

After long minutes punctuated only by Juliana's heavy breathing and the occasional phrase muttered in disgusted Italian, she spun around, hands on her hips, to face Callie. Juliana's eyes were wild with her frustration, her face pinkened with exertion and anger. She took a deep breath, then announced, "I am leaving."

Callie's eyebrows rose in surprise. "I beg your pardon?"

"I am. I am unable to remain here. Not one minute longer!" She turned away, heaving open a large wooden trunk with a litany of Italian in which Callie picked out the words for brother, bull, and artichoke.

"Juliana . . ." Callie said cautiously, "do you not think this is a bit . . . rash?"

Juliana's head popped up over the top of the trunk. "What rash? I do not have a rash!"

Tamping down her smile at the girl's misunderstanding, Callie pointed out, "Not *a* rash. You are *being* rash. Impulsive. Reckless."

Juliana cocked her head, considering the new word before she shook her head. "Not at all! Indeed, I only expected him to realize that he hated me sooner." She began to shove the dresses into the trunk, her maid looking to Callie in horror at the abominable treatment the gowns were receiving.

Callie would have laughed if the situation hadn't been so heated. "He does not hate you."

Juliana raised her head, her disbelief evident. "No? Did you *see* the way he looked at me? Did you *hear* him wish that I were gone?"

Callie couldn't help the little smile that came at the young woman's outrage—outrage that only intensified when she registered her friend's amusement. "You find this amusing?" she asked, accusation in her tone.

"Not at all—well—a bit," Callie admitted, hurrying on when she saw Juliana redden. "You see—you've never had an elder brother."

"No—and it appears that I have one who cares very little for the role!"

"Nonsense. He adores you. They both do."

"Ha! There you are *wrong*! I am nothing but a disappointment to them!" She returned to the wardrobe and began yanking shoes from deep inside, her voice muffled as she spoke, "I am . . . a commoner . . . an Italian . . . a Catholic." She threw shoes behind her as she spoke.

"I assure you, Ralston does not care about any of those things."

"Ha!" Juliana turned around to face Callie, breathing heavily. "Perhaps not! But I assure you he most definitely cares that I am the daughter of his mother . . . a woman he despises!"

Callie shook her head. "I cannot believe that he would blame you for your mother's . . ."

"That is easy for you to say, Callie. *You* did not have our mother!" Callie remained silent as Juliana began to thrust the shoes into the trunk. "Our mother was a terrible woman. Cold and utterly fascinated with herself. I remember very little of her except that she carried *uno specchio*—a mirror—with her always . . . so she could always look upon herself." She slowed her words, losing herself to the memory. "She hated to be touched. Was always afraid of wrinkled or stained skirts."

Juliana's voice became quiet as she added, "I was not allowed to touch her. 'Children have dirty hands' she would say, 'when you are older, you will understand.'" She shook her head. "But I do not understand. What kind of woman would not want her daughter to touch her? Not want her sons? Why would she leave us all?"

She looked down at the trunk, overflowing in a jumble of silks and satins, shoes and undergarments. "I dreamed of brothers— whom I could touch. Who would allow me to be messy. Who would play with me. And protect me. *Una famiglia.*" A small smile crossed her face. "And it turns out that I have them. She gave them to me."

"That is something very good that she has done for you." Callie moved to kneel next to Juliana, putting one arm around the younger girl.

"And now I have ruined it."

Callie shook her head. "Arguments happen. I promise you that he does not want you to leave."

Juliana looked up at Callie, her blue eyes so like Ralston's. "I could love them."

Callie smiled. "Good. As it should be."

"But what if there is no place for me here? I am nothing like them. And, yet, what if I do not belong anywhere else?"

Callie held the younger girl in her arms as Juliana considered the questions—the answers to which would decide her future.

And in the long moments they sat in silence, Callie realized that only Ralston could make Juliana see that she had a rightful place here.

She had to find him.

Fifteen

"Juliana did not deserve your censure."

Ralston turned away from the large window overlooking the back gardens of Ralston House and met his twin's blue gaze. "She called her dance master an idiot."

"To be fair, she wasn't entirely off the mark." Nick crossed the study, offering Ralston a tumbler of scotch, which he gladly accepted. The two stood silently at the window, watching the sunlight play through the leaves, casting mottled shadows across the lush green garden.

After a long moment, Ralston looked at Nick. "Are you defending her?"

"Not at all. But your response was overmuch. She is more delicate than she seems."

Ralston took a long drink of scotch. "Considering the murderous look she gave me, I'm not so certain that there is anything delicate about her at all."

"Would you care to tell me what has set you off?"

"No," Ralston said.

Nick left the window, moving to a large chair by the fireplace. Once seated, he took a long drink, waiting. The look Ralston cast over his shoulder at his brother would have sent a lesser man running from the room. Instead, Nick leaned back in his chair, and said, "It seems that after seeing Lady Calpurnia and me waltzing, you promptly took leave of your senses."

"That's rather overstating it."

"I don't think it is, Gabriel. You terrified the pianist, fired the dance instructor, and sent our sister fleeing the room, not to mention your insinuation that I was rather less than a gentleman."

"Are you saying that you weren't flirting inappropriately with the lady?" Ralston's tone was bordering on peevish.

"Flirting? Yes. Inappropriately? No."

Ralston looked back at the garden. Of course Nick hadn't been flirting inappropriately.

As they'd matured, the twins had taken wildly divergent paths to shake off the mantle of their mother, who had so thoroughly destroyed the Ralston reputation. While Gabriel had enjoyed living up to the low expectations of the *ton* when it came to his womanizing ways, Nick, instead, had escaped those expectations altogether, spending nearly a decade on the Continent, entirely immersed in his work with antiquities. Certainly, his brother had had his fair share of women, but Ralston had never known Nick to attach himself to one publicly enough to garner even a modicum of gossip. The result? Women chased after both twins, but for vastly different reasons. Ralston was a well-known libertine; Nick was the perfect gentleman.

"In fact, we were talking about you," Nick added, drawing a look of surprise from his brother. The younger St. John took the chance to drive his point home. "Tell me something. How does Lady Calpurnia happen to know that you play?"

There was a pause as Ralston processed the question. "That I play what?"

"The piano," Nick said, as though speaking to a child.

"I don't know."

Nick sighed deeply. "You may avoid it, but it's rather obvious, Gabriel. The only way she would know that you play . . . that you're a *virtuoso* as she put it . . . is if she'd witnessed it. And I don't believe I've ever seen you play outside of your bedchamber. It's not exactly a habit that marquesses run around boasting of."

He paused, waiting for his brother to speak. When Ralston said nothing, Nick continued, "So you've taken her to mistress."

"No." Ralston's response was instant and vitriolic. He spun toward his brother, his muscles tense with barely contained violence. "She's not my mistress. And I'll see the next man who speculates such at dawn. I don't care who he is." The threat was clear.

It was Nick's turn to look surprised. He blinked. "Well. That was enlightening. I'll confess I'm happy to hear it. I had hoped she would not relinquish her honor so easily."

When Ralston did not respond, instead glowering at his brother, Nick continued, "You understand, of course, that she is not the typical female with whom you tend to find yourself entangled."

"We are not entangled."

"No, of course not." Nick waved a hand idly in the air and spoke wryly. "It's quite common for you to come at me twice in one day over a woman."

"I am attempting to keep her reputation intact. She is inexorably intertwined with Juliana. We cannot risk any gossip finding its way to our doorstep," Ralston said, attempting to head Nick off.

"You've never cared much for reputations before," Nick said wryly.

"I've never had a sister before."

Nick raised an eyebrow in disbelief. "I don't think this about Juliana at all. I think this is about Lady Calpurnia. And I think you're risking more than her reputation."

"You needn't feel it necessary to defend her honor to me, Nick. You saw the look she gave me before going after Juliana. I wouldn't be surprised if that were the last I saw of Lady Calpurnia Hartwell."

"And you would be happy with such a turn of events?"

"Certainly."

"Then it would be fine if I were to court her?"

The words hit Ralston like a physical blow. He tensed, eyes narrowing as he met his brother's amused, knowing gaze.

"I see it would not be fine. Intriguing."

"You go too far, Nick."

"Probably. But someone must remind you of the truth."

"Which is?"

"Calpurnia Hartwell is not your kind of woman, Gabriel."

"And what kind of woman is she?"

"The kind that wants love."

"Love." Ralston spat the word. "Callie knows better than to believe in fairy tales. One doesn't get to be her age without understanding that love is a fool's errand."

"Callie, is it?" Nick asked.

"You're lucky I don't lay you out right now," Ralston growled.

"Mmm," Nick replied, noncommittally. He held his brother's eyes for a long moment before standing and making his way to the door of the room. Once there, he turned back. "Just tell me one thing. The truth this time. Are you after her?"

Yes. "No," Ralston scoffed. "What on earth would I want with such a plain, missish creature?" *Not so plain; not so missish.* Ralston pushed the thought aside. "Have you ever known me to pursue a woman like her? I need her for Juliana's sake. That is all. It is not my fault if the girl finds me attractive."

Nick nodded once at the words before pulling open the door,

which had been ajar, to reveal Callie, wide-eyed and pale-faced. If Ralston were less in control of his emotions, he would have cursed violently.

It was obvious that she had overheard.

ALL THOUGHTS OF Juliana gone from her mind, Callie looked from one brother to the other and opened her mouth to speak, feeling that she must say something.

There was nothing to say, of course. Ralston had said quite enough.

She took a deep breath, his words seeming to echo around her. *What on earth would I want with such a plain, miss-ish creature?* Well. At least now she knew the truth. Surely there was some comfort to be found in that.

None right this moment, of course, but . . . surely at some point . . . sometime in the future . . . the pain of his words hit her like a physical blow.

And then she felt the anger, surging around her like a vicious, welcome storm.

And she wanted nothing but to strike back at this arrogant, self-important man who seemed to be no kind of gentleman.

"Well," she said, sarcasm seeping into her tone, as she pushed through the doorway to face Gabriel, "you seem to have a rather inflated view of yourself, my lord."

Twin sets of ink black eyebrows shot up at her words and, while she did not take her eyes from the marquess, she heard Nick's surprised cough, followed by, "I do believe I will seek out Juliana. Perhaps she is faring better than my other sibling."

He bowed low, despite Callie's summarily ignoring him, and left the room, closing the door behind him with a soft click.

The sound spurred Callie into motion. "How dare you?"

Gabriel moved toward her. "I did not mean . . ."

She held up one hand to stay his words. "You ruined your sister's dancing lesson, not to mention the rest of her afternoon."

He stopped, surprised by the shift in topic. "She rather ruined it herself, don't you think?"

"No. I think you ruined it for her. And for the rest of us." She pulled herself up to her full height, squaring her shoulders. "And I would thank you to remember that, since you need me for Juliana's sake, you would do well to steer clear of our lessons before making a hash out of any more of them."

He blinked at her icy words before saying coolly, "You seemed to be enjoying yourself."

She lifted her chin, defiant. "As a matter of fact, I was. It is unfortunate that the afternoon ended so abruptly." She looked down her pert nose at him for a long moment before turning on one heel to leave the room. Her fingers had barely touched the handle of the door when she turned back. "You owe your sister an apology."

He scoffed. "For what?"

"She is young and alone and terrified that she will disappoint you, Lord Ralston. You may say whatever you like about me, but do try to remember that she is delicate. And she needs you."

"I am not a monster."

She smiled, the expression not reaching her eyes. "No. Of course not."

He had the distinct impression that she did not necessarily believe the words.

She turned back to the door, making to leave, and he spoke, his words flying across the room. "Is he an item on your list?"

"I beg your pardon?" she asked, stiffly, turning with all the disdain of a Queen.

He pressed on, as though speaking to a simpleton. "Nicholas, Callie. My brother. Is he an item on your list? *Number three: Land St. John?*"

Callie's eyes widened. "You think I've put your brother on my list?"

"That's exactly what I think." His eyes flared with a barely contained emotion that she couldn't quite identify. "Did you?"

She couldn't help the laugh that bubbled up at the ridiculous query. "No, Ralston. I didn't. I assure you that were there a conquest on my list, it would not be your brother."

"Who would it be?"

Against my better judgment, it would be you, *you cabbagehead.* "I am through with this conversation." Callie made to turn back to the door. And then he was next to her, grabbing her hand firmly, spinning her toward him. The warm heat of his skin sent a shock through her; she fought to ignore it.

"I am not through with it."

"Lord Ralston," Callie said, eyes flashing with unbridled anger, "you appear to be laboring under the misapprehension that I am in some way beholden to your whims. Allow me to set you to rights. You may be able to direct your servants and your family as you see fit, but I fall into neither of those categories. And while I may be a plain, missish, *passive* creature, I am through with being ordered about by you. I am leaving."

He rocked back on his heels at her ire. "I never called you passive. There is nothing passive about you."

With a tug, she extricated her hand from his grasp. She glared up at him, and for a fleeting moment he thought she might do him bodily harm.

When she turned on one heel and reached for the door, he flattened his palm against the cool mahogany, blocking her exit. "You may not be my servant or my family, Calpurnia, but we do have an agreement."

She froze at the words, gaze locked on his hand. "I have lived up to my end of the bargain."

"Juliana's behavior this afternoon indicates otherwise."

"Oh, please." Callie scoffed. "We both know she is ready."

"I know no such thing. I shall be the judge of her preparedness."

"There were no such stipulations made when we discussed the agreement."

"Nor were they expressly *not* made. I am making them now. You received what you requested. Or, have you forgotten?" The words sent a shiver down her spine. He was standing behind her, and she could feel the warm kiss of his breath on her bare neck, sending a river of heat through her.

"I have not forgotten." The words came unbidden, and she closed her eyes.

He laid a hand on her arm and, with virtually no pressure, turned her to face him. When he met her eyes, the anger that had been there was gone, replaced by something much more complex. "Neither have I. And not for lack of trying."

Before she could begin to consider the meaning behind his words, he settled his mouth upon hers, robbing her of thought.

"I've tried to forget that kiss . . . and the carriage ride . . . and the fencing club . . . but you seem to have taken up residence . . . in my memory."

As he spoke between long, drugging kisses that consumed her senses, he guided Callie across the study and into a large chair near the fireplace. Kneeling in front of her, he cupped one cheek in a strong, warm hand, and met her gaze with a searing look. Shaking his head as though he couldn't quite understand what had come over him, he kissed her again, growling low in the back of his throat. Her hands found their way into his thick, dark hair as he caught her bottom lip in his teeth, nibbling and licking at it until she thought she might perish from the intensity of the feeling. She whimpered at the sensation, and he rewarded the sound by deepening the kiss, giving her everything she desired.

He broke off the kiss as one of his hands found its way under her skirts, caressing up the inside of her leg. He shifted her against him, running his lips across her cheek to the curl of her ear, sucking and nibbling and licking as he spoke to her, the scandalous words more sensation than sound.

"Such soft skin . . ." he said, as his fingers played along the inside of her thighs, driving her mad with desire as heat pooled at their juncture. "I've been wondering what you felt like here . . ." He shifted to gain better access to the skin high on the inside of her thighs, so close to the spot where she most wanted him. "Now that I know . . . I'm going to be consumed with thoughts of how this soft, lovely skin will feel against me . . ." He placed a soft, lush kiss on the column of her neck as his hand moved higher, closer to the center of her.

Her hands rushing across his chest and shoulders, eager for the feel of him, Callie sighed, squirming against him, desperate for his hands in that secret, dark place that she had just recently come to understand. He smiled against her neck, deliberately pulling back, lightly tracing his fingers back down her legs. He moved away from her and she opened her eyes.

"I'm not going anywhere, Empress," he said with a wicked smile. "I merely want a better look."

He had lifted her skirts even higher before she fully comprehended the meaning of his words and struggled to sit up. "No . . ." she said, embarrassed by the very idea that he might want to *see* such an intimate place.

He reached up, running one hand to the back of her neck and pulling her toward him for a searing kiss. When she had softened against him once more, he released her from the caress and said, "Oh, yes, Empress."

He pushed her skirts high on her legs and gently parted her thighs once more, running his strong, knowing hands along the skin there. "So smooth and soft," he murmured, placing soft, wet kisses on the inside of one knee and following a warm, wicked path up her leg, coaxing her open once more. Callie closed her eyes against the vision of him moving so sinfully against her, but could not help but open for him when he asked—she was entirely under his control, a victim of his passionate assault.

When he reached the junction of her thighs, he pulled back, marveling at the dark, glistening curls that shielded her sex. Brushing his fingers lightly against the soft down, he sent a shock of sensation through her. Her eyes opened, and she met his heavy-lidded gaze. He spoke, his voice coursing through her as his fingers played at her entrance. "I've imagined this moment, late at night, in the privacy of my bedchamber. I've thought of you, like this, open to me . . . entirely mine."

The words sent a flood of liquid fire through her.

"I've imagined touching you like this . . . opening you, caressing you . . ." As he spoke, his actions mirrored his words, parting the delicate folds of her sex, stroking her wet heat. She gasped at the sensation, lifting her hips toward him, silently pleading for more. He circled the firm nub of her sex gently with the tip of his finger and watched as a shock of feeling coursed through her.

She moved toward him again, but this time he let his hands slide away from her . . . from the place where the world seemed to begin and end, and she cried out her disapproval. For a moment, she thought he would end it there, but instead he set his lips softly to the spot where her thigh and torso met.

When he lifted his head from the kiss, he said, "Do you touch yourself, lovely?" He ran his finger through the wet heat of her.

Callie squeezed her eyes shut at the question . . . she couldn't speak . . . couldn't answer him . . . couldn't meet his gaze, dark with restrained passion. But he would not allow her to escape.

"Empress," the nickname coaxed, as a single finger played at the entrance to her. "Answer me. Do you?" The words were barely a whisper, a lush, wanton sound that she couldn't possibly respond to. That she couldn't possibly *not* respond to.

She nodded, catching her lip in her teeth on a tiny whimper, the color raging across her cheeks a mixture of passion and embarrassment as his white teeth flashed and his fingers resumed their unbearable stroking.

"Here?" The word was a breath of sound, brushing against the sensitive skin of her thighs as he inserted a finger deep within her, and set his thumb to the tight place that set her aflame. "Do you touch yourself here?"

She gasped her reply. "Yes!"

A second finger joined the first, rubbing against the very heart of her, sending bolts of pleasure through her body—which was no longer her own to control. It was his. *As she had always known it would be.*

"What do you think about when you touch yourself here?" The words were spoken against her skin as he kissed across her torso toward the place where his hands were robbing her of thought. She bit her lip—she couldn't tell him—couldn't answer.

He placed a soft kiss on her rounded belly, looking up at her. "Empress . . ." His tone was cajoling, making her want nothing more than to tell him anything—everything.

His fingers delved deep, thrusting and stroking against her, his thumb circling the little button of fire that made her blood rush. She arched toward him, eager for more as his fingers retreated. Opening her legs wider, she whimpered at the loss of him, only to gasp when he blew on the soft hair that covered her mound, sending all coherent thought from her head.

"Lovely . . ." His tone was lazy; if it weren't for his harsh breathing, she would have thought he was unmoved by the situation.

His thumbs separated the folds guarding the heart of her and,

for a moment, she struggled, embarrassed by his actions, morti-
fied by his interest as he dragged his gaze up her body to meet
hers—his piercing blue eyes held a promise that she did not fully
understand, but for which she was desperate.

"Callie . . ." His breath hit the heart of her, hot and intense.

"I—" Words escaped her as he blew firmly on her—a cool
stream of air teasing the exact place where her pleasure seemed to
pool. She gasped. He was killing her.

"Who do you think of?"

She couldn't bear it.

"You."

The word ended on a cry as his mouth rewarded her for her
honesty. The sensation of his mouth on her turned Callie inside
out. Her hands plunged into his hair as his tongue stroked, laving the soft, moist skin of her inner lips, tasting her wet heat
with tiny circular movements that threatened to rob her of breath
and sanity. She sighed at the pleasure he wrought, lifting against
him, boldly asking for more even as she felt a wave of embarrassment course through her.

When his tongue found the swollen, aching nub at the center
of her and circled it firmly, sending a wave of pleasure through
her, Callie cried out his name and grasped his shoulders, in a twin
attempt to push him away and lift toward him. In response, he
grasped her hips firmly, holding her still as his lips closed tightly
around the secret place, and he sucked, bringing her to the brink
of pleasure with his lush, knowing mouth.

"No . . ." Callie panted, shaking her head against the powerful
feelings coursing through her, "Gabriel . . . stop . . ."

He ignored her, licking more firmly, sucking more deeply, moving one hand to thrust a knowing finger deep inside her to coax
forth more of her sweet rain. And then, as though he knew precisely what her body needed, he began to move faster, his fingers

and tongue in perfect unison, chasing away all rational thought, bringing with them a wave of passion and unfathomable pleasure. Just when she thought she couldn't bear any more, the wave crested, and Callie shattered, unable to do anything but give herself up to the sensation, pulsing against him, crying out his name as the world tumbled down around her.

His mouth softened against her, his fingers stilling as she regained awareness of the day, of the room. He lifted his head, watching her intently as she opened her eyes and met his gaze, filled with passion and satisfaction and something else she couldn't identify. Stretching toward her, he took her mouth with a dark intensity that she did not recognize; the kiss felt more brand than caress.

Pulling away, he spoke, his voice harsh. "You do want me."

The words pierced through the haze of emotion that had consumed her, and she stiffened immediately. With vivid clarity, she recognized the meaning in his words. It was not passion that had driven him to make love to her in his study in broad daylight, but rather a need to prove himself and his prowess. This was nothing more than a competition; she was nothing more than a prize to be won.

He didn't want her . . . *of course he didn't. She was plain and missish.*

The thought sent a vicious chill through her, and Callie sprang into motion, pushing at him with all her might, knocking him off-balance, suddenly desperate to get away from his mouth and hands and heat. She stood, haphazardly setting her skirts to rights as she stumbled past him and hurried toward the door of the room, putting distance between them.

"Callie—" he said, standing and following her. She turned at her name and, surprised to see him so near, she held one hand out as though she could stop him from coming closer. As though she could prevent him from becoming too deeply entrenched in her heart. *As though it weren't too late for that.*

Hair mussed, cravat untangled, waistcoat unbuttoned, Ralston appeared every inch the portrait of debauchery. In that moment, there was no question that Gabriel St. John, the Marquess of Ralston, was a rake of the highest caliber. He'd likely had this very interlude with countless other women—likely to prove the same point. Callie shook her head, disappointed in herself. She so obviously meant nothing to him. *How could she not have seen that?*

Because you didn't want to see it. You're Selene. Doomed to love a mortal in eternal sleep. She closed her eyes at the thought, willing the tears not to come. At least, not until she was out of the room. Out of his house.

He raised an arrogant brow, his harsh breathing echoing around them. "Do you deny it?"

Hurt flared, and she could no longer hide it. When she spoke, her voice was small. "I don't deny it. It's always been you."

She watched him react to the words, watched him register the truth in them. And then she said, "I just wish it were anyone else." And with that, she turned and—pride be damned—she fled.

He watched her go, unmoving. When he heard the main door to the house close, signaling her exit, he swore roundly, the vicious sound echoing around the room.

MUCH LATER, RALSTON sat at his piano, willing the instrument to perform the task it had done throughout his life—to help him to forget. He played with rigor—with a strength that brought unbridled sound from the instrument. The notes came fast and furious, his fingers flying across the keys as he closed his eyes and waited for the music to drive Callie from his mind. *It's always been you.*

The music enveloped him, dark and venomous, stinging his senses as he lingered at the keys in the lower register, pouring his emotion into his playing. The sound, aching and lyric, punished him, reminding again and again of Callie's expression, so wounded, so pained, just before she had escaped the house. Before she had escaped him.

I just wish it were anyone else.

He swore, and the sound was swallowed up by the piano. Her cool response to him—so very deserved—had nevertheless left him consumed with a desire to possess her. To brand her his own.

He'd pushed her to the limits of her awareness of herself, of her body, of her emotions. He'd known what he was doing; he'd sensed that he was going too far. But he couldn't have stopped if he'd wanted to. He'd been just as entangled in the moment as she had been. The king himself could have entered the study, and Ralston would have been hard-pressed to stop.

The truth of it shocked him, and his fingers paused on the piano keys. He shook his head, as if he could clear it of her memory. What was it about this woman? This plain, unassuming woman whom he had never before noticed? *There is nothing about her that is plain or unassuming now.*

And he hated himself for describing her as such.

No . . . Lady Calpurnia Hartwell was coming into her own in a spectacular way—entirely new and thoroughly different from every woman he had known before her. And it was her heady combination of innocent curiosity and feminine will that had lured him into behaving the way he did.

He wanted her. Viscerally. In a way he'd never wanted any woman before her.

Of course, he could not have her.

Nick had been right; Callie wanted love. Ralston had known that from the very beginning—she didn't hide her belief in the power of the emotion, her unwavering faith in it. He paused in his playing, wondering what it would feel like to believe so strongly in the power of love to do good. To bring happiness.

He shook his head, bowing low over the keys of the piano. He'd never seen that side of love. He'd only seen the pain it wrought, the soul-crushing devastation that came when it was rescinded. A memory flashed, of his father professing his undying love for his wife. A wife who walked out on her duties as wife and mother without ever looking back. Twice.

So much for love everlasting.

He swore roundly. He might not agree with Callie's assessment of love, but it did not mean that he had the right to treat her so unconscionably. He would not deny the pleasure he'd felt with her in his arms that afternoon, but he did admit his behavior was unacceptable. She deserved infinitely better.

He would apologize. Even if he did not regret his actions in the slightest.

He continued to play, the notes growing slower, more contemplative, reflecting the mood of their master.

Minutes later, a knock sounded, and Ralston stopped playing, turning on the piano bench to face the door. For a fleeting moment, he wondered if it was possible that Callie had returned, that it was she outside the door, waiting for him to allow her entrance.

"Enter."

The door opened and he registered the woman who stood silhouetted in the bright lights of the hallway beyond. His sister.

He seemed inundated with females deserving of his apology.

"Juliana, come in." He stood, reaching for a tinderbox and making quick work of lighting a candelabra nearby and waving her in the direction of a chair near the room's large fireplace. "I had not noticed that it had grown so dark."

"It is quite late," Juliana said quietly, taking her seat and waiting while he lit several more candles and seated himself across from her. When she opened her mouth to speak, he stayed her words with a raised hand.

"Please, allow me to apologize." Her eyes widened as he added, "I should not have lost my temper."

A smile flashed. "It appears that the loss of temper is yet another something we have in common, brother."

One side of his mouth kicked up. "So it does."

Juliana sighed, relaxing into her chair. "I have come to *fare la pace.*"

Gabriel extended his legs, leaning back with a smile at his sister's Italian. "I would very much enjoy making peace."

She extended a large parcel wrapped in brown paper. "In Italy, we have an expression, a gift after an argument—it is an olive branch."

He accepted the package. "It is the same in English."

She grinned. "It is nice to know that some things do not change."

"I should think you have had enough change recently."

She dipped her head. "As you say." Her gaze fell to the parcel. "Are you not curious about your gift?"

Gabriel looked down at the package, carefully wrapped and tied to best protect its contents, and he found he was filled with curiosity. How long had it been since he'd received a gift? A gift from someone who expected nothing in return? Looking back at his sister, he registered the expectant excitement on her face—her obvious hope that he would enjoy whatever was inside the simple, brown wrapping.

Yes. He was very curious.

He tore into the package, breaking the string that held the paper and shucking the wrapping. Turning the book over in his hands, he registered her thoughtfulness. "How did you know that I have a passion for Mozart?"

She smiled. "I have a bedchamber in this house, also. It is not difficult to recognize your favorite composer."

He ran his fingers across the leather-bound cover with reverence. "I shall begin reading it tonight." He met her eyes, all seriousness. "Thank you, Juliana."

She gave a small, shy smile. "You are welcome. I am happy that you like it."

"I do. Very much."

He marveled at the fact that this girl who had been through so much, who had found herself unceremoniously delivered to the doorstep of a complete stranger two countries away, would have thought to purchase a gift for him.

"I do not have a gift for you."

She laughed. "Of course you do not. Why would you?" When he seemed unable to find a decent response, she added, "We are family. This is what family does, is it not?"

He paused for a moment, thinking. "Actually, I haven't any idea if this is what family does. It has been rather a long time since I've had anyone other than Nick."

Juliana considered his words. "Indeed. Well then. Shall we make a decision now that this is what family does? At least, *our* family?"

"That sounds like a capital idea."

Juliana clapped her hands quickly and grinned broadly. "Excellent!" She added in a casual tone, "Do you know, my lord, that I have always wanted a brother who would spoil me?"

He laughed at her feigned innocence. "Really? May I suggest you discuss that particular desire with Nick?"

Her eyes widened at his jest before she burst out laughing. "I think that is a marvelous plan!" Lowering her voice to a conspiratorial whisper, she said, "Do you think he will be very extravagant?"

"One can certainly hope so."

"Indeed, she can!"

They settled into companionable silence for a few long minutes, and Juliana watched as Gabriel leafed through his new book. Finally, he looked up, and said, "When did you find time to purchase this?"

Juliana waved one hand in the air, and said, "Several weeks ago, Callie and Mariana and I were on Bond Street and discovered a bookshop there—that book came highly recommended—and Callie seemed to think that it would make an excellent gift for you."

He stiffened at the mention of Callie. "Did she?"

Juliana nodded, "I find she gives excellent counsel." When he shifted in his chair and said nothing, her eyes narrowed perceptively, and she said, "You look guilty, brother."

Gabriel looked away, eyes focusing on the candelabra he had set nearby earlier. "I did rather an excellent job of running her off earlier. I imagine she is quite . . . vexed with me at the moment."

"Ah," she said, knowing and teasing in her tone. "You are saying that Monsieur Latuffe was not the only *idiota* in the room this afternoon."

One side of Ralston's mouth twitched in chagrin. "No. It appears not." He relaxed into his chair. "Do you know, I do not think that anyone has ever spoken to me such?"

A smile flashed. "You are long overdue for a sister, my lord."

He considered her words. "I think you may be right."

"Callie, she is different from other women," Juliana said, entirely overstepping her bounds. "She is so willing to do what she must to make a situation right."

A vision flashed, Callie standing in the doorway of his study, so obviously hurt by the words she had overheard and yet so willing to defend Juliana to him—to tell him precisely where he had overstepped the bounds of brotherhood. As though her personal pride were somehow less important than Juliana's happiness.

When he turned his attention back to his sister, she was looking at him with a knowing gaze. "I see you have noticed the same."

"Yes. She is quite remarkable."

"Perhaps you should apologize for your . . ." She waved one hand, searching for the word.

"Idiocy?"

She smiled. "If you like."

He shifted in his chair, resting one leg over the other, and they grew quiet once more, each lost in thought. Finally, Gabriel spoke up, "Do you enjoy art?"

She looked up, curious. "I do."

"I should very much like to take you to the Royal Art Exhibition." He lifted his book. "To thank you for the gift."

"You do not have to thank me for the gift. Remember? This is what our family does."

He inclined his head. "Then, I would like for our family also to attend the Royal Art Exhibition."

"Ah, well then. If you are going to make a rule of it . . . I suppose I have no choice but to accept your invitation."

He laughed. "How very magnanimous of you."

"I thought so."

Gabriel leaned forward with a smile. "You know, Juliana, I think you may be long overdue for a brother."

Juliana tilted her head again, in a gesture he was coming to find rather endearing. "I think you may be right."

Sixteen

Callie alighted from the Rivington coach at the front of Somerset House and turned back to meet Mariana's smile as her sister followed her down from the carriage. The sisters were immediately surrounded by throngs of people, all scrambling for entrance to the private viewing of the Royal Academy of Art Exhibition, one of the most sought-after invitations of the season.

She watched as Mariana took Rivington's arm with a loving look, allowing the duke to guide her up the wide marble steps to the entrance of Somerset House, where the exhibition was already under way. Callie suppressed a little sigh at the obvious adoration between the two.

"My lady?"

Callie started at the words, turning to her own companion, Baron Oxford.

"Shall we?"

Callie pasted a bright smile on her face and took his offered arm. "Indeed, my lord."

They followed Mariana and Rivington up the wide entryway to the gallery, refusing to allow Oxford's odd behavior to mar the events of the afternoon. The Royal Exhibition had always been one of Callie's favorite activities of the season, as it gave Londoners a rare look at the work of the country's most revered contemporary artists. Callie loved art, and made it a point never to miss an exhibition.

"I have heard that we might see the most recent Blake etchings today, my lord," she offered as she climbed the steps.

Oxford gave her a strange look before asking disbelievingly, "You aren't really here to see the art, are you?"

Callie's confusion showed. "Certainly. I very much enjoy the fine arts. You do not?"

"I like a pretty painting as much as the next chap," Oxford said. "But no one really comes to the private viewing to see the art, Lady Calpurnia. It's about proving you are able to secure a ticket."

Callie dipped her head to keep the baron from seeing her roll her eyes. "Oh, yes. Well that is an impressive feat as well."

"Have you ever been here before?" Oxford asked, a boast already in his voice.

Callie hedged, uncertain of whether she should answer truthfully. She didn't have to.

Mariana, who had been waiting with Rivington for Callie and Oxford to catch up to them, stepped in and answered for her. "Our father was a trustee of the Royal Academy, Baron Oxford. This is one of Callie's favorite days of the year."

"Truly? I hadn't thought you would be such an . . . academic." The word sounded foreign on his tongue.

"Oh, Callie's quite brilliant when it comes to art. You should hear her speak about the Renaissance." Mariana turned a bright smile on the baron before continuing, "You don't mind if I steal my darling sister away, do you? I see a Pearce that we've been longing to have a look at."

With that, Mariana clasped Callie's arm and whisked her

through the crush of people, away from their escorts. "Ugh. He's insufferable! What on earth possessed you to accept his invitation?"

"He extended an invitation, Mari. In case you hadn't noticed, I'm not in a position to refuse them." She paused. "Besides, he's not as bad as all that."

"He's an imbecile. And a drunk," Mariana said frankly before smiling broadly in acknowledgment of the Viscountess Longwell, who tipped her head in response as they passed her. "For goodness sake, you're willing to dress as a man and sneak into Benedick's fencing club, but you won't turn down *Oxford*?"

"Shh!" Callie looked around to be certain that Mariana hadn't been heard. "Are you addled, mentioning that here? The fact is that I accepted Oxford's invitation. And now we're being rather rude."

"Pshaw. Rivington will entertain him." Mariana was distracted, standing on her toes, craning to see above the crowds. "You don't see Juliana, do you?"

Callie froze. "Juliana Fiori?"

Mariana gave Callie an odd look. "Yes, Calpurnia. Juliana Fiori. Which other Juliana would I be looking for?"

"I didn't know she was going to be here."

"Mmm," Mariana said, looking about. "Apparently Ralston offered to bring her. I promised her we wouldn't see Blake's *Jerusalem* without her."

Callie opened her mouth to speak, uncertain of what to say, only sure that she would have no choice but to leave the exhibition before she ran into Ralston. She couldn't see him. Couldn't be in the same room with him. It didn't matter that half of London would be there as well. Callie began to feel panicked.

"Ah . . . here are the ladies for whom we've been searching." Callie and Mariana whirled to face Oxford and Rivington. Oxford captured Callie's gaze and flashed a brilliant smile. "You left us, but we are excellent at tracking our prey."

"Indeed, it appears so, my lord." This afternoon was growing more and more odd. She should have remained home. That much was clear.

"Lady Calpurnia, may I escort you to see some of the paintings in the North Gallery?"

"I—" For a fleeting moment, Callie considered refusing before realizing that an afternoon with Oxford would be infinitely less awkward than an afternoon spent avoiding Ralston. "I would enjoy that very much, my lord."

"Wonderful." He offered Callie his arm. She took it, and they were off across the main gallery toward the northern exit. As they walked, he said, "We shall have to seek out the Renaissance artists here today, shan't we?"

She bit her tongue, keeping herself from explaining that, as a contemporary exhibition, there were no Renaissance artists represented at the event. Instead, she smiled mutely and allowed the baron to guide her along. When they arrived at the slightly less crowded North Gallery, Oxford turned a bright smile on her, and, with a broad gesture, said, "What do you think?"

Callie smiled up at the baron, and said, politely, "It is an excellent exhibition this year, my lord. Thank you very much for escorting me."

He leaned closer. "Come now, Lady Calpurnia. Surely you have more to say than that." Pointing to a large portrait, he asked, "What of that one?"

Callie considered the painting, a rather forgiving likeness of the king, before saying, "I think that King George must have been very happy with it."

Oxford laughed. "How very diplomatic of you."

Callie laughed as well, considering the baron. Certainly, he was a dandy and rather vapid, but he seemed in possession of a good humor and a not-unpleasant countenance. She was surprised to find that she was rather enjoying herself.

Oxford leaned in to speak close to her ear. "I had hoped we would get a chance to be apart from your sister and Rivington."

Her eyebrows shot up at the words. "My lord?"

"I know," he said, misunderstanding her reticence. "It's hard to believe that this is happening." He ran a single finger discreetly down the length of her forearm, and his smile broadened as he leaned in once more. "But indeed it is happening to you, Lady Calpurnia."

"Baron Oxford," she said, quickly, searching for a distraction to save them both from embarrassment. "I thought we were going to seek out the Renaissance paintings? I do not see them here."

"Perhaps we should look for them in a quieter, more secluded locale?" he said, his voice low. *Was that whiskey on his breath?*

Callie hedged. "I wonder if they might be back in the main gallery?"

He paused, considering her words. "I understand. You are concerned that we might be observed."

She clung to the words. "Indeed, that is precisely my concern."

He flashed his white teeth in understanding. "Of course. Let's return to the main gallery and have a better look."

Who would have thought Oxford would be so understanding?

Callie was so surprised by his change in tack that she couldn't help her own brilliant smile. They made their way back to the main gallery and passed into the throng of people inside. Once in the crush, Callie was unable to keep from pressing up against Oxford, and as she did so, she felt one of his hands running down the back of her gown, dangerously familiar. Leaping away from his touch, Callie turned to him, hand to her throat, and said, "I am quite parched. I wonder if you would fetch me some lemonade while I find my sister?"

Oxford's eyes narrowed on her in a manner she could only assume was meant to appear concerned, and he said, "Of course."

"Oh, thank you, my lord," she said, attempting coquettishness.

She watched as he turned and disappeared into the crowd, the throngs of people swallowing him up as she took a deep breath and let it out slowly. This entire afternoon had been a mistake.

"I see you have Oxford eating from the palm of your hand." The dry words startled her, so close to her ear, and she stiffened in immediate recognition.

Willing herself to remain calm, she turned to face the speaker "Lord Ralston. What a surprise," she said, her tone in direct opposition to her words. She was, all of a sudden, very tired. Tired of sparring with Ralston, tired of outsmarting Oxford, tired of being there amidst London's most beautiful people. She wanted to go home.

"Lady Calpurnia," Ralston executed a short bow, "I had hoped that you would be here."

The words, and the implication that he'd sought her out, would have elated her months ago. Today, however, she wanted nothing more than to turn on her heel and run from him. Meeting his blue eyes served only to remind her of the embarrassment and pain that he had delivered her at their last meeting. Her heart constricted at the thought of having another conversation with him, knowing that she was little more than a pawn in some game she did not understand.

She could not summon graciousness. "While I'm certain that's not entirely true, you knew I would be here. You were there when Oxford extended the invitation."

"So I was." He inclined his head as if to give her a point in their verbal game. "Nevertheless, I had hoped to see you this afternoon. Although I confess I was rather disheartened to see you smiling up at Oxford as though he were the only man in attendance."

She refused to give him the pleasure of knowing the truth. "The baron has been most accommodating."

"Accommodating," Ralston tested the word. "Makes him sound rather like furniture, doesn't it?"

She did not hide her exasperation. "Is there something you wanted, my lord?"

"An intriguing question," he said, enigmatically, before adding, "I should like to speak with you."

All of a sudden, Oxford seemed rather the lesser of two evils. "Now is not an ideal time. Perhaps another day? I am here with an escort." She turned purposefully, eager to make a quick exit.

"It appears that your escort has left you to your own defenses," Ralston pointed out wryly. "I couldn't very well allow you to navigate this crush alone. It wouldn't be at all gentlemanly."

Frustration flared. *Could he not just leave her alone?* Callie narrowed her gaze. "Yes, well, certainly you wouldn't want to appear less than *gentlemanly*." The slight emphasis on the word spoke volumes. "You needn't worry, my lord. I am certain that the baron will return presently."

"In this crowd? I wouldn't wager good money on it," he said, his tone dry.

The man was thoroughly exasperating. Callie made to escape him only to find herself unable to escape for the crush of people around them. She stamped her foot, irritated, and turned back to him. "You did this on purpose," she said, peevishly.

"You think I orchestrated these throngs to ensnare you?"

"I wouldn't doubt it."

"You entirely misjudge my power over the *ton,* Empress."

She flushed at the nickname, so intimate, before whispering. "Don't call me that."

He took hold of her elbow and guided her into the West Gallery. She protested his forcing her to follow him briefly, before she realized that removing herself from his grasp was liable to get them both noticed and set tongues wagging.

Once within the side gallery, he released her elbow but guided her to the far end of the room, through the clusters of people viewing the paintings hanging on every inch of wall to a large screen that cordoned off a piece of the enormous room.

"Where are you taking me?" she whispered, darting glances at the crowds of people surrounding them—all of whom seemed oblivious to her abduction.

He pushed her behind the screen, following her into the quiet alcove, and they were alone again. Callie was once more consumed by emotion, equal parts excitement and fear. The enormous mahogany screen had been set several feet from the wall of west-facing windows to block the sun from obstructing the views of the paintings. The screen reached far above their heads, creating a pool of brilliant sunlight and muffling the sound of the exhibition beyond.

The perfect place for a lovers' tryst. Callie pushed the thought from her head and summoned the anger and hurt that she'd been feeling in the days since her last interaction with Ralston. She could not let him have the upper hand. Not here. "Are you mad?" she whispered, irritated.

"No one saw," Ralston said.

"How could you know that?"

"Because I know." He reached out a hand to touch her face.

She flinched from his touch. "Don't touch me."

Emotion flashed in his eyes at her movement, there, then gone before she could define it. "I would never do anything to damage your reputation, Callie." The words were honest.

"Forgive me, my lord, but it rather seems that everything you do near me is a risk to my reputation." She lashed out, desperate to hurt him, eager for him to feel the pain that she had felt for the days since she'd seen him last.

One side of Ralston's mouth lifted. "I deserved that."

"And much more." She met his eyes boldly. "I told you that afternoon in your ballroom, my lord, I'm through with these interludes. And with you. You have quite extraordinarily misinterpreted my interest. Now, if you'll excuse me, Baron Oxford will be searching for me."

"You can't really be serious about Oxford."

She ignored him, instead moving to pass him and escape around the edge of the screen into the room beyond. He captured her hand as she pushed past, and the touch stopped her. He did not hold her firmly enough that she couldn't extricate herself from his grasp, but the heat of his gloved hand against her own made her look back at him, forced her to meet his eyes.

In that moment, the only thing he wanted was for her to stay with him. For her to forgive him. He'd arrived with Juliana, ready to find Callie and apologize for his boorish behavior—ready to do whatever it took to repair the obvious hurt that he had caused. And he'd located her almost immediately, beaming up at Oxford, clearly having a lovely time, as the pair had reentered the main gallery. The sight had infuriated him—Callie so lovely and happy, Oxford so foppish and simple.

She'd never smiled so openly at Ralston. And if she were to do so, he certainly wouldn't respond as Oxford had, the fool, walking away from her. No. If she ever looked at him in such a way, he'd sweep her into his arms and kiss her senseless. Hang the Royal Art Exhibition.

Hell. He wanted to kiss her senseless right then, and she certainly wasn't smiling at him.

He'd find a way to repair the damage he'd caused. But first, he had to eliminate Oxford from the equation. The stupid wager that he'd made with the ridiculous baron, was just that—stupid. Ralston now understood that he'd done nothing but taunt Oxford into proving his ability to win Callie; he was not going to give up the chase for Callie. Particularly not with one thousand pounds riding on its outcome.

"Don't get attached to Oxford," Ralston said.

"Whyever not?" Her words taunted him.

"He's a gold digger with the intelligence of a goat."

"Of course he is," she said, simply, as though he had just proclaimed the sky blue.

His brow furrowed. "Then why come here with him?"

"Because he asked."

The answer, so obvious, frustrated him. He ran a hand through his hair before pointing out, "That shouldn't be enough, Callie. For God's sake."

She smiled then, a sad, small smile that set him on edge. "You're right. It shouldn't be enough."

He felt a strange pressure in his chest at the words and, in that moment, the decision was made. Oxford couldn't have her. Ralston wouldn't allow it.

Their gazes locked for several long moments before she moved to pull her hand from his, and he found that he could not let her go. His fingers tightened around hers, unyielding. She looked to him with surprise.

"Let me take you somewhere," he said.

"My lord?"

"Where would you like to go? Surely you'll afford me the same opportunity you've given Oxford."

"It's not a competition." The words were quiet, and he sensed an underlying meaning in them that he didn't entirely understand.

Ignoring that for a moment, he repeated, "Let me take you somewhere. You choose. The theater again. A picnic with Mariana and Rivington. A damn carriage ride."

She thought for a moment. "I don't want your escort to any of those places."

"Why not?"

"I am turning over a new leaf. Nowhere plain. Nowhere missish."

He felt the words like a blow, immediately recognizing the hurtful words as his own. Damn it. *What could he say to make it right?* He ran another hand through his dark hair, setting several thick locks loose. Suddenly, the conversation seemed one of the most important he'd ever had.

"God, Callie, I'm sorry. Give me a chance to prove that I'm not entirely a cad and an imbecile."

"I don't think you are an imbecile."

"I note you did not refute the other claim," he said, with a crooked smile. "Anything you want."

She gave a frustrated sigh, looking anywhere but directly at him. Her eyes settled on their entwined hands before she met his gaze again. "Anything?"

His eyes narrowed as understanding dawned. "You're thinking about your damned list, aren't you?"

"Well, you did request I refrain from completing any other items on the list without your escort."

"Indeed, I did."

"I could always ask Oxford . . ." She trailed off deliberately, coaxing a half laugh from him.

"You are learning to play me quite well, Minx. Fine. We shall complete another item on your list. Which shall it be?"

She thought for a moment, worrying her lower lip. The action served to draw Ralston's attention away from the conversation for a brief moment, as he considered kissing her to stop the nervous habit. For a moment, he was lost in the memory of the sweetness of her mouth, the softness of her lips, the wild abandon with which she met him at every turn. He felt himself harden at the thought, and was mere seconds from taking her mouth again when her lips formed a single word.

"Gambling."

His eyebrows shot up, and he shook his head as though to clear it. Surely she hadn't just said—"Gambling?"

She nodded eagerly. "Yes. Gambling. In a gentleman's club."

He laughed. "You can't be serious."

"Indeed, I am, my lord."

"You just asked me to smuggle you into Brooks's, Callie. I think we're rather past the point where you need stand on titular ceremony."

She offered a small smile. "Very well, Gabriel. I should like you to take me gambling. At your club."

"No woman has ever breached the defenses of Brooks's, Callie—"

She interrupted him dryly, "I find that rather difficult to believe."

"Very well, no *gentlewoman* has ever breached the club's defenses. I would be exiled from its ranks if we were discovered." He shook his head firmly before continuing. "May I talk you into a game of *vingt-et-un* at Ralston House instead? We shall play for money. I can assure you the experience will be quite the same."

"I don't think it would be the same at all, actually," Callie speculated. "Part of the draw of this item is the experience of the club itself."

"Whatever for?" He was genuinely baffled.

She paused, changing tack. "Have you ever wondered what it is that women do behind closed doors at teas and after dinners? What we talk about, how we live without you?"

"No."

"Of course not. Because our lives are out in the open. We may be alone in a room, sequestered from men, but you own the houses in which we congregate, you've been in the rooms in which we cloister ourselves. There is always the possibility that you might enter, and so we set ourselves to needlepoint or idle gossip and never allow ourselves to say or do too much beyond the bounds of propriety, for fear that you might see.

"It's different for you," she pressed on, growing more impassioned as she spoke. "Men have these secret locations . . . taverns and sporting clubs and men's clubs. And there you can do and feel and experience anything you'd like. Far from the prying eyes of women."

"Exactly," he said, "which is why I cannot take you to Brooks's."

"Why should you be the only ones to have that kind of freedom? Why do you think I've got the list at all? I want to experience that sense of freedom. I want to see this secret place—this inner sanctum where men really can be men."

He didn't answer, not entirely sure how to handle this new, strong-willed stranger. "Callie," Ralston said quietly, firmly, in an attempt to bring reason to the discussion, "if you were caught, it would be the end of you. Gambling is one thing. But . . . at Brooks's?"

"Is the great Marquess of Ralston afraid of what might happen if he takes such a risk? The same man who once compromised a Prussian princess in Hyde Park?"

He blinked. "I did no such thing."

Callie couldn't help the little smile that flashed. "Ah, so we finally discover a legend that is not grounded in reality." His eyes narrowed on her as she pulled herself up to her full height and, with all the pride of a queen, said, "I don't need you, you know. I can sneak into White's on my own—using a letter of invitation from Benedick."

Gabriel gave her a look of disbelief. "He'd never write it."

"He doesn't have to," she said, matter-of-factly, "I sneaked into his fencing club without issue."

"And you needed *me* to shepherd you out of there!" he said, a touch louder than was ideal for their clandestine location.

"Are you saying you won't take me?"

"I am."

"A pity. I had looked forward to your escort."

He shook his head, dumbfounded. "You cannot do this."

"Why? Because I'm a woman?"

"No! Because you're mad! You will be caught!"

"I haven't been caught yet."

"I've caught you! Twice!"

"As I've said before," she scoffed, "you're different."

"How am I different?" his exasperation was clear.

"Well, it seems you are my partner in crime." She smiled then, a beaming grin not unlike the one he'd seen her give Oxford earlier.

He lost his bluster at the words, feeling the full force of her pleasure like a blow, and a nonsensical wave of pride coursed through him . . . pride at being the one she would turn to with such excitement, pride at being the one she would ask to escort her on such an adventure. And, in that sun-filled moment, with all of London mere inches away from their hiding place, he was struck by her beauty—her bright brown eyes and her hair, gleaming auburn in the light and her mouth, wide and welcoming and enough to bring a man to his knees.

She was really quite extraordinary.

The revelation made it difficult to breathe, so intense was the truth of it. "My God. You're lovely."

Her eyes widened in shock as she processed the words, then narrowed suspiciously. "Don't try to throw me off course with your compliments."

"I wouldn't dream of it."

"Because I'm doing this. I'm gambling. I won't be distracted from my purpose."

"Of course not."

"Certainly telling me that I'm—Well, that I'm—"

"Lovely."

"Yes. That. It won't deter me."

"I didn't mean it to."

"I'm not a fool, you know."

He took a step closer to her. "I know. I shall take you."

"Even if you won't take me—" She stopped. "I beg your pardon?"

"I said I would take you."

"Oh. Well. Then."

"Yes, I thought it was rather magnanimous of me." He lifted a finger and tucked an errant lock of hair behind one of her ears.

"I'm not lovely," she blurted out.

One side of his mouth kicked up. "Now, there," he said quietly, searching her face as if to memorize this new Callie, whom he'd just discovered, "I shall have to disagree."

And then he set his lips to hers and she was drugged by his caress and his words, both equally intoxicating. This kiss was different from all that they had shared before—softer, seeking, as though they were both discovering something altogether new. This was a concert of stroking tongue and soft lips. Gabriel lifted his head and waited for her to open her eyes; when she did, he was struck once more by her loveliness. He searched her face, watching as she returned from the sensual place where the kiss had taken her.

"You said I was plain."

He shook his head slowly, marveling at the clear, brown depths of emotion in her eyes. "There is nothing plain about you." And then, he kissed her again.

Her mouth was his banquet. He sipped at her lips, savoring their taste, their softness. Her hands found their way around his neck and into his hair—threading through the dark locks. The caress sent a shiver of pleasure through him. He ate at her, nibbling at her lips before gently laving the worried skin there with his tongue. When he pulled away and met her eyes once more, they were both breathing heavily, and Gabriel was wishing that they were anywhere but here, hundreds of Londoners mere feet away.

He had to stop. He was about to do exactly what he had resolved not to do. Had he not promised himself that he would not compromise her again? He owed her more. Better.

A vision flashed in his mind of Callie naked, spread before him in a pool of sunlight, and he pushed it aside. This was no time to indulge in fantasies that would further arouse him—as it was, his excitement was embarrassingly obvious in his breeches. Reaching up, he unwound Callie's arms from around his neck, kissing the knuckles on both hands before meeting her gaze once more.

"I owe you an apology."

Her brow furrowed. "I beg your pardon?"

He set a soft kiss to her forehead, smoothing the lines there, pulling her tightly into his arms before continuing. "An apology. For everything. For the afternoon at Ralston House, for the fencing club, God, Callie, for this afternoon, even. I have treated you quite abominably, nearly compromising you at every turn. And—I should apologize."

Callie blinked up at him, the sunlight pooling around her, turning her flushed skin the perfect shade of pink. When she did not speak, he said, "I should like to make it all up to you. I think taking you to Brooks's would be a start."

A shadow crossed Callie's face fleetingly—as though she were disappointed—and then it was gone.

Ralston pressed on. "I shall take you tonight."

"Tonight?"

"Unless you have plans to spend the evening with Oxford as well?" he said, coolly.

"No . . . I was to attend the Cavendish Ball, however. I shall have to beg off." She avoided his gaze.

"That would be ideal. If we go while the ball is in full cry, it will make the whole procedure much easier."

"What shall I wear?" she asked quietly.

A memory flashed of Callie dressed in men's clothing, wearing only tight-fitting fencing breeches, her breasts unbound and pressed against him, her skin flushed with pleasure. Feeling his own breeches tighten, he shifted uncomfortably before saying, "I suppose you're going to have to dress in men's clothing. Do you have something appropriate for a club? Or will you be wearing your fencing suit?"

She blushed at his teasing before shaking her head. "No. I have something more appropriate."

Of course she did. He refrained from asking her when she'd had cause to wear something more appropriate. *This was a terrible idea.*

Nonetheless, he'd given her his word. It was better that he escort her than someone else. Better him than Oxford. The thought of her clambering about in men's clothing with Oxford was enough to make him want to put his fist into the baron's face.

Eager to be rid of the vision of Callie and Oxford, Ralston moved to the edge of the screen, where he darted a quick glance into the room beyond to ensure they would not be seen returning from their hiding place. When he was certain they would remain unnoticed, he deftly guided her around the screen and into the main room, his pace indicating that she should attempt to appear casual as they walked through toward the main gallery. "Shall I meet you at Allendale House at half twelve?" he said, looking away from her but keeping his voice low enough that only she could hear.

She nodded. "That is an ideal time. Late enough that everyone will be at the ball, early enough not to run into them coming home." She looked up in surprise. "You're rather good at this."

He dipped his head as though accepting a compliment. "This isn't the first time I've planned a clandestine outing."

Her gaze skidded away. "No, I don't imagine it would be," she said quietly before she stopped in front of a large painting of a King Charles spaniel. She took a deep breath and continued, "The back entrance."

He gave a hint of a nod. "I made peace with Juliana." He did not know why he felt that he had to tell her, but he did.

Surprise flashed across her face, there and gone so quickly, he wasn't entirely certain it had been there at all. "I am happy to hear it. She is a good girl. And I believe she is coming to care for you deeply."

The words made him uncomfortable though he could not understand why.

Callie seemed to notice. "I am happy to hear it," she repeated.

He nodded once. "What do you think of this?" he asked, indicating the painting nearby.

She gave him an odd look. "I think it's an enormous painting of a dog."

He made a show of considering the picture and nodded seriously. "An astute observation." She gave a short laugh before he continued. "The visual arts have never been my specialty. I prefer to consider myself a connoisseur of music. As you know." The last words were spoken softly near her ear. They were meant to fluster her, to remind her of the evening in his bedchamber . . . of their first kiss. The strategy worked, and Ralston couldn't help the pleasure that shot through him at the sound of her breath catching.

"I think it best if I return to my sister," Callie said, her voice wavering slightly.

"I shall take you."

"No!" she said, a touch louder than she had planned. She paused, then continued. "I think I should go alone."

For a moment, he considered pressing the issue—forcing her to accept his escort. But he recognized a battle won when he saw one. "Indeed," he said, bowing low over her hand, before adding quietly, "Tonight, then?"

She met his gaze and held it for a long moment before she gave a small nod. "Tonight."

And then she was gone, swallowed up by the crowd.

Seventeen

$\mathcal{B}$y nine o'clock that evening, Callie was pacing her bedchamber and counting the hours until she could creep down
the back stairs and begin her next adventure. Her nerves had been
on edge since she'd escaped Ralston that afternoon. Between Oxford's constant talk of himself and odd advances toward her and
Mariana and Rivington's doting upon each other, the rest of the
exhibition had been interminable, not even seeing *Jerusalem* had
made it enjoyable.

Of course, being at home was even less diverting than being
at the Royal Academy. Callie had cloistered herself in her bedchamber immediately upon her return, crying headache to ensure
that her mother would allow her to forgo the plans to attend the
Cavendish Ball. Now she paced the little room, going quietly mad
in captivity.

She turned to the clock in the corner of the room, checking the
time once more. Ten past nine. She sighed, throwing herself onto
the bench under the bay window that overlooked the back gardens
of Allendale House.

If only Ralston hadn't made it abundantly clear that the interludes they had shared—the moments that had made her feel so alive and exhilarated—were a mistake.

She'd wanted the floor to open and swallow her whole when he'd ended their kiss and promptly apologized. While it might have been the gentlemanly thing to do, it certainly wasn't in Ralston's character to apologize unless he truly regretted his behavior.

Callie could only assume that he regretted ever getting involved with her—after all, a naïve spinster wasn't exactly the ideal companion for a first-rate rake.

But he'd called her lovely. She sighed again, pulling her legs up underneath her and playing the moment over in her mind. It had been exactly as wonderful as she'd imagined it would be— wonderful, handsome Ralston, the man she'd pined over for a decade, had finally noticed her. Not simply noticed her—said she was lovely.

And then he'd hauled off and apologized. For everything. She'd rather he'd never given her any attention at all than *regret* their time together.

Callie stood and went to the looking glass that stood in the corner of the room. Facing her reflection, she took herself in— Too-brown hair, too-brown eyes, too-short stature, too full a mouth, altogether unfashionably endowed with too-ample breasts and too-wide hips.

No wonder he'd apologized.

She sighed, wishing she could banish the memory of Ralston's earnest words, so forthright and gentlemanly that they made her want to spit.

Or cry.

She took a deep breath, willing away the stinging tears that hovered just behind her eyes. She would not cry on what was to become, she hoped, the most exciting night of her life. Exciting not because of Ralston . . . but because of her.

And a little because of Ralston.

Fine. And a very little because of Ralston. But mainly because of her.

She thought for a moment, attempting to divine whether gambling or Brooks's was more of a draw. It was impossible to decide. She would simply have to wait until she had firsthand experience. Which she would have in . . . she looked at the clock again. Twelve past nine. Was it possible that the timepiece was somehow broken? It couldn't possibly have been only two minutes since the last time she checked. She watched the hands on the clock face, waiting for the minute hand to move to thirteen minutes past. The wait was interminable. Yes. It was most definitely broken.

Callie spun on her heel and headed toward the door to the room, intending to sneak into the hallway beyond and check the actual time. Surely it was closer to eleven. She was going to have to get dressed quickly if she was going to be on time for Ralston. She had to call for Anne.

She'd barely taken a step toward the door when it flew open and Mariana burst in, closing it immediately behind her. The younger woman stood, arms akimbo, breathless—as though she had run for miles to be there.

With a quick glance to the pristine, unused bed, Mari speared Callie with a triumphant look, and said, "I knew it!" The words were spoken as though she had just invented the wheel. Or something equally world-changing.

Callie's eyes widened. "Knew what?"

Mariana pointed at her sister, her eyes flashing with excited accusation. "I knew you weren't ill!" She lowered her voice to a whisper. "You're going to complete another item on the list!"

Callie stood frozen for several long minutes before turning away and putting a hand to her head. She headed for bed. "Whyever would you think that? I was just getting up to call for one of Cook's remedies."

She spared a quick glance at Mariana, who was having none of it. "Cook's remedies?" she said, disbelief in her tone. "You could be on your deathbed and you wouldn't take one of Cook's remedies." Mari rushed to the bed and leapt upon it as though she were wearing a night rail and not a stunning silk ball gown. "What's tonight? Horse racing? Boxing? Snuff?"

Callie lay down on the bed and pulled a pillow over her face.

"I know! A brothel!"

Shocked, Callie thrust the pillow away from her face. "Mari! You are letting your imagination run wild. Of course I am not going to a brothel."

Mari's face fell. "Oh. That's a pity."

Callie leveled her sister with a wry look. "Yes. I'm sure it is. Nevertheless, I shan't be visiting any houses of ill repute tonight."

"But maybe another night?"

Callie shook her head. "It's quite extraordinary that you are mere months away from being a duchess."

Mari grinned and shrugged her shoulders in a supremely unladylike fashion. "Exactly! I shall be a duchess! Who will criticize me? Besides Mother, that is."

Callie met her sister's smile. "Aren't you going to be late for the ball?"

"I don't want to go. I want to go with you."

"I'm not going anywhere."

"You know it's a sin to lie," Mariana said, all seriousness.

"Fine. I am going somewhere, but you cannot come. If we both cry sick, Mother will know there is something amiss."

Mariana clapped her hands eagerly. "Where are you going?"

"What time is it?"

Mari's eyes narrowed. "Callie. Do not change the subject."

"I am not changing the subject! I just don't want to be late."

"It's twenty past nine."

Callie sighed and flopped back onto the bed. "This evening is *interminable!*"

"Callie!" Mariana said sharply, "Where are you going?"

Callie met her sister's eager gaze. "If half past twelve ever comes, I am going gambling."

Mari gasped. "No!"

Callie grinned. "Yes!"

"Are you going to a hell?"

"No . . . I thought it might be too easy to be caught there. I'm going to Brooks's."

Mariana froze. "Brooks's . . . as in, the men's club?"

Callie nodded, color flooding her cheeks.

"You think it will be more difficult to get caught at *Brooks's* than at a gaming hell?" Mariana shook her head in amazement. "You're mad."

"I'm not!"

"How are you ever going to . . . My God! Callie! Women aren't allowed at Brooks's! If you were caught . . ."

"I shan't be."

"How do you know?"

Callie paused, unsure of what to say. Mariana pressed on. "Callie."

"Ralston is taking me."

Mariana blinked twice. Callie waited for her sister to wrap her head around the announcement.

"The *Marquess* of Ralston?"

"The very same."

"You're going with *Ralston?*" If the words hadn't been so nerve-racking, Callie would have laughed at Mariana's squeaking voice. Instead, she worried the stitching on the blanket and nodded. "I knew it!" Mari crowed, triumphantly. "I knew it from the first time you waltzed! At my betrothal ball!"

"Mari! Hush! The whole house will hear you!" Callie whispered frantically.

"You'll be ruined if you're caught," Mariana announced, as though the idea had never crossed Callie's mind.

Callie nodded again in the silence that fell.

"Well, then. We shall have to be very careful to ensure that you are not caught." Callie took heart in Mariana's use of the word "we" as she pressed on. "It appears that you are excellently prepared for sneaking out of the house . . . but how are you planning to sneak back in?"

"I had thought to come back the same way—through the back door and up the servants' stairs."

Mariana shook her head. "It won't do. The upper doorway of those stairs squeaks horribly, and Mother will hear."

Callie considered her options. "I shall have to oil the hinges."

Mari nodded. "And watch the third step from the top. It creaks."

Callie narrowed her gaze on her sister. "How do you know that?"

"Let's simply say that Rivington and I have had need of those stairs once or twice."

Callie gave her sister a wide-eyed look. "Mariana!"

"It's a little late for *you* to be outraged. At least I'm *engaged* to Rivington!" Mariana teased. "You're meeting *Ralston* for a late-night rendezvous! My God! Promise me you'll tell me everything!"

"It's not a rendezvous," Callie protested. "He's merely helping me. We are . . . friends."

"Friends do not risk friends' reputations, Calpurnia." Mariana lowered her voice. "Have you and he . . ." She waved one hand as the question trailed off.

"Have we?" Callie pretended to misunderstand.

Mariana narrowed her gaze on her elder sister. "Callie. You know very well what I am asking."

Callie looked away. "I assure you I do not."

Mariana squealed with delight. "Yes! You do! And you *have*!" She clapped her hands. "How delicious!"

"It's not delicious."

Mariana's face fell. "Oh. What a pity. He looks as though he would be—"

"Mari!" Callie cut her off. "That's not what I meant."

"So it *is* delicious!"

Callie sighed. "It rather is."

Mari's grin was wide and wicked. "I would like to hear all about that."

"Well, you shan't. And this conversation is entirely inappropriate."

Mari waved one hand to dismiss Callie's prim statement. "You know that if you're caught together, you shall have to marry. Imagine the scandal!"

Callie closed her eyes tightly—it was only too easy to imagine the scandal. "I shan't be getting caught."

"MARIANA!!!!" Callie was saved from the embarrassing conversation by the Dowager Countess of Allendale's shrill call from belowstairs. Mariana rolled her eyes, and said, "My word that woman can screech. You should see what she's wearing, Callie. It's velvet. Canary yellow velvet. Turban to match. She looks like a furry banana."

Callie winced at the vivid image. "It's part of her charm."

"It's a miracle Rivington offered for me."

Callie smiled broadly at the dry comment. "Have fun."

Mari reached forward to give Callie a quick hug. "*You* are the one who will have fun! I shall be thinking of you all night long! Tomorrow, I want to hear everything! Promise me!"

"I promise."

Mariana stood, smoothed out her wrinkled skirts, and gave a little hop of excitement in Callie's direction before she took her leave. Callie followed her to the door, pressing her ear against the wood to listen for the sound of the family exiting the house before rushing to the window to listen for the clatter of hooves and wheels indicating their official departure for the ball. When she could no longer hear the carriage, she spun away from the window and called for Anne.

She had much to do before Ralston arrived.

Ten minutes before she was to meet her escort, Callie stole across the darkened Allendale gardens to the gate in the far wall. Opening the latch, she pulled the gate open, noting its screaming hinges. "Damn," she said, irritation in her voice. Was every hinge on the property in need of oiling?

Thanks to Mariana, however, Callie had expected that she might need the oil can Michael had fetched for her earlier that evening—without a single question as to her motives, bless him—and she had come prepared. Lifting the can in her hand, she soaked the hinge with the dark liquid, working the gate to spread the lubricant and silence the jarring noise. When she had completed her work with the top hinge, she turned her attention to the lower one.

She was so engrossed in her work that she did not hear Ralston approach.

"Now here is a gentleman of many talents," he said dryly, and she jumped in surprise at the words. Looking up at him from her crouch, she smiled before carefully adding drops of oil to the hinge and working the gate. He removed his gloves and crouched next to her, taking the oil can as he continued, "Of all the clandestine outings I've taken in my life, I will say that this is the first one that included oiling squeaky hinges."

She smiled at his casual tone. "I could not take the risk that I could be caught by my family should I return home after them."

He nodded, the movement barely perceptible in the darkness. "A clever precaution." Finishing his task, he set the oil can aside and removed a handkerchief from his pocket, wiping his hands on it and handing it to her to do the same. Rising, he reached down to help her into a standing position. He took a step back to survey her disguise. It wasn't easy to see, but this time she was wearing black and white eveningwear, entirely appropriate for the inside of Brooks's. Her boots shone in the moonlight, black breeches and black topcoat highlighting a crisp white shirt and waistcoat and a perfectly starched cravat. Anne was becoming quite adept at dressing her mistress in men's clothing. To complete the look, Callie's hair was tucked into a black top hat. Lifting her cane with a flourish, she asked in a low tone, "Well, my lord? What do you think?"

"I think that, though diminutive, you should pass just fine. Assuming the lights inside Brooks's are similar to those here. In your garden. In the dead of night." His lips set in a firm line as he considered her, then shook his head. "One would have to be an imbecile not to know you're a woman. This is going to be a disaster."

Pulling his gloves back on, Ralston began to walk the short distance to his coach. She followed, pointing out, "You didn't notice I was a woman in the fencing club."

He gave a noncommittal grunt.

"I find that people see what they *expect*, my lord, as opposed to what is there."

He opened the coach door and handed her up into the darkened interior. As she scrambled across the seat to make room for him, she could have sworn that she heard him say, "This was a terrible idea," before he joined her, pulling the door closed behind him and knocking on the roof to set the carriage in motion.

They rode in silence, Callie attempting to ignore Ralston's obvious second thoughts when it came to smuggling her into his club. She had come this far . . . she most certainly was not turning back. The drive wasn't far, and when the carriage arrived, Callie sat forward on her seat to get a better look out the window. As she pressed her face to the glass, Ralston produced a large greatcoat and handed it to her. "Here. Put this on."

"But, I—"

"This is not negotiable," he cut her off in a clipped tone. "It is my membership on the line if you get caught."

"Not to mention my reputation," she said under her breath.

He gave her a firm look. "Yes. Well, tonight I'm rather more concerned with my club. Put on the cloak; pull the collar up; keep your head down. Do not meet anyone's eye. Stay close to me. Do not look at anyone. And for God's sake don't use that ridiculous voice you think sounds manly."

"But, I—"

"No, Callie. I promised you I'd take you gambling at Brooks's. But I did not promise to do it your way."

She sighed. "Fine."

He opened the door and hopped out of the carriage, striding to the door of the club without giving her another glance. She watched for a moment, surprised that he so easily ignored his gentlemanly instincts—leaving her, instead, to fend for herself in alighting from the coach. She did so, slamming the door behind her.

The coach door banged shut with a too-loud crash, drawing attention from Ralston and several others on the street. As several heads spun toward her, Callie's tentative steps faltered. She met Ralston's brilliant blue gaze with her panicked brown one and watched as he raised one brow just enough for her to read his thoughts.

Are you quite finished?

She dipped her head, hiding her face in the ample collar of his greatcoat, and headed for him. When she was a few steps away, he entered the club, throwing the door open wide enough for her to catch it and follow him inside.

Callie's first thought upon crossing the threshold was that Brook's was stunning. She hadn't known what to expect, but it was not this. The wide marble entryway boasted the wealth and stature of the men who were members—all lovely planes and gilded edges.

She caught her breath at the space, outfitted like the finest London homes in deep masculine colors and rich woods. And there were men *everywhere*. They stood in little pockets of conversation in the foyer, acknowledging Ralston with quick nods as he passed through the large entryway and led Callie down a long corridor toward the back of the building. Trying to be discreet, she peeped into the rooms that stood open, some large and warmly lit, where clusters of men were engaged in billiards, cards, and discussion, and others, small and intimate, hosting just a handful of occupants who drank port and smoked.

Callie slowed down as she passed each doorway, cataloging the activities and those present inside, eager to absorb every bit of this mysterious, fascinating place. As Ralston led her deeper into the maze of corridors, the number of open doors dwindled and the hallway became darker and more quiet. As they passed one room, Callie noted the door was ajar and the room inside warm and golden with candlelight. She heard a distinctly feminine laugh from within, and she froze midstep, unable to help herself from taking a closer look.

Peering through the crack in the door, Callie's eyes widened as she took in the scene beyond. There were three men inside, each wearing a domino mask, each seated in one of three large leather chairs arranged in a tight circle. The men, though relaxed in their chairs, were transfixed by the woman who stood at the center of the cluster, tall and buxom, her hair cascading down her back in a luscious mane of ebony curls. She was stunning: high cheekbones, lovely skin, perfectly kohled eyes, pouting red lips curved in a wicked, knowing smile. Callie was transfixed by her—just as the men inside seemed to be—for it was obvious that the woman was a courtesan.

She wore a gown that was not for public view—a bold, sapphire silk with a tightly fitted bodice that appeared more corset than dress. Her breasts nearly spilled from the top of the dress as she bent low over one of the men. Callie held her breath as he reached out and grazed the side of one breast, his eyes transfixed on the woman's feminine bounty. She gave a low laugh as he touched her, boldly placing her hand over his and guiding him to touch her breast more firmly. He did as he was directed, and one of the other men reached for the hem of the courtesan's gown and began to raise it, baring long legs and, finally, her rounded bottom. Callie gasped quietly as he caressed the woman's behind.

The gasp turned into a little squeal as Ralston grabbed her arm and pulled her from the spot where she had been frozen. He growled close to her ear, "This is exactly why men's clubs are not for women."

"It appears that particular room is most definitely for women," she replied tartly.

He did not respond, instead guiding her into the next open doorway before closing and locking the door behind them. When she heard the lock click ominously in the silence, she whirled to face Ralston, who was glowering at her from his position—pressed against the closed door.

"Did I not make myself clear? You were to stay close to me and not to look at anyone."

"I didn't!"

"So you were not just peering into a room full of people?"

"I wouldn't call it *full*," Callie hedged. His gaze narrowed at her words. "It's not as if they saw me!"

"They could have!"

"They were rather busy," she pointed out. "Perhaps you could explain something to me?"

His gaze turned wary. "Perhaps."

"How is it that one woman is . . . enough . . . for three men?"

Ralston raised his eyes to the ceiling and made a choking sound. After a moment, he looked back at her. "I don't know."

She gave him a look of disbelief. "She must be a very talented courtesan."

He raked a hand through his hair before saying in a strangled tone, "Callie."

She plunged ahead, innocently, "Well, that was what she was. Wasn't it?"

"Yes."

"How very fascinating!" She smiled brightly. "I've never met a courtesan, you know."

"I could have surmised as such."

"She looked just as I imagined they did! Well, she was rather prettier."

Ralston's eyes darted around the room as though he was looking for the quickest escape route. "Callie. Wouldn't you rather gamble than talk about courtesans?"

She tilted her head, considering his question. "I don't really know . . . both things are worth the time, don't you think?"

"No," he said with a surprised laugh. "I don't."

Ignoring him, she took in the room around them. It was decorated with Grecian friezes depicting the gods and goddesses in a variety of different scenes, and furnished with a large card table and a collection of carved wooden chairs. At one side of the room, in front of a roaring fireplace, there was a seating area complete with two overstuffed chairs and a long chaise. The walls that did not boast the enormous pieces of marble artwork were lined with bookshelves. It was a comfortable, if masculine, room.

She turned back to Ralston. "Won't others be irritated that we've commandeered this room?"

Ralston removed his gloves and hat and placed them on a small table by the door. "I doubt it. By this time of night men are usually fully ensconced in whatever . . . pursuits they are planning for the evening."

"Pursuits." She repeated dryly, mimicking his actions with her own hat and gloves before removing his greatcoat and hanging it on a nearby stand. Turning back to him, she noted his sharp gaze. "You're not still angry with me, are you? We arrived with no difficulty. No one out there even knows I am in here."

A long moment went by as he gave her outfit a thorough perusal. He shook his head. "I just find it impossible to believe that not one man in this entire club noticed that you're no more a man than you are a giraffe."

One side of her mouth kicked up. "I should think they would have noticed if I were a giraffe. And why do you say that? Don't you think the disguise is a good one?" She looked down at herself, suddenly uncertain. "I know I have rather a . . . figure, but I think I've hidden it . . . well, as much as I can."

When he spoke, his voice was low and dark. "Callie. It would take a blind man not to notice your figure in those clothes. No man I have ever known has had such a lovely—"

"That's quite enough, my lord," she cut him off, primly, as though she weren't standing in the middle of Brooks's with one of London's most notorious rakes, wearing men's clothing. "It's getting late. I would like to learn to gamble now, if you don't mind."

He gave a little smirk and held out a chair, indicating that she should sit at the card table. She moved to take the proffered seat, keenly aware of his nearness. When he had seated himself across from her at the table, he lifted the deck of cards that had been set there, and said, "I think we should begin with *vingt-et-un*."

For the next few moments, he explained the rules of the game—helping Callie to understand the strategy required to ensure that her cards were valued as closely to twenty-one as they could be without exceeding the number. They played several rounds, Ralston letting her win before, on the third and fourth games, he beat her roundly. On the fifth game, she was thrilled that she had reached twenty when he flipped over his cards and showed his twenty-one.

Frustrated by another loss, Callie burst out, "You cheated!"

He looked at her, wide-eyed with feigned outrage. "I beg your pardon. If you were a man, I would call you out for that accusation."

"And I assure you, my lord, that I would ride forth victoriously on behalf of truth, humility, and righteousness."

He chuckled, shuffling the cards. "Are you quoting the Bible to me?"

"Indeed," she said primly, the portrait of piousness.

"While gambling."

"What better location to attempt to reform one such as you?" she said, humor twinkling in her eyes. They shared a smile before he dealt the cards, and she continued, "It would be rather fortuitous, however, if you were to call me out, though. I should like to attend a duel."

He froze for a fleeting moment, before shaking his head in surrender. "Of course you would. Is there anything on this list that won't shock me?"

She checked her cards casually before saying, "Oh, most assuredly not."

"Well, considering it seems that it has become my particular role to help you complete the items, I must ask . . . how are you enjoying this one?"

She wrinkled her nose as she considered the question. "The club is quite remarkable. I feel certain that I would never have had such an experience if not for you, my lord."

"Gabriel," he interrupted.

"Gabriel," she corrected herself. "But I will say that I am rather uncertain as to what it is about gambling that is so very compelling. To be sure, it is a fine pastime, but I fail to see what it is about the process that lands so many in debtors' prison."

He leaned back in his chair and watched her carefully. "You don't see it, lovely, because you have nothing at risk."

"At risk?"

"Indeed," he said, "the appeal of the tables is enhanced by both the thrill of winning *and* the fear of losing."

She considered the words before nodding thoughtfully. "Shall we play for money, then?"

He inclined his head toward her. "If you'd like."

She changed her mind. "You don't care about losing money."

"Not particularly."

"Then it's not a risk for you."

"It doesn't matter if there is no risk for me. This is your night. Only you have to feel the edge of risk. I'm merely your able assistant."

She couldn't help the smile that broke at the trivial description. "Oh, no, Gabriel," she said, and he stiffened at her free use of his given name. "If we are to play a legitimate round of cards, I should like you to feel that you might lose."

His blue eyes glittered across the table. "Name your terms."

Excitement flared. "All right, for every round I win . . . you must answer a question. Truthfully."

His brows snapped together. "What kind of questions?"

"Why?" she teased. "Are you afraid you will lose to me?"

He leaned forward. "All right, Empress, but for every round *I* win, you must grant me a favor . . . of my choosing."

A thrill went through her at the words, followed immediately by an acute sense of terror. "What kind of favor?"

"Why?" he repeated. "Are you afraid?"

Yes. She met his eyes firmly. "Of course not."

"Excellent," he said, dealing the cards quickly. "Then let's make this interesting, shall we?"

All of a sudden, gambling seemed to Callie like a wonderfully addictive pastime. Every turn of the cards had her breath catching in her throat as she sought ways to beat Ralston. And, on the first round, she did . . . although she couldn't help but wonder if it wasn't possible that he'd let her do so.

Not that she cared. She wanted her answer. She leaned back in her chair and watched for several moments as his long, graceful fingers collected the cards from the table, stacking them carefully and idly shuffling them while he waited for her question. She met his eyes. "Tell me about courtesans."

He gave a short laugh, shaking his head. "I agreed to answer questions. That wasn't a question."

She rolled her eyes. "All right, then. Are there often courtesans here?"

"Yes."

When he didn't elaborate, she pressed, "And do they often entertain groups of men?"

"Callie," he said, matter-of-factly, "what are you really getting at?"

She wrinkled her nose. "I'm just having trouble understanding how she was—that is . . . what they were going to—I mean . . ."

He smiled a wry smile and waited for her to finish.

"Oh . . . you know what I mean."

"I assure you I do not."

"There were three of them and only one of her!"

"Were there?"

"You are insufferable! You told me you'd answer my questions!"

"If you were to ask a question, love, I assure you I would answer it."

"Could she really be expected to . . ." she paused, searching for the word.

"Pleasure?" He offered, amiably.

"Entertain. All three of them?"

He began dealing the cards again. "Yes."

"How?"

He looked up at her, and offered her a wolfish grin. "Would you really like me to answer that?"

Her eyes widened. "Uhm . . . no."

He laughed then, a deep, rumbling laugh unlike anything she'd ever heard from him, and she was stunned by the way it transformed him. His face was immediately lighter, his eyes brighter, his frame more relaxed. She couldn't help but smile back at him, even as she admonished, "You're enjoying my discomfort."

"Indeed I am, Empress."

She blushed. "You shouldn't call me that."

"Why not? You were named for an empress, were you not?"

She closed her eyes and gave a mock shudder. "I prefer not to be reminded of the hideous name."

"You should embrace it," he said, forthrightly. "You're one of the few women I've met who could live up to such a name."

"You've said that before," she said.

He turned a curious look on her. "I have?"

She met his eyes and immediately regretted bringing up the decade-old memory, so insignificant to him—so very meaningful to her. She spoke quickly, trying to end the moment. "Yes. I don't remember when. Shall we play?"

His eyes narrowed on her slightly before he nodded. She was so flustered during the next round that he won easily, twenty to her twenty-eight.

"You should have held on nineteen," he offered casually.

"Why? I still wouldn't have won," she said, grumpily.

"Why Lady Calpurnia—" she was certain he used the name to provoke her, "I believe you are a sore loser."

"No one likes losing, my lord."

"Mmm. And yet it seems you have."

She sighed. "Get on with it. What do you want?"

He watched her, waiting for her to meet his gaze. "Take down your hair."

Her brow furrowed. "Why?"

"Because I won. And you agreed to the terms."

She considered his words briefly before lifting her hands and removing the pins that held her hair in place. As it fell in soft, brown waves around her shoulders, she said, "I must look silly, dressed in men's clothing with all this hair."

His gaze hadn't left her as she'd released her locks from their tight restraint. "I assure you, 'silly' is not the word I would use."

The words, spoken in the dark voice she was coming to adore, set her pulse racing. She cleared her throat. "Shall we continue?"

He dealt the cards again. She won. Attempting to sound cool and collected, she said, "Do you have a mistress?"

He froze briefly in collecting the cards, and she immediately regretted the question. She didn't really want to know if he had a mistress. *Did she?*

"I do not."

"Oh." She wasn't sure what she had been expecting him to say, but it hadn't been that.

"You don't believe me?"

"I believe you. I mean, you wouldn't be here with me if you could be somewhere with someone like . . ." She stopped, realizing that her words could be misunderstood. "Not that I think you're here to . . . with me . . ."

He watched her, his expression revealing none of his thoughts. "I would still be here with you."

"You would?" she squeaked.

"Yes. You're different. Refreshing."

"Oh. Well. Thank you."

"Mistresses can be rather difficult."

"I don't imagine you like difficult," she said quietly.

"No. I don't," he agreed. He set the deck of cards down on the table. "Why are you so interested in mistresses and courtesans?"

Not mistresses. Your mistresses. She shrugged her shoulders. "They're rather fascinating to women who aren't so . . . free."

"I'd hardly call them free."

"Oh! But they are! They can behave however they'd like, with whomever they like! They're not at all like women in society. We're expected to sit quietly while men hie off and sow their wild oats. I think it's high time that women have the chance to sow some oats of their own. And those women do."

"You have an overly romanticized view of what women like that can and cannot do. They are bound to the men with whom they consort. They rely on them for everything. Money, food, clothing."

"How is that different from me? I rely on Benedick for all those things."

He was clearly uncomfortable with the comparison. "It's different. He's your brother."

She shook her head. "You're wrong. It's quite the same. Only women like the one across the corridor get to choose the men to whom they are beholden."

His tone turned serious. "You don't know the first thing about the woman across the corridor, Callie. She is the opposite of free. I assure you. And I suggest you stop romanticizing her before it gets you into trouble."

Whether the result of the adventure of the evening or the verbal sparring with Ralston, Callie's mouth seemed to have become completely disconnected from her sense of self-preservation. "Why?" she asked. "I confess, I'm rather intrigued by the whole idea. I wouldn't necessarily dismiss an offer to become someone's mistress out of hand."

The words stunned him into silence, and Callie couldn't hide the little smirk of victory that sprang to her face as she noted his surprise. His brows snapped together as she reached across the table to lift the cards and begin dealing them. He grabbed her hand, stilling her motion and drawing her gaze to his, which glittered with an emotion she couldn't quite place except to know it was not a good thing. "You don't mean it." His tone brooked no refusal.

"I—" She sensed danger and spoke the truth. "Of course not."

"Is it on the list?"

"What? No!" Her shock was real enough to convince him.

"You are too valuable to play the mistress to some society dandy, Callie. It's not a glamorous role. Not a romantic one. Those women live in gilded cages. You should have a pedestal."

She scoffed. "Thank you, no. I would prefer not to be handled with kid gloves and apologies." She tugged her hand from beneath his. The warmth of his touch was too much. Too close to what she really wanted—to what she'd wanted for her whole life.

"Apologies?"

She closed her eyes for a brief moment, shoring up her courage. "Yes. Apologies. Like the one you delivered so beautifully this morning. If I were anyone else . . . your opera singer . . . the woman across the hall . . . would you have apologized?"

He looked confused. "No . . . but you are neither of those women."

Frustration flared. "You and the rest of society believe that it's better for me to be set upon a pedestal of primness and propriety—which might have been fine if a decade on that pedestal hadn't simply landed me on the shelf. Perhaps unmarried young women like our sisters should be there. But what of me?" Her voice dropped as she looked down at the cards in her hands. "I'm never going to get a chance to experience life from up there. All that is up there is dust and unwanted apologies. The same cage as hers"—she indicated the woman outside—"merely a different gilt."

He watched her carefully, unmoving, as the words poured out. When he did not respond, she looked up at him, only to find his expression shuttered. *What was he thinking?*

"Deal the cards."

She did, and they played the next round in silence, but it was clear he was no longer playing a harmless game of twenty-one. She knew from his hard face that he would win, and her heart pounded in her chest at the thought—what would he do in the face of her outburst?

When he won, he threw his cards into the center of the table. In silence, he stood, moved to the sideboard and poured two glasses of scotch. Returning, he offered her one of the tumblers.

She took it and sipped the amber liquid, surprised when she did not sputter and cough as she had in the tavern. In fact, the liquor served only to enhance the warmth that had spread through her as she waited for Gabriel to name his next favor.

Turning away from her, he moved to one of the overstuffed chairs by the fireplace and relaxed into it. She watched as he stared into the fire, wondering what he was thinking. Was he considering taking her home? She'd certainly said enough not only to embarrass herself but also him. Should she apologize?

"Come here." The words cut through the room, even though he didn't redirect his attention from the dancing flames.

"Why?"

"Because I will it."

An hour ago, she would have laughed at the imperious sentiment but, for some inexplicable reason, at that moment, Callie was drawn to the command. She stood and went to him, stopping mere inches from his right arm. She waited, the sound of her own blood pounding in her ear, the sound of her breath seeming to fill the room.

The wait was torturous.

And then he turned to her with an imperious look in his brilliant blue eyes, and said, "Sit."

It wasn't what she had expected. She moved stiltedly to take the other chair, but stopped as he added, "Not there, Empress. Here."

She turned back to him, surprise and confusion in her eyes. "Where?"

He reached out a hand. "Here."

The word echoed through the room. *He meant for her to sit on his lap?* She shook her head "I couldn't."

"You wanted to try the role on for size, lovely," he said, the words warm and coaxing. "Come. Sit with me."

She knew without his having to say any more that this was her chance to experience it all. *With Ralston.*

She moved to stand directly in front of him and met his eyes. She did not say anything; she did not have to. Within seconds, he had pulled her down onto his lap and covered her lips with his.

There was no turning back.

She gave herself up to the adventure. And to him.

Eighteen

The kiss was darker, more deliberate, more intense than any they had shared previously, and Callie had the immediate sense that Ralston was giving her the experience for which she had asked. The idea thrilled her—that this man, whom she had been pining for years, would be the one to show her the enticing, wicked place that she was so eager to know.

His tongue stroked her bottom lip as his hands roamed over her, freeing the buttons of the waistcoat she wore and deftly shucking the layers off her shoulders and down her arms before pulling the hem of her shirt from the waistband of her breeches. His warm, powerful hands settled on the soft, bare skin just above her breeches, and he took the opportunity to plunder her mouth. He searched and stroked, sending ripples of pleasure pooling deep within her as his hand stole upward, toward her breasts. She was overwhelmed by the combination of sensations from his wicked mouth and knowing fingers, and she could do nothing but wait for him to touch her where she wished . . . how she wished.

He pulled back sharply as his hand reached the linen bindings and he cursed—eyes flashing.

"Don't bind them again," he said, breath harsh, matched by her own. He caught the back of her head in the palm of his free hand and speared her with an unyielding blue gaze. "Ever."

The words were spoken in a dark, possessive tone, and she shook her head, assuring him of her compliance with his wishes. "I won't."

He held her eyes for a long moment, as if to divine the truth of her words. Satisfied, he claimed her mouth for a long, drugging kiss, sliding the cambric shirt up and releasing her mouth only long enough to pull the garment over her head. Resuming the kiss, he tossed the shirt aside, the white cloth fluttering through the air unnoticed as he returned his hands to her body, seeking and finding the end of the linen binding. Just when she was certain that he would begin to unwrap the cloth, his hands spread wide and he released her mouth again. The combination of his warm, firm hands upon her, the cool air against her lips, the hardness of his thighs beneath her, and the sound of their mingled breath was enough to rattle Callie's senses, and it took her a moment to open her eyes.

When she did, their gazes collided. Her breath caught as she read the passion in his gaze—barely controlled. She felt his chest rise and fall against her before he spoke. "Shall I free you, lovely?"

The words sent a liquid shock through Callie. Their earlier conversation flashed in her mind, and she recognized the underlying meaning in them. Her mouth dropped open, and his eyes followed the movement. As though unable to resist, he leaned forward and nibbled on her moistened bottom lip before pulling back and rephrasing the question, one finger running lightly along the straining flesh above the linen wrap.

"Shall I loose you from your cage?"

The words, laden with sensual promise, weakened her. He was offering her all the adventure and excitement she'd ever wanted— the things she could not commit to her list, could not admit to herself, even in her most personal of moments. How could she refuse?

She nodded her assent.

It was all he needed.

He slowly unraveled the long, linen bindings, pushing away her hands as she reached to help him. "No," he said, his voice full of promise and possessiveness, "you are my gift. I shall unwrap you."

And he did, slowly releasing her breasts until they spilled into his hands and, as he had the last time they had found themselves in that position, he set his mouth to her angry flesh and soothed her. He made love to the red skin, marred by the creases in the tight linen, running tongue and teeth and fingers across her. Her hands moved of their own volition, her fingers plunging into his soft, dark hair to hold him close to her as her own head tipped back, the weight of her long, heavy tresses combining with the heady sensations he caused to steal her strength.

His hands stole around her to keep her steady as his mouth took its toll—calling forth a gasp as he suckled softly on the hardened tip of one breast, sending waves of excitement coursing through her. She had never felt so wonderful, so female, so *alive*. And all because of him. The thought faded as he moved his attention to her other breast, lifting her as though she weighed nothing and rearranging her so that she straddled his lap, providing him with better access to her bounty. As he moved her, the loosened bandages fell to her waist and her list, freed from its hiding place, landed on his lap, brushing his forearm on its path. Distracted by the strange feeling, he looked at the folded paper sandwiched between them and picked it up, offering the square back to her. She accepted it, marveling at the rush of feeling that originated at the spot where their fingers touched. Holding his gaze, she tossed the paper to the side—heedless of where it landed.

He clasped her to him, pulling her closer. His hands were everywhere, caressing her bottom, her legs, her breasts, lifting her mass of hair to bare her neck to his hot, wet mouth. He followed the column of her neck up to lick the soft lobe of one ear, then back to rain kisses along her collarbone and down to her straining nipples once more. He worshipped her breasts, sucking and licking across their straining tips as her hands traveled their own path of discovery, finding their way beneath the collar of his coat, over his broad shoulders, down the chiseled muscles of his chest.

She set her fingers to the buttons of his waistcoat, tugging on the fastenings, uncertain of how she should proceed. He released one rose-tipped breast and met her eyes boldly. "Take what you want, Empress."

From the moment they'd started down this sensual path, he'd encouraged her to ignore the boundaries she met, to act boldly, with conviction. Tonight was no different. His words spurred her into action. Her fingers moved clumsily down the row of buttons, opening his waistcoat, baring his thin linen shirt. She paused, uncertain. She nibbled her lower lip as she considered her next step.

He watched, eyes like slits, refusing to make her decision for her but unable to resist clasping the back of her head and taking her worried lip with his own, licking and sucking until they were both panting. Pulling back, he relaxed into the chair, covering her hands on his chest and watching as she tried to regain her composure. "What will you do with me, now?"

She tilted her head, nervous, before saying, "I should like for you to be wearing fewer clothes."

He cocked a smile at her prim wording—so antithetical to the moment. His reply was gravelly, sending a shiver of pleasure through her. "Well, I certainly couldn't deny a lady."

He shrugged out of his coat and waistcoat, lifting against her to do so. The movement forced him to press against her, and he groaned at the soft core of her cradling him. Divested of his outer layers, he let himself fall back to the chair, clasping her hips tightly as he did so, unwilling to allow the sensation of her against him to end. Pushing against her again, he watched as she sighed with pleasure at the pressure—just where she was desperate for it.

Holding her gaze, he lifted again, sending a wave of passion through her once more. "Is that what you want, lovely?"

The question came on a pant of breath, and she noticed that he was as affected by the movement as she was. In response, she smiled boldly and ground herself against him in a firm, circular motion. His hands moved instantly to her hips to hold her tight to him. His eyes narrowed, and she felt powerful in the face of his passion.

She shook her head boldly, unwilling to look away from him. "Even fewer clothes."

He smiled again, sitting up and easing his back from the chair before lifting the hem of his shirt from the waistband of his breeches. Pulling the shirt over his head, he sent it along the same path that hers had traveled earlier.

Watching her watching him, he set his fingers to the tips of her breasts, teasing the flushed skin there. "Now what, Empress?"

She swallowed at the sight of him—magnificent and corded and muscled and *male*—it was the first time she had seen a man without a shirt, and her mouth was suddenly dry. Dragging her gaze up to meet his, she said, "May I . . . touch you?"

He gave a little laugh at the words. "Please."

Her eyes slid down to his chest and she set her hands to him, her fingers softly running up the sides of his torso, playing delicately over the planes of his chest. She ran one thumb over a flat nipple, and her eyes widened as it puckered, and the cadence of his breathing shifted. She repeated the motion, and he growled low in the back of his throat. She looked up at the sound, worried. "Did I hurt you?"

"No." The word came out on a harsh exhale. To prove it, he kissed her roundly, stroking deep inside her mouth, and mimicked the motion, rubbing his thumb across the turgid peak of one of her breasts until she whimpered with frustration. He spoke against her lips. "Does it hurt you?"

She shook her head, taking a shaky breath. "No." She stroked him again. "But it aches. In a good way. In a wonderful way."

He nodded. "Indeed. It does."

She watched her thumb as it traced slow circles around him, then leaned in and set her mouth to his chest. She could feel the thrum of his heart as she traced her lips across his warm skin, and she wondered what would happen if . . . her mouth found his nipple and she laved the straining flesh there.

He hissed in a breath, plunging his fingers through her hair as she repeated his earlier caresses with warm, lavish strokes of her tongue. He allowed her to explore with hands and mouth until he could no longer bear it, eventually pulling her up for another kiss. He ate her mouth until she had lost all coherent thought, until she was nothing but a puddle of femininity in his arms. It was as though he knew the moment she crossed over into the experience of pure pleasure, because he lifted her in his arms at that moment and, without breaking their kiss, settled her on the long, low chaise.

Callie stretched out along the chaise as he followed her down, the length of him spilling heat over every inch of her skin.

"I want you naked, Empress." The words were hot against her ear as he took her lobe in his teeth and sent shivers through her. "Let me worship you."

She couldn't resist him, couldn't resist the words that she'd dreamed of for years. Instead, she took hold of one of his hands and boldly shifted it to the fastenings of her breeches. The movement gave him all the permission he required and, within moments, he had removed her boots and breeches, and Callie was naked, laid bare just for him.

Ralston stopped and took her in, his hands stroking down her lush body, molding to her skin, flush with equal parts passion and embarrassment. She tried to cover herself, but he wouldn't allow it, his hands staving hers off in playful movements as he drank her in. She gave up on hiding her breasts, but could not stop herself from covering the thatch of brown curls that marked her most private place.

He lifted her hand from there and replaced it with his own. He kissed her deeply before pulling back just enough to speak. "Are you embarrassed, my lovely?"

At her nod, he pressed the heel of his hand firmly against her, enjoying the feeling of immense satisfaction that coursed through him when she sighed her pleasure against his mouth. "Don't be . . . let me cover you."

At the words, Callie burst into shocked laughter, which he shared intimately until he slid one, warm finger between the plump lips of her sex and turned her laughing into a gasp of pleasure as he found the opening of her inner flesh and stroked deep inside her.

"You are so very beautiful, my love."

She closed her eyes, the combination of erotic caress and coveted endearment too much for her to bear. He claimed her mouth again. "I've never known such passion. Such responsiveness. You make me want to tie you up and have my way with you." An image flashed through her mind of her bound, defenseless against the onslaught of his caresses. She opened her eyes in surprise and met his amused gaze. Reading her thoughts, he continued, "Someday, Empress, I shall show you just how much pleasure such an interlude can bring . . . but, tonight." His thumb rubbed gently through her aching, swollen flesh, seeking and finding the tight bud of pleasure there. She arched into the caress as he continued, "Tonight, I want you touching me as well." He traced small circles with his finger, drawing frustrated cries from Callie as moisture rained down into his palm. He set his lips to hers, and whispered, "So wet . . ." A second finger joined the first, thrusting deep, stretching her as her body clenched around him. "So tight . . ."

He spoke against her parted, moist lips as she pushed against him. "So beautiful."

He was pushing her farther and farther to the brink, his mouth and hands everywhere at once. She was his pianoforte; he played her body and her mind with his warm hands and wicked words. She focused on his hand, on the deep slide of his fingers as they worked her into a frenzy, on the firm, wonderful stroke of his thumb, circling the place to which all of her energy seemed to have fled. She rocked against him, begging for more, crying his name.

And then he was between her legs, spreading them wide and holding her down as he set his mouth to the place where she most desperately needed him. His tongue flicked and laved with intensity that she could not bear—the powerful lash of the caress robbing her of breath and of thought and of everything but feeling. She let her hands fall to his head, her fingers clenching wildly in his hair as he worked her swollen, desperate flesh with fingers and tongue and lips until she thought she might die if he ever stopped. She could feel a rolling wave of pleasure building, higher and higher as his caresses grew faster and harder, as the tip of his tongue flicked boldly across the peak of her sex, his mouth tugging at her until she lost her mind. She lifted her hips from the chaise as she felt the crest of pleasure peak and the wave crashed over her and she cried out and clung to him—the rock at the center of her tilting world.

His caresses gentled, and he brought her back to the moment, soothing her flesh before lifting his head and looking up at her. He caught his breath when he met her eyes, which burned with passion and feminine knowledge. She extended one, beckoning hand out to him, and said, "Come here."

The words sent a shudder through him, and he couldn't stop himself from stretching out beside her again. Her hands ran along his side, stroking down to his breeches where she could see the fabric straining across the hard ridge of him. She traced one finger along the length of him and reveled in the hitch of his breath. With a smile borne of feminine power, she repeated the caress more firmly, and he grasped her hand, stilling the movement.

Meeting her eyes, he spoke, breath harsh. "A man only has so much willpower, Empress. If you touch me like that, I cannot guarantee I will be able to restrain myself."

Callie freed her hand from his grasp and set it to the side of his face, guiding him down for another kiss. This time, she controlled the caress. It was her tongue that stroked the inside of his warm mouth, her lips that played across his firm, full lower lip. When she ended the caress, she traced her hand back down his torso to the buttons of his breeches. Holding his gaze, she used shaking fingers to release the straining placket of fabric from its fastenings. Sliding her hand inside, she found his straining length and grasped him firmly in her eager hand. His eyes darkened as she spoke, a tremor in her voice the only indication of her nervousness. "What if I were to touch you like this?"

Callie held her breath as Ralston took in her words. He went utterly still for a long moment, and Callie wondered if she had severely miscalculated her actions.

And then he moved. He captured her mouth with a groan deep in his throat. He stilled her hand with his own, meeting her gaze. There was something about her eagerness and her innocence—

about the passion that flared in her eyes even as she delivered such exquisite pleasure—that slayed him. As he looked into her velvety brown eyes, he realized that he'd never met a woman like her. She was a study in contradictions, all passionate innocence and adventurous primness and shy exploration. The heady combination was enough to fascinate even the most hardened of cynics—and he was indeed fascinated.

He wanted her. Fiercely. He shook off the thought. She deserved better. For once in his life, he would play the gentleman. He closed his eyes against the vision of her naked, open to him, welcoming and more freely passionate than any woman he'd ever known.

He should receive a medal for what he was about to do.

He lifted her hand away from the straining length of him, placing a warm, wet kiss in her palm, and spoke, unable to keep his hands from stroking the length of her, eager for the feel of her soft, smooth skin. "I think I should get you home."

Her eyelids flickered, the only indication she gave that she heard him. He saw the doubt flash in her eyes and wanted nothing more than to pull her to him and tell her exactly what he *wanted* to do rather than *thought* he should do.

"But, I don't want to go home. You said you would release me from my cage. Are you reneging?" The question was teasing and seductive, a siren's call as she pressed against him—the unskilled movement setting his pulse pounding.

He kissed her again, unable to stop himself from taking some of the sweetness she offered. When he released her mouth, she sighed against his lips. "Please, Gabriel . . . show me how it can be. Let me taste it. Just once."

The words, so honest and open, cut straight through him, and he realized that he'd been doomed from the start. He could not refuse her.

And then his breeches were gone and he was above her, settling between her legs, allowing her softness to cradle him. He kissed along the column of her neck, his hands stroking her breasts, tweaking the tips until they were hard and straining for his mouth. He settled his lips once again to the rosy peaks, wringing cries of pleasure from her. Her hands fell to his shoulders, stroking his warm skin, reminding him of the pleasure that he found over and over in her eager arms. And that pleasure would soon be magnified a hundredfold.

He pressed against the soft, downy hair at her core, feeling the warmth and wetness that waited for him there, and it took all of his control not to plunge deep inside her, not to drive himself to the hilt. Instead, he moved lightly against her, drawing a sigh from her with the sweet friction he caused. She lifted against him, seeking something she couldn't name, and he lifted away from her, meeting her impassioned gaze with a wicked, teasing grin. "What do you want, lovely?"

She lifted again, trying to increase their contact, and, again, he pulled back. She narrowed her eyes on him. "You know what I want."

He pulled her pouting bottom lip between his teeth and suckled gently before moving his hips firmly against hers, giving her precisely what she'd been seeking. "Is that it, Empress?"

She gasped and nodded as he repeated the motion, drawing more of her sweet rain down to moisten the soft, swollen lips that cradled him. It was his turn to groan then. "Oh, God, Callie . . . you're so sweet." He thrust again, the tip of him rubbing against the place where all her pleasure seemed to pool.

She sucked in a harsh breath at the sensation. "I want—" She started to speak, then stopped, uncertain.

"Tell me, love." He laved the spot where her jaw met the soft skin of her neck with his roughened tongue as one hand idly stroked a turgid nipple, and he moved against her in a rhythm that was certain to drive them both mad.

"I—I don't know what I want." She ran her hands down his back, lifting against him again, drawing a harsh exhale from him. "I feel so—" He lifted his head to watch her search for the word . . . "Empty."

He rewarded her for the words, so raw and wanting, kissing her passionately, tongue thrusting deep into her mouth. Then he moved slightly, fitting his hand between them and, with the tip of one finger, he traced the entrance to the core of her. "Here, love?" he whispered against her ear, the words more caress than sound. "Do you feel empty here?" He pushed the finger deep inside her as she sighed his name. "Do you want me here?"

She bit her lip and nodded.

"Say it, Empress. Tell me." A second finger joined the first, stretching. Filling.

"I want you."

"Where?" The fingers thrust in unison, showing her the answer.

"Gabriel . . ." The word was equal parts plea and protest.

He smiled against her neck. "Where, lovely?"

He was killing her. "Inside me."

His fingers disappeared and she lifted her hips, the movement protesting his retreat. He placed a line of soft, velvet kisses along her collarbone as he settled between her open thighs, replacing his knowing fingers with the hard length of him—poised at the entrance to her. He took her face in his hands and met her eyes, unwilling to let her hide from him in this supremely intimate moment.

Her breath caught as he pushed just barely inside her, stretching, opening. He stilled, the hardest thing he'd ever done, as the swollen head of him was cradled in her velvet, wet heat. He watched the flicker of sensation in her brown eyes. "Does it hurt?"

She closed her eyes tightly, shaking her head. "No," she whispered. "Yes. It feels . . . I want . . ." she met his gaze, "I want more. I want all of it. I want you. Please."

The raw emotion laid bare in her words and in her look was enough to send him over the edge, but he refused to allow himself to ruin this, her first taste of passion. He paused in his movements, sipping at the tips of her breasts and returning his hand to the hard, straining nub at the core of her. He rubbed a slow circle there, watching as pleasure flared in her eyes at the caress. "Callie . . ." he whispered, "I am going to hurt you. I cannot prevent it."

"I know." The words were breathless. "I don't care."

He kissed her then, his tongue slow and seeking, stroking the soft skin as though they had all the time in the world. "I care," he whispered, his thumb stroking faster against her, causing her hips to rock against him in a rhythm that set them both aflame. "But I shall make it up to you."

He rocked against her, gritting his teeth against the sublime pleasure he felt as he moved carefully, inch by slow inch, traveling slightly deeper on each smooth thrust, then pulling out completely, giving her time to adjust to him.

And then, when she was writhing in pleasure, he pulled back and thrust to the hilt, the hard length of him stretching the untried flesh at the heart of her. She sucked in a deep breath at the pain, and he stilled above her, the muscles of his arms and shoulders and neck coiled with rigid tension. "I'm sorry," he whispered, raining kisses along her cheek to her ear.

She turned to meet his gaze with a small smile. "No . . . it's not . . . it isn't bad." She cocked her head, as though considering the sensations within her. "Is that it?"

He gave a little, strained laugh at the innocent question. "That's not even close to being it."

"Oh." She moved against him, and it was his turn to gasp.

"Oh . . . that's quite . . ." She moved again and he stilled her hips with a strong hand, unwilling to trust himself if she continued her rolling motions.

"Indeed," he said, suckling the tip of one breast idly. "It is. Quite."

He retreated almost entirely from her passage and thrust again, a smooth, long movement that chased away the residual pain and replaced it with a spark of pleasure. "Oh . . . yes."

"Yes?" he teased, repeating the movement.

This time she met his thrust with her own and sighed. "Yes," she agreed.

"My sentiments, exactly," he said, and began to move rhythmically in deep, smooth strokes designed to drive them both wild. After several long moments of his rich caresses, Callie began to move beneath him, canting her hips to increase the pressure of his thrusts.

Ralston shifted to accommodate her body's request, increasing his speed and force. Clenching his teeth against the pleasure of her body, so tight and hot around him. Callie began to cry out, little mewling cries of pleasure that made him wild, so real and honest was her passion. Never in his life had he wanted to find his release so badly; never had he so desperately wanted to hang on, to give his partner the pleasure she deserved.

"Gabriel," she keened, "I need—"

"I know," he breathed against her ear, "I know what you need. Take it."

"I can't—"

"Yes, you can."

And then he placed his thumb at the core of her once more, pressing and stroking while he thrust deep and fast, and the combination of sensations was too much. The tension that had been slowly mounting threatened to spiral out of control, to consume everything in its path, including her thought and sanity. She cried out his name and arched against him, afraid of what was about to happen—unwilling to shy away from it.

He captured her wild gaze with his own. "Look at me, Empress. I want to see you come undone. I want to watch you go over the edge with me."

"I can't—I—I don't know—how." She thrashed her head from one side to the other, panting out the words.

"We shall discover it together."

And they did. The coiled tension within her was set free, and she convulsed around him, her muscles tightening around him in a perfect prison, milking him with sweet, unbearable rhythm. She cried out his name, scoring his shoulders with her fingernails as she grabbed hold of him, and he watched her come unraveled.

And then, only then, once she had found her pleasure, did he take his own, calling out as he followed her over the edge with a force he had never before experienced. He collapsed onto her, his chest heaving in unison with her own as he attempted to regain his strength.

He lay there for a long moment, until his breathing stabilized, and he had the wherewithal to lift himself on strong arms and look down at her. Taking in her flushed, pleasure-dampened skin, her sated smile, and heavy-lidded eyes, Ralston was struck by realization.

He'd never experienced anything like this . . . anything like her. He'd never been with a woman so open and free . . . never known someone so willing to give and receive and embrace passion with such a powerful will. *He'd never known anyone like her.* His eyes raked over body, naked and beautiful and bathed in the golden, flickering firelight. She was wrapped around him in every way imaginable, and all he could think of was taking her again. Immediately. Of course, she must be sore. . .

The thought washed over him like a cold wave.

My God, she'd been a virgin.

What had he been thinking? Virgins deserved better, for God's sake. Not that he'd ever been in the situation before, but he was certain they deserved poetry and roses and *at least* a proper bed. Not a chaise longue in a men's club.

My God. She'd been a virgin and he'd treated her like a common—

He shook his head at the thought, unwilling to allow himself even to finish the sentence in his mind. He was consumed by self-loathing as he considered what he'd done. She'd trusted him. And he'd taken advantage of her. At Brooks's, for Christsakes. *My God,* What had he done?

He blanched at the thought.

She noticed. "Is something wrong?"

The words brought him back to the moment, and he found it difficult to meet her eyes. Instead, he placed a gentle kiss on one of her shoulders and sat up, ignoring the sense of loss that coursed through him as he disentangled himself from her warm, willing body.

He began to dress, noting when, after several long moments of watching him, Callie moved to do the same. He tried not to look at her, but found himself unable to resist when she turned to face away from him and pull on her breeches. His palms itched to touch her, to gather her against him and, once more, feel her softness cradling the hard angles of his body. Pulling himself from his reverie, he set to work on his cravat as she pulled on her shirt, forgoing her bindings.

She turned to search for her waistcoat and met his gaze briefly. He could not help but register the sadness in her eyes. She already regretted what they had done.

Leaning down, he lifted the length of linen that she had ignored, running it through his fingers. "Do you need this?"

"No," she said softly. "Your greatcoat is large enough to hide me . . ." She paused before adding, "That, and I promised I wouldn't bind them again."

The words, along with the erotic power they had carried earlier that evening, echoed between them, reminding him of his unforgivable behavior. She turned away from him as he said, "So you did."

He wrapped the linen into a small bundle and tucked it inside his waistcoat before leaning to retrieve his topcoat from the floor. As he did, he noted the square of paper that lay beneath it—the list that had set them on this wild course.

He straightened, opening his mouth to offer her the paper, but stopping just short of sound when he realized that she remained resolutely faced away from him, her back straight, shoulders squared as though she were about to do battle as she calmly inserted pins into her hair, restoring it to its original state.

For some reason, he did not want to mention her silly list. Instead, he tucked the wrinkled square into his pocket and waited for her to face him again.

Several minutes later, she did, and he was struck by the emotion in her eyes, liquid with unshed tears. In the face of her sadness, he felt like an utter ass. Swallowing, he searched for the right thing to say. He could see that she was waiting for him to speak, to say the words that would redeem him . . . the words that would stop the tears that threatened to spill over.

He wanted to say the right thing. He might not have been able to repair the damage he had done with his unthinking, callous behavior, but he certainly could behave the gentleman going forward. And so, he said the thing that he imagined gentlemen said in such a situation. The thing that he was certain women wanted to hear in such a situation. The thing that was sure to stop her tears.

"Please, forgive me for my behavior. Of course, we shall marry."

He waited out the long moment during which the words hung between them, while Callie's eyes widened in shock, then narrowed upon him as though his mind were thoroughly addled. He waited for her to realize that he'd done the gentlemanly thing. Waited for her to be pleased by—grateful for, even—his offer of marriage. Waited for her to say something—anything. He waited as she wrapped herself in his greatcoat, pulled on her gloves, and set her hat upon her head.

And, when she was done, and she had faced him and finally spoke, it was as though he'd said nothing at all. "Thank you for the supremely edifying evening, my lord. Would you mind very much taking me home?"

Well. At least she hadn't cried.

Nineteen

*O*f all the arrogant—pompous—horrid—men!" Callie
wrenched books from the shelves of the Allendale House
library and tossed them onto the growing piles at her feet as
she muttered aloud to herself. "'Of course, we shall marry'? I
wouldn't—marry him—if he were the last—man—in—London!"

She blew a stray lock of hair from her eyes and wiped her dusty
hands on the gray woolen dress she was wearing before surveying the damage she had caused over the last hour. The library had
been torn asunder. There were books everywhere—on tables and
chairs and in progressively less neat piles on the floor.

After a stony-silent ride home with Ralston mere hours ago,
Callie had crept back into the house and found her bed, torn between a longing to crawl under the covers never to reemerge and
an equally strong desire to march straight to Ralston House, wake
up its master, and tell him precisely what she thought he should do
with his generous, gentlemanly offer.

For several hours, she'd attempted the former . . . playing the
events of the evening over and over in her head—alternating between tears and anger at how thoroughly he'd ruined such a remarkable evening. He'd shown her precisely how amazing passion

could be, she'd seen her first glimpse of ecstasy, and then he'd gone and destroyed it. And she'd been reminded, mere moments after her discovery, that she was not destined for passion of any kind.

No, instead of Ralston saying any number of wonderful things that could have been appropriate for the precise situation in which they had found themselves—from *You are the most unparalleled female I have ever known,* to *How can I ever live without you now that I've found heaven in your arms,* to *I love you, Callie, more than I had ever dreamed* to even *Shall we have another go?*—he'd gone and mucked it up by apologizing.

And, even worse, mentioning marriage.

Not that marriage would have been the entirely wrong thing for him to mention. Indeed, she would have welcomed it, somewhere between *You are the most unparalleled female I have ever known* and *How can I ever live without you now that I've found heaven in your arms.* It would have been lovely if he'd looked into her eyes with absolute devotion, and said, *Make me the happiest, luckiest, most satisfied man in the world, Callie. Marry me.*

Certainly, if he'd said that—or, she allowed magnanimously, any variation on the theme—she would have collapsed, elated, into his arms and allowed him to kiss her senseless all the way home. And she would still be abed, dreaming of a long, happy life as the Marchioness of Ralston.

Instead, it was half past nine, the morning after what should have been the most marvelous evening of her entire life—including all those still left to come—and she was rearranging the library.

Hands on her hips, she gave a curt nod at the scene before her. "It seems as good a time as any."

Well, at least she hadn't cried.

She sneezed. First, she would have to dust.

She marched to the door and yanked it open to have a footman fetch her a duster, only to discover Mariana and Anne, heads bowed, deep in whispered conversation with a maid across the hallway.

All three heads snapped up at the sound of the library door opening, and Callie noted that the maid's jaw dropped at the sight of her. Callie spoke evenly to the servant. "I am in need of a duster." The girl looked entirely dumbfounded, as though she failed to understand the statement. Callie tried again. "To dust. The books. In the library." The girl appeared to be rooted to the floor of the foyer. Callie sighed. "I should like to dust the library *today* . . . do you think that will be possible?"

The question spurred the girl into motion, and she scurried off down the hall to do her mistress's bidding. Callie leveled Mariana and Anne with a stern look. *At least they had the good sense not to comment.*

"Oh, my," Mariana said, "it appears that it is worse than we thought."

Callie's gaze narrowed on her sister, speaking volumes, before she spun on one heel and returned to the library to begin the long process of alphabetizing the books that were now thoroughly out of order. From her spot on the floor, Callie noted that Mariana and Anne had followed her into the room. Anne stood resolutely by the closed door as Mariana perched cautiously on the arm of one chair.

They watched Callie carefully, remaining quiet for several minutes as Callie collected titles from nearby piles. Mariana broke the silence finally, asking, "What letter are you on?"

Callie looked up at her sister from amidst the towering books and said, obviously, "A."

Mari leaned over to consider a pile of books by her feet. Deftly removing one from the stack, she flashed a self-satisfied smile, and said, "Alighieri. *Inferno.*"

Callie turned back to her piles. "That's Dante. It should be shelved under D."

"Really?" Mariana wrinkled her nose at the book in her hand. "That seems odd. His surname begins with an A."

"Michelangelo's surname begins with a B and we still file him under M."

"Hmm," Mariana said, feigning interest in the conversation. "It must be the Italians." She paused briefly as the maid knocked and entered with a duster for Callie. When the girl had come and gone, closing the door behind her, Mari continued absently, "I wonder if Juliana would be filed under J or F?"

Callie's back stiffened briefly at the mention of Ralston's sister before she resumed her dusting. "I haven't any idea. Probably J."

Anne piped up. "'Tis a pity she's not an official St. John. I've always liked S."

Mariana nodded. "I do so agree."

Callie snapped her head around to look at Mariana. "What are you two trying to get at?"

"What happened last night?"

Callie looked back at the shelf she was filling. "Nothing happened."

"No?"

"No."

"Then why are you reorganizing the library?" Mariana asked.

Callie gave a little shrug of her shoulders. "Why not? I haven't anything else to do today."

"Nothing better to do than rearrange the library."

Callie wondered how difficult it would be to strangle her sister.

"A thing you only ever do when you are in search of distraction?"

And her lady's maid.

Mariana stood and leaned against the shelf where Callie was working. "You promised you would tell me everything, you know."

Callie shrugged again. "There's nothing to tell."

The words were punctuated by a knock on the door of the room.

All three women turned their attention to the butler, who was making a valiant attempt to ignore the mess that had taken over the normally impeccably organized library.

He entered, closing the door firmly behind him, as though attempting to shield them from the hallway. "My lady, Lord Ralston is here. He is requesting an audience with you."

Mariana and Anne exchanged a wide-eyed look before Mariana turned to give Callie a smug look. "Is he?"

Callie rolled her eyes at her sister and addressed the butler, "Thank you, Davis. You may tell the marquess that I am not in. He may return later in the day should he like to take a chance on my being able to receive him then."

"Indeed, my lady." The butler gave a short bow and exited the room.

Callie closed her eyes and took a deep, shuddering breath, attempting to calm herself. When she opened them again, Mariana and Anne were standing shoulder to shoulder, watching her closely. Anne said, "Nothing to tell, hmm?"

"No." Callie willed her voice to remain steady.

"You're a wretched liar," Mariana said casually. "One can only hope that Davis is slightly better than you are."

As the words hung in the air between them, the door opened once again, revealing the aging butler. "My ladies." He bowed.

"Has he gone?" Callie asked.

"Erm. No, my lady. He says he will wait for you to return."

Mariana's jaw dropped slightly at the words. "Really?"

Davis nodded once in the direction of the youngest Hartwell sister. "Quite, my lady."

Mari smiled brightly at Callie. "Well, this appears to be shaping into something of an adventure."

"Oh, do shut up." Callie turned to Davis. "Davis, you shall

have to make it clear that I am not receiving. It is far too early
for callers."

"I made that point already, my lady. Unfortunately, the marquess appears to be rather . . . persistent."

Callie gave a little, frustrated huff. "Yes. He does trend in that
direction. You shall have to persevere."

"My lady . . ." the butler hedged.

Callie lost her patience. "Davis. You are considered to be one of
the best butlers in London."

Davis preened. Well, as much as a butler could do so and retain
an appropriate level of gravity. "In England, my lady."

"Yes. Well. Do you think you could . . . buttle . . . this morning?"

Anne snorted her amusement as Davis's face fell.

Mariana turned kind eyes on the butler, and said, "She doesn't
mean to insult, Davis."

The butler was stone-faced when he replied with a sniff, "Indeed, not." He then bowed, more deeply than Callie thought he'd
ever bowed to them before and took his leave once more.

Callie sighed, returning to her task, deep within a row of
shelves. "I shall be punished for my behavior, shan't I?"

"Most definitely. You'll be served overcooked beef for the next
month," Anne said, her amusement barely controlled.

Mari inspected a pile of books there before asking casually,
"Do you think Lord Ralston will be deterred?"

"I wouldn't place a wager on it."

Callie's heart leapt into her throat at the dry words, spoken from
inside the room. She snapped her head toward the sound, but the
surrounding shelving blocked her view. At the end of the passage-
way where she stood, Callie could see her maid frozen in place,
eyes wide as saucers, staring in the direction of the door.

In the silence that ensued, Mariana turned her gaze on Callie.

Ignoring her sister's pleading look, the younger woman offered a smile befitting The Allendale Angel, and said, sweetly, "Callie, it appears that you have a visitor."

Callie's gaze narrowed. There was truly nothing worse in the wide world than a sister.

She watched as Mari hopped up from her place and smoothed out her skirts, turning to face the door—and Ralston. "It's a lovely day," she said.

"Indeed, it is, Lady Mariana," came Ralston's disembodied voice. Callie stomped her slippered foot in irritation. *Did he have to be so very calm?*

"I think I shall walk in the gardens," Mariana said, conversationally.

"That sounds like a capital idea."

"Yes. I rather thought so myself. If you'll pardon me. Anne?" Callie watched as her sister dropped a quick curtsy and left the room, the traitorous Anne fast on her heels. Callie, instead, stayed precisely where she was, hoping that she could simply wait Ralston out. A gentleman wouldn't corner her in the narrow space between bookshelves. And he'd certainly gone out of his way the night before to prove that he was a gentleman.

Silence fell, and Callie kept arranging books, willing herself to ignore Ralston's arrival. *Adams, Aeschylus, Aesop.*

She noted his footsteps coming closer; saw him out of the corner of her eye standing at the end of the shelf, watching her. *Ambrose, Aristotle, Arnold.*

Yes, she would simply pretend he wasn't there. How could he remain so silent? It was enough to try the patience of a saint. *Augustine.*

She couldn't stand it anymore. Without taking her eyes from the shelf where she was aligning the spines of the books into a perfectly straight row, she said, churlishly, "I am not receiving."

"Interesting," he drawled. "Because, it appears you have received me."

"No. You barged into my library without invitation."

"Is that what this is?" he said, wryly. "I was not sure, what, with all the shelves being empty of books."

She gave him an exasperated look. "I am rearranging."

"Yes, I gathered."

"Which is why I am *not receiving*." She emphasized the words in the hope that he would realize his rudeness and leave.

"I think we're rather past that, don't you?"

Apparently he did not mind being rude. Fine, then. She would not mind, either. "Was there something you wanted, Lord Ralston?" she said, coolly.

She turned to face him. A mistake. He was just as perfectly put together as he always was—all smooth hair and golden skin and impeccable cravat and eyebrow arched with just enough grace to make her feel like she'd been born and raised in a stable. She was immediately and acutely aware that she was wearing her grayest, drabbest, and now, no doubt, dirtiest gown, and that she likely appeared in dire need of both a nap and a bath.

He was an infuriating man. Truly.

"I should like to continue our conversation from last night."

She did not respond, instead stooping to pick up several books from the floor.

He watched her, unmoving, as though considering his next words carefully. She waited, slowly placing the books on their shelf, willing him not to say anything. Hoping he'd simply give up and leave.

He stepped closer to her, crowding her into the dimly lit space. "Callie, I cannot apologize enough." His words were quiet in their sincerity.

She closed her eyes at the words, letting her fingers trail down the spine of one of the books. She saw the letters on the cover, in shining gold plate, but she could not read them. Taking a deep breath, she steeled herself against the emotion pounding through her. She shook her head firmly, refusing to look at him—not trusting herself to look at him. "Please don't apologize," she whispered. "There is no need."

"Of course there is a need. My behavior was reprehensible." He sliced a hand through the air. "More important, however, is that I rectify the situation immediately."

His meaning was clear. Callie shook her head again. "No," she said quietly.

"I beg your pardon?" His surprise was obvious.

She cleared her throat, willing her voice to be stronger, this time. "No. There is no situation and, hence, no requirement for you to rectify it."

He gave a short, disbelieving laugh. "You cannot be serious."

She squared her shoulders and pushed past him into the light, open central area of the library. Wiping her hands on her dress, she made a show of sorting through a pile of books on a nearby table. She saw none of the titles; registered none of the authors. "I am quite serious, my lord. Whatever perceived infraction you seem to believe you committed, I assure you, you have done no such thing."

He raked a hand through his hair, irritation flashing across his face. "Callie. I compromised you. Rather thoroughly. And now, I should like to make it right. We are marrying."

She swallowed, refusing to look at him—not trusting herself to do so. "No, my lord. We are not." They were, quite possibly, the most difficult words she had ever said. "Not that I do not appreciate the offer," she added politely.

He looked thoroughly nonplussed. "Why not?"

"My lord?"

"Why won't you marry me?"

"Well, for one thing, you haven't asked. You announced."

He looked to the ceiling as though asking for patience. "Fine. Will you marry me?"

The words sent a sad thrill through Callie. Forced into it or no, the Marquess of Ralston proposing to her was definitely high on her list of most wonderful moments in her lifetime. *Tops on the list.*

"No. But, thank you very much for asking."

"Of all the damn fool—" he checked himself. "Do you want me on one knee, then?"

"No!" Callie didn't think she would be able to bear him on bended knee, asking her to marry him. That would be a cruel trick of the universe.

"What the devil is the problem?"

The problem is that you don't really want me. "I simply see no reason for us to marry."

"No reason," he repeated, testing the words for himself. "I would venture to guess that I could name one or two very good reasons."

She met his eyes finally, unsettled by the conviction in their rich blue depths. "Surely you haven't attempted to marry every woman you've compromised. Why begin with me?"

His eyes widened in shock at her bold words. The emotion was soon replaced by irritation. "Let us resolve this once and for all. You evidently think me far more profligate than I have been. Contrary to what you might believe, I have indeed proposed to every unmarried virgin I've deflowered. All *one* of them."

Callie flushed at his frank words and looked away, nibbling at her lower lip. He was obviously upset by the situation, and she was sorry for that. But, truthfully, he couldn't possibly be more upset than she was. She'd spent a glorious evening in the arms of the only man she'd ever wanted, and he'd promptly proposed to her—out of some newfound sense of duty—with all the romance of a side of beef.

And she was supposed to collapse in gratitude for the overwhelmingly generous Marquess of Ralston? *No, thank you.* She would live out the rest of her days with the wonderful memory of the night before and be happy with that.

She hoped.

"Your honorable actions are duly noted, my lord—"

"For God's sake, Callie—stop 'my lording' me." Irritation laced his tone, giving her pause. "You realize you could be with child."

One of Callie's hands went immediately to her waist at the words. She quelled the intense longing that shot through her at the idea of carrying Ralston's child. She hadn't considered the possibility, but how likely could it really be? "I doubt very much that that is the case."

"Nevertheless, there is a possibility. I won't have a child of mine born a bastard."

Callie's eyes flashed. "Neither would I. But this conversation is rather premature, don't you think? After all, the risk of such a thing is rather minimal."

"Any risk is too much of a risk. I want you to marry me. I will give you everything you could ever want."

You'll never love me. You never could. I am too plain. Too boring. Nothing like what you deserve. The words whispered through her mind, but she remained silent, instead shaking her head.

He sighed, frustrated. "If you won't hear reason, I shall have no choice but to have this conversation with Benedick."

Callie gasped. "You wouldn't."

"You have evidently mistaken me for a different man. I shall marry you, and I am not above having your brother force you down the aisle to do it."

"Benedick would never force me to marry you," Callie protested.

"It appears we will discover the truth of that statement." They stood, facing off, eyes sparkling with frustration, for several long moments before his tone softened, and he said, "Would it be that bad?"

Raw emotion burst in Callie's chest, and she could not immediately reply. Of course, marrying Ralston would not be bad. Marrying Ralston would be wonderful. She'd pined for him for years, watched him longingly from the edges of ballrooms, combed the gossip columns for news of him and his escapades. For a decade, when the doyennes of the *ton* speculated about the future Marchioness of Ralston, Callie had secretly imagined herself holding court alongside her coveted marquess.

But in all those years, she'd imagined a love match. She'd dreamed that one day he would spy her from across a crowded ballroom or from inside a shop on Bond Street, or at a dinner party and fall madly in love with her. She'd imagined them living happily ever after.

Marriages borne of regret and mistakes did not make for appropriately happy ever afters.

At her age and station, she knew that her best chance of ever marrying and having a family was to accept a loveless marriage, but agreeing to such with Ralston was simply too much to bear.

She'd longed for him for too long to accept less than love. Collecting herself, she said, "Of course it would not be bad. I'm sure you would make a fine husband. I am simply not in the market for one."

"Forgive me if I don't believe you," he scoffed. "Every unmarried female in London is in the market for a husband." He paused, considering the situation. "Is it me?"

"No." *You're rather perfect, actually.* He was going to push her until she gave him a reason. She gave a little shrug. "I simply don't believe that we would suit."

He leveled her with a blank stare. "You don't think we'd suit."

"No." She met his eyes. "I don't."

"Why the devil not?"

"Well, I am not exactly your preferred specimen of femininity."

Ralston paused at her phrasing, looking up to the ceiling as though asking for patience. "Which is?"

Callie gave a frustrated little sigh. Did he have to push her constantly? "You're really going to make me say it?"

"I really am, Callie. Because, truly, I don't understand."

She hated him in that moment. Hated him almost as much as she adored him. She waved her hand in irritation. "Beautiful. Sophisticated. Experienced. I am none of those things. I am the opposite of you and the women with whom you've surrounded yourself. I'd much rather read books than go to balls, I loathe society, and I am so lacking in experience in the romance department that I had to come to your house in the dead of night to secure my first kiss. The last thing I want is a marriage with someone who will regret such an arrangement from the moment we speak our vows." The words came out fast and furious, and she was angry that he'd pressed her into laying bare her insecurities.

She punctuated her diatribe with a muttered, "Thank you very much for forcing me to say it all."

He blinked at her, silent, taking in her words. And then he said, simply, "I shan't regret it."

The words were her undoing. She'd had enough. Enough of his kindness and his passion. Enough of the way he made her mind and her heart and her body feel. Enough of punishing herself with moments alone with him. Enough of the events of the past few weeks somehow convincing her that she might, after all, have a chance with Ralston. "Really? In the same way you didn't regret your actions in your study? In the same way you don't regret the events of last evening?" She shook her head, sad. "You've been so quick to apologize after each of those moments, Ralston, it's fairly obvious that a marriage to me is the very last thing you would choose freely."

"That's not true."

She looked up at him, her eyes filled with emotion. "Of course it's true. And, frankly, I will not put you through a lifetime of regretting your being tied to someone as . . . plain and missish . . . as I." She ignored his slight flinch at her description—the same words that he had used that afternoon in his study. "I couldn't bear it. So, thank you very much, but I will not marry you." *I have loved you too long. And too much.*

"Callie, I should never have said—"

She held up both hands to halt his speech. "Stop. Please."

He stared at her for a long moment, and she could sense his frustration at her words. And then he spoke.

"This is not over," he said, his voice firm and unyielding.

She met his unwavering blue gaze, and said, "Yes. It is."

He spun on his heel and stormed from the room.

She watched him go, listening for the main door of Allendale House to slam closed before she allowed the tears to come.

Twenty

*R*alston went straight to Brooks's, which was a mistake. If it weren't enough that she'd refused his suit and in the process made him feel like a royal ass, Callie had also ruined his club. Quite thoroughly.

In the span of twelve hours, this place that had been designed specifically for men to find comfort and solace far from the struggles of the outside world had become a mahogany-and-marble reminder of Calpurnia Hartwell. As he stood in the great foyer, awash in the drone of male conversation, all Ralston could think of was her: Callie, dressed in men's clothing, skulking down the darkened hallways of the club; Callie, peeping through open doorways to soak in the ambiance of her first—and, one would hope, only—men's club; Callie, grinning at him over their private card table; Callie, naked, the heat of their passion casting a rosy glow over her lovely smooth skin.

Casting a look down the long, shadowed path that he and Callie had taken the previous night, Ralston was struck with a perverse desire to return to the card room where they had spent the evening. For a fleeting moment, he considered ordering a pot of coffee brought to the room, where he could torture himself with memories of the night and all the many ways that he had said and done the wrong thing. He immediately decided against it, however, in the interest of preserving his own sanity.

Truthfully, he was shocked by her negative response to his proposal. After all, it wasn't every day that an attractive, young, wealthy marquess made an offer of marriage. He imagined that the days were even more rare when those marquesses were refused. How long had he been avoiding matchmaking mamas and desperate debutantes, all vying to secure the position of Marchioness of Ralston? And now, when he'd finally made the position available, the woman to whom he'd offered it had refused him.

If she thought she could simply refuse him and walk away after last night, she was entirely wrong.

Frustrated, he pulled off his greatcoat and tossed it to a footman nearby, but not without recognizing her scent on the fabric—a combination of almonds and lavender and . . . Callie. The thought brought a scowl to his face, and he admitted a modicum of pleasure at the way the footman scurried out of sight rather than be on the receiving end of Ralston's foul mood.

The emotion was fleeting, replaced by a new flare of indignation. *What the devil is wrong with her?*

He couldn't believe that she had turned him away. Surely she couldn't honestly believe that they were incompatible. She might have been a virgin, but even she must have sensed that their interaction last night—and all the others, for that matter—was far from typical. Certainly their marriage would not suffer in the bedchamber. And, if the passion between them weren't enough, there was also their well-matched intelligence, humor, and maturity. Aside from all that, she was quite lovely. Soft in all the right places. Ralston let his thoughts linger . . . a man could spend years lost in her lush curves.

Yes, Lady Calpurnia Hartwell would make him a fine marchioness.

If only she would realize it for herself.

Ralston raked a hand through his hair. When they married, she'd have title, wealth, lands, and one of the most coveted bachelors in all of England. What the hell else did the woman want?

A love match.

The thought gave him pause. She'd confessed her belief in love matches ages ago, and he'd scoffed at her, showing her that attraction was equally as powerful as the love in which she placed such faith. She couldn't honestly have refused him because she was holding out for love. He shook his head, frustrated at the very idea that she would risk her reputation and her future with a rejection of his proposal because of some childish fantasy she refused to release.

The very idea was preposterous. He'd had enough of thinking about it.

Ralston made his way to the large antechamber off the foyer, where one was always able to find a willing distraction. He entered in search of a political debate that would keep him occupied, only to discover the room virtually empty, with the exception of a small game of cards. Seated at the card table was Oxford, along with two others. They were disheveled enough for Ralston to know that the trio had likely been at the table all night.

Disgusted by the sight of Oxford's irresponsible gambling habits, and with no interest in being pulled into conversation by the group, Ralston made to exit the room as quickly and silently as he'd entered. Before he could, however, he was discovered.

"Ralston, old chap. Come and play a trick with us," Oxford called out jovially.

Ralston paused, devising a plan to best ignore the invitation, when the baron added, "Now is the time for you to win against, me, Ralston, for soon your pockets will be considerably lighter." The words, laden with meaning and followed by a round of amused noise from the table, brought Ralston around to face Oxford.

Ralston's expression steeled as he approached the table. From Oxford's ruddy-cheeked and sunken-eyed look, it was clear that he was deep in his cups. Ralston spoke blandly, indicating the piles of winnings that sat in front of the baron's companions. "It appears that my pockets are in no danger of being lightened today, Oxford."

Oxford scowled at Ralston before remembering why he'd called the baron over to begin with. "Yes, well, I shall have plenty of money to gamble away soon enough . . ." He paused, swallowing back a moment of indigestion. "You see, I'm planning to be engaged before week's end."

Ignoring the overwhelming premonition that coursed through him, Ralston tried to appear casual when he said, "To whom?"

Oxford pointed a long, pasty finger at Ralston and crowed triumphantly. "To Calpurnia Hartwell, of course! You had better count out that"—his body wavered in its seat—"thousand pounds."

The words sent a wave of heat through Ralston, which was followed quickly by a serious desire to put his fist into Oxford's smug face. It was only by pure strength of character that Ralston remained calm, and said, "You think you've got her, eh?"

Oxford flashed a toothy grin that made him look like an imbecile. "Oh, I've got her, all right. She was putty in my hands at the Royal Academy yesterday." He winked at his friends baldly.

Ralston stiffened at the words—so blatant a lie. His fists clenched at his sides, and energy pulsed through him, desperate for release, preferably in the form of tearing Oxford limb from limb.

Oxford failed to sense the tension in Ralston's corded muscles, instead pushing further. "I shall visit her tomorrow and get the proposal business out of the way. Then probably get the girl compromised by week's end to make sure that Allendale will have no choice but to welcome me into the family—though he'll likely thank me for taking on his dusty old sister with a substantial marriage settlement."

The idea of Oxford laying a finger upon Callie sent Ralston over the edge. In mere seconds, he had lifted the baron from his seat at the card table as though he weighed no more than a child. The motion startled Oxford's friends from their chairs, which went flying backward as the men scrambled to distance themselves from a fight with Ralston.

As Oxford dangled from his hands, Ralston could smell the fear on the weaker man, and the cowardice fed his disgust. When he spoke, the words were a growl. "Lady Calpurnia Hartwell is a thousand times better than you. You don't deserve to breathe her air."

Releasing Oxford, Ralston felt an acute sense of masculine satisfaction at the other man's immediate and ungraceful collapse into his chair. With an arrogant look that rivaled that of any king, Ralston added, "I wagered a thousand pounds that she won't have you, and I stand by it. In fact, I am so certain of it . . . I'll double the bet here and now."

Ralston watched, noticing the slight tremble in the baron's hands as Oxford adjusted the sleeves of his topcoat, and said, "After your boorish behavior, Ralston, I shall enjoy lightening your coffers even more."

Ralston spun on his heel and left the room, saying nothing, telling himself that his behavior had been in defense of a lady to whom he was greatly indebted.

It was easier to convince himself of that reasoning than to consider the emotions that still roiled at the idea of Callie's becoming a baroness.

* * *

CALLIE PUSHED OPEN the door to Madame Hebert's shop on Bond Street later that afternoon, eager to be done with what was certain to be another excruciating part of her day. After Ralston had stormed from the house, Callie had cried for several long minutes before receiving word that the dressmaker had completed work on the gown that she had commissioned, as well as on several pieces of Juliana's new wardrobe.

Taking the message as a sign that she could not while away the day feeling sorry for herself, Callie had prepared for an afternoon at the dressmaker's, an outing that held only slightly more appeal than a funeral. Nevertheless, she was in dire need of a distraction, and the French *modiste* was guaranteed to provide just the thing.

She'd convinced Mariana to join her for the afternoon, and the younger Hartwell sister had left Allendale House ahead of Callie to retrieve Juliana, who would spend much of the afternoon in fittings for her own dresses. Callie would have ordinarily joined the other girls, but she simply couldn't bear the thought of meeting Ralston again today—however unlikely an event that might be—and so, here she was, standing just inside the door to the dressmaker's salon, waiting for someone to acknowledge her presence.

The shop was buzzing with activity, Madame Hebert was nowhere in sight, but her assistants rushed back and forth through the curtained entrance to the fitting room, arms laden with lengths of fabric, buttons, laces, and trims. There were three other women in the front portion of the shop, considering the dresses on display, marveling at the artistry of the seamstresses' hands.

"Oh! Lady Calpurnia!" The soft, eager words, were spoken in the thick French accent of Valerie, Madame Hebert's trusted apprentice, who had come from the back of the shop and dropped a quick curtsy in Callie's direction. "Madame Hebert sends her apology that you are kept waiting. She is just finishing with another lady, but we have cleared her schedule for the afternoon, and she will join you"—she waved her hand in the air, searching for the correct phrase—"*tout de suite . . .* at once. Yes?"

"Yes, of course. I am happy to wait."

"Valerie!" Madame Hebert's voice traveled from beyond the curtain mere seconds before the Frenchwoman poked her head out into the main shop. "Bring Lady Calpurnia back. I will begin with her immediately." The dressmaker waved Callie forward with an encouraging smile. When she and Valerie were closer to the curtain, Madame Hebert added quietly to her assistant, "You may finish with Miss Kritikos."

Callie froze midstride, just outside the entrance to the fitting room. Had she heard correctly? Was it possible that Ralston's former mistress was in the room beyond? *Of course she was.* It was the perfect addition to this disaster of a day. She squared her shoulders, preparing to enter the room. Nastasia Kritikos had no reason to know Callie; therefore, Callie would simply pretend not to recognize the opera singer.

Pushing through the curtains, Callie discovered that such a task was far easier planned than performed. Nastasia stood on a raised platform at the center of the fitting room, her back to the doorway, larger than life. Callie marveled at the prima donna's hourglass form, her hips flaring in perfect concert with a bosom that women everywhere would covet. Nastasia turned from side to side, casting a critical eye at her image in an enormous mirror, taking in the details of the stunning scarlet silk gown she was wearing. The gown was beautifully fitted to Nastasia's long, lush body, its bodice secured at the back with a row of small, elegant ribbons, each tied in a perfect tiny bow.

Callie swallowed, immediately feeling pale and plain, wishing she'd chosen another day to retrieve her gown. Realizing that she was gaping in the direction of the other woman, Callie caught

herself and turned to follow Madame Hebert. Passing behind
Nastasia, Callie couldn't help but sneak a look at the opera singer's reflection and marvel at the woman's beauty. She and Ralston
must have made a stunning couple. Nastasia was grand—she
boasted the kind of beauty that women like Callie could only
dream of having, mostly because her porcelain skin and shining
black tresses and lovely, bow-shaped mouth were only part of her
appeal. More than any one physical characteristic, the opera singer's obvious confidence and self-awareness made all the difference. She owned the room the way she owned the stage—wholly
and completely.

She was magnificent.

And Callie envied every bit of the other woman as she watched
her in the reflection—from her perfect poise to her riveting violet
eyes . . . eyes that met Callie's in the mirror.

Caught staring, Callie blushed and looked away immediately,
hurrying to catch up with Madame Hebert. Callie followed the
Frenchwoman around a tall dressing screen set to one side of the
room and pulled up short when she saw the dressmaker's form
standing in the corner, draped in what was, quite possibly, the
loveliest gown she had ever seen.

Madame Hebert met her eyes with a little, knowing smile. "It
pleases you?"

"Oh, yes . . ." Callie's fingers itched to touch the fabric, to stroke
down the cascade of silk that was more lovely than she remembered.

"Excellent. I think it is time you see it as it is meant to be . . . on
you. Don't you agree?"

The seamstress turned Callie around and set to work on the buttons of her day dress. Indicating the collection of undergarments
that had been set out next to the dress, the dressmaker said, "We
will begin with lingerie."

Callie immediately shook her head, "Oh, I couldn't . . . I have plenty of underthings . . . I do not need new ones."

The dress loosened into her hands as Madame Hebert spoke. "I assure you, you do need them." She helped Callie out of her corset and chemise, saying, "The most confident of women are those who believe in every scrap of fabric that they wear. They are the ones who are as happy with their drawers as they are with their gowns. You can tell the difference between a woman who wraps herself in beautiful silks and satins and she who wears . . ." The *modiste* paused as she dropped Callie's worn chemise to the floor. " . . . otherwise."

Callie slipped into the new, lovely undergarments adorned with little details—satin ribbons, little, hand-fashioned flowers in lovely colors, lace panels that added a touch of femininity that she had never before considered necessary in unmentionables. As the layers were draped over her, she felt rather silly for enjoying the sensation of lovely silks and satins against her skin, but Madame Hebert had been right. There was something quite decadent about wearing such frivolously beautiful underclothes—especially when Anne was the only person who would ever see them.

As if she were reading Callie's thoughts, the dressmaker leaned in, and whispered, "And, let us not forget, one never knows who might someday unwrap such a present, *oui*?" Callie blushed fiercely at the words, followed by the Frenchwoman's knowing laugh.

And then she was in her gown, which seemed to fit her perfectly. Madame Hebert looked pleased as Punch as she walked a slow circle around Callie, noting each minute detail of the gown. Satisfied, she met Callie's wide-eyed gaze, and said, "Now, out into the fitting room and we shall have a closer look."

Following the *modiste* back into the main room, Callie noted that Nastasia was still on her platform as Valerie worked to hem the red gown. Pushing aside the immediate sense of insecurity that consumed her, Callie stepped up to take her place on the empty second platform in the room. Madame Hebert gently turned her toward a large mirror placed nearby, and Callie's eyes widened in surprise as she realized that she was the woman in the reflection. She shook her head. She'd never seen herself this way—thoroughly transformed from prim and plain to . . . well, quite remarkable.

Her breasts were perfectly highlighted by the low cut of the gown, looking lush and full without appearing vulgar, the drape of the silk over her curving waist and hips and stomach made her appear well proportioned rather than too plump, and the color— the most lovely, shimmering blue she'd ever seen, gave her usually too-red skin the appearance of strawberries and cream.

A smile broke out on her face. Madame Hebert had been right. This was a dress made for waltzing. Callie couldn't resist spinning in excitement toward the dressmaker. "Oh, it's lovely, Madame."

The *modiste's* smile matched Callie's. "Indeed. It is." She tilted her head, looking critically at Callie's reflection, and said, "It needs to be raised a touch in the skirt. Excuse me—I shall fetch a girl to help me pin."

The Frenchwoman disappeared through a nearby door, and Callie looked back at her reflection, taking in the drape of the fabric, the lovely cut—so uniquely different from anything that was in London ballrooms at present, so perfectly suited to her un- fashionable figure.

"Hebert is a genius, is she not?"

Callie's eyes flew to the looking glass, where she met a pair of probing violet eyes, doubly reflected in their mirrors. With a small, polite smile, she said, quietly, "She certainly is."

Nastasia's eyes flickered to Valerie's reflection, and she watched as the girl pinned a section of her hem before saying casually, "Ralston has always liked her work."

Callie looked away at the words, uncertain. She'd never spoken to someone's mistress before. Certainly not to the mistress of the man she loved.

Nastasia pressed on, sounding bored. "You do not have to shy away from me, Lady Calpurnia. We are not girls, just out of the schoolroom, but women, yes? I know he is with you, now. It is the way of the world, my dear."

Callie shook her head, her mouth falling open in shock. "He isn't . . . with me."

The opera singer raised a perfectly sculpted eyebrow. "Are you really going to tell me that Ralston hasn't seduced you?"

Callie blushed, looking away again, and Nastasia laughed. The sound wasn't mean-spirited, as Callie would have expected, but entertained. "You didn't expect him to do it, did you? But I shall wager you enjoyed every minute of it. Ralston is a rare breed of man . . . one who cares more for his lovers than for himself." Callie's cheeks flamed as the Greek woman pressed on, frank. "I have had many lovers . . . and only one other who was as generous as Ralston. You are lucky he was your first."

Callie thought she might perish from embarrassment right there. On the spot.

"May I offer you a piece of advice?"

Callie's head snapped up, and she watched the raven-haired beauty in the mirror. Nastasia was no longer looking at her, but instead off through a large window through which the afternoon sun poured into the fitting room. After several long moments of silence, Callie's curiosity got the better of her. "Please."

Nastasia spoke, the words coming from far away. "When I was eighteen, I met the first of those men. Dimitri was generous and kind and a remarkable lover . . . everything I had dreamed of . . . everything I hadn't known I longed for. It was inevitable that I fell in love with him. And it was a love that surpassed anything I'd ever known . . . anything I'd ever heard of—mythic in its proportions. He was the only man I would ever love." She paused, sadness passing over her face so quickly that Callie was not entirely certain it had been there to begin with. "But he could not love me in return. The capacity for that kind of emotion . . . it was not in him. And, so, instead, he broke my heart."

Tears sprang to Callie's eyes, unbidden, at the sadness of the other woman's story. She couldn't contain her curiosity. "What happened?"

Nastasia gave a small, elegant shrug. "I left Greece. And my voice carried the day."

Valerie stood, finished with her task, and Nastasia seemed to return from far away. Her eyes cleared as she inspected the young woman's work in the mirror. "Ralston is your Dimitri. Guard your heart well."

There was a pregnant pause as the two women each considered their own reflections. "If you could do it again . . . would you have taken him without love?" Callie blurted out the question, regretting it as soon as the words were spoken.

Nastasia thought for a long moment, her face a portrait of sadness. When her eyes met Callie's in the mirror, they were liquid with emotion. "No," she whispered. "I loved him too much for it to be one-sided."

Callie brushed away an errant tear as Madame Hebert returned, apprentice in tow, unaware of the conversation that had taken place. Nastasia turned her head to the dressmaker. "Lady Calpurnia's gown is beautiful," she said, "I should like one of the same fabric."

Madame Hebert spoke in clipped tones. "I am sorry, Miss Kritikos. The fabric is no longer available."

Nastasia gave Callie a frank appraisal, from head to toe. "Well, then, it appears you are making a habit of receiving those things that I desire, Lady Calpurnia." She offered a small smile. "May you have better luck than I. That dress will certainly help."

Callie dipped her head in acknowledgment of Nastasia's words. "Thank you, Miss Kritikos. And, may I say, I think you are a brilliant talent."

Nastasia stepped from her platform and sank into a deep, gracious curtsy, finally acknowledging Callie's social position. "You are too kind, my lady." With that, she and Valerie exited to a side dressing room, where Callie could only imagine there were other garments for Nastasia to consider. She watched the other woman leave, surprised and saddened by the direction of their conversation.

Returning her attention to the curious dressmaker, Callie offered her a small, watery smile. She knew what Madame Hebert was thinking. What could an opera singer and the sister of an earl possibly have to say to each other?

The *modiste* had been running her salon for too long to risk insulting her patrons with questions about their personal lives, however, and her business acumen forced her to turn her focus to Callie's hem.

Madame Hebert adjusted the length of Callie's skirt, then issued instructions to the young apprentice and left the room. The girl began to pin Callie's dress in silence, and Callie played the conversation with Nastasia over in her mind. The singer's words had been powerful; Callie had felt them like a blow. She had known the truth, of course, that Ralston would never be able to love her the way she desired, but hearing Nastasia's story—sensing its truth—had intensified Callie's sadness from earlier in the day.

She watched her reflection in the mirror as her tears blurred it. She could be as beautiful as the woman in the mirror every day, but it would not make Ralston love her. And, perhaps, if he were anyone else—someone whom she loved less, or not at all—she would have embraced his offer of marriage and accepted. But she had dreamed of being his for too long. He had quite ruined her for a marriage of convenience. She wanted everything from him: his mind, his body, his name and, most of all, his heart.

Perhaps refusing him had been a mistake. Perhaps she should have jumped at the opportunity to be his marchioness. To be the mother of his children. Callie's heart clenched at the idea of little dark-haired, blue-eyed babies clinging to her skirts. But it seemed that Nastasia was right. The worst misery would come not from being without him but being without *all* of him.

Callie heaved a little sigh, willing her morbid thoughts away for this moment, as she discovered this newer, lovelier version of herself. A burst of familiar laughter came from the front of the shop, and she forced herself to smile as Juliana and Mariana hurried through the curtain, stopping short at the sight of Callie.

"Oh, Callie . . ." Mariana said in a hushed, reverent voice. "You look beautiful."

Callie dipped her head at the compliment, so uncommon. "No."

Juliana nodded her head eagerly. "It is true. You are beautiful!"

Callie's cheeks reddened. "Thank you."

Mari walked a slow circle around her sister. "It's a stunning gown, Callie . . . but there's more . . . there's something . . ." She paused, looking up into her sister's big, brown eyes. "You *feel* beautiful, don't you?"

The words brought a smile to Callie's eyes. "I rather think I do, actually."

Juliana laughed. "*Brava!* It is time you feel beautiful, Callie." When Mariana nodded encouragingly, Juliana continued, "I have thought you were lovely from the beginning of our acquaintance, of course. But, now, with this dress . . . you must wear it to the ball. *Dovete!* You *must*." Three nights hence marked the Salisbury Ball, when Juliana would make her official debut to the *ton*. The young woman clapped her hands, excitedly. "We shall have our coming out together! With new dresses! Although I cannot imagine that any of mine will be anything so beautiful as this one!"

Mariana nodded her agreement, and Callie looked from one girl to the other, overwhelmed. "Oh, I do not imagine this dress will be ready by the ball. It must be hemmed, and I'm certain that Madame Hebert has much more important customers than I."

"If you need it for the ball, my lady, you shall have it for the ball." The words came from the *modiste,* who had reentered the room to check on the progress of her assistant. "I shall hem it myself and have it delivered first thing in the morning on one condition." She leaned in close to Callie, and said, "You must promise that you will dance every waltz."

Callie smiled, shaking her head. "I am afraid that is not my decision to make, Madame."

"Nonsense," the dressmaker scoffed. "In this dress, you shall be leaving hearts in your wake. The men, they shall be chasing after you."

Callie laughed at the unlikely image the words painted, only to discover that none of the other women found the idea remotely amusing. Her laughter died away, and Mariana spoke. "They shall, indeed!"

Juliana smiled a thoughtful smile, cocking her head as she took Callie in. "I agree. I cannot wait to see Gabriel's response to this! You are a vision!"

Mariana looked to her friend and spoke matter-of-factly. "Oh, Ralston is a foregone conclusion, I'd venture to guess."

Callie sputtered at the bold, inappropriate conversation, a blush flooding her cheeks. Were her feelings for Ralston that obvious? *Had Juliana said anything to her brother?*

Her discomfort was ignored; the girls continued to titter between themselves as Madame Hebert guided Callie back behind the dressing screen.

Once there, Callie risked a look at the dressmaker, noting the woman's knowing smile just before she said, quietly, "The Marquess of Ralston is after you, is he?"

Callie shook her head in response to the bold question, immediately answering, "No. Certainly not." With a little noise of acknowledgment, Madame Hebert began to unbutton Callie's dress, remaining silent long enough for Callie to think the conversation was over.

It was only after she stepped out of the pool of aethereal blue silk that the *modiste* added, as though Callie had not spoken, "Well, if Ralston is your target, be certain to wear the lingerie, my lady. He shall enjoy it as much as you do."

Callie blushed furiously as the dressmaker gave a little, knowing laugh.

Twenty-one

$\mathscr{C}$allie and Mariana stood on the edge of the Salisbury ballroom, watching the steady stream of attendees arrive. The enormous space was bathed in the golden light of thousands of candles flickering high above in enormous crystal chandeliers. The room was mirrored along one wall, doubling the light and giving the illusion that it was twice its size and that all of London had turned out for the ball. Of course, all of London just might have done so. The ball was packed with people—women in silks and satins of every imaginable hue gossiping in small clusters, men in dark formal attire talking politics and Parliament.

Callie stood up on her toes and looked around the room, concerned that they might have missed Juliana's entrance. The hour was growing late for arrivals, and the last thing that a new addition to the *ton* needed was to be unfashionably late to her first ball. *Surely Ralston understood that,* Callie thought to herself as she searched for the younger woman.

There had been little doubt that the Salisbury Ball was the ideal place to launch Juliana into society. The annual event, one of the largest and most inclusive of the season, was hosted by the very dear and very kind Earl and Countess of Salisbury, whom

Callie had always considered one of the most gracious couples in London. When her father had passed away, it had been Lord and Lady Salisbury who had offered the most support—for both Callie's devastated mother and for young, ill-prepared Benedick, who had been in dire need of the tutelage that the earl had offered. The Salisburys were friends, and they would welcome Juliana and Ralston without question. Of that, Callie was certain.

Assuming, of course, they ever arrived.

Callie gave a little sigh. She was as nervous as she had been on the night of her own coming out.

"They shall be here," Mariana said calmly. "I don't know Ralston nearly as well as you do, but I know enough of him to be certain that he would not miss this evening." She turned an impish gaze on Callie. "And when he sees you in this dress, he will be very happy that he did not miss it."

Callie rolled her eyes at her sister and said dryly, "A bit much, Mari, even for you."

Mariana laughed and gave a delicate shrug. "Perhaps . . . but true, nonetheless. Hebert has outdone herself. It is a stunning gown."

Callie looked down at herself, at the drape of blue silk across her bodice and the full, lovely skirt that swayed perfectly when she walked. The fabric, which she had only ever seen in sunlight, took on an entirely different sheen in candlelight. It shimmered as though it were alive, like the bluest of oceans. She gave a little smile at the memory of her image in the mirror tonight. Gone was the dusty old lace-capped spinster; this gown had transformed her.

"They're here."

Callie's reverie was cut short by Mariana's whisper, and her gaze flew to the entrance of the ballroom, marked by a wide staircase, just long enough to offer attendees an ideal look at those entering the festivities. There were masses of people crowded along the edges of the stairway and on the platform above, but it was impossible to miss the trio that had just arrived.

Juliana was relieved of her pristine white cloak and stood, back straight, perfectly still, in a soft empire-waisted dress of the palest of pinks. It was the perfect gown for the evening—beautifully crafted without being ostentatious, expensive without being gaudy. Just behind her, moving almost in unison, stood Ralston and St. John, shucking their greatcoats to flank their sister. They were twin portraits of determination, each surveying the crowd below as though preparing to do battle. The corner of Callie's mouth twitched in amusement. London society just might be the closest thing to battle that the people in this room would ever see.

Callie's gaze settled on Ralston as her heart pounded in her chest, noting the firm set of his jaw and the cool determination in his eyes—so blue that she could see them from where she stood, halfway across the room. And then he was looking at her. She warmed as his gaze lingered, taking her in. Unconsciously, she sighed, a deep, resigned sigh, and Mariana gave her a little nudge with her elbow. "Callie, do try not to appear as though you're thoroughly infatuated with the man, will you?"

Callie snapped her head around to her sister, and whispered harshly, "I am doing no such thing!"

"Mmm. And I am Queen Charlotte," Mariana said dryly, ignoring her sister's glare before adding, "And so it begins."

Callie followed the direction of Mariana's gaze and noted Juliana being presented to the countess and earl. She watched as the young woman fell into a perfectly executed curtsy, eyes downcast, serene smile pasted on her face. The long column of her neck gave her a swanlike grace that was sure to be the envy of every woman in the room who was watching. And they were all watching.

At Callie's shoulder, Mariana let out a little sound of satisfaction. "She did that better than I've ever done!"

Callie ignored Mariana, instead turning her attention to the rest of the ballroom and taking note of the stares directed at Juliana from every direction.

This was not going to be easy.

"I heard that she is illegitimate—by the mother." A feminine whisper came from Callie's left, and she turned to see the Duke and Dowager Duchess of Leighton, each staring at Juliana. Callie's breath hitched in anger as she registered the disdain on the duke's handsome face as his mother continued, "I cannot *imagine* why Salisbury would have let her in the door. It's not as though Ralston's reputation is much better. I'm sure he's sired a few on the wrong side of the blanket himself."

The words, so thoroughly inappropriate and, at the same time, so very expected, were too much. Callie cast a long, quelling look at the duchess—a look meant to be seen.

The Duke of Leighton noticed and matched Callie's stare with a cool one of his own. "Eavesdropping is a terrible habit, Lady Calpurnia."

A year ago, Callie would not have had the courage to respond—but with a pointed look in the direction of the dowager duchess, she said, "I believe I could think of a worse habit, Your Grace."

With that, she headed across the ballroom to save Juliana from these vipers.

Mariana was fast on her heels. "Well done, sister!" Mariana applauded her boldness. "The look on their faces! Priceless!"

"They deserved it. Their snobbery is unconscionable," Callie said absently, focused entirely on getting to Juliana's side and placing her squarely under the protection of the Allendale name for the evening. It would not stem the gossip, but it most certainly would help matters.

As they pushed through the throng of people, the pair passed Rivington, and Mari placed a quick hand on her betrothed's arm, speaking so only he could hear. "Come and meet Juliana, Riv." Of course, Rivington had met the girl before, but the duke knew immediately what Mariana really meant. *Come and stamp her with the approval of a dukedom.* He followed without pause.

Callie pushed past the last cluster of people to find Juliana standing in an empty area, several feet from the various clusters of revelers nearby who appeared to be so enthralled with their own conversations that they could not bear to interrupt themselves to meet Juliana. Callie knew better. So did everyone else. Ralston and St. John stood on either side of their sister, looking entirely ready to do bodily harm to half of London. Callie met Ralston's gaze briefly, noting his obvious anger at this society that so easily shunned those it did not immediately accept. How many times had she felt precisely the same way as he did in this moment?

She could not stop to sympathize with him, however. His sister needed her. "Juliana!" she said, her voice high and clear and obvious to those standing nearby, keenly aware of the power of the moment. "I am so happy that you are here! Mariana and I have been waiting for your arrival!"

Mariana clasped Juliana's hands in her own, and said, "Indeed we have! The evening has been quite dismal without you!" She turned eager eyes on Rivington. "Rivington, don't you agree?"

The Duke of Rivington bowed low over Juliana's hand. "Indeed. Miss Fiori, I should very much like to accompany you for the next dance," he said, his tone warm and a touch louder than usual. "That is, assuming you have not already promised it to another?"

Juliana shook her head, overwhelmed by the moment. "No, Your Grace."

Mariana beamed up at her future husband, and said, "I think that is an excellent idea!" She then leaned in to Juliana and whispered conspiratorially, "Mind he doesn't tread on your toes."

The foursome laughed at Mari's jest, and Rivington guided Juliana into the center of the room. Mariana and Callie watched as the two took their place and Juliana received her first public acceptance—in the form of a dance with one of the most powerful men in England. The sisters looked to each other, unable to hide their wide, proud smiles.

"I find I should very much like to dance myself," came a voice close behind them. They turned to find St. John smiling at them. "Lady Mariana, never say you have promised this one to someone else?"

Mari looked down at her dance card and laughed. "Indeed I had, my lord," she whispered, "although, it appears that my partner has chosen your sister instead."

Nick shook his head, a tragic frown upon his face. "I shall endeavor to make it up to you, my lady."

"That would be the gentlemanly thing to do," Mari said with a brilliant smile, and allowed him to guide her onto the floor.

Callie watched them go, amused. It was almost enough for her to forget that they'd all summarily left her with Ralston. Almost enough.

Uncertain of what to say in light of their last conversation, she turned and met his unreadable gaze. Nervous, she decided on the safest topic. "Lord Ralston," she said, "it appears your sister is in fine form this evening."

"Indeed. Thanks to you and your family."

"Rivington is proving himself to be an excellent soon-to-be member of our motley crew." Callie's lips curved in a quiet smile as they watched the dancing couples.

One side of Ralston's mouth kicked up. "I am indebted to him." He looked at her, spearing her with a serious look. "And to you."

His eyes darkened and narrowed as they passed over her, and Callie detected a slight shifting of his weight. And it was then that she knew . . . he had noticed her dress. *Ask me to dance.* She knew that it was a terrible idea—that the very last thing she should do was allow herself to be swept away by Ralston tonight—mere hours after refusing his proposal of marriage and resolving to remain far, far away from him. *Ask me to dance so that my first waltz in this gown is with you.* She quashed the little voice, resolving this moment to stop her silly flights of fancy. Dancing with Ralston was a decidedly *awful* idea.

"Lady Calpurnia, would you care to dance?"

At first, Callie was legitimately confused by the words, which she had willed Ralston to speak but that instead came from an altogether different direction—over her right shoulder. She blinked uncertainly, barely noting Ralston's thunderous expression before understanding dawned, and she turned to face Baron Oxford.

No! She resisted the urge to stomp her foot.

She could not refuse his offer; not only would it be the height of impropriety to do so, Callie was certainly in no position to refuse any offer to dance. It wasn't as though they came fast and furiously. She darted a little glance in the direction of Ralston, briefly wondering if he might step in and claim the dance for himself. She would not deny it if he were to say that he had requested the waltz in question.

But he said nothing, instead watching her with that cold, unreadable gaze. She turned back to Oxford. "I would very much like to dance, my lord. Thank you."

The baron extended his hand to her, and she settled her palm in his.

When their hands touched, he flashed a broad grin that did not wholly reach his eyes. "Excellent."

Ralston watched as Oxford guided Callie into the waltz, fury coursing through him at the sight of the other man's arms wrapped around her—touching her. Only years of training in restraint stayed him from storming out onto the ballroom floor and wrenching her from the clutches of the fortune-hunting dandy.

It should be me dancing with her, for God's sake. Ralston berated himself as he followed their path around the dance floor, Oxford's tall frame towering over Callie as he swept her through the room, turning her into a swirl of blue. As if the events that had transpired—her thorough dismissal of him and his marriage proposal—had not smarted enough, now she was in Oxford's arms, dressed like an angel.

Where the hell had she found a dress like that? It fit her beautifully, embracing and celebrating the lush, feminine shape of her, highlighting her lovely breasts, the subtle curve of her hips, her voluptuous figure. It was a dress designed to enhance and embolden and drive men mad. It was a dress that served only one purpose—to tempt men into removing it.

At that moment, Oxford and Callie turned in such a way that she was facing Ralston head-on. He met her gaze and was shaken by the sadness in her eyes. There was something about her tonight that was different, more tragic, from other nights. He knew instinctively that he was the reason for her sadness—that he had made a thorough mess of everything, mucking up his marriage proposal, somehow leading her to believe that he didn't really want to marry her.

He bit back a curse as Oxford and Callie were swallowed up by the teeming crowd of dancers. He could see the shimmering blue of the gown peeking out at him as the wave of people ebbed and flowed, and his mood descended into blackness as the couple moved farther and farther away.

Ralston began to prowl his way around the outside edge of the ballroom, unwilling to allow them to move completely out of sight. As he passed clusters of people, he nodded his acknowledgment halfheartedly, attempting to move slowly enough not to spark curiosity but quickly enough to keep up with the swirling dancers.

"Lord Ralston, it is such a pleasure to see you in attendance this evening," purred the Countess of Marsden as he pushed past her.

He stopped, unable to be rude despite the woman's predatory look. Ralston wouldn't have been surprised to see her dart her tongue across her rouged lips salaciously. "Lady Marsden," he said, affecting a bored tone that he knew would irritate the countess, "I am happy to have been able to oblige. I should very much like to pay my respects to your husband," he said, pointedly. "Is he here?"

The countess's gaze narrowed on him, and he knew his aim had struck true. "No. He isn't."

"Ah," he said, already moving away, distracted. "A pity. Do give him my regards."

He looked back at the dancers to find Juliana laughing up at Rivington as he whirled her across the ballroom, showing all of London that, half sister or no, foreign or no, Juliana Fiori was as fine a dance partner as any in the room. A burst of emotion flared in Ralston's chest as he watched his new sister—who had so quickly found a way into his heart—smile up at the duke as though it were the most natural thing in the world for her to be dancing with one of the most revered members of the aristocracy. The *ton* would be hard-pressed to find fault with the girl, although it would try its very best to do so. Between him and Nick and the Rivington and Allendale families, however, Juliana would be protected—as much as she could be. Forming an alliance with Callie had been one of the best decisions he could have made to ensure Juliana's acceptance into society.

Callie.

She was remarkable. Even as she had pushed and prodded and refused him, she had delivered on every one of her promises, turning Juliana into a debutante that would make any brother proud. Lord knew he couldn't have done it on his own, not even with his newly honorable intentions. It was only because of Callie that Juliana was here tonight. She was a vital part of Juliana's success. And, somehow, she had become a vital part of his life.

The thought spurred him on; all of a sudden, he knew he had to get Callie alone once more. It was no longer that he *had* to marry her out of respect for propriety and responsibility. It was that he *wanted* to marry her. Perversely, it seemed that the more she denied him, the more he wanted to marry her, infuriating though she was. Now he just had to convince her that she wanted it, also.

He scanned the crowd, frustrated, searching the writhing mass of bodies for her—eager for a glimpse of blue satin, eager for the dance to be over so that he could steal her away for a private conversation.

The music came to a swirling crescendo, and the couples whirled to a stop. Ralston watched as they began to promenade from the floor as the orchestra paused in its playing. He saw Juliana and Rivington find Mariana and Nick and resume their earlier conversation, but there was no sign of Oxford and Callie.

Where the hell had they gone?

AFTER THEIR WALTZ, Oxford guided Callie to a small, private antechamber off a long, dark corridor beyond the Salisbury House ballroom. The doors to the hallway had been left open to increase the flow of air into the stifling ballroom and Oxford led her into the secluded area after their waltz, insisting they enjoy a quiet moment together.

Eyeing the doorway, left barely open, Callie offered Oxford a wavering smile. "Thank you, my lord, for your escort," she said, graciously. "I forget how very cloying balls can be."

Oxford took a step closer. "Please, do not think of it."

Callie inched away as he closed the distance between them. "I find I am rather parched, my lord. Perhaps we could return to the ball and find the refreshment room?"

"Or, perhaps, we could distract ourselves from thirst with . . . other pursuits?" He paused. "Darling."

Callie's brows rose at the endearment. "My lord," she said in protest as he stepped closer, forcing her up against the wall next to the door to the hallway. Nervousness coursed through her. "Baron Oxford!" she exclaimed, uncertain of his motives.

He leaned in, closer. "Rupert," he corrected, "I think it is time we dispense with formalities. Don't you?"

"Baron Oxford," she said firmly, "I should like to return. Now. This is highly inappropriate."

"You won't think so when you hear what I have to say," he replied. "You see . . ." he stopped on a long, lingering pause. "I'm offering you the chance to be my baroness."

Callie's eyebrows shot up at his words.

He noted her surprise and tried again, this time speaking to her as though she were a child. "You have the opportunity to marry. Me."

Dear Lord, was there not a single man in London in possession of an ounce of romance when it came to marriage proposals?

Callie swallowed back a nervous laugh, edging toward the door. "My lord. I am quite honored that you would think of me . . ." She paused, attempting to find the appropriate words to delicately refuse.

And then his arms had snaked around her and his lips were on hers, wet and soft and not at all pleasant. His tongue pushed into her mouth, and Callie recoiled from the touch, her hands flying up to his shoulders to stay his advances. He mistook the movement for a caress and pressed on, towering over her, crowding her into the wall until she felt the hard edge of the doorjamb pressing into the back of her as he pulled back briefly to whisper, "Do not be shy. We shan't be caught. And if we are, we are betrothed."

Callie leaned away from the baron, shaking her head at his unmatched arrogance. The idea that she would simply collapse into gratitude at the mere hint of a proposal would have stung if it weren't so preposterous. Pushing against him with all her might, Callie said, "I am afraid you are severely misguided." He stopped his advancement as she squeezed out from between him and the wall. "I have no intention of marrying you. I should like you to leave."

Oxford blinked twice, as though unable to comprehend her decision. "You cannot be serious."

The irony of the situation was not lost on Callie. After twenty-eight years of waiting for someone, anyone, to show interest in her, two men propose to her and she rejects both suits. *Was she mad?*

"Indeed, I am quite serious. It appears that you have mistaken my friendship."

"Friendship!" Oxford sneered, sending a bolt of fear through Callie at the harsh change in his tone. "You think I'm looking for friendship? On the contrary. I'm looking for a wife." He spat the words at her as though she were addle-pated.

Callie recoiled instinctively from him, surprised by this new Oxford—gone was the brightly smiling vapid dandy, replaced by an angry, unpleasant man. "Then it appears you have been laboring under a misapprehension that I am seeking a husband."

Oxford's lip curled, and he spoke, rudely. "Come now. You cannot expect me to believe that you haven't been dreaming of this. Isn't this the moment of which all aging spinsters dream?"

She pulled herself up to her full, proud height. "Certainly, Lord Oxford, we dream of proposals of marriage. We simply do not dream of them coming from you."

She watched as rage passed over him, and he stiffened, his face turned a shocking shade of red. Ordinarily, she would have taken some pride in such a transformation, but instead, fleetingly, she thought he might strike her. He did not, instead pulling back and freeing her from his stifling closeness. She watched as rage turned to disgust, and she finally saw what he really felt for her—complete and utter disdain.

"You are making a terrible mistake," he warned.

"I sincerely doubt that." Callie's words turned cold, her defenses raised. "This conversation is over."

He stared at her, eyes glittering with anger, as she turned resolutely away, returning her attention to the dark gardens beyond. "I'm the best offer you'll ever have. You think anyone would actually *want* a piglet like you?" The words were meant to sting, and they did. She kept her back straight as he exited the room, and she listened to his footsteps disappear, returning him to the ballroom, before she came back to her chair.

And then she let out a long sigh, feeling the strength leave her as Oxford's horrible words repeated themselves over and over inside her head. Of course, he was right. She'd received two proposals in her lifetime, and neither of them had had anything to do with her. Oxford had needed the money he would receive from her dowry, and Ralston . . . Ralston was attempting to keep her reputation intact which, while honorable, was not exactly the most romantic of notions. Why couldn't someone, somewhere, want her for her?

Tears sprang to her eyes at the thought. *What a thorough mess.* She bowed her head and slumped, her shoulders squeezing the back of a padded chair positioned near the door as hard as she could, her muscles protesting the movement. She took deep, cleansing breaths and wondered how long she could stay in this room without being missed.

"You should not be here by yourself."

She stiffened at the firm words, but did not turn around, unwilling to show her tear-stained face to Ralston. "How did you know I was here?"

"I saw Oxford coming from this direction. Did something happen? Are you all right?"

Instead, she whispered into the darkness, "Please go away."

There was a pause, followed by a shift in the air around them as he stepped closer, reaching out to her. "Callie?" he said, and the quiet concern in his voice tore at her heart. "Are you all right? My God. Did Oxford touch you? I'll kill him."

She took another deep breath. "No . . . No. He did nothing. I am fine. I should just appreciate your leaving before my . . . reputation . . . becomes an issue."

He gave a little laugh. "I think we're rather past that, don't you think?" She didn't respond, and he pressed on, speaking to the back of her head. "That's part of why I came to find you."

She kept her viselike grip on the chair. "Ralston, please. Just leave."

"I cannot," he stepped closer, setting his hands to her shoulders as he spoke, his tone at once pleading and enticing. "Callie, you must give me a chance to convince you that my offer is a good one. Please. Marry me."

It was all too much. She couldn't bear it. Tears came again, fast and uncontrollable and entirely embarrassing. She stayed quiet, willing herself not to make a sound to give away her sorrow. He whispered again, close to her ear, the words so tempting and lovely. "Marry me."

She bowed her head again. "I cannot."

A pause. "Why?"

"I—I don't want to marry you." The untruth was almost too much to bear.

Anger began to edge into his voice. "I don't believe you."

"It's the truth."

"Look at me and say it."

There was a long pause as the words hung between them, and Callie considered her options. She had no choice. She turned and looked at him, thanking her Maker that her face remained in shadow as she did. Her voice trembling, she repeated, "I don't want to marry you."

He shook his head slowly. "I don't believe you. You do want me. Do you think I haven't noticed how compatible we are? Intellectually? Physically?" When she didn't respond he said, "Shall I prove it to you again?" His lips were so close to hers, and she was so aware of him. The breath of his words caressed her in a way that made her want nothing more than to close the scant distance between them and take the kiss she yearned for. "You know I shall give you everything."

She closed her eyes against the words and their dark promise. "Not everything," she said, sadness in her tone.

"Everything I can give you," he vowed, reaching up to touch her face and pulling back when she flinched, almost violently.

"And what shall happen when that is not enough?" The question fell between them.

He brought a hand down hard on the chair behind her, and Callie flinched at the sound that his palm made on the wood. "What more do you want, Callie? I'm rich. I'm handsome . . ."

She cut him off with a pained, frustrated laugh. "Do you think I care about any of that?" she said, angry and sad and hurt all at the same time, "I'd have you poor and ugly—I don't care—as long as you—"

His gaze narrowed on her as she stopped the flow of words. "As long as I, what?"

As long as you loved me.

She shook her head, not trusting herself to speak.

He let out a harsh breath and tried again, confusion making him frustrated and angry. "What do you want from me? Name it, and I'll give it to you! I'm a marquess, for God's sake!"

That was it. She'd had enough. "I don't care if you're the bloody king. I'm not marrying you!"

"Why the hell not?"

"Any number of reasons!"

"Give me one decent reason!" He was so close to her, so angry, and she said the first thing that came into her head.

"Because I love you!"

They were both surprised by the words. He recovered first. "What?"

She shook her head, tears spilling over. When she spoke, her voice was laced with self-deprecating humor, her only defense against this awful, awkward moment. "Please, don't make me say it again."

"I—" He stopped, uncertain of his words.

"You don't have to say anything. In fact, I'd prefer you not say anything. But there it is. I can't marry you. Because it would kill me to spend the rest of my days with you when you are only marrying me out of some newfound—and misplaced—sense of honor and duty."

He watched her for long moments, followed the tears as they traveled, unhindered, down her cheeks. "I—" He repeated, for the first time in his life entirely without words.

She couldn't bear to look at him. "Do you remember the night in your bedchamber?" she whispered. "When we negotiated the terms of our transaction?"

The night everything changed. "Of course I do."

"Do you remember you promised me a favor? Of my choosing? In the future?"

A feeling of cold dread settled in the pit of his stomach. All of a sudden, he knew what she was going to say. "Callie, don't do this."

"I'm asking you to honor that promise. Right now. Please, just go away."

The pain in her voice was heartbreaking, and Ralston itched to touch her, to comfort her. Instead, he raked his hands through his hair, cursing violently. "Callie—" He stopped, not knowing what to say but determined to say something, anything, that would convince her that she should marry him.

She held up a single hand, and Ralston had a fleeting moment of surprise at its steadiness. "Please, Gabriel. If you care for me at all," she repeated, "please, just go away. Go away and leave me alone."

And, because it was the one request she'd made that he could honor, he did.

Callie sat for a long while in the quiet room, allowing the darkness to surround her. The tears that came were fleeting, soon replaced by a bone-deep sadness that came with the sense of finality that the interaction with Ralston had brought.

For, in that moment, she knew with utter certainty that she would be alone forever. Refusing Ralston's suit so summarily had ruined her for all others. For, if she could not have him, she would never want anyone else.

Perhaps she had made a mistake. Perhaps she could have loved him enough for both of them. But could she survive a lifetime of knowing that he never really wanted her? That he had proposed simply because it was the thing to do? That, left to his own devices, he would have found someone infinitely more worldly? Infinitely more beautiful? Infinitely . . . more?

No. She couldn't bear it. Refusing him had been her only option.

She wiped a stray tear from her cheek and sniffled quietly, knowing she should return to the ball but unable to make the effort.

"Callie?"

The whisper, barely a sound, came from the doorway and Callie snapped her head around to face Juliana, who was peering through the dim light to confirm that the woman in the darkness was, indeed, her friend.

Dashing another tear from her cheek, Callie sat up in her chair, facing the younger girl. "Juliana, you should not be here, alone!"

At the words, Juliana closed the door firmly behind her and crossed to Callie, sitting on a nearby ottoman. "I am quite tired of being told what I should and should not do. *You* are here, are you not? I am not so alone now!"

Callie smiled a watery smile at the girl's defense. "That much is true."

"And it looks as though you could use a companion, *amica*. As could I."

Callie blinked, focusing on Juliana's face, registering her blue eyes, rounded and . . . *hurt?* Callie pushed her own sadness aside, and said, "What has happened?"

Juliana waved one hand with what Callie knew was feigned dismissiveness. "I wandered away from the celebration and became lost."

Callie's look softened. "Juliana, you cannot allow them to upset you."

Juliana's lips twisted wryly. "I am not upset. Indeed, I find myself eager to show them what I am capable of."

Callie smiled at the younger girl, "Yes! That is how you must face them. Proud, and strong, and wonderfully *you*. They shall not be able to resist you. I guarantee it!"

Juliana's face shadowed for a moment—so fleeting that Callie almost missed it. "Some shall resist me, it seems."

Callie shook her head, placing a warm, reassuring hand on the other girl's knee. "I vow they shan't be able to for long."

"May I tell you something?" Juliana bowed closer until their foreheads almost touched.

"Always."

"I have decided to stay here. In England."

"You have?" Callie's eyes widened as the words registered. "But, that's wonderful!" She clapped her hands with pleasure. "When did you come to your decision?"

"Just moments ago."

Callie sat back. "The *ball* decided your fate?"

The younger woman nodded firmly. "Indeed. I cannot simply allow these aristocratic nobs . . ."—she paused, pleased with her use of the slang—"to scare me off. If I were to return to Italy, who would set them to rights?"

Callie laughed. "Excellent! I shall take great pleasure in watching them all tumble!" She squeezed Juliana's hands in hers. "And your brothers, Juliana . . . they shall be *thrilled*."

Juliana beamed. "Yes . . . I suppose they will." Her expression quickly turned serious as she looked into Callie's eyes. "However, I am not certain that Gabriel deserves such good news."

Callie looked down at her lap.

It was Juliana's turn to take Callie's hands in hers. "Callie, what happened?"

"Nothing happened."

Your brother merely broke my heart. That is all.

Juliana waited for Callie to look up again and, when she did, her eyes liquid with tears, the younger woman searched her gaze for answers. After a very long moment, Juliana seemed to find what she was looking for.

Squeezing her friend's hands, she said, "You must face him proud, and strong, and wonderfully *you*."

The words, an echo of those Callie had spoken only moments

earlier, sent her tears spilling over, coursing down her cheeks in long, silent tracks.

Instantly, Juliana moved to perch next to Callie on the chair, pulling her into a strong, powerful embrace.

And, as Juliana held her, Callie whispered the words she could no longer deny.

"But what if I am not enough?"

Twenty-two

Ralston exited the ball immediately. Leaving the carriage for his siblings, he departed on foot, heading in the direction of Ralston House, no more than a quarter of a mile away.

For his entire life, he'd been avoiding precisely this moment: He had eschewed relationships with women with whom he had too much in common; he had avoided matchmaking mamas at all costs, out of fear that he might actually *like* the women they attempted to foist upon him. He'd grown up in a household destroyed by a woman, marred by an unrequited love that had eaten away at his father, who had eventually died of the affliction—too heartbroken for too long to fight the fever to which he had ultimately succumbed.

And now, he was faced with Callie, fresh-faced, open-hearted, charming, intelligent Callie, who seemed to be everything that his mother had not been, and yet, was equally as dangerous as the former marchioness. For, when she'd looked at him with those stunning brown eyes and professed her love, Ralston had lost his ability to think.

And when she had begged him to leave, he had known precisely what his father had felt when his mother had left—the sense of complete and utter helplessness, as though he were watching a part of himself being stolen away but could do nothing at all to stop it.

It was a terrifying feeling. And if it was love, he wanted none of it.

It was raining, a fine London mist that seemed to come from all directions, casting a shining, wet glow over the darkened city and rendering umbrellas useless. Ralston was blind to the wet, his thoughts clouded by a vision of Callie, tears streaming down her face, devastated—and all because of him.

If he were honest with himself, he would admit that he'd been destined to make a mess of the situation since the moment she'd arrived on the threshold of his bedchamber—all big, brown eyes and full, tempting lips—asking him to kiss her. If he'd paid closer attention, he would have realized then that she was going to wreak marvelous havoc on his perfectly satisfactory life.

Tonight she had given him an opportunity to walk away—to return to that life. To spend his days at his men's club, and his sporting club, and his taverns and to forget that he'd ever found himself entangled with an adventurous wallflower who appeared to be entirely unaware of society's boundaries.

He should have leapt at the chance to be rid of the vexing woman.

But now there were memories of her in all of those places. And now, when Ralston considered his life prior to the night she'd barged into his bedchamber, it didn't seem satisfactory at all. It seemed sorely lacking in laughter and in conversation and in entirely inappropriate visits to taverns and clubs with adventuresome females. It was lacking in wide smiles and lush curves and insane lists. It was lacking in Callie.

And the prospect of returning to a life without her was dismal, indeed.

He had been walking for several hours, having passed Ralston

House multiple times as he roamed the darkened city, mind racing. His greatcoat was soaked through when he finally looked up, only to find himself outside Allendale House. The house was dark, save for a light in a lower-level room facing the side gardens, and Ralston stood for a long moment considering that golden glow.

The decision was made.

He knocked on the door and, when the aging butler, whom he'd terrorized previously, opened the door, eyes wide with recognition, Ralston had one thing to say. "I am here to see your master."

The butler seemed to sense the importance of the matter because he did not argue the lateness of the hour or speculate that, perhaps, the Earl of Allendale might not be in. Instead, he indicated that Ralston should wait and shuffled off to announce the visitor.

In less than a minute, he was back, taking Ralston's sopping coat and hat and indicating that he should see his way into the earl's study. Ralston entered the large, well-lit room and closed the door behind him to find Benedick leaning on the edge of a large oak desk, eyeglasses on the tip of his nose, reading from a sheaf of papers. He looked up when the latch clicked. "Ralston," he acknowledged.

Ralston dipped his head. "Thank you for seeing me."

Benedick cocked a smile, setting the papers down on his desk. "I was having a rather boring evening, frankly. You are a welcome distraction."

"I'm not sure you'll think so after you hear what I've come to say."

One of the earl's eyebrows lifted. "Well, then, I think you should come out with it, then, don't you?"

"I've compromised your sister."

At first, there was no indication that Benedick heard Ralston's confession. He did not move, or take his gaze from his visitor. And then he came to his full height and slowly removed his glasses, setting them on top of the papers he'd discarded before walking toward Ralston.

Standing in front of Ralston, Benedick said, "I assume we are talking about Callie?"

Ralston's gaze did not waver. "Yes."

"I don't suppose that you are overstating the situation?"

"No. I've compromised her. Quite thoroughly."

Benedick nodded thoughtfully, then punched him.

Ralston didn't see the blow coming; he reeled backward, pain exploding in his cheek. When he straightened, Benedick was shaking off the residual sting in his hand calmly. He said, apologetically, "I had to do it."

Ralston nodded calmly, testing the tender skin around his eye. "I wouldn't have expected anything less."

Benedick moved to a low table nearby and poured two tumblers of scotch. Offering one to Ralston, he said, "I suppose you had better explain yourself."

Accepting the glass, Ralston said, "It's quite simple, actually. I've compromised your sister, and I should like to marry her."

Benedick sat down in a large leather chair and watched Ralston carefully for a moment. "If it is so simple, why did you arrive at my home sopping wet in the middle of the night?"

Taking the chair across from the earl, Ralston said, "Well, I suppose it is simple to me."

"Ah." Understanding dawned. "Callie has refused you."

"Your sister is infuriating."

"She does have a tendency to be so."

"She won't marry me. So I am here to enlist your help."

"Of course she will marry you," Benedick said, and a wave of relief coursed through Ralston—far more powerful than he would have liked to admit. "But I shan't force her. You're going to have to convince her."

The relief was short-lived. "I've tried. She won't hear reason."

Benedick laughed at the surprise and frustration in Ralston's voice. "Spoken like someone who did not grow up with sisters. They never hear reason."

Ralston gave a small smile. "Yes, I'm beginning to see that."

"Has she told you why she won't marry you?"

Ralston took a long pull of scotch and considered his reply. "She says she loves me."

Benedick's eyes widened before he said, "That seems like a reason *to* marry someone."

"My thoughts exactly." He leaned forward in his chair. "How do I convince *her* of that?"

Benedick leaned back in his chair, met Ralston's scowl and took pity on him. "Callie is a hopeless romantic. She has been since she was a little girl. It's the natural result of our being the products of a complete and utter love match, her reading every romantic novel she could get her hands on over the last twenty years, and my own encouragement of her resistance to the institution of the loveless marriage. I'm not surprised she won't marry you without the promise of love. So, it raises the question: Do you love her?"

"I—" Ralston stopped, his mind racing. *Did he love her?*

One side of Benedick's mouth kicked up as he watched the thoughts play over Ralston's face. "You shall have to do better than that when she asks you, old man."

"I would make her a good husband."

"I do not doubt it."

"I've the money, the lands, the title to do it."

"If I know Callie, she doesn't care about any of that."

"She does not. Which is yet another reason why she is legions better than I deserve. But you should care. So I am telling you."

Benedick's rich brown gaze locked with Ralston's firm one, and understanding passed between them. "I appreciate it."

"Then I have your blessing?"

"To marry her? Yes, but it is not my agreement you must secure."

"I shan't force her. But in order to convince her, I need some time with her. Alone. I should like it sooner rather than later."

Benedick took a sip of scotch and watched Ralston carefully. Noting the frustration in his eyes, the tension in his form, the earl took pity on the man whom his sister was running ragged. "If Callie is half as distraught as you appear to be right now, she is in the library."

Ralston's brows snapped together. "Why would you tell me that?"

One side of Benedick's mouth kicked up. "Suffice it to say I don't like the idea of my sister even half as distraught as you look. Try the library. I shan't bother you. But, dear God, don't get caught by my mother, or there will be hell to pay."

Ralston smiled halfheartedly at Benedick's jest. "I shall try my best to keep a low profile, but, to be honest, your mother demanding I make it right might be the best way to secure precisely what I want." He stood, squaring his shoulders as though he were about to do battle. Looking down at Benedick, he said, "Thank you. I promise that I shall consider it my life's work to make her happy."

Benedick tipped his glass at the marquess in acknowledgment of the vow. "As long as you make it your day's work tomorrow to secure a special license."

Ralston nodded his head in solemn confirmation that he would marry Callie as soon as humanly possible and left the room, crossing the darkened, quiet foyer to the door of the library. He set his hand to the door handle cautiously and took a deep breath to calm his racing pulse. He'd never been so on edge; so concerned with the outcome of a conversation; so willing to do whatever it took to get what he wanted. And yet, here he was, certain that the next few minutes would be the most important of his life.

He pushed open the door, his eyes immediately finding her in the dim light. She was curled in one of the large leather chairs positioned by the fireplace, her back to the door, one elbow propped on the arm of the chair, holding her chin as she stared into the flames. He noticed the swath of blue satin that spilled over the edge of the chair to just barely brush the floor; she was still in the lovely blue dress she had been wearing at the ball earlier in the evening. She sighed as he closed the door quietly and approached her, noting the column of her neck, the soft skin that ran along her collarbone and down to the trimmed edge of her gown. He took a moment to stand behind her, admiring her relaxed form, as she said, "I really don't want any company, Benny."

He didn't say anything in response, instead moving stealthily around the edge of her chair and seating himself on the ottoman that she had pushed to the side when she had sat down. She turned her head as he sat, her breath catching as she sat straight up and put her feet to the floor.

"What—what are you doing here?"

He leaned forward, his elbows on his knees, and said, "I tried to stay away. But there are some things I must say."

She shook her head, eyes wide. "If you're caught . . . Benedick is in the other room! How did you get in?"

"Your brother let me in. He knows I'm here. And, I am afraid, Empress, that he is on my side."

"You told him?" She was aghast.

"I did. You gave me little choice. Now, be quiet and listen, for I have much to say."

Callie shook her head, not trusting herself to stand firm in her decision if he showered her with pretty words. "Gabriel—please don't."

"No. This is both of our lives you're playing with now, Callie. I won't have you making decisions without all the information." She tucked her feet up under her and the image of her, curled into a little, sad ball, tugged at Gabriel's heart. "You love me. Don't you feel that you owe it to yourself to hear what I have to say on the matter?"

She squeezed her eyes shut and groaned in embarrassment, "Oh, God. Please don't bring it up. I cannot believe I told you."

He reached out and ran a finger down her cheek, he spoke in a deep, gravelly tone, "I shan't let you take it back, you know."

She opened her eyes, and the look in them was wide and clear and nearly stole his breath. "I don't take it back."

"Good," he said. "Now listen to me." He didn't know where to begin, and so he spoke the words as they came. "My mother was very beautiful—dark hair, brilliant blue eyes, delicate features, like Juliana. She was barely older than Juliana when she left us—fled to the Continent to escape her family and her life here. My memories of her are vague, but I remember one thing with complete certainty. My father was mad for her.

"I can remember sneaking out of my bed to eavesdrop on their conversations late at night when I was small. On one particular evening, I heard the strangest noise coming from my father's study, and I crept down the stairs, curious. The hallway was dark—it must have been very late—and the door to the study was ajar."

He stopped, and Callie sat forward in her seat, a sense of dread coursing through her at the story, this critical memory. She waited for him to continue. She would have waited all night.

"I looked in, and I could see the graceful line of my mother's back, so straight and unfeeling—the way she always was with Nick and me. She was standing at the center of the room in a perfectly pressed, unwrinkled gown of the palest lavender . . ." He paused, and spoke the next words with surprise, "It's amazing how the details come so fresh so long after . . ." And then the story started up again.

"She was facing my father, who was kneeling at her feet—*kneeling*—both hands wrapped around one of hers, and he was crying." The words were coming easier now, and Callie watched as his eyes glazed over, recounting the memory. "The sounds I had heard from above stairs were my father's sobs. He was keening, begging her to stay. He pressed her cold, passionless hand to his cheek and professed his undying love, telling her that he loved her more than life, more than his sons, more than the world. He begged her to stay, repeating the words again and again, telling her again and again that he loved her, as though the words could stop her dispassionate glances, her cool responses to him, to her sons.

"She was gone the next morning. And so was he, in a sense." He stopped, his mind stuck in the moment over twenty-five years earlier. "I swore two things that night. First, I would never eavesdrop again. And second, I would never become a victim of love. I started playing the piano that day . . . it was the only thing that could block out the sound of his sorrow."

When he looked to Callie again, he noted the tears streaming silently down her cheeks, and his gaze cleared instantly. He reached out and took her face in his hands, brushing away the errant teardrops with his thumbs. "Oh, Callie, don't cry." He leaned in and kissed her softly, his lips warm and welcome against hers. Placing his forehead against hers, he smiled. "Don't cry for me, Empress. I'm not worth it."

"I'm not crying for you," she said, placing her hand against his cheek. "I'm crying for that little boy who never had a chance to believe in love. And for your father, who obviously never experienced it either. Because that was infatuation, not love. Love isn't one-sided and selfish. It is full and generous and life-altering in the best of ways. Love does not destroy, Gabriel. It creates."

He considered her words and the emotion in them, her vehement belief in the emotion that he had been avoiding for his entire adult life. And he told her the truth. "I cannot promise you love, Callie. The part of me that could have . . . that might have been . . . has been closed off for so long. But what I can tell you is this . . . I will do my damnedest to be a kind and good and generous husband. I will work to give you the life you deserve. And if I have my way, you will never doubt how much I care for you."

He came off the ottoman, onto his knees, and Callie could not help but see the parallel between that moment and the story he had told about his parents. "Please, Callie. Please, do me the very great honor of becoming my wife." The words came on a fervent, poignant whisper, and Callie was lost. How could she deny him after all he had confessed? How could she deny herself?

"Yes," she said, quietly, barely loud enough for him to hear.

One side of his mouth kicked up. "Say it again."

"Yes," she said, this time firmer, more certain. "Yes, I'll marry you."

And then his hands were in her hair, scattering her hairpins, and his lips were on hers, stealing her breath, and she was touching him—this remarkable man whom she'd loved for so long and who was finally, finally hers.

Callie sighed into Ralston's mouth—noting that he tasted of scotch and something more exotic, more male—and a feeling of complete and utter elation coursed through her. This was Ralston, her future husband, and he was making her feel so warm and wonderful and alive. And then he was kissing down the column of her neck, whispering her name like a litany as he lifted her arms over his shoulders and set his lips to the expanse of white skin above the neck of her gown. Callie gasped as his strong hands spread wide across her torso, stealing up to cup her breasts in a gesture of complete and utter possession.

"This gown," he said, the words coming thick and liquid, "is sinful."

Callie couldn't help her smile as he leaned back to watch her breasts lift against the satin edge of the dress. "Do you think so?"

"Indeed. It is made to drive men crazy . . . to reveal all your luscious curves"—he ran a finger beneath the satin lazily, just far enough to graze the edge of a nipple—"without showing off anything. It's a torturous viewing experience," he added, wickedly, as he pulled the edge of the gown lower, exposing the straining tip of one breast to the cool air and his hot mouth. He suckled briefly, until Callie was writhing against him, then, releasing her, he said, "When we are married, I shall buy you one in every color."

She giggled at the words, the laughter fading into a sigh, then a low moan as his mouth worked its magic on her tender, sensitive flesh. He drew the sound out for as long as he could before he remembered their location.

"It occurs to me," Gabriel said, pulling back, "that this is a highly inappropriate place for us to be in such a delicate position, lovely, what with your entire family mere moments away." He met her gaze, and the liquid heat in her eyes consumed him for a moment and, with a little groan, he took her mouth again in a hot, open, consuming kiss that stole reason and thought for several long minutes. When he pulled away again, leaving them both breathless, he restored her dress to its original position with a soft, nibbling kiss on the delicate skin of her breast.

"I cannot stay, Empress. You are too much temptation, and I am nowhere near strong or good enough to resist you." He spoke the words quietly at her ear, his nose buried in her hair—hair he no longer considered brown, but a rich myriad of chocolate and mahogany and sable that was fast becoming his favorite of all colors. "I shall return tomorrow. Perhaps we could ride on the Serpentine?"

Callie didn't want him to leave. Didn't want the night to end. Didn't want to risk the possibility that this was a very dear, very wonderful, very realistic dream. "Don't leave," she whispered, placing one hand boldly at the nape of his neck and turning to capture his lips in a lingering kiss. "Stay."

He smiled, setting his forehead to hers. "You are very bad for me. I am trying to turn over a new leaf—I am trying to be more gentlemanly."

"But what if I want you to stay a rake?" she teased, her fingers trailing down his neck and chest, fingering the buttons on his waistcoat. "A libertine, even?" She slipped one fastening from its seat and he grabbed her errant hand, bringing it to his lips for a swift kiss.

"Callie," he said, his voice thick with warning as she set her free hand to the second button on his coat.

"What if I want the rogue, Gabriel?" The question was soft and sweet.

"What are you saying?"

She kissed across the firm square line of his jaw and whispered to him, shyness in her shaking voice, "Take me to bed, Gabriel. Give me a taste of scandal."

His breath quickened at the words, and he realized that leaving her would be the noblest thing he had ever done. His reply came deep in his throat, "I think you've tasted rather a lot of scandal in the last few weeks, Empress."

"But, once we're married, it's back to plain old Callie. This could be my last chance."

A shadow of self-doubt crossed her face, and he took her head in both of his hands. "Make no mistake, lovely, there is nothing plain about you." He kissed her again, stroking until she broke away, panting.

Meeting his gaze with her most smoldering, inviting and irresistible look, she tried again. "Come upstairs, Gabriel."

There was a long pause, and Callie thought she might have pushed him too far. He stood, reaching down to her and pulling her up to stand in front of him. "You realize that, if we're caught, we shall have to marry immediately."

A thrill coursed through her. "I do."

"And that you shan't have the enormous wedding of which your mother has no doubt dreamed for ages."

Callie shook her head. "I never wanted that wedding anyway. Mariana can have it for both of us." Her hands slid up his arms toward his broad shoulders.

"And that your mother will never forgive me for ruining her elder daughter." His arms wrapped around her, pulling her closer.

"Oh, she shall forgive you. Marquesses rarely receive the full force of a mother's wrath. And, have you forgotten, good sir, that I am already ruined?"

A dark, wicked grin flashed. "An excellent point."

"There is a servants' stairwell that leads straight to my room," she whispered. "The hinges on the doors are beautifully quiet. I oiled them myself."

He chuckled. "'Twould be a pity to let such diligence go to waste. By all means, my lady, lead on."

They crept up the stairs—avoiding the third from the top—and into Callie's bedchamber. The door closed behind them with a soft click, and the air thickened immediately. Callie was instantly nervous. The siren from earlier was gone, and she was consumed with awareness.

Here she was, in the room where she'd slept for her entire life, with Ralston, who overpowered the space, his strength and *maleness* so incongruous within the dainty little room. She looked down at her hands, clasped tightly together, and wondered if she would ever be used to him so close in such an intimate place. *Surely not.*

And then he was touching her—lifting her chin and taking her mouth and pulling her against him in the most complete of ways— and thought was lost.

His hands made quick work of the long line of buttons on her gown. She felt the fabric loosen and the cool air brush against her flushed skin, and she knew that he was staying and that this night would be the most important of her life—the night she accepted Ralston's suit, the night she professed her love, the first night of the rest of their life together. And she could not deny the remarkable rightness in his being there, his hands and mouth on her as he removed her dress to reveal—

"Oh, my. Empress."

His words pulled her from her thoughts. His gaze was locked upon her, taking in the beautiful silk lingerie, the delicate fabric that clung to her curves, hinting temptingly at what it hid. He reminded her of a wolf—hungry and eager to snare its prey—and her breath caught as his eyes met hers, desire rife within them.

She blushed. "Madame Hebert told me I needed them."

His eyes darkened to a rich, midnight blue. "Madame Hebert was right." He toyed with a little satin ribbon at the edge of her chemise. "How do they make you feel?"

Her eyes fluttered closed as a wave of embarrassment coursed through her. He turned her around, setting his hands to the laces of her stays, his words hot and soft against her ear. "How does it feel to be draped in warm silk?"

She said the first thing that came to her mind. "I feel feminine."

His hands spread across her hips. "What else?"

She was breathing more heavily than usual, anticipation making her voice breathy with excitement. "I feel . . . lovely."

He rewarded her words with a soft kiss on her neck. "Good. Because you are exquisite. And . . . ?"

The word hovered between them as her corset came undone, falling to the floor unheeded. Her eyes opened at the freedom and she noticed that he had turned her to face the mirror in the room. She was unable to stop herself from watching as his hands splayed across her torso and pulled her back against him firmly. They stole upward to cup her breasts, testing their weight, and she gasped, both at the heady combination of his warm skin branding her through the silk and his hands stark against the pale blue of her chemise. She was riveted by their reflection, feeling at once shy and sensual and wondering if she should turn away.

And then she realized that he was watching her—reading the play of emotions across her face in the dim reflection. And his voice was dark and wicked at her ear. "Do they make you feel wanton?"

"Yes," she confessed. "They make me feel . . ." She paused, searching for the word. "They make me feel alive."

He made a small sound of approval deep in his throat. "They make me feel alive as well." And then he was lifting her in his arms and carrying her to the bed and she was naked and the silk was forgotten, replaced by his wonderful heat and mouth and hands.

He kissed across her collarbone and she smiled as he lingered over the faint scar on her arm, where his foil had cut her during their fencing lesson. "I'm so sorry I hurt you, lovely," he whispered, worshipping the pink line with his lips and tongue.

Her head rolled back and forth on the pillow as his hands

stroked down her body, stealing her strength. She opened her eyes and let all her desire show. "Never apologize for that afternoon. I wouldn't change a moment of it." She took his face in her hands and pulled him up for a searing kiss.

After several long minutes, he began to kiss down her body, and her hands fell to his shoulders to stay him. She whispered, "Wait."

His blue gaze captured hers, hot and arresting, and he placed a warm kiss on her soft, rounded belly. "What is it, lovely?"

"I want to touch you this time."

His teeth flashed, white in the dim light. "If I remember correctly, you touched me last time, and I couldn't bear it for long."

"I wonder if you'd be willing to try it again?"

One dark eyebrow rose as he considered the question. There was a pause, before he grinned and stretched out next to her on his back, hands stacked under his head, naked and unabashed. "I'm yours for the taking, Empress."

I'm yours. The words echoed in her mind, sending a thrill though her. He was hers. This was the first in a long line of nights when she would be able to touch him, to feel his marvelous heat. He was hers. A smile played across her lips at the very thought.

"You look like the cat that got the cream."

"I rather *feel* like the cat that got the cream," she said, marveling at his body, the strength of his corded muscles, the dark, soft hair that dusted his chest, narrowing to a thin line that led to . . . *oh, my.* It was the first time she'd been able to see him in his entirety. He was long and hard and large enough that she marveled at the truth that they actually fit together.

Sensing her thoughts, he said, "Touch me, darling."

She couldn't refuse the dark, inviting words, and she set her hands to him, running them over his chest, and down to the part of him that made her so nervous. He flinched as she touched him softly, just lightly enough to drive him slightly mad. She pulled back immediately. "Did I hurt you?"

"No," he said, his voice shaking with tightly leashed passion. "Do it again." She did, wrapping her fingers around the hard, silken length of him and caressing him with an innocence that threatened to slay him. With a groan, he placed his hand on hers, and his strong, skilled fingers guided hers, showing her just how to hold him, just where to stroke him, just how to please him.

What she lacked in skill she more than made up for in eagerness, and Ralston soon found himself harder and heavier than he had ever been. Her warm hand moved more and more firmly as she gained confidence and he reveled in her touch until his breath was ragged and harsh and he realized that if her hot little fingers stayed upon him much longer, he would not be able to hold back.

And then she spoke, and he thought he might lose his mind. "May I . . . kiss you?"

He let out a harsh laugh and spoke through gritted teeth. "No."

"But you have . . . with me."

"Yes, Empress, and someday I will happily allow you to respond in kind. But tonight I cannot . . . for I already want you too much."

"Oh," she said, "I understand." Her eyes revealed that she wasn't entirely certain she did.

He lifted her hand from him and rolled to cover her with his body, settling between her silken thighs, the length of him pressing against the heart of her, where she was wet and willing and aching for him. "I want you too much to allow you such free rein. Your touch is already threatening my sanity." His voice lowered as he began to rain kisses across her breasts, suckling first one hard, waiting nipple, then the other, wringing a soft cry from her. "I would much rather spend the rest of the evening inside you, until neither one of us can think."

He pressed against her again, rubbing against the hard, eager nub of her sex and sending a ripple of pleasure through her. "Don't you agree?"

"Oh, yes," she sighed, as he repeated the motion.

He nipped at her shoulder, his lips curving in a smile. "I thought you might."

With a single, delicious thrust, he was inside her, and she belatedly realized that there was no pain, no discomfort as there had been the first time, but only a rich, welcome fullness that made her feel utterly complete.

He stopped, seated to the hilt. "Are you all right, lovely?"

"Yes, I'm quite wonderful," she said, her tone a mix of pleasure and awe. She shifted beneath him, and he groaned, moving against her several times before retreating until nothing but the very tip of him remained inside her, and she thought the loss of him might make her mad.

"Gabriel," she sighed. "Please."

He rewarded her, filling her again, pushing her further, higher, shifting and moving until the angle of his movements was perfect, and she cried out.

He stopped, whispering in her ear teasingly, "Careful, Empress . . . you'll get us caught." Her eyes widened at his words, and he smiled. "It makes it even better, doesn't it . . . the threat of discovery?"

As if to test her willpower, his fingers stroked just above where they were joined, skillfully playing in the nest of curls, finding the tight bud of pleasure there and stroking it until she was biting her lower lip to keep silent. And then he was moving again, building the sweet friction between them, coaxing her into abandon while whispering heated reminders to stay quiet. She couldn't stop herself, and he captured her mouth in a soul-stealing kiss to keep her from calling out as she shattered beneath him, pulsing around him, giving him a taste of heaven.

And when she tore her lips from his to whisper "I love you," over and over like a litany, he was lost, too, barely controlling his own cries of pleasure as he spilled inside of her.

After several long moments, he lifted his weight from her, and she gave a little sigh of protest at the loss of him. He lay next to her, immediately pulling her into his arms. When Callie rested her cheek upon his chest, she whispered her love one more time, so softly that he barely heard the words.

Gabriel lay there for a long time, watching her sleep, taking in her simple, powerful beauty and wondering at the intensity of the moment, of the evening. As he breathed her in, he was overcome with a ragged emotion—foreign and unsettling—and he wondered fleetingly what he had brought upon them.

$\mathscr{C}$allie woke to the sound of rustling paper.

She opened her eyes at the noise then, disoriented in the dim, gray light that marked the predawn hour, closed them once more. The fire in her room had gone out hours ago, and she cuddled closer to the source of heat next to her, stretching against the smooth, warm skin . . . before realizing precisely to whom the skin in question belonged.

Her eyes flew open, and she met Ralston's bold, amused gaze.

"Good morning, Empress." She felt more than heard the words as they rumbled in his chest, filled with sleep, and she blushed. After all, it wasn't every day that she woke to a man in her bed. She wasn't entirely sure how to respond, but she felt certain that ignoring him was highly improper. Pulling away from him in a desperate attempt to restore a semblance of ladylikeness to her person, she said, "Good morning. What time is it?"

"Just before five," he answered, one arm snaking around her and pulling her back to her original position, pressed against his very warm, very hard, very *naked* body. "Altogether too early to leave this bed."

"We shall be caught!" she whispered.

"I shall leave before that will happen, lovely," he promised, "but first, I must return something to you." He lifted his free hand and, in horror, she recognized the paper he held. Her list.

She lunged for it, and he easily held it away from her, forcing her to squirm across his chest, reaching for the parchment. She quickly realized that she was fighting a losing battle and stopped, turned accusing eyes on him. "*You* had it!"

"You needn't look at me as though I stole it, lovely." He spoke with mock affront. "You misplaced it. I merely rescued it for you."

"Well," she said, her voice sweet, "I am very lucky to have you as my savior, aren't I?" She reached out for the paper. "I should like it back."

"I shall be happy to oblige, of course," he said, waving the paper idly in the air, "but don't you think that, considering our new relationship, I should be let in on your little list? After all, I shouldn't like to be taken unawares by your eccentric activities once we're married."

Callie's eyes widened. "No! You can't! You promised you wouldn't look!" She wriggled against him again, resuming her quest to rescue her list from his clutches.

"Yes, well, that's what you get for attaching yourself to a renowned cad," he teased, groaning as her lush breasts pressed against his chest. He stilled her with one hand. "Be careful, Empress, or I shall have to prove myself a rogue once more."

She was filled with feminine understanding at the power her nakedness had over him. She slithered against him, deliberately rubbing across one of his nipples, and reveled in the hissing sound of his breath. "Minx," he growled, stealing her lips for a deep kiss. Ending the caress, he said, "No. You shan't distract me. Let's have a look at this list."

Recognizing defeat, Callie buried her face against him, cheeks flaming, as he read the list. What would he think of her? What would he say? She waited, the hair on his chest tickling her nose, for him to respond to her ridiculous list.

He was silent for a long while. And then he said, "Which of these did you do first?"

And she wanted to die of embarrassment. She shook her head.

"Callie. Which one came first?"

She answered, the words muffled by his chest.

"I can't hear you, love."

She turned her head, pressing her ear to where she could hear the strong, steady beat of his heart. "Kissing."

His chest rose and fell as he took a deep breath. "The night you came to Ralston House."

She nodded, face on fire. "Yes," she whispered.

"Why me?"

He'd asked the question in his bedchamber that night, and she'd answered with a half-truth. But this morning, as dawn crept across the sky in long, pink streaks, Callie found that she did not want to lie. She wanted him to know her. Even if it risked everything.

"Because I wanted it to be you. From the beginning. I wanted my first kiss to be with you."

"The other day," he said quietly, stroking his hand along the soft skin of her shoulders, "at Ralston House. You said it had always been me. What does that mean?"

She stiffened against him, and he waited while she considered his question. She did not meet his eye when she said, "I've loved you for ages. For longer than I should have, I imagine."

"How?"

She paused long enough for him to think she might not answer. "We met once. I was young and impressionable. You were charming and unobtainable and . . . I couldn't help myself." She looked away again, staring into nothing. "You're rather difficult to ignore."

"Why do I not remember?" he asked softly.

"I'm not exactly a legendary beauty." A ghost of a smile flashed and her gaze fell to his chest, where her fingers idly stroked the smattering of dark hair there. "I'm rarely noticed, actually."

He captured her hand, stilling it, and forced her to meet his eyes. "I don't know how I didn't notice you, Callie, but I can tell you that I was rather an imbecile not to have done so." She caught her breath at the words, so honest, so forthright.

His eyes returned to the paper. "You have some items to cross off this list."

She followed the direction of his gaze, reading. "Gambling," she agreed, "I shall cross it off the moment I am again in possession of the list. Should that ever happen again," she added meaningfully.

He looked back at her, his eyes dark and serious despite her attempt at lightheartedness. "Not just gambling, Callie. It's time you realize how beautiful you are."

She looked away at the words, but he captured her chin in his hand and forced her to meet his gaze again as he spoke. "You are, quite possibly, the most beautiful woman I've ever known."

"No . . ." she whispered, "I am not. But it is very kind of you to say it."

He shook his head firmly. "Hear me well. I cannot begin to list all the things about you that are beautiful—a man could lose himself in your eyes; in your lovely, full lips; in your silken hair; in your soft, luscious curves; in your creamy, perfect skin and the way you blush and turn it the color of an exquisite, ripe peach. And that's without considering your warmth, your intelligence, your humor, and the way I am utterly drawn to you when you enter a room."

Tears sprang to her eyes at the words—words she desperately wanted to believe.

"Never doubt how beautiful you are, Callie. For your beauty has quite ruined me for all others. And, frankly, I rather wish I'd found you years ago."

So do I, she thought. What if he'd noticed her all those years ago? What if he'd courted her then? Would she have had a life filled with romance and passion? Would she have avoided the deep, heart-wrenching loneliness that she'd so long denied?

And what about him? Would he have learned to love?

Her emotions played across her face and, while he couldn't have known precisely what she was thinking, he seemed to understand nevertheless. He took her lips in a passionate kiss and she matched it, pouring a depth of feeling into the caress and stealing his breath.

When the kiss ended, he offered her a wicked grin. "I shall just have to make up for lost time, I imagine." And she couldn't help but laugh at his rakish tone. "Would you like to cross another item off this list today?"

"I should like that very much. Which do you propose?" She turned to look at the list as he let it fall from his fingers, unwanted, and he pulled her atop him. She gasped at the feel of him firm and warm beneath her, the smoothness of his skin between her thighs.

"I think it's time you try riding astride." As she took in his meaning, the words sent a liquid heat straight to the core of her, where she could feel the hard length of him pressing against her in the most intimate of ways.

"You can't mean . . ." She paused as his hands lifted her into a seated position, cupping her breasts and rubbing his thumbs across her fast-hardening nipples.

"Oh, but I do, indeed, mean, Empress." His words were soft and tempting as he pulled her down just far enough to provide him access to the tips of her breasts. He kissed first one, then the other, while running his hand down her back to caress her rounded but-tocks, rearranging her, opening her thighs. He released one turgid nipple with a lingering lick and watched her with heavy-lidded eyes as he guided her to sit straight up. His hands moved again, leaving fire in their wake, finally finding the place where she ached for him and stroking the slick, wet folds of her sex, and rolling his thumb over the hard, wanting nub of pleasure that seemed to belong to him now.

She whispered his name in the early-morning light, and he spoke in soft encouragements, "That's it, Empress, come for me. I want to watch you fall apart above me . . . so passionate . . . so beautiful."

The words were sinful, wicked and tempting and perfect, and it took all of Callie's will to shake her head, placing her hands on his chest to support her weight. "No . . ." she protested. "I don't want to . . . not without you with me."

The words rocked him to his core, and he could think of little else but being inside of her, driving her to the edge and toppling over with her. "Please, Gabriel," she pleaded. "Please make love to me."

He never had a chance.

In seconds, he had lifted her and positioned himself at the entrance to her warm, luxurious heat, and he allowed her to feel her power over him as she sank down onto his shaft, seating herself to the hilt. Her eyes were wide with the newfound pleasure of this movement, and in that moment he adored her—her eager uncertainty making her thoroughly irresistible.

He set his hands to her hips, guiding her up, then back down, slowly, showing her the movements, encouraging her exploration. "That's it, beautiful," he whispered, watching as her voluptuous body rose and fell on him in sweet torment. "Ride me." And she did, finding her own marvelous rhythm—one that he thought would certainly kill him if he didn't so desperately want to live to see the ecstasy on her face when she found her release.

He didn't have to wait long. She perfected the angle, tiny little gasps of pleasure marking each step she took toward the ultimate goal, and he held on to her hips, his grasp firm and encouraging as she reached for completion. "Take it, Empress," he said hoarsely, as he watched her crest on a wave of pleasure, eyes closed, back arched, head thrown back in complete abandon as she moved against him. "Take what you want."

Her eyes opened, and he read the desire in her gaze. "Come with me," she said, not understanding the erotic power of the words. He could do nothing but give her that for which she had asked. He flexed beneath her as she lost her strength and fell against him, catching her cries with a kiss, rolling her to her back and continuing their movements until the pleasure shattered around her again. Only then did he give himself up to the powerful pulsing release that made him never want to leave her arms or her bed again.

Minutes later, as they lay tangled together, dazed in the aftermath of their loving, Callie began to chuckle silently against Gabriel's side. Lifting his head to find her grinning a wide, silly grin, he drawled, "What is it that has you so amused, lovely?"

"I was simply thinking"—she stopped to catch her breath from the laughter and started again—"I was merely thinking that if that is what riding astride is like, the female population is missing out on one of life's finer experiences." The last word was lost as she dissolved once more into giggles.

He caught her against him in a fierce hug and sighed, unable to keep himself from smiling up at the ceiling as he said, "You know, Empress, men do not appreciate laughter at this particular moment. It's devastating to the self-confidence."

Her head snapped up and she took in his amused countenance. "Oh, my apologies, good sir," she teased. "I would hate to damage such a fragile ego as that of the Marquess of Ralston."

With a playful growl, he pinned her to the mattress. "Minx. You shall pay for that." And he began to kiss down the side of her neck, nibbling across her collarbone until she sighed with pleasure.

"If this is how I must pay for it, my lord, you may guarantee I shall tease you a great deal in the coming months."

"More than months, I hope," he drawled, distracted by her lovely white breasts. "Years. Decades, even."

"Decades," she repeated, awestruck. *My God. He's going to be my husband.*

"Mmm-hmm," he murmured against her skin before pulling away from her. "Which is why, despite how very difficult it shall be for me to leave you warm and lush in your bed, I shall console myself with the fact that, very soon, I shan't have to do so ever again."

She watched as he dressed, marveling at his magnificent form before he leaned over her to deliver her a soft, wonderful farewell kiss. "Will you be at the Chilton Ball tonight?"

"I had planned to be."

"Excellent. I will see you then. Save me a waltz." He kissed her again, savoring the taste of her. "Save me all of them."

She smiled. "That will certainly cause a stir."

"Indeed, but I believe our reputations can handle it." He winked. "I shall have special license in hand by then. How would you feel about marrying tonight at Chilton House and being done with the whole thing?"

Warmth burst in her chest. "I think it shall give any number of members of the *ton* the vapors."

"An added bonus, then," he said, before giving her a long, lingering kiss. And then he was gone, leaving her dazed and exhausted and happy.

She was almost instantly asleep. And when she dreamed, she dreamed of him, and of their future together.

* * *

"OH, CALLIE! A marquess!"

Callie rolled her eyes at her mother's exclamation and looked across the carriage to her siblings for support. It didn't take long to realize that they would be no help at all. Mariana was smirking, obviously thrilled that hers had been relegated to second-most-exciting upcoming marriage for the duration of the evening, and Benedick looked as though he was seriously considering leaping from the moving vehicle to avoid their mother's chirping excitement.

"I cannot believe you caught a marquess, Callie! And *Ralston* at that! And *you*, Benedick," the dowager countess turned her attention to her eldest child, "I cannot believe that *you* kept Ralston's plans from me for so long!"

"Yes, well, Callie and Ralston were eager to keep their courtship a secret, Mother." The countess burst into a flurry of chatter as Benedick raised an eyebrow and mouthed, *From all of us.*

Callie couldn't keep her slippered foot from flying. "Oy!" Benedick exclaimed, reaching down to rub his wounded shin.

"Oh, I am sorry, Benny," Callie said sweetly. "It must be the nerves making me jumpy."

Benedick's eyes narrowed as their mother spoke, "Of course it is your nerves! Oh! To think! Our Callie! Betrothed! To *Ralston*!"

"Mother, please do attempt not to make a production of the news this evening, will you?" Callie pleaded. "I shouldn't like to embarrass Ralston."

Benedick and Mariana let out twin bursts of laughter at the idea that the dowager countess was at all capable of such decorum. "A bit late for that, don't you think, Callie?" Benedick teased, as the carriage rolled to a stop and he leapt out to hand down his mother and sisters.

Before she exited the carriage, the countess placed a comforting hand on Callie's leg. "Nonsense, Callie. Ralston's been around long enough to know how these things are. He'll forgive an elated mother."

Callie groaned as her mother exited the carriage. "I should have asked Ralston to elope."

Mariana grinned broadly. "Now you know how I feel." With a wink, she was gone, after the dowager countess.

By the time Callie was out of the carriage, her mother had already started up the steps to Chilton House to eagerly share her news with anyone who would listen, and Callie had a sinking feeling that this was going to be the most awful night of her life. She looked into her siblings' laughing eyes, and said, "You two are no help."

The eldest and youngest Hartwell children smiled, unable to contain their amusement. "Shouldn't you try to find Ralston, Callie? Before Mother has worked her magic, that is," Mariana said helpfully.

"Is that what it is? Magic?" Callie turned to watch as their mother, a beacon in lime green—complete with enormous lace-and-ostrich-feather headdress—spoke excitedly to Lady Lovewell, tapping her fan excitedly against the arm of the most-renowned gossip of the *ton*. "Dear Lord," Callie breathed.

"I've tried prayer myself," Benedick said genially. "It doesn't seem to work with her. I believe she's made a deal with the Maker."

"Or with someone else," Callie posited, adjusting her shawl and following in her mother's wake, the sound of her siblings' laughter trailing behind her.

Once inside, Callie tried desperately to find Ralston in the crush of people that filled the ballroom to bursting. She stood just inside the room attempting to appear casual as she turned in a slow crescent, searching for him. Her height, or lack thereof, made the task particularly difficult, however, and eventually, with a sigh, she instinctively made for Spinster Seating.

She had just rounded the corner of the ballroom and had Miss Heloise and Aunt Beatrice in her sights when at her shoulder, a deep, familiar voice spoke quietly. "Where are you off to, Empress?"

A thrill coursed up her spine and she turned toward Ralston, unable to keep her pleasure at his finding her hidden. Of course, once she was facing him—all tall, broad, handsome, impeccably dressed, and starched-cravatted him—she was instantly shy.

What did one say, after all, to one's fiancé, whom one had last seen in one's bedroom, as he sneaked out just before daybreak?

He lifted one arrogant brow, as though he were reading her thoughts. She heard the beginning strains of a waltz as he took one of her gloved hands in his. "I should like very much to dance the first waltz with my betrothed," he said casually.

"Oh," she said, quietly. She let him guide her to the dance floor and sweep her into his arms.

After several moments of silence, he spoke again. "So. Where were you heading?"

She shook her head, unable to lift her gaze from his cravat. "Nowhere."

He pulled away slightly, tilting his head to look at her. "Callie," he said, in a tone that she was certain no female had ever been able to resist. "Where were you going?"

"Spinster Seating," she blurted, immediately regretting the words. It wasn't as if people actually *called* it that.

He blinked once, his eyes moving to the elderly ladies several feet away, then back to her. One side of his mouth kicked up. "Why?"

Her cheeks flamed. "I . . . I don't know."

"You're not a spinster anymore, beautiful," he said, close to her ear.

"Don't call me that." Callie darted her gaze around to see if anyone was looking at them and might have heard. It appeared that *everyone* was looking at them. Her mother had worked quickly.

He turned her quickly, regaining her attention. "But it's true," he said, feigning innocence. "You are very soon to be the Marchioness of Ralston. I'm not saying that you cannot still socialize with Misses Heloise and Beatrice," he teased. "I'm simply saying you'll have to rename the area in which you do it."

She couldn't help her smile. "I would much prefer to waltz with you than sit with them, my lord." The words came quickly, and she wondered immediately if she had been too forward . . . if she were pushing him too far. After all, Ralston never seemed to like society before, there was certainly no reason why he should begin to attend social events now. She risked a glance up into his knowing, amused eyes.

"I would prefer that, myself, my lady."

She played the lovely words over and over in her head as he whirled her across the room, and she basked in the knowledge that she would dance again, and often, with him once they were married. Callie looked past him to see Juliana watching them, a bright smile on her face. She turned to Ralston, and said, "You told your brother and sister about us."

"I thought it better they hear it from me than from your mother."

Callie winced at the words. "I'm so sorry, Gabriel, I tried to keep her quiet."

He chuckled. "You should have known better than to even attempt it. Let her have her fun, lovely."

"You shan't feel that way for long," Callie warned.

"Well then, I think we had best enjoy my magnanimity while it lasts, hadn't we?"

He swirled her to a stop as the music faded, and they made their way to Juliana, who threw herself into Callie's arms with a quiet squeal. Callie laughed at the younger girl but couldn't help being caught up in the excitement of the evening and the news that she and Ralston were to be married.

She had no time to chat, however, when a quadrille began and Nick joined them, bowing low and asking her to partner him. She happily accepted her future brother-in-law's offer, and the two were soon halfway across the room. After the quadrille, she was instantly partnered for a country dance, a second quadrille, a minuet, and so on until she had danced every dance during the first hour of the ball. And she was having a lovely time.

As she promenaded around the room with Lord Weston, a charming young man in line for a dukedom, she wondered at the strange turn of events. *From Spinster Seating to the belle of the ball and all it took was a marriage proposal.*

She paused. A marriage proposal from Ralston.

Ralston.

And then, as though she'd conjured him up, he was there, at her side. Taking her elbow, he guided her around the edge of the ballroom. "Are you enjoying yourself?" he asked, all innocence.

"You know very well that I am," she said through her teeth. "You did this on purpose!"

He surprised her with a quick turn, moving through a barely open doorway from the stifling ballroom out onto a small, secluded balcony. "I don't know what you're talking about."

She turned to look at him, silhouetted in the golden light from the ballroom beyond. "You made them all dance with me! Because of my list! How embarrassing!" She took a deep breath, spinning back around to face the darkened garden, and repeating, "How very embarrassing!"

"Callie," Ralston said, confusion in his tone. "I honestly haven't any idea what you are about."

She looked up at the starlit sky. "Dance every dance," she said quietly. "Ralston, I've never danced so much in my life as I did this evening. You cannot possibly tell me you had nothing to do with it. You saw the list."

"I can, indeed, tell you that I had nothing to do with it," he argued, "because I had nothing to do with it."

She turned back to face him. "It's quite sweet, actually, that you would work so diligently to help me complete the items on my list. I suppose I should thank you."

"You can thank me, lovely, but I honestly didn't have anything to do with it." He took a step closer to her. "Shall I prove it to you?"

She could feel the heat coming from him, welcome in the crisp spring air. "Please."

"I don't enjoy watching you dance with other men. I would much prefer we never attend another ball so I never again have to stand by as a line of rogues take the opportunity to touch you inappropriately."

She gasped indignantly, "They were not inappropriate!"

"You shall have to get used to my being the judge of such things." He came closer, leaving scant inches between them. He lifted a hand to brush an errant curl from her face. "They were inappropriate. Especially Weston."

She laughed then. "Lord Weston is madly in love with his wife." Lady Weston was widely considered one of the most beautiful women in London.

"She pales in comparison to you," he said earnestly, the words rich and wonderful around her.

Callie blushed. "You really didn't do it?"

He shook his head, a smile playing across his lips. "I really didn't, Empress. But I am not surprised they wanted to dance with you. You are, after all, quite remarkably beautiful this evening."

He lifted her chin, and she was at a loss for words. "Oh?"

"Indeed," he said, cupping her cheeks, turning her head just enough to ensure the perfect angle of the kiss. He sipped at her lips, teasing her with little nibbling kisses along her soft, full bottom lip before taking her mouth in a deep, passionate kiss that weakened her knees. His silken tongue stroked along her bottom lip, delving inside to taste her sweetness. She sighed into his mouth, eager for more, desperate for them to be anywhere but here—anywhere where they could revel in each other. She pressed closer to him, eager for more of his warmth, and as a ribbon of fire curled in her stomach, he emitted a low growl in the back of his throat.

"I should have known you'd be out here mauling her, Ralston. Ensuring that you have won?"

Callie pulled back instantly at the words, spoken from the entrance to the ballroom. Even without seeing the speaker, the loathing in his tone sent a chill down her spine.

Ralston stiffened and turned to face the newcomer, attempting to block her with his size. "Oxford," he said, his tone laced with warning.

"I heard the news of your pending nuptials," Oxford said as Callie moved out from behind Ralston to face the Baron herself. "I'll confess I was rather surprised to discover that you've discovered such an interest in Lady Calpurnia, Ralston."

"I would think very carefully before you say any more, Oxford," Ralston said through gritted teeth.

"But why would I do that?" Callie noticed the baron sway with the words, and she couldn't help but wonder if perhaps he were foxed. "I've got nothing to lose, you see. I've already lost, haven't I?"

At that moment, Mariana and Benedick stumbled out onto the balcony, interrupting the conversation. "Callie," Mariana said breathlessly. "You should come with me."

Callie's eyes widened. "Why? What has happened?"

Mariana met Ralston's eyes with a scathing, imperious look. "Nothing yet, thankfully." Turning back to her sister, she repeated, "You must come with me. Now."

Callie shook her head, backing up until she could feel Ralston's nearness. Taking in Oxford's smirking grin, Mariana's pleading gaze, and Benedick's stoic one, she turned to Ralston. "Gabriel?" she asked, confusion and uncertainty in the single word.

"Callie. Go with Mariana," Benedick interrupted.

Callie turned on her brother. "I will not. I will not leave before someone tells me precisely what is happening." Shifting her gaze to Mariana, she said, "Mari?"

Mariana sighed. "It is being said that Oxford and Ralston placed a wager upon you."

The idea was so preposterous that Callie laughed. "What kind of wager?"

"They are saying inside that Ralston bet Oxford that he could not win your hand." Benedick's eyes did not leave Ralston—his loathing barely contained. "And, when he discovered that Oxford was close to winning you—he took you for himself."

"They're saying that you've been compromised, Callie, and that is why Ralston . . ." Mariana trailed off.

Callie laughed again. "How very dramatic. Can you imagine?" She turned her smiling eyes on Ralston, expecting him to share in her amusement. In the face of his hard, unmoving expression, however, truth dawned. "Oh." She looked to smug Oxford. "Oh."

"Poor girl. You thought he actually wanted you," he said with a smirk.

"Stop, Oxford." Ralston's words were ice-cold.

Callie turned on him. "You made a wager? On me?"

"Indeed he did," Oxford said with a boastful tone, as though he was happy to be in the thick of the moment that would forever change her life. "He bet me that you wouldn't marry me. And when it looked like I might win, he doubled the wager and courted you to ensure that he'd win. I suspect that it didn't hurt that aligning himself to your family would also guarantee his sister a sound place in society."

Callie did not remove her gaze from Ralston. "Is it true? Did you wager on me?"

There was a beat as Ralston searched for the right answer. And, in that moment, Callie knew.

Ralston took a step toward her, and she backed away, Mariana placing a reassuring hand at the small of her back as he said, almost desperately, "It wasn't like that."

"How much?"

"Callie." Mariana whispered, trying to avoid a scene, but Callie held up a hand to stay her words.

"How much, my lord?"

He looked away. "Two thousand pounds."

Callie felt as though the breath had been knocked out of her.

"When?" she whispered.

"Callie—"

"When?" She repeated, louder.

"The afternoon of your sister's betrothal ball."

Callie's face fell. "The day you asked me to dance."

His eyes widened as he registered the timeline. "Callie—"

"No." She shook her head. "And when did you double it?"

When he did not answer, she turned to Oxford. "When did he double it?"

Oxford wavered. "Tuesday."

The morning he proposed. He'd still thought of her as nothing more than a wager only a short time ago.

"I should have known," she whispered, the sound so sad, so raw, that Ralston thought his heart would break. "I should have known you didn't really . . . you couldn't really . . ." She trailed off. She took a deep breath before she looked up at him, her enormous brown eyes glistening with unshed tears, and said, "I would have helped you with Juliana anyway. I would have done anything you asked of me."

The truth of her past unwavering devotion overwhelmed her, and a single tear tracked down her cheek before she wiped it away in irritation. She could barely hear the sounds of the ball beyond for the blood pounding in her ears as a wave of familiar insecurity crashed over her.

She had been so very very stupid.

How many times had she told herself that Ralston was not for her? That she was too plain, too plump, too inexperienced and uninteresting to capture his interest? How many times had she been warned? By her family, her friends, his *mistress,* for God's sake. And yet she had allowed herself to believe that the fantasy could be real. That, one day, the world had tilted just so on its axis and Ralston had fallen for her. And here he was . . . wagering on her future. Playing with her emotions and her love as though she were a toy to be used, then cast aside.

And she felt so very cast aside.

It was so easy to believe that she meant so little to him. So tempting to fall back into the comfortable invisibility that came with being a passive wallflower whom so few people really noticed.

And that was what hurt the most.

Pulling herself up to her full height and squaring her shoulders before she spoke, emotion gone from her voice. "You really have won, my lord. For, not only am I not marrying Lord Oxford, I am not marrying you, either. I release you from our betrothal. You are free to resume your life of self-indulgence and profligacy."

He opened his mouth to speak, to stay her, to explain everything—his silly pride, his ridiculous, irrational anger in the face of the idiot Oxford—but she cut him off before he could speak. "I only ask that you stay as far away from me as possible."

And then she was gone, pushing past Benedick and Oxford into the ballroom beyond, Mariana following closely behind.

Ralston moved to follow, twin bursts of uncertainty and pride coursing through him at her newfound strength, at her powerful confidence, at her unwillingness to compromise her desires. He wanted to capture her and tell her the whole truth—that he didn't care about Juliana's coming out or about his family's reputation or about anything else.

"Leave her." The words, hard and unfeeling, came from the Earl of Allendale, who had placed himself between Ralston and the entrance to the ballroom the moment his sister had escaped.

"I never wanted to hurt her. The wager means nothing. I don't need the money, Allendale. You know that."

"I do know that. And I don't fully understand what possessed you to continue with this ridiculous game." Allendale remained unmoving, daring Ralston to come at him. "Nevertheless, you *have* hurt her. And if you go near her again, I shall trounce you. As it is, we shall have a beast of a time dealing with a broken engagement."

"The engagement is not broken." Ralston's voice was steel.

"You should let it go, Ralston. She is not worth it," Oxford said cheerfully.

Ralston turned to face the all-but-forgotten dandy who had single-handedly destroyed the best thing in his life, and said, "What did you say?"

"I said she's not worth it," Oxford pressed on, oblivious to the hardened planes of Ralston's face—to the harsh stiffening of his body. "Certainly, the best thing about spinsters is that they're eager for a toss, but you can't really mean to tell me you need to resort to one as plain and uninspiring as that one. Although, it did appear that she was more than willing to lift her skirts for you . . . and I suppose that is something."

Benedick stiffened, and fury, hot and quick, coursed through Ralston at the words, so demeaning and unpleasant, directed at the woman he planned to make his wife. Because there was absolutely no question that Callie was going to be his wife.

Drunk or no, Oxford would pay for his words.

Reaching out, Ralston grabbed Oxford by the lapels of his top-coat and slammed him against the stone wall that marked one edge of the balcony. The force of the blow took the breath out of the baron, and, gasping for air, he slumped to the ground, clutching his chest.

Ralston looked down his long, elegant nose at the vile creature at his feet, and said, "You just impugned the honor of my future marchioness. Choose your seconds. I will see you at dawn."

Leaving Oxford sputtering on the ground, Ralston spun on one elegant heel to face Benedick. "When I am done with him, I am coming for your sister. And, if you intend to keep me from her, you had better have an army at your side."

Twenty-four

Callie brushed aside her tears as she sat curled on the window seat in her bedchamber, considering the events of the evening.

How could she go on without him? And, at the same time, how could she go on knowing that every moment of their time together had meant so little to him—designed only to win him a wager and launch his sister into society.

It couldn't be possible. Every ounce of her rejected the thought that he would have used her so callously.

And yet, he hadn't denied it.

And why should she not believe it? The Marquess of Ralston—inveterate rake—would not have thought twice about using her for his personal gain. Hadn't he done so? From the very beginning? He'd bargained his kisses for her support of his sister. Why should she have ever believed he might have changed?

She'd so believed he could—that decades marked by disdain for emotion could have been nothing more than a faint memory in his checkered past. That she could love him enough to prove to him that the world was worth his caring, his trust. That she could turn him into the man of whom she had dreamed for so long.

That was perhaps the hardest truth of all—that Ralston, the man she'd pined over for a decade, had never been real. He'd never been the strong and silent Odysseus; he'd never been aloof Darcy; never Antony, powerful and passionate. He had only ever been Ralston, arrogant and flawed and altogether flesh and blood.

And, he'd never pretended to be anything else. He'd never plied her with false professions of love, never fooled her into believing that he was anything more than what he was. He had even said it himself; he'd only needed her for Juliana's sake.

Juliana's sake and two thousand pounds, it seemed. Not that he needed the money.

That almost made it worse.

She bowed her head as another wave of tears came on a crest of sadness.

Oh, Callie. How did you come to be such an idiot?

Even as she'd come to know the real Ralston—the Ralston who was not cut from heroic cloth—Callie had failed to see the truth. And, instead of seeing her own heartbreak coming, she had fallen in love, not with her fantasy, but with this new, flawed Ralston.

And, while she had been so caught up in the idea that *he* might change, tonight it was clear that the powerful metamorphosis she had witnessed was not his.

It was hers.

And it was due almost entirely to him.

She stared blindly at the crumpled, stained list clutched in her hand—the list that had begun as hers but that had somehow become *theirs*. Her heart clenched as she realized that Ralston had been an integral part of this new, bold, adventurous Callie, that he had guided her through each item on the paper. She was forever changed because of him.

How would she survive such heartache? How would she forget that she was so very much in love with him?

She had no idea.

She did know, however, that she could not spend one more moment in this room. She leapt from her seat and crossed the bedchamber with purpose, pulling open the door and moving silently through the quiet house to Benedick's study. She was going to try her hand at getting foxed again. Men seemed to take comfort in the experience when they were at their lowest lows; what was stopping her from doing the same?

Entering the room, she halted just inside, surprised to find her brother seated behind his enormous desk, staring off into the distance. He turned toward her at the sound of her feet on the wooden floor, and she watched as a shadow passed over his face. "Callie," he said, and there was something in the way he spoke her name that made tears well in her eyes once more. "It's four o'clock in the morning."

"I'm sorry," she said, beginning to back out of the room.

"No." He waved a hand in her direction, beckoning her to come inside. "Stay."

She did, closing the door softly behind her before padding over to the desk and seating herself in a comfortable chair across from him. She pulled her bare feet up under her. "You know," she said, her voice trembling with unshed tears, "when I was a little girl, I used to sit in this chair, in my nightgown, and watch Father shuffle papers around that desk. For the longest time, I didn't understand why he had so much work to do. I mean, wasn't everything—the title, the house, the land, the things—weren't they simply his?"

Benedick nodded at her words. "I felt the same way. Imagine my surprise when I discovered that all those things actually make work, and that Father wasn't pretending."

She smiled a watery smile. "It's amazing. Here I am, in my nightgown, in this chair, looking at you. So little has changed."

Benedick met her eyes. "Callie?"

The tears came then, silent and quick, running down her cheeks. She shook her head, looking down at her lap, worrying the fabric of her nightgown. "I thought I could change him."

Benedick sighed.

"I see now that I cannot. I just . . . I thought I could convince him to love me."

He sat for a long time, considering his words carefully. "Callie . . . love grows. Not everyone has an instant love match like Mother and Father. Like Mariana and Rivington. Ralston has been alone for a long time."

Tears welled. "I love him," she whispered.

"Is it not possible that he might love you as well?"

"He wagered two thousand pounds on my future, Benny."

A ghost of a smile played across his lips. "I will not deny the fact that he was something of an imbecile to do such a thing . . . but I cannot imagine that the wager was anything more than a point of pride."

"Pride?"

He nodded. "Male pride."

Callie shook her head. "Your gender is utterly bizarre." She shrugged her shoulders. "But that doesn't mean he loves me. I am not sure he cares for me at all."

"That's ridiculous." Benedick waited for her to look at him. "I would like nothing more than for you and Ralston never to see each other again, Callie, with the level of scandal that the two of you created tonight—and that's not even considering the count-less other scandals that you've most definitely orchestrated out-side of my knowing—not that I ever want to know about them." He paused. "However, you forget that I saw him last night. He came to me before he went to you in the library. He cares for you. I know it, or I never would have given him my blessing."

"You're wrong," Callie whispered. "I thought I could love him enough for both of us. But I cannot."

Silence fell between them, and Benedick watched as tears stained his sister's cheeks. Finally, he spoke. "Callie . . . Ralston called Oxford out tonight."

Callie's head snapped up. She was certain that she had misunderstood her brother. "I—I beg your pardon?"

"He's challenged Oxford to a duel."

Callie shook her head, attempting to clear it of the fog that had just come over her. "No. It can't be true. Are you sure it was he? And not St. John? They are twins, you know. It can be confusing."

"Yes, Callie. I am aware that they are twins. I am also quite certain that the dueling parties are *Ralston* and Oxford, as I witnessed the whole thing. And, considering the duel is over you . . ."

"Me?" Callie squeaked. "Ralston would never duel over me. I'm not worth risking his life. I mean, it's not as if he loves me, Benedick," she scoffed, meeting his concerned gaze. Benedick remained silent as she considered the words. "Oh, my God."

"He may not love you, Callie. But I'd wager he feels something rather impressive for you, or he and Oxford would not be choosing their seconds as we speak."

He was risking everything for her.

If that was not change, what was?

Callie's eyes widened. "Oh, my God." She leaned toward him, reaching across the desktop to grab his arm. "Benedick, you have to take me there."

"Callie . . ." Benedick shook his head. "I cannot take you there. You know that."

She shot up from her chair, announcing, "Benedick! He could die!" And she went tearing out of the room, up the wide center staircase and back into her bedchamber, Benedick hot on her heels.

She threw open her door with a crash and rushed to her armoire to retrieve a dress from inside. "He could be killed!" she cried.

Benedick closed the door behind him, attempting to keep Callie calm with a soft, steady tone. "He won't be killed, Callie. Duels rarely go that route anymore."

She turned to him, arms laden with muslin. "Am I mistaken in how they operate, Benedick? Twenty paces, turn, and *fire*? A *pistol*? A *loaded* pistol?"

"Well, yes," Benedick conceded the point, adding, "but death is not usually the expected outcome. I mean, one could go to prison for killing someone in a duel, for heaven's sake."

"Ah, so it's a sort of gentlemen's agreement?"

"Exactly."

"Really more for show than for purpose."

"Quite," he said, pleased that she understood.

Her eyes narrowed on him. "And, what if one of the gentlemen in question is a poor shot?"

Benedick's mouth opened, then closed.

Callie shook her head and moved behind her dressing screen. "You're taking me."

Her nightgown was almost immediately tossed over the top of the screen. Benedick threw up his hands at the indignity of the moment and turned his back to the general area. "I am not taking you, Callie. You shall wait here, as women do."

"I most certainly shall not! I am no longer meek and biddable!"

"You labor under the misconception that you were ever meek and biddable!"

Benedick turned to find Callie dressed and yanking on a pair of walking boots. Her eyes flashed. "You have two options, Benedick. You may escort me like a good brother, or you may stand aside as I leave this house and travel through London in the dead of night by myself."

"You'll never find it."

"Nonsense. You forget I am well acquainted with a public house or two in this city. I'm sure news of a duel involving one of London's best-known aristocrats travels fast."

His eyes widened. "I shall lock you in!"

"Then I shall climb down the trellis!" she announced.

"Damn it, Callie!"

"Benedick, I love him! I've loved him for a decade. And I had him for one day before I made a complete and utter mess of things. Or he did. I'm still not sure about that. But you cannot really believe I won't fight to save him?"

The words hung between them as brother and sister faced off.

"Please, Benny," she said softly, plaintively. "I love him."

The Earl of Allendale gave a long sigh.

"Lord, deliver me from sisters. I shall call for the curricle."

"ARE YOU SURE you want to do this?" Nick leaned against a lone rowan tree, hunching his shoulders against the cold morning mist and watching as Ralston checked his pistol. "You could be killed."

"I shan't be killed," Ralston said distractedly, looking across the wide expanse of field that Oxford had chosen as the location for their duel.

"Better men than you have said as much, Gabriel. I don't want to have to put you in the ground."

"It would serve you well," Ralston said morbidly as he meticulously packed the gun with powder. "You'd be a marquess."

"I have been around you long enough to know that I do not actually want to be a marquess, thank you."

"Well then, I shall endeavor to retain my title."

"Excellent."

Silence fell as the brothers waited for the arrival of Oxford and his second. The duel was set for dawn, and the field was bathed in a pale gray light that stole the color from the lush spring landscape and turned the setting bleak.

After several long minutes, Ralston said, "I cannot let him get away with saying such things about her, Nick."

"I understand."

"She deserves so much more."

"She deserves you. Alive."

Ralston turned to his brother, meeting his gaze firmly. "You must promise me something."

Nick knew immediately what Ralston was going to say. "No."

"Yes. You must. You're my brother and my second. You haven't a choice but to hear and accommodate my last wish."

"If this is your last wish, I shall follow you into hell to ensure that you pay for it."

"Nevertheless." Ralston looked up at the sky, pulling his great-coat closer for warmth. "Promise me you'll take care of her."

"You will take care of her, yourself, brother."

Brilliant blue gazes met. "I swear before you and God that I will. But if something should happen, and this morning should go awry, promise me you'll take care of her. Promise me you'll tell her . . ." Ralston paused.

"Tell her what?"

Ralston took a deep breath, the words bringing a tightening in his chest. "Promise me you'll tell her that I was an idiot. That the money didn't matter. That, last night, faced with the terrifying possibility that I had lost her . . . I realized that she was the most important thing I had ever had . . . because of my arrogance and my unwillingness to accept what has been in my heart for too long . . ." He trailed off. "What the hell have I done?"

"It appears that you've gone and fallen in love."

Ralston considered the statement. The old Ralston might have scoffed at the words—so pedestrian and fantastic and terrifying—

instead, he felt warmth spread through him at the idea that he might love Callie. And that she might love him back. Perhaps he had, indeed, "gone and fallen in love."

Nick continued, unable to keep the smug smile from his lips. "Shall I tell you what I would do if I discovered I'd been a royal ass and had lost the only woman I'd ever really wanted?"

Ralston's eyes narrowed on his brother. "I don't imagine I could stop you."

"Indeed not," Nick said. "I can tell you I wouldn't be standing in this godforsaken field in this godforsaken cold waiting for that idiot Oxford to shoot at me. I would walk away from this ridiculous, antiquated exercise, and I would find that woman and tell her that I was a royal ass. And then I would do whatever it takes to convince her that she should take a chance on me despite my being a royal ass. And once that's done, I would get her, immediately, to the nearest vicar and get the girl married. And with child."

A vision flashed of Callie full and rounded with his child, and Ralston closed his eyes against the pleasure of it. "I thought that allowing myself to love her would turn me into Father. I thought she would make me weak. Like him."

"You're nothing like Father, Gabriel."

"I see that now. She made me see it." He paused, lost in the memory of Callie's big brown eyes, her wide, smiling mouth. "My God, she's made me so much more than what I was."

The statement, filled with surprise and wonder, was punctuated by a shout from across the field as Oxford, Lord Raleigh, his second, and a doctor came into view.

Nick swore under his breath. "I'll confess, I'd hoped that Oxford was soused enough last night not to remember."

He took the pistol from Ralston and walked out to meet Raleigh and arrange the rules of the duel. As was customary, Oxford approached Ralston, fear in his eyes, and extended his hand. "For what it's worth, Ralston, I apologize for what I said about Lady Calpurnia. And, I thought you'd like to know that, while I do not have the two thousand now, I shall find a way to pay the debt."

Ralston stiffened at the reference to the stupid wager that had caused so much pain and unhappiness. He ignored Oxford's proffered hand, and instead met the baron's concerned gaze, and said, "Keep the money. I have her. She's all I want."

The truth of the statement was rather overwhelming to Ralston, and he found himself exhausted by the very idea of a duel now that he'd discovered just how much he wanted to be with Callie. Why was he standing in a cold, wet field when he could be sneaking into Allendale House, climbing into her warm, welcome bed, and showering her with apologies until she forgave him and married him immediately?

Nick and Raleigh returned quickly, eager to be done with the events of the morning. As Raleigh informed Oxford of the rules, Nick guided Ralston away from the others to say quietly, "Twenty paces, turn, and fire. And I have it on good authority that Oxford plans to aim wide."

Ralston nodded, acknowledging that aiming wide would leave both parties with their honor and lives intact. "I shall do the same," he said, swinging his greatcoat off and trading it for the pistol Nick offered.

"Good." Nick folded the coat over his arm. "Let's get this done, shall we? It's freezing."

"One . . . Two . . ." Ralston and Oxford stood back to back as Raleigh began to count off their paces. As he walked slowly to the rhythmic calling of the numbers, "Five . . . Six . . ." Ralston thought of Callie, all bright eyes and warm smiles. "Twelve . . . Thirteen . . ." Callie, who was likely fast asleep in her bed at that very moment. "Sixteen . . . Seventeen . . ."

He couldn't wait to be done with Oxford so he could go to her.

He would apologize and explain everything and beg her to marry him and . . .

"Stop! No!"

The shout came from across the field, and he turned toward it, knowing before looking that Callie was there—that she was running toward him. And all he could think was that Oxford was going to aim wide, and if he chose to fire in her direction . . .

Ralston didn't pause. He ran.

"Twenty!"

The sound of a single pistol's report echoed across the field.

And Ralston was falling to his knees, watching Callie's big brown eyes—eyes he had been thinking of all morning—widen in horror, and her mouth opened and her scream rent the early-morning silence, followed by Nick's swear and Benedick's call of "Doctor!" and Oxford's high, nasal cry of, "I aimed wide!"

And as the bullet ripped through his flesh, Ralston was consumed with a single thought: *I never told her that I loved her.*

He watched as Callie collapsed to her knees in front of him and began to push his coat back, running her hands across his chest, searching for the wound.

She was alive.

Relief coursed through him, hot and disorienting, and all he could do was watch her, repeating to himself that she was alive and unharmed over and over until the truth of it resonated. The rush of emotions he'd felt in the scant moments before he'd been shot—the fear that he might have lost her, that she might have been hurt—stole his breath.

He hissed in pain as she jostled his arm and she froze, looking up at him with tears in her eyes, saying, "Where are you hurt?"

He swallowed around the knot that formed in his throat at the picture she made, so worried, so pained, so very in love with him. And all he wanted to do was take her in his arms.

But first, he wanted to shake her.

"What the hell are you doing here?" he exploded, not caring that her eyes went wide with surprise.

"Gabriel," Nick interjected softly, using a knife to cut away the sleeve of Ralston's coat, "have a care."

"I will not!" Ralston turned back to Callie. "You cannot simply traipse across London whenever you damn well please, Callie."

"I came to save you—" Callie started, then stopped.

Ralston gave a harsh laugh. "Well, it appears you did an excellent job of getting me shot instead."

He barely registered Oxford's arrival and defensive pronouncement of, "I aimed wide!"

"Gabriel." Nick's words took on a warning tone as he ripped the sleeve of his brother's coat from his shirt. Gabriel winced, certain that Nick was taking pleasure in his pain. "Enough."

"And you!" Ralston turned on Benedick. "What the hell were you thinking? Bringing her here!"

"Ralston, you know as well as I do that she cannot be stopped."

"You need to get your women under control, Allendale," Ralston said, turning back to Callie. "When you're my wife, I'm going to lock you up, I swear before God!"

"Gabriel!" Nick was angry.

Ralston didn't care. He turned on his brother as the surgeon knelt next to him and inspected the wound. "She could have been killed!"

"And what about you?" This time, it was Callie who spoke, her own pent-up energy releasing in anger, and the men turned as one to look at her, surprised that she had found her voice. "What about you and your idiotic plan to somehow restore my honor by playing with guns out in the middle of nowhere with *Oxford*?" She said the baron's name with disdain. "Like children? Of all the ridiculous, unnecessary, thoughtless, *male* things to do . . . who even *fights* duels anymore?!"

"I aimed wide!" Oxford interjected.

"Oh, Oxford, no one cares," Callie said, before turning back to Ralston, and saying, "You were worried about me? How do you think I felt knowing that I might have arrived and you might have been *dead*? How do you think I felt when I heard that gunshot? When I saw the man I love fall to the ground? Of all the selfish things you've done in your life, Gabriel . . . and I feel certain that you've done rather a lot of selfish things . . . this one is by far the most arrogant and obnoxious of them all." She was crying now, either unwilling or unable to stop the tears. "What am I supposed to do if you *die*?"

The fight went out of him in the face of her tears. He couldn't bear the thought of her worrying about him. He brushed off the doctor and cupped her face in his palms, ignoring the pain in his arm as he pulled her to him and spoke firmly. "I'm not going to die, Callie. It's just a flesh wound."

His words, a repeat of those she'd said to him all those weeks ago in the fencing club, elicited a watery smile. "What would you know about flesh wounds?" she asked.

He smiled. "There's my empress." He kissed her softly, oblivious to their audience, before he added, "We shall simply have matching scars." She grew teary again, eyeing his wound skeptically before he repeated, "I'm not going to die, lovely. Not for a very long time."

Callie raised a brow in a gesture she'd learned from him. "I'm not certain I believe that, Gabriel. It appears you're not a very good shot."

Ralston turned a narrow gaze on his brother as Nick snickered at Callie's wry words before turning back to her. "For the record,

Calpurnia, I'm an excellent shot when not worried that you might find yourself in the way of a bullet."

"Why were you worried about me? You were the one in the duel!"

The surgeon probed at his wound, sending a bolt of pain down his arm. "My lord," the surgeon said as Ralston hissed in pain, "I'm afraid I'm going to have to remove the bullet. It won't be comfortable."

Ralston nodded to the doctor, who was removing a collection of rather wicked-looking instruments from his bag in preparation for the procedure.

Callie gave a nervous look at the tools, and said, "Are you sure you want to do this here, Doctor? Perhaps we should go somewhere less . . . rustic?"

"Here is as good a place as any, my lady," the doctor responded amiably. "It isn't the first bullet I've removed in this particular field, and I feel certain it won't be the last."

"I see," she said, her tone making it clear that she did not, in fact, see.

With his free hand, Ralston took hold of one of hers. When he spoke, it was with an urgency she'd never heard from him. "Callie—the wager."

She shook her head. "I don't care about the stupid wager, Gabriel."

"Nevertheless," he winced as the doctor prodded at the wound. "I was an idiot."

She eyed the doctor's movements skeptically before agreeing. "You were, indeed. But I was something of an idiot as well—for believing the worst. And then Benedick told me you were here . . . and I was so very worried that you might be shot. And then I went and *got* you shot."

"Better than getting *you* shot—which would have caused me a great deal of heartache. You see, Empress, it appears that I have fallen quite thoroughly in love with you."

She blinked twice, her eyes wide, as though she hadn't entirely understood his words. "I beg your pardon?" she whispered.

"I love you. I love your extravagant name and your beautiful face and your brilliant mind and your ridiculous list and your taste for adventure, which I imagine is very likely going to be the *actual* cause of my death. And I very much wanted to be able to tell you all that before you were shot in a field."

The men around them turned away in unison, embarrassed and eager to escape the exceedingly private moment that was taking place despite both their presence and the garish wound in Ralston's arm.

Callie didn't care that they had witnessed it. She only cared that she had heard it correctly. Refusing to take her eyes from Ralston's, she said, "I—You—Are you certain?"

One side of his mouth kicked up. "Quite. I love you. And I am rather ready to get on with a lifetime of doing so."

"Really?" She was smiling like a little girl told she could have an extra pudding after dinner.

"Indeed. There is one thing, however."

"Anything." She didn't care what he wanted as long as he was in love with her.

"Nick!" He called, adding, when his brother turned back, "Would you mind very much finding my pistol? Callie needs it."

Callie laughed roundly, understanding his motives instantly, and the noise carried across the field and drew the attention of the other men. "Gabriel, no!"

"Oh, yes, my little hellion," he said, humor and love in his tone. "I want this list done with. It is a danger to your reputation and to my person, evidently. And, since you've just this morning crossed off *Attending a duel*, I feel confident that we might as well kill two birds with one proverbial stone and give you a chance to fire a pistol, don't you?"

Callie held his gaze for a long moment, reading his thoughts, before she broke into a wide smile, and said, "All right. I shall do it. But only to please you."

His laughter carried across the field even as he grimaced at the pain in his arm. "How very magnanimous of you."

"Of course, you realize what will happen when this item is complete?"

Ralston's gaze narrowed. "What will happen?"

"I shall have to begin a new list."

He groaned. "No, Callie. Your time for lists is over. It's a miracle I survived this one."

"My new list only has one item."

"That sounds like a very dangerous list."

"Oh, it is," she agreed happily. "It's very dangerous. Particularly to your reputation."

Now he was curious. "What is the item?"

"To reform a rake."

He paused, the meaning of her words sinking in before he pulled her to him and kissed her thoroughly. When he pulled away, he set his forehead to hers, and whispered, "Done."

Epilogue

$\mathcal{C}$allie attempted to appear casual as she escaped the stifling ballroom of Worthington House and made her way down the wide stone steps into the darkened gardens below. She felt a jolt of excitement as she passed into the shadows of the hedge maze beyond. The darkness, combined with the heavy warmth of the summer evening and the sweet, heady scent of lavender from the blooming bushes beyond heightened her senses as she navigated the twists and turns of the maze.

After the duel, word had spread far and fast that Lady Calpurnia Hartwell and the Marquess of Ralston had been spied in a scandalous embrace, in public no less. If that were not enough, the gossipmongers added, the location of said embrace had been, moments earlier, the location of a *duel*.

She came upon a wide clearing, at the center of which stood a great marble fountain gleaming in the moonlight. She stopped just inside the clearing, still so familiar after so many years. Her heart began to race as she approached the fountain, reaching out one hand to run her fingers through the cool water that bubbled down the bodies of the cherubic statues.

As she did, strong arms captured her from behind, pulling her flush against a broad, firm chest. She couldn't keep the smile from her lips as Ralston whispered wickedly into her ear, "I wasn't at all certain what to expect when a footman delivered a scandalous invitation to a clandestine meeting." He set his lips hotly to the nape of her neck, licking the skin there and sending a chill down her spine, welcome in the warm night. "You are a serious risk to my reputation, Lady Ralston."

She sighed at the caress, before replying, "You forget, my lord, that I learned everything I know from you." She turned in his arms, running her fingers through his hair as she met his smiling eyes. "You have turned me into quite the libertine."

Yes, both their reputations had taken hits.

Not that either of them cared one way or another.

They had been married in less than a fortnight. Between Oxford's help in denouncing the rumors about wagers and duels and his own courtship of Callie and the fact that Ralston was obviously thoroughly smitten with his new bride, it was difficult for anyone to speculate that the hasty marriage was anything short of a love match—and the *ton* seemed more than willing to forgive both the marquess and his new marchioness for their perceived infractions.

"And, what an extraordinarily lucky man I am to have such a rake for a wife," he said, before taking her lips in a kiss that left her breathless and weak-kneed. "You may lure me into the darkness at any time, my love. In fact"—he paused, he kissed down the length of her neck, his lips leaving a fiery path in their wake—"I should very much like for you to take me home and have your way with me. Do you think we could leave immediately?"

She laughed, enjoying every moment of their scandalous conversation. "As this is the first ball we have attended as husband and wife, I don't think we can escape under cover of darkness without ruining all chances of being invited to balls in the future."

He ran his tongue along her collarbone, one hand stealing up to capture her breast, murmuring, "Would that be so bad? Think of all the things we could do at home, instead. I assure you, love, you would not want for excitement in the evenings."

She giggled at the words, the sound turning into a sigh as he stroked one turgid nipple through her gown. "Yes, well I think perhaps Juliana would be sad to have to miss society. She's beginning to fit right in, don't you think?"

He met her gaze thoughtfully. "Indeed. I never thanked you for convincing her to stay with us."

"I cannot imagine any woman, sister or otherwise, wanting to leave you once she'd found you, Gabriel." She smiled up into his vibrant blue eyes. "I am afraid you are quite saddled with me."

"Excellent." He spoke against her lips. "Because I shall never allow you to leave."

They kissed deeply, reveling in each other for long minutes until Callie pulled back, just barely, to meet his gaze. "I think I've loved you for my entire life."

His blue eyes flashed in the silver moonlight. "And I shall love you for the rest of mine, Empress."

She leaned her head back, smiling at the night sky, and he caught his breath at the vision of her, so exquisite, so beautiful.

"Do you know that the first time you ever called me Empress was here? In this garden?"

He cocked his head to one side, thinking. "How is that possible?"

She stepped out of his embrace, turning to the fountain again. "It was ten years ago. I was just out and hiding in the maze, desperate for something to distract me from my miserable failure of a first season. And there you were." She skimmed her fingers through the water in the fountain idly, her thoughts on that evening long ago. "Little did I know you would distract me for a full decade."

He kissed her again, worrying her full, bottom lip until she sighed, then said, "I plan to distract you for much longer than that." He captured her hand and kissed the tips of her fingers before saying, "While I know I should be sorry for your years of waiting, I confess, I am thoroughly pleased that you waited for me to open my eyes and finally see you, love." He pulled her back into his embrace, adding, "But I am rather frustrated that I didn't simply see it then . . . for we'd have a decade of happiness and a brood of children to show for it."

"And two fewer scars."

He laughed. "And that, my little hellion."

She stroked his cheek idly, basking in the warmth of his touch. "You make an excellent point, but then I wouldn't have had my list. And you wouldn't have benefited from the items on it. Consider tonight's item, for example."

One rogue brow rose. "Tonight's item?" His eyes darkened with passion, and he pulled her close to him, reveling in the feel of her wrapped around him. Lifting her against him, he carried her to a nearby bench and settled her upon it before he knelt beside her and slipped his warm hands beneath the hem of her gown to caress her ankles. The touch held the promise of much more, and Callie gave a little laugh that turned into a sigh as his hands stole up the inside of her leg.

"Indeed," she said, a mysterious smile playing across her lips as she wrapped her arms around his neck. "*Tryst in a Garden.*"

His mouth hovered just above hers and he spoke in a dark whisper, "Far be it from me to deny you an adventure."

The story of the St. John siblings continues
with Nick's romance in

Ten Ways
to Be Adored
When Landing a Lord

About the author

About the book

Insights,
Interviews
& More . . .

Read on

Meet Sarah MacLean

Courtesy of the Author

New York Times, Washington Post, and *USA Today* bestselling author Sarah MacLean's historical romance novels have been translated into more than twenty languages. A leading voice in the romance genre, Sarah is a columnist and the cohost of the weekly romance podcast *Fated Mates.* She lives in New York City. ❧

Behind the Book

I'm Sarah MacLean. I read romance novels and I write them.

Whenever I introduce myself to the world—on panels, on podcasts, in readers' guides—I begin this way, and always in this order. Romance reader first; romance reader always. There are days when I can imagine packing in the pen, for sure (not today, thankfully!), but I'll never not be a romance reader.

Lady adventurers who were happy to man the guns for themselves got me through middle school. High school was marked by casino owners and scoundrels, and the heroines who brought them to their knees. College brought me unmarried wallflowers and brilliant bluestockings who refused to follow the expected path, and instead forged their own.

In the years since? Thousands of books, thousands of characters, each refusing to let the world claim them. Refusing to let the world dictate to them. Refusing to let the world hold them back. Characters who choose the other path. Characters who changed their worlds. Staked their claims. And broke the rules.

So, it's no surprise, on reflection, that when I wrote my first romance novel, *Nine Rules to Break When Romancing a Rake,* I wrote about a rule breaker. Looking back, it's pretty clear that I sat down and opened up a vein when I wrote this one . . . filling it with all the things ▶

Behind the Book *(continued)*

I loved about the books that brought me to the genre. Handsome rakes! Twin brothers! Meddling mamas! Beautiful sisters! Scandals! Fencing! Wagers! Men's clubs! Heroines in trousers! Duels! No wonder *Nine Rules* is my longest book; it's full of all my favorite romancey bits.

And perhaps the best romancey bit of all: the heroine who not only finds love, but finds herself in the balance.

The joy of writing historical romance is this: as authors we get the best of both worlds. We get the magic of the candlelit ballroom, the gorgeous gowns, the fencing, the scoundrels, the trips to the opera, the power and title and prestige that comes with the dateline, but we also get to hold a mirror to the world in which we live now. The way we love now. The way we fight the rules we're asked to follow. The way we change them. That's where Callie comes in.

We meet her at a breaking point, or rather, at a point when she might allow herself to be broken. Instead, she makes another choice. Forges a different path. Burns her bonnet and heads off to do the wildest thing she can imagine—find a rake, and romance him, and set her new life in motion.

If being a romance reader has taught me anything, once that's done, literally anything is possible. Adventure, passion, hope, joy, partnership, love, future. All of it.

The curvy, wallflowery rule breaker

and her wickedly handsome hero
added romance writer to my bio. In
the decade since, casino owners and
scoundrels and brilliant bluestockings
and (more) unmarried wallflowers and
lady adventurers all became part of the
MacLeaniverse . . . and they're all
waiting to meet you.

In the meantime, whether it was your
first time with Callie and Ralston or
they're old friends, I hope you enjoyed
Nine Rules, and I hope that Callie's list
inspired you just a little bit. Enough to
find a rule of your own . . . and break it.

Please write and tell me all about it.

Much love,
Sarah ᕗ

Reading Group Guide

1. The prologue happens ten years before the main story unfolds: What essential elements of Callie and Ralston's relationship does the prologue seed?

2. Callie begins the book as a wallflower, destined for a life of spinsterhood. She chooses to transform herself, and we love her for that. What makes us root for her? How do you see yourself in her journey?

3. The nine rules Callie breaks are not revolutionary in the twenty-first century, but the list still resonates. Why is she drawn to activities that powerful men of her time took for granted? Why is she convinced that these activities hold the key to her transformation? Which item on her list would you most like to break?

4. In what ways does Ralston embody the "classic rake" archetype we see in historical romance? In what ways does MacLean flip the script on the rake and remake him in a modern form?

5. "Wallflower brings a rake to his knees" is a beloved romantic trope, in large part because of the power dynamic between the characters.

How does Callie claim power? How does Ralston cede it? How do these scenes show us what it means to be "powerful" in a relationship?

6. Who were your favorite side characters in the book? What makes a side character a good prospect for a book of their own? How does your answer to that question help you understand why Nick becomes a hero (*Ten Ways to Be Adored When Landing a Lord*), but, to date, Benedick has not?

7. The Happily Ever After (HEA) is an essential component to any romance novel. Discuss the ending of *Nine Rules to Break When Romancing a Rake* and the lead-up to the HEA. What was satisfying about it?

8. Published in 2010, *Nine Rules to Break When Romancing a Rake* is considered a modern romance classic. Many readers have a deep, abiding love for Callie and Ralston. What are the ingredients that make this such a beloved romance?

9. Sarah MacLean often speaks of romance as a reflection of the world not during the time in which the book is set, but of the time during which it was written. Thinking ▶

about the world in the year 2010, what can you see in *Nine Rules* that is clearly "of a time"? What about the book still feels timeless?

10. What would be on *your* list of rules to break (romancing a rake optional!)? ～

Sarah Recommends

There's nothing in the world Sarah enjoys more than recommending romance. Whether you've been reading historical romance for years or are new to the genre, you can't go wrong with one of these books. Find many more on her website at sarahmaclean.net/recommended.

- *How the Duke Was Won* by Lenora Bell
- *Heart and Hand* by Rebel Carter
- *Wanted, A Gentleman* by KJ Charles
- *Any Duchess Will Do* by Tessa Dare
- *Never Kiss a Duke* by Megan Frampton
- *Honeytrap* by Aster Glenn Gray
- *Dalliances & Devotion* by Felicia Grossman
- *Waking Up with the Duke* by Lorraine Heath
- *A Caribbean Heiress in Paris* by Adriana Herrera
- *The Wisteria Society of Lady Scoundrels* by India Holton
- *The Beast of Beswick* by Amalie Howard
- *When Beauty Tamed the Beast* by Eloisa James
- *Forbidden* by Beverly Jenkins ▶

Sarah Recommends *(continued)*

- *The Virgin and the Rogue* by Sophie Jordan
- *Marrying Winterborne* by Lisa Kleypas
- *Dare to Love a Duke* by Eva Leigh
- *Love and Other Scandals* by Caroline Linden
- *Her Night with the Duke* by Diana Quincy
- *The Bittersweet Bride* by Vanessa Riley
- *Unmasked by the Marquess* by Cat Sebastian
- *The Prince of Broadway* by Joanna Shupe

Discover great authors, exclusive offers, and more at hc.com.